Other books by MJ Duncan

Second Chances

Veritas

MJ Duncan

This is a work of fiction. Names, characters, places, and incidents are products of the author's imagination or are used fictitiously and are not to be construed as real. Any resemblance to actual events, locales, organizations, or persons, living or dead, is entirely coincidental.

ISBN: 0692023968

ISBN-13: 9780692023969

Chapter 1

It was getting late, and Lauren Murphy knew that she had to be up before dawn the next morning to begin her new job, but she was content to enjoy what was left of her first night in Saint Thomas sitting on the sweeping patio at Jack's. The restaurant was across the street from her hotel, and it fronted the western edge of the harbor in Charlotte Amalie, which gave her breathtaking views of both the boats moored in the harbor as well as the island's lush mountains.

The sound of plates shattering against the concrete patio behind her had her turning in her seat to inspect the damage, and she shook her head as she forced herself to turn back around. *Not my kitchen, not my problem,* she thought as she smoothed her hands over the napkin on her lap.

It was still hard for her to believe that she was not in the kitchen at Clarke's on the Upper West Side, her black chef's coat buttoned primly to the neck and her sleeves rolled to her elbows. It was, after all, what she had done every night for the last ten years. She had dedicated herself to her craft, spending practically every night since she graduated from the Culinary Institute of America in one high-end kitchen and then another, steadily working her way up through the cutthroat New York restaurant scene, until, at thirty-two, she was considered amongst the best of the best—despite the fact that she still only held the title of sous chef. The recognition was nice, it certainly made the hours she put into her career worthwhile, but she had reached the point where she was too exhausted to care.

She stretched her legs out beneath the table and sighed as she ran a hand through her hair. New York was the last thing she wanted to think about. She had taken the job as a private chef aboard a charter yacht for a few weeks to take a break from the stress of constantly trying to be the best and just enjoy cooking again. And, as a bonus, she would get to explore a part of the world she had always been fascinated by as a girl growing up in the Midwest.

A lithe figure cutting purposefully through the tables just to her right drew her attention, and a slow smile tweaked her lips as she studied the new arrival. The woman was tall, with an athletic build and luscious sun-bronzed skin, both of which were shown off to utter perfection by her tight jeans and fitted tank top. Her hair was cut in a shaggy pixie style, the short auburn strands windblown in a most appealing way, and the smile on her face was absolutely enchanting. Lauren unabashedly ran her eyes over the woman's body, lingering on the ample swell of her breasts and the taut curve of her ass. It had been far too long since she had taken a woman to bed.

Her ogling was interrupted by her waiter setting the glass of wine she had ordered in front of her. "Is there anything else I can get you?"

"Just the check, please." Lauren nodded her thanks as she reached for her glass, and the moment he was gone she immediately looked for the beautiful brunette.

It did not take Lauren long to find her standing at the bar, chatting up a leggy blonde in a red spaghetti-strap sundress. The light from the bar made it easy for her to see the way the brunette leaned in closer to the blonde, tan fingers trailing lightly over her forearm as she said something that made her laugh.

The return of her waiter with her check forced Lauren's attention away from the women, and she cleared her throat softly as she dug in her purse for her wallet. She slid her credit card into the leather folder he was holding out for her without even bothering to glance at the tab, and dropped her wallet onto the table. "Here you go."

He nodded and hurried off to the register beside the kitchen to run the card, and her eyes drifted back to the two women at the bar. The brunette leaned in to brush a light kiss over the blonde's cheek before whispering something in her ear. Though Lauren knew her staring was incredibly rude, she could not look away. The blonde nodded in response to whatever it was the brunette had suggested, and Lauren bit her lip as she watched the blonde drag a playful finger down the middle of the brunette's chest before sliding sensuously off her barstool and sauntering toward the parking lot.

The brunette flashed a friendly wave at the bartender as she followed the blonde, and Lauren's eyes widened in surprise when she saw the bartender and some of the waitstaff exchanging money in the wake of her exit.

"Did they seriously bet on whether or not she could pick that girl up?" She shook her head, leaned back in her chair, and picked up the wine glass she had been idly spinning on the tabletop as she had watched the two women at the bar. Lauren sipped at the drink and gazed softly at the spot the brunette had been standing only minutes before, wistfully thinking that she would have quite liked to trade places with the beautiful blonde.

Her waiter returned a few minutes later, smiling politely as he held up the back of her card to her. "I'm sorry, but you wrote on here that I'm supposed to check your ID?"

"Of course." Lauren pulled her driver's license from her wallet and held it out for him. "Here you go."

"New York," he observed, making a show of holding the front of the credit card to the ID to double-check that the names matched.

"Yep."

He handed her both her credit card and the receipt for her to sign. "I hope you enjoy your vacation, then."

"Thanks, but I'm not on vacation. I'm going to be chef on the *Veritas* for a couple of cruises." She waved a hand at the gleaming red and white catamaran that was moored at the end of a dock near the mouth of the marina. "I start tomorrow."

"I see," the waiter drawled, a slow grin tweaking his lips.

Lauren frowned. His smile was entirely too knowing and amused. "What?"

"Nothing." He shook his head. "I'm sure you and Grey will get along just fine."

Lauren's frown deepened. There was definitely something going on that she did not understand, and it apparently had something to do with the captain of the *Veritas*. "What do you mean? Do you know Grey Wells?"

The waiter laughed and nodded. "Everybody knows Grey, but just forget that I said anything. Don't worry about whatever you've heard, most of it isn't true. People like to make up stories to amuse themselves, but even Wells can't sleep with *that* many women. Good luck on your first sail tomorrow," he added, smirking as he knocked lightly on her table before turning on his heel and heading over to another table where the customer was waving a hand to catch his attention.

Lauren chewed her lip thoughtfully as she slipped her credit card back into her wallet, and could not help but wonder what, exactly, she had gotten herself into by accepting the chef's position aboard the *Veritas*.

Chapter 2

The barest hint of sun was beginning to peek over the eastern horizon, setting fire to the cobalt sea that seemed to stretch to infinity, when Lauren made her way down an otherwise empty dock the next morning. A light onshore breeze tickled her bare legs, and she marveled at how nice it was to be wearing shorts in early November.

She slowed to a stop beside the stern of the *Veritas,* and hitched the duffel bag she was wearing like a backpack higher on her shoulders as she studied the yacht that would be her home for the next two and a half weeks. Light from the main salon poured out onto the back deck through open sliding glass doors, casting a golden hue over the two tables that framed the surprisingly roomy space. Modern classical music, full of lilting flutes, heavy beats, and energetic violins was playing over the yacht's speakers, and Lauren knew that even if she called out to make her presence known, whoever was inside the yacht would not hear.

Nerves she had managed to subdue until that moment flared inside her, making her stomach flutter uncomfortably, and she drew a deep breath to solidify her resolve before she climbed aboard. Her arrival was effectively masked by the music playing, and she made her way slowly across the deck toward the open doors in search of the yacht's captain.

The salon was empty, which gave her time to just stop and take it all in for a moment. A gleaming banquette dining area with cream-colored leather cushions was at the far left side of the room, and a matching sofa filled the right. Bookshelves were built into the wall behind the banquette and the sofa, and a colorful red and gold rug covered the floor in front of the couch. To her right was a small desk area with a computer and what she imagined had to be a satellite telephone. The galley was on her left. It was U-shaped and a much smaller space than she was used to working in, but very modern, with stainless appliances and black granite countertops. From where she was standing, she could see a decent-sized fridge, as well as a four-burner stove with a built-in grill above a single oven, and the sink anchored the peninsula that separated the galley from the rest of the room. Three barstools with leather seats that matched the banquette and the sofa were tucked under the overhanging counter, and Lauren's mind instantly imagined using the space as both a prep-area and an eating area.

Lauren was so lost in her examination of the galley that she failed to notice when she was no longer alone, and she jumped with someone cleared their throat behind her.

"May I help you?"

The voice was a low, rough alto that sent pleasant shivers rolling down Lauren's spine. "I'm sorry…" she began to apologize as she turned around, but the remainder of her apology died on her tongue when she found herself looking at the woman from the bar the night before.

If Lauren had thought the brunette was beautiful from a distance, it was nothing compared to how she looked up-close. She was perhaps an inch taller than her own five foot ten inch frame, and her eyes, the one feature Lauren had not been able to catalogue the night before, were a warm brown, flecked with streaks of gold that gave them a hypnotic depth that was nearly impossible to look away from. Lauren was acutely aware of the way the brunette's eyes swept slowly over her body, and her stomach lurched at the almost horrified look that was on her face when their eyes met again. The brunette's face seemed to pale as they stared at each other, and Lauren found herself thrown completely off-balance by the entire situation. The woman in front of her did not look upset at finding a stranger on her boat. She looked stunned. Like there was something about Lauren that absolutely terrified her.

The strange silence seemed to go on forever, until Lauren blurted, rather inelegantly, "I cook."

The brunette nodded slowly, a look of understanding and panic flashing in her eyes. "Lauren Murphy?"

"Yeah." Lauren looked back over her shoulder at the galley and shrugged. "I'm the, uh, new chef."

"Right," the brunette muttered, forcing a small smile as she held a hand out in greeting. "Grey Wells. Welcome aboard the *Veritas*."

"Thank you," Lauren murmured as she reached for Grey's hand, and it was then that she remembered her waiter's words from the night before.

Not even Wells can sleep with **that** *many women.*

But, Lauren surmised as she shook Grey's hand, her waiter was wrong. She had no idea how many women Grey was rumored to have bedded, but she had no doubt that the brunette could pick up pretty much any woman if she tried. Grey was simply too beautiful to ever be turned down. Lauren smiled shyly at Grey as she released her hand and turned back toward the galley. "I'll need to check the pantry to make sure I have everything I need before I head over to the farmer's market to pick up the fresh produce for the trip."

Grey nodded, clearly relieved that Lauren seemed more interested in examining the boat than making nice with her. "It's stocked with pretty much everything that I think you could possibly need, but I'll let you look for yourself after we get your things stowed away. So—" she clapped her hands, grateful for the opportunity to look anywhere but at Lauren, "—I'll give you a quick tour, and then we can get to it. This is the salon." She waved a hand at the open space they were standing in. "Galley, dining room, lounge, and navigation center. Through there—" she pointed at a narrow oval-shaped doorway that was nestled between the dining area and the lounge, "—are two guest cabins that share an en suite. The other guest cabins are along the starboard side, both with full en suites."

Lauren looked at the stairs by the desk Grey had called the navigation center and nodded. Grey was obviously trying a little too hard to sound upbeat, and when she glanced at her out of the corner of her eye, she noticed that Grey was studiously avoiding looking at her. There was a stiffness to her posture that told Lauren she was anxious about something, and Lauren could not help but wonder what in the world she had done to make her act that way.

"Crew cabins are this way," Grey continued, waving a hand for Lauren to follow her as she made her way past the galley and down five narrow steps to the landing that separated the *Veritas'* two other cabins. Floor-to-ceiling cabinetry filled the outer wall of the small area, and she pointed at the door that was at the stern. "My cabin is there, yours is at the bow. You have your own en suite, and there is a closet with drawers inside it for your things. All cabins have televisions that are wired to the boat's electronic entertainment system, so you'll have full-access to the digital library. The boat also has WiFi via satellite, if you need to check emails or go online while we're out on the charters. The WiFi network is called Veritas, and the password is *opensesame*—all lowercase, no spaces."

Lauren looked at the oval doorway that led to her cabin. "Got it."

Grey nodded and tried her best to appear calm. Her heart rate spiked as her eyes locked onto Lauren's, and she immediately looked back toward the salon, desperate for some kind of an escape. "Excellent. Well, the Muellers won't be here until midday, so you have some time now to stow your gear. I'm assuming you have a copy of the food profile they filled out when they scheduled their charter?"

Lauren nodded, even as her mind clicked through the basics. Family of five. No allergies. Three young boys who are adventurous eaters but do not like anything too spicy. "I do."

"Awesome. Well, when you're done unpacking, I'll show you the pantry. You can dig around in there and the fridge, make notes on whatever it is you'll need that I haven't already bought, and then we can go to the farmer's market in town. There's a fishmonger I like who always has a stall there, and we can pick up the steaks, chicken, and whatever else you're going to need from the butcher on the way back to the boat."

"Okay," Lauren said, her brow furrowing slightly.

Grey forced a smile that was more akin to a grimace, and hooked a thumb over her shoulder. "Great. I'll be on deck, just come on up when you're ready."

Chapter 3

Standing at the *Veritas'* helm, the one place that had been her sanctuary over the last three years, Grey ran her hands through her hair and looked out over the familiar expanse of Charlotte Amalie's harbor. Now that she was no longer fighting to control herself for appearance's sake, her hands shook, and she was seriously tempted to fire Lauren before she had prepared a single meal. Grey knew that it was not really an option—there was no way she was even close to being capable of preparing the meals for the next two cruises that Lauren had signed-on for—but that knowledge was not enough to keep her from thinking about it.

She took a deep breath, held it for five seconds, and then let it go. And then she did it again. And again. Eventually, the regulated breathing calmed her racing heart and eased the shaking in her hands, but it did little to stop her mind from spinning.

The past came back to her in flashbacks. A warm smile. Gentle eyes. Tender touches. Whispers of affection that were laced with so much emotion that her heart would skip a beat. Harsh fluorescent lighting. Beeping Machines. And then nothing. Always nothing.

If there was one road Grey could not allow herself to travel, it was that one. She knew that time was supposed to heal all wounds, but the gaping hole in her heart was just as all-encompassing as ever, and she had yet to find anything that could make it go away. Drinking herself into a stupor worked to a degree, as did losing herself in the desperate embrace of a woman whose name she never particularly cared to learn, let alone remember, but neither of those coping mechanisms were going to work for her now because she had guests arriving in a few hours and a new chef making herself at home below deck.

She could not help but be pissed at Lauren's presence on her boat, and she latched onto that anger as she pulled her phone from her pocket. She did not even have to look at the screen to pull up the number she needed, and she gritted her teeth as the call rang through. She knew that what she was about to do was not at all fair, but she was too upset to care. "You fucking suck," she greeted her best friend the moment she picked up.

Kelly Kipling laughed. *"Sometimes, yes. But why, exactly, do I suck this time?"*

"Lauren Murphy," Grey muttered, rolling her eyes and running a frustrated hand through her hair. "You were supposed to find me a goddamn chef for a couple cruises."

"And, judging by her résumé, I did. She graduated first in her class from the Culinary Institute of America. From the handful of people I talked to while checking her references, I can tell you that she's widely regarded as one of the best sous chefs in New York, and everybody is expecting her to be given her own kitchen sooner, rather than later. Her bosses at Clarke's have nothing but great things to say about her. I found you a better chef than you usually get pillaging the local hotel kitchens—mine included, by the way. She didn't seem interested in relocating, but she looks so good on paper that I was hoping after a couple weeks down here she might be more open to persuasion. So, what's the problem?"

Grey chuckled darkly and shook her head. "She's a redhead. Wild fucking curls, gorgeous fucking hazel eyes, the whole nine yards."

"Oh," Kelly murmured. *"Sorry?"*

"I thought you interviewed her."

"I did interview her, Grey. Over the phone," Kelly said, her tone softening. *"It's not like I can jet up to New York to interview a chef for a short-term position like the one you were trying to fill. I mean, I do have three hotels to oversee on the island here, never mind the two on Saint John, and the one on St. Croix."*

Properly chastised, Grey sighed and nodded. "Yeah, I know." The Kipling family had been a fixture in the Virgin Islands for generations, and Kelly was the general manager for Kipling Resorts, overseeing the family's empire. It was because none of the chefs for her hotels were available for the next few weeks that Grey had asked Kelly if she could help her find somebody to work on the *Veritas*. "I'm sorry…"

"It's fine, Grey, don't worry about it. Look, you just have to make it through two cruises and then you'll be rid of her. Just give her a chance, and don't rip her head off just because she looks like—"

"Don't even go there, Kip."

"Fine," Kelly sighed. Really, she should have known better than to try and say Emily's name. *"Look, I am sorry. About all of it."* She paused for a beat and then added, *"So, you leave this afternoon?"*

"Yeah. We'll be out for nine days. I'm just going to follow my usual loop through the BVI and back for this one, nothing spectacular." Grey held her breath at the sound of footsteps making their way up the stairs to the bridge, and her heart thudded heavily in her chest when Lauren came into view. "I, uh, gotta go."

"She's there."

Grey nodded, unable to tear her gaze away from Lauren, who flashed her an apologetic smile and quickly backed down the stairs. "Yeah. We need to go do some grocery shopping to stock up for the trip."

"Good luck. Call me when you get back. Or, you know, whenever you need to."

"Will do." Grey blew out a loud breath and added, "Look, I'm sorry I went off on you. Thanks for listening."

"That's what I'm here for," Kelly murmured, her voice tinged with concern. *"Be good."*

Grey laughed, the sound devoid of any genuine mirth, but she was grateful for the normalcy of the quip when her entire world felt like it was spinning out of control. "When am I ever good?"

"There's a first time for everything, Wells. I'll talk to you later."

"Yeah. Later." Grey shoved her phone into her pocket and started for the stairs, knowing that they really did need to get going if they were to get back in time to put everything away before the Muellers arrived. Lauren was sitting at one of the tables on the back deck that was sheltered by the bridge, and Grey's breath caught in her throat at the small smile the redhead greeted her with. It was not fair that she should have to try and continue to survive, day after day, while being confronted with a reminder of all that she had loved and lost.

"Sorry about interrupting," Lauren said.

Grey shook her head and glanced toward the salon. The ache in her chest was easier to ignore if she did not actually look at Lauren. "Don't worry about it. It's not a big deal. I was just talking to a friend. I'll, um, just show you to the pantry so you can see what we've got, and then we can head out."

"I went ahead and found it on my own before I came looking for you. Hope that was okay." When Grey nodded, Lauren continued, "Anyways, I have my list ready."

"Excellent." Grey waved a hand at the dock and motioned for Lauren to disembark first. "Then let's get going."

Chapter 4

Lauren loved farmer's markets. There was something about the combination of fresh air and interacting with people who were proud of the produce they had brought to sell that never failed to make her smile. It was difficult, however, for her to find any enjoyment in this particular trip. She did not like confrontation, but she found herself almost wishing for it as Grey continued to avoid her. At least then she would know what it was about her that irked the brunette so. She had given up trying to draw Grey into conversation after her eighth failed attempt, and they had ended up wandering the market in a tense silence that set Lauren on edge.

She double-checked her list and glanced up at Grey, who was standing a good four feet away from her and looking like she would like nothing more than to drop the cooler full of fish she was carrying and run away. "I just need to pick up a few herbs, and then I'll be done."

Grey nodded and looked around the bustling stalls around them, and Lauren sighed as she made her way over to a small table that was covered with different herbs. She set the bags of fruits and vegetables that she was carrying onto the ground, and began quickly sorting through the bundles of aromatics that were piled in small wooden crates on the long rectangular table. Everything looked to be at the peak of freshness, and it did not take her long to find what she needed. She stowed the herbs she had chosen on top of their other purchases in her bags as Grey paid, and she forced herself to smile when Grey turned toward her.

Grey pocketed her change and looked at a spot that was just over Lauren's right shoulder, grateful that the mirrored lenses of her sunglasses hid the fact that she was not looking her in the eye. "What's next?"

Lauren looked at her list again, even though she had checked it only moments before. "We have everything but the meats from the butcher."

Grey glanced at her watch. The polished steel hands stood out easily against the orange face, telling her that it was just after eight o'clock, and she nodded. "It all should be ready and waiting for us." She had called the butcher and placed Lauren's order while she drove to the market. The call served two purposes: first, the food would be ready when they arrived; and second, it gave her a few minutes respite from the tension that surrounded her and Lauren. She really was trying to behave as normally as possible, but she knew by the cautious glances Lauren kept shooting her way that she was failing miserably at it. *Of all the chefs in the world…* she lamented silently. She cleared her throat and waved a hand toward her car. "The butcher is on the way back to the marina."

Lauren nodded, picked up her bags, and headed toward the half of the parking lot that was actually being used for its intended purpose. She wandered toward the back row of the lot to where they had parked, and stopped behind Grey's red Mini Cooper. She remained quiet as she stowed her bags in the back of the car, and glanced only once at Grey as she slipped into the passenger's seat.

More of the modern classical music Grey had been listening to earlier poured from the speakers as Grey started the car, and Lauren sighed as she looked out the window. At least now there was some music to fill the tense silence between them. Despite her growing frustration, Lauren could not help stealing quick glances at Grey, who was staring purposefully out the windshield. Grey's jaw was clenched tight, the corded muscles of her forearms visible as she gripped the steering wheel much harder than was necessary. It was obvious that she wanted to be anywhere else at that moment, and Lauren pursed her lips as she looked away again.

Though she was doing her best to not look at Lauren, Grey did not miss the hurt that had flashed across Lauren's face before she turned toward her window. Guilt swept through her, and she gave herself a sound mental head-slap. It was not Lauren's fault that her mere presence was driving her insane. And, like it or not, she also knew that the two of them needed to be at least passably friendly with each other once the Mueller family arrived later that morning. "So, um…you're a chef in New York?"

"I am," Lauren said softly. Her eyes flicked over toward Grey, whose grip on the steering wheel seemed to have somehow managed to become even tighter, and sighed as she looked back out her window.

"What made you decide to do this?" Grey kept her eyes on the road ahead as she waved a hand to indicate the whole Virgin Islands, working-on-a-boat thing.

Lauren shrugged. "I haven't had a proper vacation in ten years and, well, I had a bunch of time saved up because the restaurant kept letting me rollover the days I didn't take. The idea of doing nothing was not at all appealing because I'm one of those people who need to always have something to do. A good friend of mine had rented a yacht and cruised around the Caribbean last summer for her honeymoon, and I figured that signing-on as a private chef was a good way to get out of New York for a bit and still keep busy."

Grey chuckled. "So, you're spending your first vacation in a decade working."

"On a beautiful yacht, sailing around the Caribbean, yes," Lauren replied. "Kelly Kipling, the woman I interviewed with, said that I would have time to snorkel and explore whatever islands we make port at, and I actually love cooking, so it seemed like a win-win kind of deal."

"You will have plenty of time for all of that," Grey said, daring to glance at Lauren as she pulled to a stop in front of the butcher's. A small smile was tweaking Lauren's lips, like she was pleased they had just managed to have an actual conversation that was halfway-normal. Grey's heart clenched as she drank in Lauren's profile, her eyes lingering on the rogue curl tickling the side of Lauren's cheek, but she forced herself to ignore it as she quickly climbed out of the car. Now was not the time for her to worry about anything other than getting ready to sail later that afternoon.

Grey nodded in response to the small, grateful smile Lauren gave her when she held the door to the butcher shop open for her, and turned her attention to the man who was standing behind the counter. Eddie Jones was wearing one of his typically gaudy Hawaiian shirts covered in big-breasted women wearing coconut bras and grass skirts, and Grey smiled when she recognized it as the one she had given him for his birthday the year before.

"Grey!" Eddie hollered, a wide smile lighting up his face as Grey slapped his hand in greeting. "I have everything you wanted right here. You wanna have a look?"

Grey glanced at Lauren and arched a brow questioningly. If it were up to her, she would just grab the stuff and go, but she knew from the way Lauren had dug through the produce stands earlier that she would want to see what he had pulled for them.

"Yes, please," Lauren said as she stepped up to the counter. She smiled at the appraising look the butcher gave her. "Hi. I'm Lauren Murphy."

"Eddie Jones." He shook her hand. "You're not from around here, are you?"

Lauren shook her head. "New York, actually. I'm just down here for a few weeks."

"And you chose to work for this one?" Eddie teased, smirking at Grey.

"Shut up," Grey grumbled as she shot him a playful glare.

Lauren glanced over at Grey. "I did," she said, though the words sounded less assured than she would have preferred.

"Smart girl." Eddie winked and turned his attention to the pile of wrapped meats that were stacked beside him. "So, here's what I have for ya…" He showed Lauren the steaks, sausages, ground beef, and chicken he had prepared according to Grey's order. He carefully rewrapped each bundle after Lauren nodded her approval and set them into a large brown paper bag. When the last white-paper package was placed inside the bag, he folded the top over and slid it across the counter beside the register. "I'll put it on your tab," Eddie told Grey.

"Sounds good, man. Thanks," Grey said as she reached for the bag. She grunted softly as she hefted it off of the counter, and forced herself to smile as she glanced at Lauren. "You ready?"

"Of course," Lauren murmured. She looked back at Eddie and added, "It was nice to meet you."

Eddie nodded. "You too, Lauren Murphy. Good luck."

Lauren flashed him a small smile and nodded. "Thanks." *I have a feeling I'm going to need it,* she added silently to herself as she looked back at Grey, who was already halfway out the door.

Chapter 5

Lauren was in the galley prepping the burgers she was going to make for lunch when the sound of excited voices spilled through the open sliding doors into the salon. The Mueller family had finally arrived.

Lauren looked over her shoulder at the clock on the range, and was shocked to see that three hours had passed since she and Grey had returned to the *Veritas*. She had spent the time preparing as many of the ingredients she would be using during the next couple days as she could, while Grey stayed as far away from her as possible, checking and re-checking the boat's mechanicals to make sure they were ready to sail. The break from the inexplicable tension that simmered between them had been a blessing, and Lauren sighed as she felt her stomach twist uncomfortably when she looked at Grey, who was already on the back deck greeting their guests. Whatever it was that had Grey behaving so strangely obviously had something to do with her, because the genuine smile lighting the brunette's face now showed none of the strain that had been directed toward her earlier.

Both of the parents and all three boys were smiling as they nodded in response to whatever it was Grey was saying, all of them obviously thrilled to be on the boat, and Lauren wiped her hands off on a dishtowel as she walked out of the galley to greet them.

Though Lauren was sure that none of their guests noticed, it did not escape her attention that Grey's smile dimmed the moment she set foot on deck, and she forced herself to act like she did not notice it as she approached the group.

Grey took a deep breath and held it as she watched Lauren saunter out of the salon like she had done it a thousand times before. Lauren had changed into the shirt she had given her—a white ClimaCool polo with *Veritas* stitched in red over the right breast—and seeing her in the polo made Grey regret giving it to her. It was hard enough to look at Lauren and not be assaulted by the ghosts of her past when the redhead was in her regular clothes, but when she was in uniform… Grey sighed and focused her attention on the Mueller boys, who were dressed in matching blue and red patterned boardshorts and white rash guards and were practically vibrating with excitement. "This is Lauren Murphy." Grey waved a hand at Lauren. "She'll be the one preparing all our meals."

"It's a pleasure to meet you all," Lauren said, tipping her head in greeting.

"I'm Will," the husband introduced himself, smiling as he shook Lauren's hand. "And this is my wife Kim, and our boys Reid, who's five, and Peyton and Max, who are seven."

Lauren nodded and shook Kim's hand before turning her attention to the boys. All three took after their mother with their honey-blond hair and bright blue eyes, though they had their father's olive-toned skin. "How's it going, guys?" she asked, holding her hands out and getting high fives from each of them. "You hungry?"

"Starving!" Reid announced dramatically as his brothers nodded their agreement.

"Great." Lauren grinned at them and arched a brow questioningly. "How do burgers sound?"

Grey smiled at the way the boys cheered and jumped up and down eagerly in response to Lauren's question. Taking families out on cruises was always fun because the kids got so excited about everything. And the younger they were, the more amplified that excitement became, which made the trip all the more enjoyable for her.

Because she knew that they were running on a tight schedule to get out of port before the seas kicked up later that afternoon, Grey clapped her hands and drew everyone's attention back onto herself. "Well, while Lauren makes lunch, why don't I show you guys to your cabins so you can unpack a bit. After lunch, we'll leave for Saint Frances Bay. It's a short sail, and you'll have plenty of time to swim or explore the beach before dinner."

The kids needed no further encouragement as they ran off to find their rooms for the trip, and Grey chuckled as she led Will and Kim inside, giving them basically the same spiel she had delivered to Lauren earlier that morning. "This is the salon…"

Lauren hung back on the deck and watched through the open doors as Grey showed the Muellers around, and only wandered inside once the family had disappeared down the starboard stairs to the cabins Reid and Will and Kim would be using. She smiled at Max and Peyton when the boys sprinted back into the salon to check out their cabins again, and she chuckled under her breath at the sound of them bouncing on one bed, running through the small bathroom that joined their rooms, and then jumping on the other bed.

Lunch was definitely a more active affair than Lauren was used to, but the boys' excitement over being on "a real sailboat" was palpable, and she found her own anticipation for the trip building as she listened to them talk about everything they hoped to see and do. She was no stranger to being on the water, but the

Caribbean promised far more adventure than the lake she had grown up on could ever do, and by the time the burgers and oven fries were polished off, she was just as ready as the kids were to get underway.

Lauren collected everybody's plates and carried them into the kitchen, waving off Kim's offer to help, though she did smile gratefully at Grey when the brunette brought all the condiments inside and put them back in the fridge. Lauren rinsed off the plates and loaded them into the dishwasher, and she was pleasantly surprised when Grey picked up a dishtowel to dry the baking sheet for her. "Thank you," Lauren murmured as she watched Grey put the baking sheet away in its proper place.

Grey glanced at Lauren and nodded as she hooked the door shut with her heel. She was halfway to the sliding doors by the time the cabinet door clicked shut, the magnet in the frame holding it closed. She did not look back as she wandered through the salon to the back deck, and she took a deep breath as her eyes swept over the familiar contours of the marina. The promise of having the wind in her face as they skipped across the sea made the weight that had settled on her chest all morning completely disappear, and she was suddenly itching to go. To motor to the mouth of the harbor, hoist the mainsail, and let the wind carry her away. Even the sound of Lauren's quiet footsteps coming out of the salon behind her did little to dampen her spirits, and Grey was still smiling when she turned to look at her. "Can you throw the lines?"

Lauren's breath hitched at the sight of Grey's smile. Grey was radiant. Her smile was wide, carefree, and brimming with a zest for adventure, and Lauren was shocked at how strongly she reacted to it. She stared into Grey's eyes that seemed to sparkle, and nodded once, not trusting herself to speak.

"All right. Start with the bow, then do the spring line, and save the stern for last. I'll be up on deck following you, so you can just toss them to me, okay?" Grey's smile grew wider when she was answered with another small tip of Lauren's head. "Awesome. Wait for me to get up to the helm before you throw the stern line, just in case the current decides to do something weird. As soon as you get the last one free, jump onto the dive platform and make sure you keep the line away from the props."

"I got it." The skin on Lauren's arm tingled where it brushed against Grey's as she edged past her, and she shook her head as she hurried down the stairs to jump onto the dock.

Lauren worked quickly, untying the lines and tossing them up to Grey, who coiled them around her arm before stowing them safely away, and less than five minutes later, she was back on the small square dive platform with the stern lines in her hands. She wrapped the ropes around her elbow and fist as she made her way up to the deck, dropped them into the small storage compartment Grey had left open for her, and flipped it closed with the side of her foot.

The Muellers were sitting at the starboard-side table on the back deck, looking out over the harbor with wide, eager eyes as Grey began pulling smoothly away from the dock. Wanting to give the family some space to enjoy the start of their vacation, but still wanting to experience the departure for herself, Lauren made her way along the port-side hull to the trampolines that stretched across the bow.

Standing at the helm up on the bridge, Grey stared out over the horizon, feeling more content than she had all day. The wheel beneath her hands was solid and warm, and she could feel the pull of current sliding around the rudders. She was in her element, totally in-control of everything, and she relished the calm that knowledge gave her.

Sailing had always been her escape. She had spent her childhood on the much cooler waters off the coast of Rhode Island racing two-man catamarans with her father, and when she had gone west to UC San Diego for college, she spent the majority of her weekends at Mission Bay sailing casually around the bay or taking on whomever she could goad into a race. Salt water ran in her veins, and when she was away from the sea for too long, she would actually become ill.

Movement in her periphery drew her eyes down, and she held her breath as she watched Lauren lower herself gracefully onto the starboard trampoline. Though she would be the first to say that the twelve years she had spent since college sailing the Caribbean had been a dream, the last three had been more of a nightmare: an all-encompassing, never-ending horror that she could not escape.

She thought she had been doing a decent job deluding herself into believing that she was okay, that the alcohol and the faceless women she lost herself in were enough—until she walked into the salon earlier that morning to find Lauren Murphy staring at the galley like it was the most incredible thing she had ever seen. Lauren's fiery red curls had thrown a blinding spotlight on her futile struggle to forget, and she was left wondering how she had ever managed to convince herself that she was okay.

Chapter 6

The back deck of the *Veritas* was bathed in a combination of light from the moon overhead and the warm glow of the lights from the salon that spilled through the open sliding doors. The sun had set half an hour earlier, leaving the sky a mix of blues and blacks, dotted by stars that burned brightly in the darkening heavens. Lauren spent the afternoon in the kitchen finishing the prep she had not done earlier that day, while Grey busied herself with making sure the sails and rigging were all properly stored after their afternoon at sea and the Muellers spent the time in the water: swimming, jumping off the side of the boat, and teaching the boys how to snorkel.

Grey hummed quietly under her breath as she popped the last bite of her Mahi-Mahi into her mouth and chewed it slowly, letting the flavors of the lemon-soy marinade and the pineapple salsa Lauren had piled on top of the fish flood her taste buds. She had eaten more than her fair share of gourmet meals over the years, that was just one of the perks of captaining a charter yacht, but she had never tasted anything as wonderful as the meal Lauren had just prepared. The ingredients were simple—fish, wild rice, and steamed vegetables—but the things Lauren had done with them were out of this world. "That was seriously amazing."

The quiet compliment made Lauren blush, since Grey had gone out of her way to avoid her all day long, and she smiled shyly as she tipped her head in a small bow. "Thank you."

"You're welcome," Grey murmured, forcing herself to hold Lauren's gaze for an extended beat before it became too much for her and she had to look away. It was still too hard to look at Lauren and not be reminded of all she had lost, but at the same time, she was finding it harder and harder to *not* look at her either. She could not explain it, but there was something about Lauren that just called to her.

"Dinner was absolutely incredible," Kim Mueller agreed. The sentiment was echoed by her husband and all three boys, who were bookended by their parents at the table opposite Grey and Lauren.

Lauren smiled. "I'm glad you all enjoyed it. Would you like dessert now, or would you rather wait a bit?"

"Dessert!" the boys yelled, bouncing in their seats and drumming their hands on the table excitedly.

Grey chuckled and shot a questioning look at Will and Kim, who simply smiled indulgently at the boys and nodded their approval. Grey grinned and winked at the boys as she slid out of the banquette and began gathering the Muellers' plates. "Looks like you guys don't have to wait."

Kim started to stand as Grey took her plate. "I can help."

"Nonsense. Stay and enjoy your family," Lauren said, shaking her head at Kim as she stacked the boys' plates to make them easier to carry. "We got this," she added, glancing at Grey, who nodded her agreement.

The dirty plates were set into the sink to be dealt with later, and Lauren smiled gratefully at Grey as she opened a cupboard near the stove and pulled out a saucepan. "Thank you for helping bring everything in. Would you like some dessert?"

"It's not a problem. And, sure. Are we having the brownies you made this afternoon while everybody was swimming?"

"We are." Lauren held the small saucepan beneath the tap at the sink and, once there were a few inches of water in it, placed it onto the stove and set the burner beneath it on high. "Would you mind pulling a jar of hot fudge sauce from the pantry? I'm going to do sundaes."

"Of course," Grey murmured, turning to retrieve the bottle of gourmet hot fudge sauce from the pantry. She twisted the top off on her way to the stove, and set it into the saucepan. "Bowls?"

"Please." Lauren moved the glass baking dish that held the brownies she had made earlier onto the counter beside a large chef's knife. An ice cream scoop was placed next to the knife, and then Lauren pulled a small container of fresh whipped cream that she had prepared just before dinner from the fridge, along with a large tub of vanilla ice cream from the freezer.

"You're spoiling those boys," Grey pointed out with an amused smile as she set seven bowls onto the counter beside Lauren's supplies. She leaned against the counter beside the range and watched Lauren peel back the plastic wrap that was covering the brownies.

Lauren laughed and began cutting the brownies into squares. They had not yet completely cooled, and she moaned softly as she popped a small piece into her mouth. "Forget the boys, this is my favorite dessert."

"Really?"

"Yes, ma'am," Lauren drawled as she carefully lifted a large brownie square from the baking dish and set it into a bowl. "Don't get me wrong, I love me some cheesecake, but this is the best. Brownie, ice cream, hot fudge, a little whipped cream…" Her voice trailed off and she shook her head, sending an errant curl into her face. "There's nothing better than that."

Grey cleared her throat, her eyes glued to the rogue tendril tickling Lauren's cheek. Her heart skipped a beat as she stared at the juxtaposition of warm red ringlets and flawless alabaster skin, and she found herself torn between wanting to reach out and tuck the hair behind Lauren's ear, and screaming in frustration because Lauren was not who she wanted her to be. With her wild curls pulled back into a messy ponytail that left the elegant slope of her neck exposed, the gentle curve of her jaw and the light dusting of freckles over her cheeks, it was almost too easy to pretend that Lauren was somebody else. It would be so much easier for her if there was *something* about Lauren that was easy to dislike—an obnoxious voice, bad attitude, terrible teeth, anything she could fixate on to keep herself from feeling so drawn to her—but Lauren was perfectly alluring, and Grey could not help but hate her a little for that.

She was so lost in her thoughts that she missed whatever it was Lauren said next, and she startled when Lauren turned, knife cradled loosely in her hand, to level her with an expectant look. "I'm sorry?"

Lauren's brow dropped as she looked at Grey. She had been mindlessly chattering away as she worked, pleased that Grey was actually engaged in a genuine conversation with her, but the far-away, almost haunted look in Grey's eyes told her that she had been wrong. "I asked you how the fudge was looking."

"Oh." Grey's eyes dropped to the glass jar on the stove that she had been idly stirring. She lifted the spoon and watched the chocolate sauce pour from the end in a silken ribbon. "It's good."

"All right," Lauren said, forcing herself to smile as she dropped a generous scoop of ice cream onto a brownie and handed it over to Grey. "Just hit that sucker with the fudge, and then I'll put the whipped cream on."

"This looks really good," Grey murmured as she began spooning hot fudge onto the sundae.

Lauren nodded and turned to hand Grey a second bowl. Her eyes grew wide when she saw how much fudge Grey had poured onto the ice cream, and she hurried to yank the bowl out of her hand. "That's too much!"

"Psht." Grey shook her head as she took the fudge-less bowl Lauren was holding out for her. "It's hot fudge. It doesn't count unless it's too much. Besides, the boys will love it."

There was really no way for Lauren to argue either of those points, and she chuckled as she turned back to the counter to finish preparing the next sundae. "Who wouldn't?"

Grey smirked and set the second completed bowl onto the counter beside the first. "Exactly."

Once they had finished preparing sundaes for everybody, Grey grabbed the three she had overloaded with hot fudge and took them out for the boys. Lauren followed with Will and Kim's desserts, and could not help but laugh at the jubilant, wide-eyed look that lit each of the boys' faces as they stared at the bowls of hot fudge.

"Hey boys, why don't you have some hot fudge with your ice cream," Kim laughed.

"All Grey's fault," Lauren shared as she handed Kim her bowl.

Will took his with a grateful smile, and looked at it for a moment before he elbowed Reid playfully and asked, "Wanna trade? You got more chocolate sauce."

Reid, who had already managed to cover half his face with fudge, shook his head and pulled his bowl closer to himself. "Mine!"

"Would you like more hot fudge?" Lauren offered.

"Nah, I'm good," Will chuckled.

"If you're sure…" Lauren smiled and turned back to the salon for her own bowl.

After the desserts had been polished off and the boys had licked their bowls clean with gleeful giggles, Lauren gathered the dirty dishes and carried them into the galley. It took a little bit of Tetris mojo to get everything into the dishwasher, but she eventually managed to fit everything in. She smiled to herself as she wiped the counters down with a dishtowel, pleased that the Muellers had enjoyed the meal, and blew out a loud breath as she turned to survey her temporary kingdom. She had not really known what to expect when she decided to become a private chef on a luxurious yacht, but it had been a nice change of pace from the hectic pace of the kitchen at Clarke's.

Her eyes skipped over the empty salon, drinking in the sight of gleaming light wood and rich red and gold accents, and her breath caught in her throat when she finally spotted Grey leaning against the dining table, the knuckles of her left hand white as she strangled the neck of the guitar she was holding. Lauren frowned as she took in the conflicted expression darkening Grey's features, and she licked her lips nervously as she held her gaze. "Grey?"

Grey shook her head, not trusting herself to speak. She had been on her way back outside to play some music for the Muellers while the boys wound down for bed when she spotted Lauren working at the sink, her lean body swaying slightly to a song only she could hear. Memories of another redhead doing the exact same thing flooded her mind, and she had barely grabbed onto the edge of the table before her knees threatened to give out beneath her. Even now, with Lauren staring back at her with a bewildered look on her face, Grey could not move.

The air between them seemed to crackle with electricity as they held each other's gaze, and Grey finally felt herself released from the magnetic pull of Lauren's stare when the redhead turned to watch an energetic blur in Spiderman pajamas bolt through the salon for the back deck. The loss of visual contact was enough to spur Grey into motion, and she shook her head as she headed for deck. It was all she could do to not run, as her heart raced and her body all but trembled with the need to escape, to find some kind of space that would give her time to try and understand what had just happened.

Chapter 7

Grey had not slept so badly in years. It took her what felt like forever to get comfortable, and once she finally did fall asleep she had been immersed in dreams that broke her heart all over again, leaving her gasping for air when she bolted awake. After the third time it happened, she gave up on trying to get any sort of rest. She swore under her breath as she ran her hands through her hair, and shook her head as she slid out of bed.

The sky outside the salon windows was still muddled in the charcoal hues of night when Grey wandered up the stairs to the main cabin, and her step faltered when she spotted Lauren in the galley preparing breakfast.

Fucking hell, she thought as reached out to steady herself against the side of the refrigerator. She had just been hoping to grab a cup of coffee to while away the minutes before the sun began to rise and it would be safe for her to hit the water for a punishing swim that would burn off the anxiousness that had settled in her muscles over the last twenty-four hours.

Lauren was barefoot, with her hair pulled back in a messy twist of a bun, wearing a pair of short blue boardshorts and a pale gray Henley whose sleeves were shoved halfway to her elbows. Grey's eyes slid slowly over Lauren's legs, noting the subtle play of muscles as Lauren shifted her stance to reach for something she needed. Her gaze lingered on Lauren's ass, which was barely covered by her shorts before sweeping higher, taking in the way Lauren's shoulders curved into her neck and her ridiculously sexy hair.

Grey hated the way her heart beat faster when she looked at Lauren. Hated the way her stomach flipped whenever their eyes met. She did not want to find Lauren attractive, but she did.

God help her, she did.

Though the voice of self-preservation in the back of her mind screamed for her to slink back down the stairs to her cabin, Grey instead stepped forward into the galley, figuring that she may as well try and deal with her unwelcome attraction toward her temporary chef. She did not miss the way Lauren tensed when she realized that she was no longer alone, and Grey offered Lauren a small smile as she pulled her favorite mug and a pod of her favorite roast from the cupboard above the coffee machine. "Good morning."

Lauren looked up from what she was doing and smiled hesitantly at Grey, unsure of where things between them stood after the way Grey had run out on her the night before. "Good morning. I wasn't expecting anyone to be up yet."

"Couldn't sleep," Grey muttered as she glanced at the glass baking dish in front of Lauren. "Whatcha making?"

"Crème brûlée french toast."

"Looks good. You want some more coffee?" Grey tipped her head at Lauren's empty cup. She could hear the tenseness in her tone, but she was relieved to see that Lauren did not seem to notice it.

"That would be great, thanks," Lauren murmured, smiling as she handed her mug to Grey.

Grey took the plain red mug without a word and set it down on the counter as her mug finished filling. While she waited, she watched Lauren cover the glass dish with a sheet of foil and set it into the fridge beside a second dish that she had already prepared. She glanced at her watch to double-check that it was, in fact, stupid-early o'clock, and arched a brow questioningly at Lauren as she switched out the mugs and put a fresh coffee pod into the machine. "How long have you been awake?"

"A while," Lauren confessed with a shy smile, not wanting to admit that she had lain awake for most of the night trying to figure out what she had done to make Grey so uneasy around her. She started rinsing out the dishes she had used to prepare breakfast and asked, "So, how long have you been doing this?"

"The charter thing?" The machine beside Grey stopped spitting coffee into Lauren's mug, and she set it down beside the sink. "Eleven years."

Lauren looked up in surprise. "Really? What'd you do, start doing this right out of college?"

"Pretty much. I came down here when I was twenty-three," Grey said as she walked out of the U-shaped galley and sat down at one of the barstools on the opposite side of the peninsula. The physical barrier helped her feel more at ease, and her pulse slowed to a more regular tempo as she watched Lauren over the rim of her mug.

"Wow." Lauren pursed her lips thoughtfully as she debated which question she could ask next that wouldn't have Grey shutting down on her and running from the room. "And what made you want to captain a charter yacht?"

Grey looked out the glass doors to her left, her eyes tracing the contours of the mountains surrounding the bay that stood in dark contrast to the slate blue sky. "I sailed around by myself for a year, but that got boring pretty fast, so I figured it was the easiest way to do what I loved and not be totally alone."

"You own the *Veritas*?" Lauren's eyes grew wide as she looked around the salon of the seventy-five-foot catamaran. She had no idea how much a boat like this would cost, but she knew that it had to be *at least* a few million.

"Yep," Grey said, a proud smile quirking her lips as she looked around her boat. She caught the look of disbelief Lauren was giving her and shrugged. "I was a computer science major at UCSD back before it was cool to be a computer science major, and wrote a couple algorithms that streamlined internet searches, effectively weeding out irrelevant data to return more accurate results, and was able to sell them for a tidy profit."

"Holy shit. You invented Google?"

Grey laughed and shook her head. "No. I just wrote a couple programs that made sites like Google work better."

"Damn," Lauren drawled as she started washing the things she had used to prepare breakfast.

Grey chuckled. "Anyways, I grew up racing two-man cats with my dad, so coming down here and buying a boat seemed like a no-brainer. And the rest, as they say, is history." She took another sip of her coffee and watched Lauren thoughtfully dry a glass mixing bowl. "What about you? What made you decide to go to culinary school?"

"I just always loved cooking." Lauren rolled her eyes as she set the bowl aside and reached for the dirty saucepan that was sitting on the stove. "And, well, New York seemed like a great adventure after growing up in the Midwest."

Pleased that they were managing to have an actual, albeit simple, conversation, Grey asked, "Where in the Midwest?"

Lauren's brow dropped as she stopped scrubbing the saucepan she had been cleaning. "Didn't you look at my résumé before you hired me?"

"Nope." Grey shook her head. "Kelly Kipling is a good friend of mine, and I trusted her to find me a chef because I usually just steal hers for charters."

"Her chefs?"

"She's the general manager for Kipling Resorts here in the islands."

"Oh. I see," Lauren drawled as she resumed cleaning. "I was wondering why, when I spoke with her on the phone, she asked me if I had ever considered heading a hotel kitchen."

Grey laughed and leaned back in her chair. "She's always looking for new talent, and she was quite impressed with your résumé. So, anyways, back to the point: where in the Midwest are you from?"

Lauren rinsed the soap from the saucepan and turned off the water. "Um, the Minneapolis area," she answered as she picked up a dishtowel and began drying the pan. "How about you?"

"Newport, Rhode Island." Grey sipped at her coffee as they fell into a slightly uncomfortable silence now that the easy get-to-know-you type questions had been exhausted. She watched as Lauren finished drying the cookware and put it away, and then leaned back against the counter with her coffee mug in her hands. Grey's eyes traced Lauren's long fingers that were wrapped lightly around the red and blue ceramic mug she was holding, and she shook her head as she forced herself to look away. "So, um," she started, trying to find another avenue of conversation to follow, "do you have a boyfriend back in New York?"

"I haven't had a boyfriend since I was in the ninth grade." Lauren smiled as she watched understanding dawn in Grey's eyes. "Not really my thing, ya know?"

Grey nodded slowly, hating the way her heart seemed to leap into her throat at what Lauren had just revealed. "I, uh…" She looked down at her nearly empty mug and then at the sky outside that was still too dark for her to safely hit the water, and sighed. She needed space. "I should go shower and stuff before the Muellers get up," she muttered, forcing herself to smile at Lauren as she slid off of her barstool.

"Yeah," Lauren murmured, her brow furrowing with confusion as she watched Grey leave. The sound of Grey's cabin door clicking shut echoed quietly through the salon, and Lauren frowned as she turned to look out the window, unable to help but wonder why her being gay would make Grey so flustered.

Chapter 8

Grey knew that she needed to apologize to Lauren for running out on her. Not just because it was the second time she had done so in a relatively short amount of time, but because she had done it right after Lauren had come out to her. She of all people understood how badly her reaction could be taken, and she hated the idea of Lauren thinking that she was neither safe nor welcome aboard the *Veritas* because of who she was.

No matter how much Grey knew that she needed to apologize, Fate seemed determined to keep her from doing so. She had intended to do it when she returned to the salon after showering, but Kim was already awake and chatting amiably with Lauren in the galley, and the day just got busier from there. Breakfast was followed by a quick sail to Leinster Bay for a morning of snorkeling where the boys spent more time running around the boat and jumping off the side into the water than they actually spent in the water itself. Lunch, followed by another short sail, and then clearing-in with British customs took up the middle of the afternoon, and as soon as their paperwork was in order she was back at the helm, sailing toward White Bay to tie-up for the night. Between dinner prep and playing hostess, she never had more than a minute or two alone with Lauren, and she knew that it was going to take more than a rushed "I'm sorry" to smooth things over.

It was not until much later that night, when the dessert dishes had been cleared and put away and the Muellers were huddled around the port-side deck table playing a spirited game of Go Fish before the boys went to bed, that Grey finally had the opportunity to track Lauren down. Never truly being alone with Lauren should have made it easier for her to deal with the confusing mix of attraction and guilt that bubbled inside her, but for some reason it only left her feeling anxious. It was irrational and completely unexplainable, but the professionally polite distance they had maintained when dealing with each other all day just felt *wrong*.

She eventually found Lauren sitting on the trampolines at the bow of the boat, and she took a deep breath to steel her resolve before she called out to her. "I'm sorry."

The words were soft, the voice unmistakable, and Lauren's gaze was cautious as she looked up at Grey, who was holding a tumbler of a sable-colored alcohol out for her. It was clearly meant to be an olive branch, and she sighed as she reached out and took it. She was no closer to understanding why Grey had run out on her earlier, but if Grey was willing to try and talk about it, she was more than willing to listen. "Thanks. What is it?"

Grey lowered herself onto the trampoline beside Lauren, and sighed as she lifted her eyes to the stars that shone brightly against the inky backdrop of the night sky. "Scotch. This is definitely a scotch kind of conversation."

Lauren sipped at her drink. It was smooth, with an unmistakable toffee flavor that was layered with citrus, cinnamon, and something else Lauren couldn't quite identify, and she hummed approvingly as she swallowed. "What's the label on this?"

"Auchentoshan, Three Wood. It's a distillery in the Scottish lowlands." Grey took a generous swallow, not bothering to savor the taste of the alcohol, just using it as a numbing balm for the wounds she was about to rip open. "I'm sorry."

"You said that." Lauren pulled her knees up to her chest and wrapped her arms around her shins, the tumbler in her right hand dangling loosely from her fingertips.

"Well, I mean it." Grey took another drink, smaller this time, and turned to look at Lauren, who was regarding her with an expectant look, one thin brow arched questioningly as she waited for her to continue. "I was an ass."

"Yeah, well," Lauren murmured with a small shake of her head, "I don't know if I'd go quite that far."

"I would."

The dejection in Grey's tone made Lauren stop and look at her. The circles under Grey's eyes were impossible to miss, even in the low light, and the resigned curve of her shoulders signaled utter defeat. Lauren sighed and leaned forward just far enough to catch Grey's eye. "Hey. It's okay."

"No, it's not." Grey shook her head. "I just…it wasn't because you told me you were into women."

Lauren chuckled wryly and shot Grey a knowing look. "I would hope not. That would be pretty hypocritical of you, don't you think?"

"How…?"

"I was at Jack's on Friday night." Lauren nodded as she watched understanding dawn in Grey's expression. "I watched you pick up that blonde. She was pretty."

"She was a distraction," Grey muttered as she looked back up at the stars. "They're always just a distraction."

Lauren sighed and took another sip of her drink as the hollowness of Grey's voice melted away any lingering frustration she might have felt toward her. There was obviously more to Grey's story—a painful reason that Grey's eyes looked so haunted whenever she caught her staring. Lauren had spent the day wishing for some kind of an explanation as to why Grey kept dancing around her, becoming friendly and then bolting away as if burned, but she realized that she did not want it. Not like this, anyway. "Look, don't worry about this morning. We're good."

Grey let out a shaky breath, relief flooding through her as she looked into warm hazel eyes that stared unblinkingly back at her. "You serious?"

"Yeah." Lauren nodded.

"I…" The genuine smile curling Lauren's lips was enough to convince Grey that Lauren meant it, and she sighed, her entire body relaxing at the reprieve. "Thank you."

"No problem." Lauren lifted her glass in a silent toast before she took a small sip and turned her attention toward the horizon. She kept her gaze trained on the line where the inky black sea and the deep indigo sky met, purposefully ignoring Grey's eyes that she could feel on her. She could have filled the air with meaningless chatter, but she enjoyed the quiet, and she had a feeling that Grey might need it too.

Grey stared at Lauren, baffled by her forgiveness. She knew that she did not deserve such kindness, not after the way she had behaved from the moment they first met, but there was a serenity in Lauren's expression that told her it was real.

The silence that stretched between them was gentle and easy, a far cry from the tenseness that had surrounded them the day before, and the longer it lasted, the more relaxed Grey became. She felt the weight on her shoulders begin to lift ever so slightly, and she found herself able to breathe more fully than she had in a long time. It was surreal, how much better she felt sitting in silence beside a woman she barely knew—a woman who reminded her too much of someone she would never forget. It was strange and scary and kind of amazing, but the shadow of loss that had been her constant companion these last few years became less overwhelming with every breath she took.

Time passed in a hazy blur, and Grey was surprised when she realized that the lights from the bedrooms that overlooked the bow had been turned off, leaving the *Veritas* illuminated by only the moon and the stars overhead. She could not remember the last time she had felt so at peace, and she selfishly wished that she had thought to bring the bottle of scotch out with her so that they would have an excuse to spend the rest of the night right where they were. It had been too long since she had felt this content, and her stomach dropped in disappointment when the sound of Lauren yawning quietly beside her signaled that it was all about to end.

Lauren smiled apologetically at Grey. "I should probably go to bed. I need to wake up early again tomorrow to get breakfast ready."

"What are we having?" Grey asked, trying to extend the moment as long as possible, knowing the contentment she was feeling would disappear with Lauren.

"I haven't really decided yet. Is there anything special that you would like?" Lauren asked.

"Waffles."

Lauren smiled at Grey's quick reply, and nodded as she pushed herself to her feet. "All right. I'll make waffles." She leaned down to give Grey's shoulder a light squeeze, hoping the gentle touch would reassure Grey that things between them were still okay. "I'll see you in the morning."

Grey sighed and relaxed into the touch, soaking up the warmth it provided. "See you in the morning."

Chapter 9

Lauren was sitting at the dining table nursing a cup of coffee and reading a book on her iPad when Grey wandered into the salon just after dawn the next morning. Hair still damp from her shower and wearing a pair of short white shorts and a faded red Lifeguard t-shirt, Grey looked relaxed and rested, and Lauren smiled when the brunette's gaze traveled from the waffle machine on the counter in the galley to her. "Good morning," she murmured, being careful to keep her voice down since everyone else was still sleeping.

"You're really making waffles," Grey said, her voice tinged with excitement as she made her way into the galley to make herself a cup of coffee.

"I told you I would. I'm going to fancy them up a bit and make cinnamon roll waffles, but if you'd prefer them plain, I can just not add the swirl and stuff to yours."

Grey shook her head. "You don't need to make anything special for me."

"It's not a big deal," Lauren assured her. "It's just the toppings that would be different."

"Nah, what you're planning on doing sounds great." The coffee machine shut down with a hiss and a splutter, and Grey smiled shyly at Lauren as she picked up her mug. "I just really like waffles."

Lauren chuckled and smiled as she leaned back in her seat. "Yeah, I got that."

The playful twinkle in Lauren's eyes made Grey's stomach flutter, and she ran a hand through her hair as she looked at her. A good night's sleep had done little to shed any light on why, exactly, she felt so at ease around Lauren, but she had decided while she was in the shower to just go with it. There was something about Lauren that drew her in, and the more she thought about Lauren, the harder it became to even think about avoiding her.

Grey cleared her throat softly and hitched a thumb toward the back deck. "Would you, maybe, want to come up to the bridge and watch the sunrise?"

Pleased that the détente they had reached the night before still seemed to be holding, Lauren nodded. "Sure. That sounds great."

The early morning air was cool but not uncomfortably so, and Lauren could not help but smile as she sat down on the sunbathing mat that was laid out in front of the helm up on the bridge. The sky along the horizon was streaked with orange and gold, while the space above clung stubbornly to the darker shades of night in the face of the rising sun. The air stirred with the ever-present trade winds blowing out of the east, and gulls swooped majestically overhead, their excited cries ringing in the new day as they dove for their breakfast.

"Not bad, huh?" Grey asked as she sat down on the opposite end of the red mat from Lauren.

"Not at all." Lauren nodded and sipped at her coffee. She looked out at the horizon and smiled. "I used to go out with my dad on our boat when I was a kid to watch the sunrise. The mornings were usually cooler than this, and a lake in Minnesota obviously has nothing on the Caribbean, but I've always loved this time of day where everything is new and fresh and quiet."

"You probably don't get a lot of quiet in New York."

"You can find it," Lauren murmured, her eyes still trained on the horizon. "Not easily, of course, but if you go into the middle of Central Park early in the morning like this, you can almost forget that you're on an island with over a million and a half other people."

"Yeah, I couldn't do living in a big city like that." Grey shook her head. "I need space."

Lauren tipped her head at their surroundings and hummed softly under her breath. "Well, you've got plenty of that here."

Grey nodded and sipped at her coffee. "Yeah."

They watched the sun inch incrementally higher in a relaxed silence that was reminiscent of the one that had surrounded them the night before, each of them comfortable to simply enjoy the moment. It was a gift, Grey knew, to find somebody who knew how to let go and just exist in the moment without having to fill the air with meaningless words. Kip could do it for a short amount of time, but Grey always knew that her friend was struggling to keep quiet. In fact, besides her father, and now Lauren, she had only ever found one person who would just sit with her like this and not say a word.

Sitting up on the bridge watching the sunrise while nursing her first cup of coffee on the day had been part of her daily routine with Emily, and she was surprised to find that she did not resent Lauren for reminding her. She had spent the last few years remembering the happier times they had shared, the big moments that marked their years together, but she had forgotten about this. Had forgotten about how they would just sit up here and watch the sunrise. It was one of the little things that seemed insignificant, a simple routine that did not mean much in the grand scheme of things—but looking back on it now, Grey realized that it was the little things that meant the most.

She swallowed around a lump in her throat and shook her head. *How could I have forgotten about this?*

Lauren had no idea what made her turn to look at Grey, but the absolutely shattered look in the brunette's eyes rocked her to her core. "Grey?"

"I'm fine," Grey murmured, closing her eyes and scrubbing a hand over her face. "I'm fine."

Grey was obviously anything but fine, but Lauren accepted the lie at face value, not wanting to push. "Right, well…I'm getting hungry. You wanna help me go make some waffles?" she asked, offering Grey both a distraction and an opportunity to be alone, depending on what she needed.

Having something else to focus on sounded like a godsend, and Grey drew a shaky breath as she ran a hand through her hair. "Making waffles sounds great."

"Good." Lauren nodded and pushed herself to her feet. "You can be my sous chef."

Grey smiled in spite of the pain that was radiating through her chest. "Oh, I can, can I?"

"Absolutely." Lauren winked at Grey. "Besides, everybody who loves waffles needs to know how to make these. They're orgasmic."

"Orgasmic, huh?" Grey absently pressed her free hand to her chest, trying to ease the feeling of aching loss that threatened to cripple her.

Lauren nodded. "Bet your ass."

"You sound pretty sure of yourself," Grey pointed out as she dropped her hand to her side.

"Well, yeah," Lauren scoffed as she turned and headed down the stairs. "I mean, I am pretty awesome."

Grey shook her head and followed Lauren into the galley, and she smiled when the redhead threw an apron at her. "You're seriously going to make me cook?"

"I am." Lauren arched a brow challengingly at Grey.

Grey slipped the apron over her head and tying the strings around her waist and gave Lauren a disbelieving look. "I could have sworn that I was paying you to cook the food."

Lauren pulled a large glass mixing bowl full of batter from the fridge and set it down beside the waffle machine. "Come on. Orgasmic waffles do not cook themselves."

"What does orgasmic mean?" a little voice piped up, making both Grey and Lauren jump.

Reid wiggled himself up onto one of the barstools and looked at the two women expectantly.

"It, um…" Grey muttered, shooting Lauren a desperate look begging for help.

"It means really good," Lauren explained, biting the inside of her cheek to keep from laughing. "But, you should probably just say 'really good'."

"Okay." Reid folded his arms on the counter and looked interestedly at the waffle machine. "Can I have a really good waffle?"

"Absolutely, buddy." Grey smiled and plugged in the waffle machine. She turned to look at Lauren, whose shoulders were trembling with silent laughter, and shook her head as she muttered, "Way to teach the kid new vocabulary words, Murphy."

Lauren finally lost it at that, and started laughing as she grabbed the squeeze bottle full of the melted butter, brown sugar, and cinnamon mixture she would use for the cinnamon roll swirls and set it by the batter. "I know!" she hissed, glancing sideways at Grey. She laughed harder at the playful smirk Grey was giving her and shook her head. "Just…get ready to make some really good waffles, Wells."

"Right, because I'm paying you to put me to work," Grey said, nodding sagely.

Lauren grinned and slapped a ladle into Grey's hand. "Exactly. Now, check the waffle machine and see if it's hot enough to start cooking."

Chapter 10

Grey leaned back in her chair at the helm and rested the balls of her feet on the bottom of the wheel to keep the *Veritas* sailing in a straight line toward Sandy Spit as she pulled a wrinkled photograph from her pocket. The edges were worn and creases cut unforgivingly through the image, remnants of the time when she could not go anywhere without the picture of the two of them together because it had been her heart until hers began actually beating again.

"God, I miss you, Em," she murmured, her voice low and rough as she touched Emily's smiling lips with her finger.

She glanced up toward the bow. The water ahead was smooth and free of traffic, and she took advantage of the calm to lose herself in her memories of Emily. Of their first kiss, stolen behind a potted palm at Kip's birthday party. Of the way Emily would sing in the shower, loud and carefree despite the fact that she was, quite possibly, the most tone-deaf person on the planet. The way Emily would smile at her, soft, open, and awed, and the way that smile made her fall in love with her all over again every time she saw it.

Her gaze landed on the ring on Emily's left hand, and tears sprung to her eyes as she remembered the night she had proposed. Anchored in an otherwise deserted bay on Cooper Island, she had made her best attempt at a fancy dinner—though only the grilled shrimp had ended up edible—and even now her heart pounded with the memory of how nervous she had been when she took Emily's left hand into hers and got down on one knee. She dearly wished she could remember what she had said to actually propose, but she would never forget the smile that lit Emily's face when she had said yes. Neither of them had any idea how hard the next few months would be, and Grey was glad that they at least had those few stolen moments of happiness. That they got those few weeks to bask in the idea of a happily ever after before Fate gleefully ripped it from their grasps.

Grey was so wrapped up in her memories that she was aware of nothing but the feeling of the boat's rudders tugging against the wheel beneath her feet. Her eyes would glance up toward the water in front of them every now and again out of habit, but she was not really seeing it. All she could see was Emily.

She was so lost in her thoughts that she did not hear Lauren calling for her, and she jumped at the feeling of a gentle hand on her shoulder and automatically tried to hide the picture in her hand, flipping it over as she turned to find Lauren standing beside her. "Um, hi."

"Hey." Lauren's eyes flicking down to the picture she had not noticed until Grey had hastily tried to hide it from her. She lifted her eyes to meet Grey's, and her stomach dropped at the raw pain she saw looking back at her. "Sorry to interrupt, but Kim was wondering how much longer it would be until we reached the snorkel spot for the morning."

Grey looked down at the chart plotter on her dash. "Probably about fifteen minutes or so. Is everything okay?"

"Yeah." Lauren smiled at the way Grey arched a questioning brow at her. "Max and Peyton just got busted for smacking Reid in the head with a couple of swimming noodles, and she wanted to know how long to leave them in time out. You seriously didn't hear the screaming?"

"No." Grey looked down at the picture in her hand. She did not know what in the world possessed her to do it, but she flipped it back over to show it to Lauren. "I guess I was distracted."

"Understandable," Lauren said, her eyes following Grey's. She tried to hide her surprise at how alike she and the woman in the picture with Grey looked, but her mouth still fell open a little bit in surprise. She was taller than the other woman, whose head had only come up to Grey's shoulder, with a darker complexion and far more freckles, but their hair and eyes were alike enough that they could have easily passed as cousins. "She's pretty."

Grey nodded and smoothed her thumb over the edge of the photo. "Yeah. She was."

"Oh…" Lauren's voice trailed off as she did not know how she should respond to Grey's use of the past tense. "I…"

"She's my fiancée. Or, was," Grey offered quietly. "Emily. She, uh, she died…a little over three years ago."

"Shit." Lauren's right hand hovered in the air above Grey's shoulder for half a second before she gave it a gentle squeeze. Suddenly Grey's '*they're all just distractions*' comment from the night before made perfect sense. "I'm so sorry, Grey."

Grey closed her eyes, drawing strength from the touch even as a feeling of guilt surged through her because of it. "Thanks."

Lauren's gaze dropped to look at the picture of Emily as Grey's shoulder relaxed beneath her palm, the brunette's head turning ever so slightly toward her, like she was trying to lean into the touch without actually doing so. Grey's expression was so heartbreakingly fragile that Lauren found herself needing to look away, and her breath caught in her throat when she saw Kim's head pop into view.

"Hey," Kim called out.

Lauren bit her lip at the way Grey tensed at the sound of Kim's voice, and sighed when Grey sat up straighter, rolling her shoulders to try and shrug her hand off. "We'll be there in about fifteen minutes," she told Kim.

"Closer to ten," Grey piped up, her voice only a little rougher than usual as she shoved the picture between her leg and the seat.

Kim's eyes flicked between the two women and she nodded as she flashed them an apologetic smile, clearly aware that she had interrupted something private. "All right, thanks."

Lauren looked down at Grey, who was staring resolutely ahead with jaw clenched tight and her hands squeezing the life out of the wheel. Everything about Grey screamed to be left alone, and two days ago, Lauren would have done just that. But she remembered the way Grey had leaned into her only moments before, the way her body had relaxed as took the comfort Lauren was offering, and she could not find the motivation to leave. Not when Grey was clearly hurting, and definitely not when she might be able to do something to help ease that pain. Lauren licked her lips nervously as she laid her hand gently back on Grey's shoulder and she let out the breath she had not realized she was holding when Grey relaxed into her touch. Lauren smiled sadly and slid her hand across the back of Grey's shoulders to pull her into a one-armed hug, nothing too much or too confining, but just a light embrace to let Grey know that she was not alone.

As Lauren felt Grey sink into her side, she wished she was better with words so that she could thank Grey for sharing Emily with her. But words had never been her strong suit, and instinct had her turning her head to press a gentle kiss to Grey's temple. It was what her best friend always did to make her feel better when she needed it, and it was not until her lips came into contact with Grey's skin that she realized what she was doing. Her breath caught in her throat as she froze, and then she pulled away as if burned. "I'm sorry," she murmured, her arm dropping to her side. "So sorry," she repeated as she turned and hurried down the stairs.

Grey had frozen at the feeling of Lauren's lips on her skin, and she only let out the breath she had unconsciously been holding once she was sure Lauren had gone. She pulled the picture of her and Emily out from under her leg, and she could not contain the few tears that slipped silently down her cheeks as she looked at the face of the woman to whom she had once promised forever.

Chapter 11

Sandy Spit was a small island that sat just off the northern coast of Jost Van Dyke, with a wide sandy beach around its perimeter and lush tropical foliage filling its middle. It was a quintessential Caribbean islet—the kind of island pirates in the movies were stranded on after a mutiny, with nothing but a bottle of rum and a flintlock pistol loaded with a single shot to put the poor bastard out of his misery once the alcohol had run out and reality set in—and because of that, it was a popular stopping point for many charters operating in the islands.

The sound of music playing greeted Grey when she returned to the *Veritas* from ferrying the Muellers over to the spit, and she smiled as she tied the dinghy's bow line off to a cleat beside the starboard dive platform. It had been a while since she had last heard *Inside Out*, but she had no problem picking up the chorus as she skipped up the stairs to the back deck. Her step faltered, however, when she spotted Lauren sitting at the starboard table, her long legs stretched in front of her and crossed at the ankle while the fingers of her left hand played with a loose curl beside her temple, but she recovered quickly under Lauren's unsure gaze and smiled as she tipped her head toward the salon. "Nice choice."

Lauren smiled somewhat nervously, still unsure as to whether or not she had overstepped her bounds earlier that morning. It had felt natural to try and soothe Grey like that, but the time between then and now had given her plenty of opportunity to replay that brief moment over and over again until she was convinced that she had royally fucked up. "Thanks. I know it's not the classical stuff you like, but…"

Grey waved her off. "It's fine." She ran a hand through her hair, and shivered when her thumb brushed over the spot at her temple where Lauren had kissed her earlier. "You, ah…reading?" she asked, forcing her attention away from the way Lauren was chewing her lower lip nervously and onto the iPad on her lap.

"Yeah. Figured I'd take advantage of the peace and quiet before I need to go start getting things ready for lunch." Lauren turned off the tablet and set it down onto her legs. "How about you?"

Grey shrugged and glanced back at the spit, noting that a couple more boats had arrived in the few minutes she had been talking to Lauren, and that a handful of people had taken to the shallow waters by the beach. "I was probably going to just watch the water. I actually had to jump in after a kid last season because he wasn't a strong enough swimmer to fight the current that wraps around the eastern edge of the island."

Lauren nodded, relieved that Grey was not going to bring up what had happened earlier. "Ah. So you actually earned that lifeguard tee you wore yesterday."

"I did," Grey said as she slipped into the banquette at the table opposite Lauren.

"In college?"

"High school." Grey grinned. "I grew up swimming competitively so the lifeguard thing was a natural fit. And, as an added bonus, I got paid to ogle all the girls in bikinis. Win-win."

"Sounds like it," Lauren chuckled. "You're lucky. I waited tables at the local country club through high school. Not a bikini in sight, there. But, well, I probably wouldn't have wanted to see the old women who came into the club's dining room in bikinis. Were you any good?"

Grey smirked. "At ogling girls?"

"At swimming." Lauren rolled her eyes. "We're all good at ogling girls, Wells."

"I was all right." Grey shrugged modestly. "Made zones pretty much every year, but once I got to San Diego, I realized I would rather spend my free time sailing rather than swimming laps, so I gave up racing."

"Do you still swim, like, just for fun?"

Grey nodded and let her attention drift back toward the water. "I usually hit the water in the morning before everybody wakes up. I just haven't these last few days because… Well, you know."

"Yeah," Lauren murmured, casting an apologetic look in Grey's direction. "I'm sorry about that."

Grey waved off the apology. "It's not your fault. It was just a lot for me to wrap my head around."

"I'll bet," Lauren agreed.

"Yeah." Grey ran her hands through her hair and sighed. "You look so much like Emily that it just kind of threw me for a loop. Ya know?"

Lauren nodded understandingly. "How did you guys meet?"

"Kelly Kipling set us up." Grey smiled at the memory. "She threw herself a birthday party at the Schooner, one of her family's hotels on Saint Thomas, and I was on my way to the bar to get a drink when I saw Emily. I remember thinking to myself how beautiful she was, and then when Kip introduced us...that was it for me. I was hooked."

"Love at first sight," Lauren said, smiling wistfully at Grey's story.

Grey nodded. "Pretty much. Anyways, after about a year of seeing each other whenever I was on the island, she quit her job as an advertising rep for Kip and became my first mate."

"How long were you two together?"

"Three years, four months, and thirteen days." Grey's gaze grew unfocused as she stared out over the water, and she cleared her throat softly. "Can we, uh, talk about something else?"

"Of course."

"It's not that I don't want to tell you about her, it's just that it's…"

"It's fine, Grey," Lauren assured her gently. "I get it. This whole situation is pretty strange."

"You could say that again."

Lauren nodded. "So…what's your favorite movie?"

Grey arched a brow at Lauren, clearly passing judgment on her choice in conversational topics. "*Wind*."

Lauren chuckled. "I should have known that you'd pick a movie about sailing."

"Have you ever even seen it?"

"Um, yeah, Jennifer Grey is in it."

Grey smiled. "Okay, how about you? What's your favorite movie? *No Reservations*?"

"Ha, no." Lauren shook her head. "I mean, I'm always up for some Catherine Zeta-Jones, but no. That movie was awful. Um…I'd have to go with *The Cutting Edge*." She saw the smirk that tweaked Grey's lips before the brunette covered it with her hand and looked away, and she pointed a warning finger at her. "Don't laugh!"

"I'm not," Grey chuckled. "I just…really? *The Cutting Edge*?"

"Shut up." Lauren waved a hand a Grey. "You like *Wind*."

"Yeah." Grey nodded. "As an avid sailor who grew up in Newport freaking Rhode Island, my favorite movie centers around the most prestigious sailing regatta in the world."

"Yeah, well, I grew up in Minnesota. We do some skating up there," Lauren grumbled. "And Moira Kelly was hot in that movie."

"So you have a thing for bitchy spoiled brats?"

Lauren laughed. "No. And I'm not going to get into a discussion about a character from a movie that you obviously hate."

"Aww, you're no fun," Grey teased. "And I don't hate the movie, I just don't think it's favorite movie material. But, fine. What's your favorite television show?"

"Of all time? *The West Wing*," Lauren said automatically, giving Grey a look that dared her to argue. "But *Warehouse 13* is also right up there for me. You?"

"Favorite show of all time has to be *Buffy*. But I binge watched the first two seasons *Once Upon a Time* during the off season this year and actually really liked it," Grey admitted with a small smile. "The first season, anyways. The second one just kind of annoyed me."

Lauren nodded. "I gave up on the show in the second season because I hated what they were doing to Regina's character. To me, that's one of those shows that are better in fic than in real life."

"You read fanfiction?" Grey asked, looking over at Lauren in surprise.

"It's fun to read stories about characters I love from television or whatever where they actually do something about the subtext." Lauren shrugged. "Besides, since you knew *exactly* what I meant when I said 'fic'...you obviously do too."

Grey nodded and held her hands up in surrender. "I do. And, let's be honest, most shows are better in fic than they are in real life."

"Absolutely," Lauren looked down at her iPad that she had more than a hundred such stories downloaded onto, and then back up at Grey. "I think I'm going to go make something to snack on. You want anything?"

Grey looked out over the water and nodded. "Sure. I'll come help."

"I can bring it out to you if you want," Lauren said as she got to her feet.

"Are you trying to get away from me?"

"You caught me," Lauren drawled, rolling her eyes. "Seriously though, if you think you should play lifeguard, I can bring you something to snack on."

Grey waved a hand at the water between them and the island. "The water is actually pretty calm and it looks like everyone over there is content to stay in the shallows, so there's no reason for me to stay out here."

"You just want to keep making fun of me for liking *The Cutting Edge*," Lauren said, grinning over her shoulder at Grey as she made her way into the salon.

"I have no idea what you're talking about, Toe Pick." Grey winked at Lauren as she slid onto a barstool. "So, we've covered movies and television shows… I'm guessing you're a Twins fan."

Lauren shook her head as she set a couple apples and a chunk of gouda onto a cutting board so that she was facing Grey. "I actually grew up rooting for the Cubs because my dad played in their farm system for a while."

"Seriously? That's awesome."

"Yeah. He was a pitcher, but he blew out his shoulder and that was the end of it." Lauren pulled a paring knife from the drawer in front of her. "Since you're a New England girl, I'm guessing you're a Red Sox fan."

"Absolutely." Grey nodded. "So were you a softball player?"

Lauren smiled and shook her head as she began slicing one of the apples into wedges. "My dad would have liked that, but no. I was a decently-awful basketball player though."

Grey chuckled. "I bet you weren't that bad. I mean, the fact that you're tall had to've helped."

"You would think so, but the fact that I was constantly tripping over my own feet made my height rather irrelevant," Lauren replied drolly. She looked up at Grey as she began coring one of the wedges. "I mostly played left ben—" She dropped the piece of apple she had been holding and her knife. "Shit!"

Grey frowned as her eyes automatically dropped to the slash of blood seeping from Lauren's thumb. "Stay there, and I'll go grab the first aid kit." She hopped off her barstool and hurried down the steps to the small landing between hers and Lauren's cabins to retrieve the kit from one of the cupboards.

Only vaguely aware of what Grey was doing, Lauren turned to the sink, flipped on the tap, and pinched her injured thumb under the stream. This was not the first time she had accidentally sliced through her own finger. Cuts and burns were an unfortunate hazard of her job, but it had been a while since she had gotten herself quite this good. She rested her elbows on the edge of the sink and let her head fall between her shoulders as she became dangerously lightheaded. "Fuck."

"How bad is it?" Grey dropped the first aid kit onto the counter and reached for Lauren's hand.

Lauren shook her head. "I'll be fine," she protested weakly as Grey's fingers wrapped gently around her wrist and turned her hand so that Grey could see the cut. "I just need a band aid."

"Just lemme see," Grey murmured, wiping Lauren's hand dry with a paper towel and then leaning in to inspect the wound. It was a clean slice across the pad of the thumb and, she was relieved to see, did not look like it was quite deep enough to require stitches. It was, however, bad enough to need some butterfly sutures. She held Lauren's left hand in her own and she rustled through the first aid kit with her right. "You need a little more than a band aid."

"I've had worse." Lauren pinched the cut closed with her good hand as she watched Grey pull antiseptic wipes, gauze, butterfly sutures, and a band aid from the kit and set them onto the lid of the first-aid kit.

"I'm sure you have." Grey motioned with her head for Lauren to let go of her injured thumb as she tore the top off an antiseptic wipe package with her teeth. "This is gonna sting," she warned half-a-second before she swiped it across the cut.

"Fucker," Lauren hissed, gritting her teeth.

"Sorry," Grey murmured with a small smile. She looked up through her lashes at Lauren and leaned in to blow lightly over the cut to help the stinging alcohol dry quicker as she opened the package of Steri-Strips she would use to close the cut up. She had to use the small pair of scissors in the kit to cut them to size, and her brow furrowed in concentration as she stretched two strips over the cut, pulling the sliced skin together. Blood trickled from the wound, and she sighed as she covered it with a piece of gauze and held it in place. "Once the bleeding slows, I'll cover this with a band aid," she said as she cradled Lauren's injured hand in both of her own.

Though she knew that she was more than capable of applying pressure to her own wound, Lauren simply nodded, lulled into agreement by the feeling of Grey's thumb stroking lazily over the back of her hand. Her heart skipped a beat at the way Grey stared at her, warm brown eyes clouded with concern and something else she could not quite identify. She had no idea how long they stood there, Grey caressing her hand while she held the gauze to her thumb, but when Grey finally pulled it back to inspect the wound, the dressing was soaked with blood.

"Bleeding has pretty much stopped." Grey flicked the edge of her thumb nail over the butterfly sutures to make sure they were still holding, and then let go of Lauren's hand to retrieve the band aid she had pulled out of the kit. She carefully wrapped the bandage around the pad of Lauren's thumb, being careful to not let the bandage's adhesive come into contact with the Steri-Strips holding the wound closed. If it needed to be changed later, she did not want to risk pulling them off.

The silence between them crackled with electricity as she smoothed her thumb lightly over Lauren's. Every breath took more effort to take-in, and the feeling of Lauren's fingers wrapping almost hesitantly around her hand made her pulse race. Her eyes dropped to Lauren's lips, and she licked her own impulsively as the urge to kiss the redhead swept through her.

Lauren noticed the way Grey's attention had dropped to her mouth, and she flashed Grey a small, lopsided smile as she gently pulled her hand away. It would be easy to give in to the attraction she felt toward Grey, but she knew that it would be a mistake. "Um…thank you, for fixing me up," she murmured. "I guess I should start cleaning up this mess."

"Oh." Grey took a step back and ran a hand through her hair. "Yeah. Of course." The walkie-talkie clipped to the waist of her shorts crackled to life, and she frowned as she pulled it free, surprised to be hearing from the Muellers when they still had an hour of play time left on the island. "This is Grey."

"Do you have a first aid kit? Max cut his foot," Kim said without preamble.

"Yeah." Grey's eyes flicked over at the still open kit on the counter. "I'll bring it over right now."

Lauren watched Grey pack up the orange waterproof kit. Grey's posture was stiff, her movement lacking her usual confident fluidity, and Lauren's heart sank when Grey turned to her and she saw the uncertainty dulling her eyes. "I'm sorry."

Grey forced a small smile and nodded. "Pretty sure you didn't mean to almost cut your finger off, so it's okay. I'm gonna go patch up Max, and I'll be back in a few," she said as she hefted the case off the counter. It bumped lightly against the side of her knee, and she added, "Just try and go easy on the knives while I'm gone, just in case."

Chapter 12

"This is the island that inspired Stevenson's *Treasure Island*." Grey glanced over at Lauren as she furled the sails and let the *Veritas* drift into Benures Bay on the northern side of Norman Island.

"Really?" Lauren pushed her sunglasses up onto her head looked around the empty bay. "I loved that book when I was a kid."

"Me too." Grey smiled and let her eyes sweep over Lauren's profile. She had spent the afternoon replaying that moment in the galley over and over again in her mind, trying and failing to make sense of the relief and disappointment she was feeling about it all. She had not missed the searching looks Lauren had thrown her way from the moment she returned from patching-up Max's foot, but she was grateful that Lauren seemed content to pretend like it had never happened. "The treasure caves are on the southern side of Pirate's Bight—the main bay we sailed past to get up here."

"Really?" Lauren's eyes sparkled with interest as she looked at Grey. "Why didn't we stay down there?"

Grey chuckled and shook her head. "Pirate's Bight isn't a good place for kids. Things tend to get a little wild, there's way too much drinking happening in that bay. Last time I was there, there was literally an orgy happening on the tramps of the boat next to us."

"Oh." Lauren nodded slowly. "I see. That's… Wow."

"Yeah." Grey laughed and ran a hand through her hair. "It was pretty nuts. Anyway, that's why I figured we'd just stay up here instead."

"Good idea." Lauren's eyes drifted over Grey's face, and she sighed softly under her breath. She knew that pulling away from Grey earlier had been the right thing to do, but a part of her wondered would have happened had she not. "So, are we going to visit the caves tomorrow, then?"

"Nah. They're fun to explore, but they're also dark, and I don't think it'd be good for the boys. We'll head over to the Indians instead." She hitched a thumb at the archipelago they had passed ten minutes earlier. "It's easier snorkeling, and there are lots of coral and fish to look at."

Lauren turned to look at the cluster of rocks jutting out of the water. "Are there even any mooring balls out there?"

"There are, but we'll have to hit it early to grab one because they fill up fast. I'm thinking I'll get us over there at first light, and then we can do a quick breakfast before they hit the water."

"Okay." Lauren looked back at the bay they were motoring across, her eyes sliding over the low hills that spilled down onto the water. A feeling of giddy excitement filled her as snippets of the story she had not read in years flashed across her mind. She was at Treasure Island. "I'm just gonna go get my phone real fast to take a picture…"

Grey smiled and nodded. "Go for it." She shook her head as she watched Lauren scamper down the stairs, and chuckled softly as she turned her attention back to the water in front of her.

After Lauren had returned to the bridge and taken a good dozen pictures of the bay and the island, she turned with a smile to

Grey as she slipped her phone into the back pocket of her shorts. "So what's the plan for tonight?"

"Eh…probably the usual. More water-time for the Muellers, one of the boys will end up crying, and then we'll have dinner and just hang out until they all go to bed. Is there anything you'd like to do?"

Lauren shrugged. "I don't know."

"Aww, come on." Grey slowed the *Veritas* to a crawl as they neared a mooring ball at the eastern edge of the bay. She pushed her sunglasses up onto her head and gave Lauren a searching look. "There's gotta be something. Snorkeling? Swimming? Taking the kayak out for a spin?"

Lauren laughed and arched a playful brow at Grey. "Are you trying to get rid of me?"

"Not at all." Grey shook her head. "I'm just trying to get you to do a little vacationing on your working vacation."

Lauren smiled and gave Grey's arm a light squeeze. "I'm good. But thank you."

"You sure?" Grey blew out a quiet breath and gave Lauren a look that clearly said she did not believe her. "Because I know that I've pretty much ruined these first few days of your trip. You deserve to have a little fun."

"Grey." Lauren shook her head. "Please, don't. I've had lots of fun."

"Yeah right." Grey rolled her eyes. "I was a total bitch to you the first day we met. Then there was the whole me running out on you when you told me you were gay thing, and then this morning…"

"Yeah, well…" Lauren looked out over the water and tucked her hair behind her ears. Grey was right, her first few days aboard the *Veritas* had been an unmitigated train wreck, but that did not change how she felt about them. "Even with all that, I've still had fun."

It was clear that Lauren was serious, and Grey's expression softened as she looked at her. "You're crazy."

The warmth in Grey's tone was unmistakable, and Lauren sighed as she looked back at her. "Maybe," she agreed, tipping her head in agreement. She held Grey's gaze until the moment felt like it was becoming too much, and then smirked and added, "But I've never claimed to be sane."

Grey laughed. "Well, obviously. I mean, your favorite movie is *The Cutting Edge*, for fuck's sake."

"It's not a bad movie!"

"It's not a great one, either." Grey grinned at the look of indignation that flashed across Lauren's face and nodded as if to confirm her own point.

"You know what, Wells…" Lauren chuckled as she started for the stairs. "I would love to continue this, but I need to get back to work. Those lines aren't going to secure themselves to that mooring ball, you know."

"No, they surely aren't." A small smiled tugged at Grey's lips as she watched Lauren walk away, and before she knew what she was doing, she was calling out to her. "Hey, Lauren…"

Lauren stopped with one foot on the top step and turned to look back at Grey. "Yes?"

"I…" Grey ran a hand through her hair and shrugged. How could she possibly put into words everything she was thinking when none of it made any sense? All she knew for sure was that she was glad Lauren was there with her. "Thank you."

Lauren smiled and nodded. "You're welcome," she answered softly, holding Grey's gaze for an extended beat before she turned and disappeared down the stairs.

Chapter 13

Grey watched the Muellers swim off into the middle of the coral gardens that filled the Indians as she waited for Lauren to finish changing so that they could head out as well. She had been pleasantly surprised by how easy it had been to talk Lauren into going snorkeling with her, and she smiled as she turned the dive mask in her hands over to inspect the lens. She looked up at the sound of Lauren clearing her throat from the doorway, and she was only dimly aware of the way her mouth fell open when she looked at her.

"Goddamn," Grey whispered as her eyes roamed greedily over Lauren's body that was shown off to utter perfection by the navy blue halter-top bikini she was wearing.

Lauren smiled at the look of obvious appreciation on Grey's face and gave the brunette a quick once-over as well. She bit her lip as her eyes dragged over the defined plane of Grey's abs, and she sighed when she eventually forced her eyes back up to Grey's. She was going to have a hard time not staring at her. "Hi."

"Hi." Grey cleared her throat softly and looked at the snorkeling gear that was laid out on the table beside her. "Here, let's get this fitted for you," she said as she handed Lauren a mask.

Lauren slipped the strap over the back of her head and pulled the mask down over her eyes. "Okay."

"How's it feel?"

Lauren pushed on the front of the mask and nodded. "Good."

"We can always make it tighter when we're in the water if it isn't sealed right." Grey waited until she saw Lauren nod again before she lifted a snorkel off the table. "Right, well, your snorkel, milady."

Lauren eyed the bright red snorkel in Grey's hands warily. "It's clean, right?" she asked as Grey clipped it onto the strap of her mask.

"Yes, it's clean." Grey rolled her eyes as she gave the snorkel a light tug to make sure it was on tight. "All of this is my personal gear. I never lend it out to guests, and I can swear to you that you're not going to catch any communicable diseases from using it."

"If I get sick…"

"You are more than welcome to kick my ass. And if I get sick from using it after you…"

Lauren laughed and shook her head. "You won't."

"Well then, yay everybody for being disease-free," Grey drawled. She winked at Lauren as she pulled her mask on, and then picked up her fins. "Do you have any questions?"

"Nope. I'm good." Lauren picked up the remaining fins from the table and looked out at the rocks behind Grey. "Let's go."

Once they were both in the water and Grey was sure that Lauren's equipment was fitted properly, she slipped her snorkel into her mouth and started toward the Indians.

They swam side-by-side through a gap between two of the jutting rocks, and Grey smiled when Lauren grabbed her arm and pointed at a burst of purple coral with the most excited look on her face. Grey followed Lauren around the gardens, occasionally touching Lauren's arm to get her attention when they happened upon something she thought Lauren would like. Though she had swam at this particular spot more times than she could count over the years, Lauren's excitement over every reef fish or different grouping of coral made Grey feel like she was seeing all for the first time as well.

Sunlight cut through the water in golden rays, making the coral lining the walls of the shallow pool practically glow, and Grey was only dimly aware of the fact that she had all but stopped swimming just to watch Lauren. She smiled sheepishly when Lauren turned toward her, one hand held out in a 'what are you doing?' type of gesture, and shook her head as she hurried to catch up.

She had no idea what she was doing. She just knew that she did not want to stop.

They explored the gardens for a couple hours, eventually meeting up with the Muellers. The boys had fun showing off their skills, and Grey found herself laughing more than she had in longer than she could remember. It was the perfect morning, just sun and fun and the water she loved, and Grey's smile was as wide as everyone else's when she finally climbed back onto the *Veritas.*

"That was incredible," Lauren enthused as she wrapped a towel around her waist.

"Yeah." Grey watched a drop of water make its way slowly down Lauren's stomach, and she smiled as she looked up into Lauren's eyes. Her breath felt light in her chest when their gazes locked, and she nodded slowly. "Absolutely incredible."

Chapter 14

Grey's face was a mask of concentration as she backed the *Veritas* toward its assigned berth in Soper's Hole Marina. The marina was situated on the northern edge of Frenchman's Cay, a small island connected to Tortola's West End by a sandbar and a small bridge, and at one time the sheltered bay served as Blackbeard's base of operations. The village itself was small, and the buildings overlooking the harbor were painted in a rainbow of bright, pastel colors. Like Sandy Spit, this was a stop she usually worked into most of her charters—it was a great location to give her guests a taste of the islands, and it also gave them a place to stretch their legs after being cooped up on the boat.

She inched the *Veritas* closer to the dock in small bursts, revving the cat's twin engines to guide them slowly into the slip. Her brow was furrowed as she focused on the distance between the rear dive platforms and the dock, and she bumped the throttle forward just enough to bring the boat to a stop as she watched Lauren leap onto the dock with the stern line grasped firmly in her hand. Lauren was pulling the starboard line tight when Grey hopped down beside her, port line in hand. Once she had looped the line around a cleat, they pulled together guiding the boat back until the bumpers were snug against the dock.

When they were done, Grey turned to Lauren and offered her a small smile. "Nicely done."

Lauren grinned and gave Grey a purposefully awful salute. "Thank you, Cap'n."

"That is the worst salute I have ever seen," Grey chuckled, shaking her head.

"Are we good to go into town now?" Kim called out, interrupting whatever retort Lauren looked ready to hurl in Grey's direction.

"Absolutely." Grey waved the Muellers down. She and Lauren helped the boys make the short hop onto the dock and, once they were all assembled, she pulled a key from her pocket. It was attached to a bright red foam keychain that would float if accidentally dropped into the water, and she smiled as she handed it to Kim. "This is a key to the salon doors, just in case either of us aren't here when you guys get back."

Kim nodded and slipped the key into her purse. "Any suggestions for where we should go?"

"The shops are all fun to poke around in." Grey shrugged and hooked a thumb toward the bright buildings behind her that fronted the wide boardwalk. "And Pusser's Landing is good for dinner. Downstairs is more laid back than up, and there's usually some kind of live entertainment, so if the boys are still wiggly they would be able to get up and move around without disturbing anyone."

"Oh, I think that's where we'll be then." Kim looked at her boys, who were already running down the dock toward town, eager to explore, and shook her head as she slipped her hand into Will's. "Here's to hoping they can run off some of that energy." She smiled affectionately at her children's backs, and sighed as she looked back at Grey and Lauren. "Enjoy your night. We'll see you guys later."

Grey waited until the Muellers were on their way before she hopped back onto the boat, and she looked over her shoulder at Lauren as she climbed the steps to the back deck. "Are there any provisions we need to stock up on since we're here?"

"I don't think so." Lauren shook her head as she followed Grey into the salon. "I mean, we pretty much have everything I'll need for the rest of the trip, unless you can think of something."

"Not really. I do want to offload our trash and top off the water and fuel, though."

"Okay. So, what do you need me to do?"

"Nothing. I'm just going hook up the water, and then I'll call down to the harbormaster's office for a trash pickup. There's not that much, but I'm not in the mood to haul it all over to the dumpster myself."

"Works for me." Lauren pursed her lips thoughtfully and added, "What about the fuel?"

"The dock's on the other side of the harbor—" Grey waved a hand in the general direction of the refueling station, "—so we'll just hit it in the morning. We actually have more than enough gas to finish this cruise, I just always fill up whenever I can."

Lauren nodded. "Makes sense."

"Yeah." Grey ran a hand through her hair and looked around the salon. Her eyes drifted to the spot in the galley where they had been standing the day before when she had almost kissed Lauren, and her pulse spiked at the memory of it. Somehow, in a span of only four days, she had gone from wanting to fire Lauren, to wanting to kiss her. She closed her eyes and took a deep breath as that truth began to truly sink in.

She was genuinely attracted to Lauren. For the first time in three years, she wanted another woman in a way that had nothing to do with forgetting her pain and everything to do with simple desire. She did not want to let go of the hurt and sorrow she had worn like armor these last few years. She did not want to forget

Emily. But she was finally ready to admit to herself that letting go of the hurt and pain she had worn like armor for so long did not mean that she was forgetting Emily. It simply meant that she was moving on.

Grey could not ignore the way her stomach fluttered when she turned to look at Lauren, and she sighed. She would never forget Emily, could never possibly forget her, but she wanted this. And, even though Lauren had been the one to pull away, Grey knew that she had not imagined the spark she felt between them. Two weeks was not enough time for anything serious to develop, but maybe, just maybe, it was enough time for her to learn to live again.

"I…" Grey cleared her throat softly and gave Lauren a small smile. She tried to ignore the way her heart was racing, but she could hear the way it made her voice tremble ever so slightly. "After the trash gets picked up, would you want to maybe go over to Pusser's for some diner? Take advantage of your night off?

Grey's smile was soft and hopeful, and Lauren found herself returning it as she nodded. "That sounds great." She looked down at herself and sighed. Though they were clean, her shorts and shirt were not exactly appropriate for going out. "Would I have time to shower?"

"Of course." Grey's breath caught as Lauren's eyes turned back to her, sweeping slowly up her body in a deliberate once-over. It was not the first time she had caught Lauren looking at her like that, but it was the first time she was willing to acknowledge what it did to her. She arched a brow when Lauren's eyes landed on hers, looking darker than usual and somewhat embarrassed at having been caught, and added, "I'll probably grab one too after I get the trash unloaded, so take as long as you want. The Muellers have a key, we're not in a rush."

Lauren nodded once. "All right." She licked her lips as she held Grey's gaze, and then smiled shyly as she finally looked away and disappeared down the stairs to her cabin.

Grey stared at the empty stairway for a moment, feeling the way her heart fluttered with anticipation in her chest, and shook her head as she pulled her phone from her pocket to call the harbormaster.

Chapter 15

Grey kept stealing glances at Lauren as she led the way to the stairs that led to the second floor dining room above the bar at Pusser's Landing. Lauren's flowing ankle-length skirt sat low on her hips and swished seductively around her legs as she walked, and her teal tank hugged her lithe torso to perfection, but it was her hair that had Grey so captivated. From the moment Lauren had set foot aboard the *Veritas*, her hair had always been up, but tonight she had opted to leave it down. Her curls were soft around her face and tickled the backs of her shoulders, and Grey's fingers itched to comb through the fiery tresses.

The curls seemed to take on a life of their own, bouncing lightly with every step, and Grey was so captivated by it that she flat-out missed the first stair and ended up lunging for the handrail to keep her feet. "Shit," she hissed under her breath as she skipped quickly up a handful of steps before resuming a more relaxed pace.

Lauren chuckled at the way Grey tried to act like nothing had happened. "Looks like my clumsiness is rubbing off," she teased, her eyes glued to Grey's ass. Grey had changed into a pair of cream-colored linen slacks that hugged her backside to delicious perfection, and Lauren was completely hypnotized by the flex of taut muscles beneath the fabric.

Grey glanced over her shoulder at Lauren, and her pulse jumped at the hungry look darkening Lauren's eyes. "No knives for either of us tonight, I guess."

A light blush tinted Lauren's cheeks when she realized that she had been caught staring, and she cleared her throat softly as she shook her head. "Kids menu for everyone, then."

"Dear god, no," Grey chuckled. She led Lauren over to the hostess' station, and smiled as she held up two fingers. "Two, please." She glanced back at Lauren as the hostess gathered their menus and added, "But, I mean, if you want fish sticks and stuff..."

"Yeah, no. I think I'll risk the knives." Lauren fell into step beside Grey as they followed the hostess to their table, her eyes sweeping over the half-empty dining room. They were led to a small table that was pushed up against the balcony railing, and she nodded appreciatively at the view of the marina below. "Wow."

Grey smiled and gallantly pulled Lauren's chair out for her. "Not a bad view, eh?"

"Not at..." Lauren's voice trailed off as she looked over at Grey, who was bent slightly at the waist as she held onto the chair, making the open collar of her pale blue camp shirt flare, giving Lauren the barest peek of black lace against the supple swell of her breasts. She cleared her throat softly and smoothed her skirt over the backs of her legs as she hurried to sit. "Um, not a bad view at all," she finished lamely, licking her lips nervously as she looked back out over the water and offered up a silent prayer that Grey had not noticed her staring. The knowing look Grey gave her as she sat down across the table told Lauren that she had not been so lucky, and she hid her face behind her menu the moment the hostess handed it to her.

"The specials tonight, which you'll find in your menu, are the Caribbean lobster and the pineapple curry shrimp," the hostess recited in a bored tone as she handed a menu to Grey. "Your server, Jameson, will be with you shortly. Enjoy."

"Thank you," Grey murmured. Once the hostess left, she chuckled and opened her own menu, even though she already knew what she was going to order. She had not intended to give Lauren a little show when she pulled her chair out for her, but she was both amused and flattered by Lauren's reaction. "See anything that looks good?"

Lauren let her menu fall and shrugged, refusing to rise to playful twinkle in Grey's eyes. "I don't know. The lobster?"

"Not worth it." Grey shook her head. "I mean, it may be because I grew up in New England and everything, but the lobster here in the islands just isn't that great. Their shrimp curry is pretty good though."

"What are you getting?" Lauren asked, her forehead furrowing thoughtfully as she looked back down at her menu.

"Conch fritters and the jerk chicken salad."

Lauren chuckled at how quickly Grey responded, and looked up at her through her lashes. "I take it that's what you order every time you come here?"

"Pretty much," Grey admitted with a grin. "No matter what you order, though, you gotta have a Painkiller to drink."

"I do, huh?" Lauren flipped to the front of her menu where the restaurant's drinks were listed. The Painkiller was at the top of the mixed drinks menu, obviously the house special—a blend of dark rum, cream of coconut, pineapple juice, orange juice, and nutmeg. Lauren nodded as she flipped back to the entrees. "Sounds good."

"It is," Grey assured her with as smile, her attention shifting from Lauren to the waiter who stopped beside their table.

"Welcome to Pusser's Landing. My name is Jameson, and I'll be your server tonight. Can I start you off with something to drink?"

"Two Painkillers," Grey ordered for them both. "And can we get an order of conch fritters?"

Jameson nodded as he scribbled their order on his notepad. "Of course. Would you like to order your entrees now as well?"

Lauren shook her head and did not bother to look up as she said, "I need another minute."

"Not a problem," Jameson assured her with a smile as he backed away to place their drink order and appetizer orders.

Grey rested her elbows on the edge of the table and perched her chin on her folded hands. Not wanting to make Lauren feel self-conscious, she pretended to look out over the harbor even though she was really watching Lauren read through the menu out of the corner of her eye. It was like watching a silent play. Lauren would silently mouth an occasional word or phrase that caught her attention, and then her forehead would either crinkle in disgust, or a look of pure surprise would light her face as she nodded in agreement with what she was reading. The longer Grey watched Lauren, the more she wished she knew which of the restaurant's dishes elicited each reaction, and she felt almost disappointed when Lauren finished reading and set the folded menu onto the table beside her.

Island service is habitually slow, and tonight was no different, so by the time Jameson returned with their drinks, Lauren had long since finished studying the menu. She waved a hand at Grey to go ahead and order first as she skimmed the menu one last time, before going ahead and ordering the jerk chicken salad as well. She smiled at the surprised look Grey gave her as their waiter disappeared. "I just figured that it has to be good if you order it every time."

"No, it is. I was just thinking that you'd want something more island-y."

"The menu has burgers on it, Grey," Lauren said, her voice tinged with laughter. "I don't think a chain restaurant whose menu consists of burgers, pub grub, and Anglicized fish dishes is the place to expect quality Caribbean fare."

"Not really, no," Grey agreed, chuckling as she reached for her drink. "We'll have a few days off before the next cruise because it's only a five-day charter. I'll take you to a couple of local spots on Saint Thomas that have some awesome island food. Sound good?"

Lauren smiled and reached out to run a finger around the rim of her glass, catching a few flecks of nutmeg on the pad of her index finger. "That sounds great." She put her finger in her mouth, curious as to whether or not the bar used freshly ground nutmeg on the drinks. She was pleased to see that they did, and she hummed approvingly as she wiped her finger dry on her napkin. "Is there a reason the next charter is only five days?"

It was clear from the look on Lauren's face that she had not meant for the whole sucking-her-finger-clean thing to be a tease, that it was just a matter of her tasting an ingredient in the drink, but knowing that did not lessen Grey's reaction to it. Her mouth was suddenly dry—impossibly, been-walking-through-a-desert-for-weeks-with-nothing-to-drink dry—and she could swear that a heater somewhere nearby had been turned on high. Her expression must have shown some of her discomfort because Lauren was looking at her inquiringly, and she shook her head as she took a generous swallow of her drink, hoping that the blended ice would help keep her face from flushing. "What?"

"I said, is there a reason the next charter is only five days?"

"Right," Grey drawled, rubbing her hands on her thighs. "Um, probably the cost. A five-day cruise is not a lot cheaper than the eight, but there is a little bit of a break."

"Makes sense." Lauren picked up her drink and took a tentative sip. The Painkiller was not nearly as creamy as a Piña Colada, but the orange juice really carried the flavors of the drink well. "Not bad." She nodded thoughtfully to herself as she set her glass back down on the table. "So, will it be a shorter version of the cruise we're on now, then?"

"Pretty much. Unless the client requests certain stops, or is someone I've taken out before, I usually stick to the same general itinerary."

Lauren leaned back in her chair and tucked her hair behind her ears as she looked around the dining room. "So, I gotta ask, what, exactly, is a 'Pusser'? Please tell me it's not island slang for a certain part of the female anatomy."

Grey laughed and shook her head. "It's not," she said as she picked up her drink and leaned back in her chair, mimicking Lauren's posture. "Although, that would be pretty awesome. But, no. Pusser is actually slang in the Royal Navy for purser, which would now be called the ship's supply officer. The Pusser was in charge of handing out supplies to the men, including rations of rum, so the rum rations became known as 'Pusser's rum'."

"So the Royal Navy sells rum?" Lauren asked, arching a brow in surprise as she reached for her glass again.

"No. They used to produce it to ration out to their sailors, but that stopped in… I want to say 1970."

Lauren sipped at her drink and grinned. "That couldn't have been a very popular decision."

"Probably not," Grey agreed with a nod. She looked up at their waiter, who was carrying a plate of conch fritters.

"Can I get you ladies anything else?" Jameson asked as he set the appetizer plate in the center of the table.

Grey arched a questioning brow at Lauren and, when she shook her head, said, "I think we're good for now, thanks."

Lauren dipped the tip of her fork into the sauce that came with the fritters to taste it. "That's actually pretty good."

"It's better on the conch than a fork," Grey teased, waving a hand at the plate. "I got these for us to share. Go for it. Help yourself."

"Thank you." Lauren picked up one of the smaller fritters from the plate. She dipped it in the sauce and took a tentative bite. The beer batter was amazing, though she had expected as much considering they were in the British Virgin Islands, and the conch meat was perfectly sweet. "This is really good."

"I know, right?" Grey said, finally putting her drink down and reaching for a fritter. "Pusser's does some awesome bar food."

Lauren spun her fritter around in her hand to dip the side she hadn't eaten off of into the sauce. "So why didn't we just sit downstairs?"

"I just thought it would be nice to share a little bit nicer dinner than at a bar," Grey said with a small shrug. "But, I mean, we can always go down there now, if you'd prefer. I'm sure they'd be able to bring our orders there instead."

Lauren smiled and shook her head as she tried to ignore the way her stomach fluttered at the idea of Grey wanting to spend a nicer evening with her than simply going out and hitting a bar for a quick meal. "This is great, really." She looked over the railing at the crowd that was beginning to fill the plastic chairs that sat between Pusser's bar and the marina now that a band had begun playing. "Maybe after dinner we can go down and listen to the music, have another drink or something?"

The idea of spending more time alone with Lauren sent a pleasant thrill down Grey's spine, and she winked at Lauren as she nodded. "I think that can be arranged, Ms. Murphy."

Lauren cleared her throat softly as she reached for her drink, hoping a generous swallow of the cocktail would cool the heat that she could feel rising up in her cheeks in response to Grey's flirty wink. "Good."

Chapter 16

"Best drinking story…" Lauren drawled, smiling as she took a sip from her third Painkiller. They had come down to the bar over an hour ago, and were seated at a small, slightly wobbly plastic table near the boardwalk that ran along the water's edge. Music from the two-man band set up to the left of the bar filled the air, and occasionally one of the tourists filling the tables around them would find the courage to get up and sing along with them. "I don't really have one."

"Bullshit," Grey chuckled, shaking her head. "Everybody has a drinking story."

Lauren rolled her eyes. "I have one, but it's not crazy or anything—just one of those 'you had to be there' type funny stories." Seeing Grey nod expectantly, she sighed. "Fine. Back when I was in my final year of culinary school, my girlfriend at the time and I spent our spring break touring Britain. After doing the whole London thing for a week, we hopped a train north to Edinburgh."

"Because haggis is amazing?"

"Ha ha, no. It's not as bad as everyone makes it out to be, though." Lauren grinned at the way Grey's face twisted in disgust. "It's kind of like black pudding. Anyways, we were on our way back to the taxi queue at the bottom of the hill after exploring the castle, when we saw a sign for The Witchery. Being the culinary geeks that we were, we had read about the bed and breakfast's restaurant, so we decided to go check it out. We wandered through a corridor that led to a little courtyard, and ended up in a vestibule that was elevated above a stunning dining room. Painted ceiling, french doors overlooking a private terrace, it was amazing. If you're ever in Edinburgh, you *need* to go there."

"Sounds like it."

"Anyways, we ordered a bottle of wine with our dinner, which later became two with dessert, and, well, you've seen how clumsy I can be…"

Grey arched a brow in agreement as she lifted her glass to her lips. "Are there knives involved in this story?"

"No." Lauren chuckled and shook her head. "So, clumsy ass that I am, I knock the bottle of wine off the table with my elbow, and it shatters on the floor, spilling what had been a rather excellent Pinot Noir all over the place. Our waiter comes running over with a stack of towels in his hands and we're both apologizing and everybody's watching us, and he just looked at us, grinned, and said, 'What a waste of perfectly good alcohol' as he started cleaning up the mess."

"What a waste of perfectly good alcohol," Grey repeated with a laugh.

Lauren nodded. "Exactly. So we start giggling like mad because, well, we're both pretty well toasted, and, that was it. I wasted perfectly good alcohol."

"Aww, that's cute," Grey drawled, smiling at Lauren over the rim of her glass.

"Shut up," Lauren muttered, rolling her eyes. "I told you it wasn't a good one. So, your turn. Best drinking story."

Grey sighed dramatically. "Junior year of college, a bunch of us went out to dinner at Benihana's before a concert."

"Which concert?" Lauren interrupted.

"Does it really matter?"

Amused that Grey obviously did not want to reveal that bit of information, Lauren grinned and nodded as she lifted her glass to her lips. "Absolutely."

"'N Sync," Grey admitted, and laughed when Lauren spit her drink all over the table. "Don't be wasting perfectly good alcohol!"

"Oh my god," Lauren chuckled, shaking her head as she reached for a napkin. "You really went to an 'N Sync concert?"

"It was for my friend Cody's birthday and he had a massive crush on Lance Bass and yeah, we took him to see 'N Sync. Anyways, do you want to hear the rest of the story, or do you just want to tease me about the concert?" Grey retorted, feigning annoyance.

"Can't I do both?"

Grey laughed and shook her head. "No."

"Fine," Lauren huffed. "Continue."

"Thank you, your majesty," Grey murmured sarcastically. "So, we went to Benihana's for dinner before the concert. We all knocked back like 3 shots of tequila before the chef ever came out, and by the time he actually started cooking, we had polished off another shot and were working on bottles of Sapporo. We were, needless to say, not feeling any pain at that point."

"I'll bet."

Grey just smiled and nodded. "Right, well, the chef starts doing the whole choppy-flippy-thing, and I decide that I could do it, too. I still don't know why he gave me the knife and shit, but he did, and I started cooking."

"Oh god."

"It gets worse," Grey assured her. "So, I'm butchering the shrimp and whatever the hell else is on the griddle thing, and Cody tells me to flip a shrimp into his mouth. Drunk me thinks that sounds like a great idea, so I load a shrimp onto the spatula and toss it to him. But instead of getting it in his mouth, I ended up hitting some poor old woman who was sitting two tables away from us in the forehead." She laughed with Lauren at that and shrugged. "And, yeah, I shouted an apology that people on the street probably could have heard, the chef took his stuff back, and I sat back down in my chair."

"Sounds like a very wise decision."

"Thank you." Grey tipped her head in a small bow. "Anyway, once the food started piling up on our plates, we were too busy eating to come up with any other genius ideas and so we managed to finish the meal without getting into trouble. But, once we finished dinner, one of the waitresses comes out with a little ceramic Buddha guy with a candle on his head and a bowl of ice cream, another waitress is behind her with a Polaroid camera, and they and the rest of the waitstaff in the restaurant start singing 'Happy Birthday' to Cody. He makes a wish, blows out the candle, and then next thing I know, he has the Buddha guy, our friend Mike has the camera, and the rest of us are all following them around the restaurant in a drunken conga line, singing to random people and taking their pictures."

"And how long did that go on?"

"Maybe five minutes," Grey said, taking a sip of her drink. "At first, I think everyone was amused by our antics, but once we climbed onto chairs at an empty table and started singing *It's Gonna Be Me*—Cody's favorite song at the time—at the top of our incredibly inebriated lungs, the manager came out, took the stuff away, and asked us to never return to the restaurant again."

Lauren laughed and shook her head. "My god. The nerve of that guy."

Grey finished off what was left of her Painkiller, and grinned as she set the empty glass onto the table. "I know, right?" She glanced at her watch as Lauren polished off the rest of her drink. It was only a little after eight o'clock. The idea of ordering another round was tempting, she was genuinely enjoying herself and was not ready for the evening to end, but she knew that they should not return to the boat with anything more than a light buzz. Will and Kim were cool, but she was running a business and that did not include her being totally hammered when there were guests aboard her boat. "You wanna go get some ice cream?"

"Ice cream?" Lauren repeated, nodding as she got to her feet. "You just don't want the night to end yet, huh?"

"No," Grey answered seriously, her eyes soft as a shy smile tugged at her lips. Her heart stuttered at the blatant honesty she could hear in her answer, and she cleared her throat quietly as she held Lauren's gaze. "I just…really want some mint 'n chip ice cream and all we have on the boat is vanilla."

Lauren stared at Grey, trying to get a read on what she was thinking. She had only been teasing Grey about not wanting the night to end, but she could tell from the open look in Grey's eyes that she was serious. That, somehow over the course of the day, the weird unsettled balance between them had found its equilibrium. And, if she were being honest with herself, she did not know how she felt about it. A part of her was pleased that Grey was so much more open and friendly and even a little flirtatious with her, but she also could not forget the look that had haunted Grey's eyes earlier that morning when she had caught her staring at the picture of her and Emily. She genuinely enjoyed Grey's company, and seeing her laugh and smile filled Lauren with a surprising warmth of affection, but she could not help but wonder if all of this was simply because she reminded Grey of Emily. "I guess I could go for some ice cream."

"Yeah?"

"Absolutely." Lauren could not suppress the pleasant shudder that rolled up her spine at the feeling of Grey's hand brushing lightly over her lower back when she walked past her, and her stomach flipped at the way Grey's breath hitched in response. Yes, whatever it was that was going on between them, they were definitely treading on dangerous ground. "How far is it to the ice cream shop?"

Grey pointed at a cluster of shops in front of them as she stepped onto the boardwalk beside Lauren. "It's just up there."

They walked down the boardwalk to the ice cream shop in silence, their arms brushing together every so often, Lauren's heart skipping a beat at every light touch, and she gave Grey a small, shaky smile when she held the door to the shop open for her. "Thank you."

"My pleasure." Grey's mouth went dry when Lauren's eyes found hers, and she swallowed thickly as Lauren pushed past her into the shop. *Goddamn*, she thought, running her hands through her hair as she followed Lauren to the counter.

Lauren held her breath as she felt Grey stop behind her. Every nerve ending in her body seemed to be attuned to Grey's presence, and she both loved and hated that Grey affected her so acutely. Loved it because it had been so long since anyone had made her feel anything like this, and hated it because there was no way for her to know what any of it meant. She dimly heard Grey order a single scoop of mint 'n chip on a sugar cone, and she cleared her throat softly when the shopkeeper's eyes landed on her. "Rocky road."

It seemed like the most appropriate choice, given her current emotional state.

Lauren paid for their ice cream since Grey had paid their dinner tab while she had been in the bathroom, and then they made their way out the door to a bench that sat right at the water's edge. The pretense of enjoying their dessert made up for the lack of conversation between them, and Lauren pretended that she did not notice the way Grey kept looking at her.

Grey could not look away from Lauren as the wind blowing in off the water stirred lightly through Lauren's hair, sending the wild tresses fluttering around her face. Her fingers itched to reach out and tuck the strands behind Lauren's ears, and it was all she could do to contain the urge. The electricity between them palpable, but electricity alone was not enough for her to take such liberties. Her breath caught when Lauren turned to look at her, and a slow, lopsided smile quirked her lips when she noticed a smear of chocolate ice cream on the side of Lauren's mouth. "Hold still," she murmured as she lifted a hand to wipe it off, "you have some ice cream on your face."

Before Lauren could take care of it herself, Grey's fingers were gliding over her jaw, and a soft thumb was swiping slowly over the corner of her mouth. Her pulse raced as Grey's thumb lingered against her lips, and she frowned. "I…"

"Got it." Grey did not pull her hand away, but instead left it wrapped lightly around Lauren's jaw. Her eyes darted over Lauren's face, from her lips to her eyes that sparkled with both surprise and desire, and she let out a shaky sigh as she began to lean in closer.

"This is a really bad idea," Lauren whispered, her eyes fluttering shut as Grey's breath landed lightly on her lips. Bad idea or not, she could not find the willpower to pull away. Her stomach fluttered with anticipation as Grey's mouth hovered just out of reach, warm and soft and full of promise, and her heart leapt into her throat when she felt the air in front of her stir.

"Maybe." Grey ran the tip of her nose over Lauren's cheek. "But all the best ones are," she murmured as she closed the gap between them and finally captured Lauren's lips with her own.

Chapter 17

Kissing Grey was like nothing Lauren had experienced before. Grey's lips were so soft, almost hesitant in the way they molded to her own, like Grey was waiting for her to pull away. She knew that she should stop this, but her heart had swooped up into her throat the moment Grey's lips landed on hers, and she found herself powerless to resist.

Grey tasted like mint and cream, and the fingers against her jaw were steel silk. Lauren could feel the air shift around them as Grey leaned into her, and desire—hot, white, and all-consuming—flared in her veins as the last of her resolve to do the smart thing disappeared. She reached for Grey, her fingers twisting blindly in the loose fabric of Grey's shirt as she pulled her closer.

She could not contain the low moan that rumbled in the back of her throat when Grey's tongue swept slowly over her lower lip, tentatively seeking more. Her nipples became instantly, impossibly hard as she opened her mouth, and the shaky whimper that fell against her lips as Grey's fingers threaded through her hair sent a delicious tremor of anticipation rolling down her spine.

Grey groaned as Lauren's mouth slanted over hers, opening wider and inviting her in deeper. Her pulse pounded in her ears as Lauren's tongue swirled around her own in a sensual dance of exploration and need, and her stomach swooped and dove at the feeling of Lauren's body arching into her. Warmth she had thought she would never feel again swept through her with every languid swipe of Lauren's tongue around her own and with every flex of the redhead's fingers in her shirt. She fisted her hands in Lauren's hair, holding her in place as she took control of the kiss, every ardent clash of lips less restrained than the last. It was madness. Sheer, unexplainable insanity, and she craved more.

A shrill wolf-whistle and catcalls drove them apart, and the world they had all but forgotten slammed violently back into place. They came apart slowly, cheeks flushed with a combination of arousal and embarrassment, and Grey cleared her throat softly as she carefully untangled her fingers from Lauren's hair and made a half-hearted effort to smooth it back into place.

"I…" Grey's voice trailed off and she shrugged, her lips curling in a small smile as she looked at Lauren. Her heart raced as she held Lauren's half-lidded gaze, and she shook her head as she trailed her fingers down the sides of Lauren's throat, unwilling to let go of her quite yet. "Wow."

Lauren bit her lip and smoothed her hands over the wrinkled fabric of Grey's shirt that she had been holding onto. The lust-fueled fog that had filled her from the moment Grey's hand had landed on her face dissipated, taking the carelessness it had wrought within her away with it. Reality, cold and sharp and painful washed over her, and she sighed as she looked over Grey's shoulder at the group of twenty-something men in cargo shorts and Hawaiian shirts that had interrupted them. A part of her was annoyed that they had intruded, but there was a larger part of herself that was grateful for the interference because, no matter how much she enjoyed kissing Grey, it should have never happened.

She should have never allowed it to happen. Grey was not over Emily, and she knew that she looked too much like her for this to be a wise decision.

Grey turned to follow Lauren's gaze, and she rolled her eyes at the grins and thumbs up the men were flashing at them. "Assholes," she muttered, shaking her head as she turned back to Lauren. Her breath caught in her throat at the distant look in Lauren's eyes, and she swallowed thickly as she reached out to run a gentle finger over Lauren's kiss-swollen lips. "Lauren?"

The gentle touch pulled Lauren back to herself, and she forced a small smile as she carefully avoided Grey's gaze. "It's getting late. We should get back to the boat."

"What?" Grey's brow furrowed with confusion as she watched Lauren practically leap from the bench and wrap her arms around herself. She quickly followed, reaching out with her right hand to grab hold of Lauren's elbow. "What's wrong?"

Everything, Lauren thought. She closed her eyes, unable to stand the raw emotion burning in Grey's gaze. "Can we just talk about this back on the boat?"

Grey's eyes darted automatically to the *Veritas*, and she was relieved to see that the lights in the salon were still off. Whatever way this conversation was going to go, she knew that they were not going to want an audience. "Okay."

The air between them crackled with tension and confusion and a latent, simmering yearning for more as they made their way wordlessly back to the boat. Grey kept stealing glances at Lauren as they walked, but Lauren's expression gave nothing away and Grey wished that she had some clue of what was going on inside her head. From the way Lauren had kissed her, Grey knew that the electricity she had felt between them was not just a figment of her imagination, but she was not feeling at all encouraged by the way Lauren was walking beside her now with her arms wrapped tightly around her middle.

Once they were finally back on the boat, Grey murmured an apology to Lauren as she eased past her to unlock the sliding doors to the salon. Lauren did not make a sound as she stepped out of the way, and Grey closed her eyes as she threw the doors open, letting the heavy glass roll silently on their tracks until magnets on the frame grabbed each one and locked them into place.

Grey's stomach sank as she stepped into the salon, convinced by the way Lauren was acting that she was going to get some version of the it-was-a-mistake-and-can't-happen-again speech.

The clarity Lauren had hoped to gain during the walk back to the boat evaded her, and she sighed as she followed Grey inside. Her heart thudded heavily in her chest when the lights flickered on, and she hovered just inside the threshold as she watched Grey wander further into the salon, hoping that the physical distance between them would help her think.

She blinked hard and tried to force herself to forget the taste of Grey's kiss. If she could just forget the way her skin tingled where Grey held her, if she could just forget the way that kiss had made her feel, then she could say the words she knew she needed to say.

But when Grey turned expectantly toward her, dark eyes shining with defiance, daring her to say that it was a mistake, Lauren could not form the words. It might have been a case of desire overriding common sense, but Lauren could not force herself to say that kissing Grey had been a mistake. It had been stupid and reckless and, god, probably the worst thing she could have possibly done, but the truth was that she wanted Grey. Had wanted her from the moment she first laid eyes on her. She wanted to feel Grey's hands on her skin, and she wanted to touch her in return. She wanted to kiss Grey, her lips practically tingled with the desire to do it again, and she was just not strong enough to deny it.

Lauren held Grey's gaze as she closed the distance that separated them in four long strides. She watched uncertainty and hope flicker in Grey's eyes as she reached up to cradle her face in her hands, and she let out a soft sight as she leaned in and claimed Grey's lips with her own.

It took Grey a split-second to react to the crush of Lauren's mouth against her own, but when she did, it was like gasoline to a flame. Her hands shot out, blindly wrapping around Lauren's waist and pulling her in closer until their hips were pressed tightly together. She moaned as Lauren's hands slipped around her head, the redhead's arms locking behind her neck as a demanding tongue pushed boldly inside her mouth.

Lauren's head swam at the feeling of full breasts pressing into her own as Grey spun them around until the backs of her thighs connected with the edge of the counter. Grey's hips shifted against her, and Lauren groaned as a lean thigh snaked its way between her own. Their kisses grew deeper, hotter, and hungrier as their hands roamed over each other's bodies, fingers tangling in hair and tugging as hips rocked together in an unconscious dance of wanton abandon.

It was the feeling of an insistent hand sliding possessively over her breast that snapped Lauren from the lust-fueled fog she had been lost in, and she sighed against Grey's mouth at the feeling of Grey's thumb dragging over her nipple. It felt good. Goddamn, it felt so good, but she *needed* to know that it was her that Grey wanted. "Grey?"

Grey laid a string of kisses over Lauren's jaw to her ear. "Hmm?" she hummed softly, flicking her tongue over Lauren's earlobe as she ran her thumb in slow circles around her nipple.

Lauren reached up and covered Grey's hand with her own. "I just need to know. Is this—" she squeezed the hand on her breast lightly, "—just because I look like Emily?"

Chapter 18

Grey froze at the sound of Emily's name, and pulled her hand slowly from Lauren's breast and let it fall to her waist. She closed her eyes, leaned her temple against Lauren's, and took a long, slow breath in through her nose, inhaling the sweet scent of Lauren's perfume. She focused on the way her heart beat inside her chest, slowly, steadily, and she felt a gentle warmth radiate through her, like Emily was reassuring her that it was okay for her to move on.

She pressed a chaste kiss to Lauren's cheek and then took a small step back, not so far to lose contact with Lauren, but just enough that she was no longer pinning her to the counter. Her eyes roamed slowly over Lauren's face, over kiss-swollen lips and dark, gray-green eyes. Lauren's cheeks were flushed, and her hair was in mild disarray from the way she had been running her fingers through it. Grey shook her head as she finally answered Lauren's question. "No. This is not because you look like Emily. If anything, it's in spite of the fact that you do."

The breath Lauren had not realized she had been holding left her in a long, drawn-out stream. "What do you mean?"

Grey shrugged and ran her hands through her hair as she tried to find a way to explain it all. "I did not want to feel like this toward you," she said, perhaps a little too honestly. But, she figured, they were discussing Lauren's resemblance to her deceased fiancée, so there really was nothing that could be more of a mood-kill than *that.* "I would have fired you that first day if I knew how to cook well enough to do the job on my own."

Lauren nodded, not particularly surprised by the confession. "I thought I had done something to make you hate me and, for the life of me, I could not figure out what it was."

"You reminded me too much of her," Grey said softly. "But then…I dunno." She shook her head. "It was little things, I guess, that began chipping away at me without me even noticing. I mean, you're obviously different people, but it was hard, at first, to see that when looking at you reminded me of her. But the more time we spent together, the more I started to see it. You're much more driven—I don't think I can name one person who would choose to work during their first vacation in a decade. Emily was content to just go with the flow, not really looking to do more than enjoy life. You like the quiet, you enjoy just sitting back and taking it all in like me… I mean, Emily always sat with me like you've done these last few days, but she didn't crave the quiet. It's just…" She shrugged. "You're just different. You express yourself differently, New York brusqueness mixed with Midwestern sweetness. You move with a purpose, like every motion has to accomplish something. I don't know how to explain it."

"Grey…"

Grey sighed. "I know. All of this would be so much easier if looking at you didn't remind me of her, but I *liked* kissing you. And I would really like to do it again."

Lauren nodded slowly as she processed everything Grey had just said. "I liked it too. I would be lying if I said that I'm not attracted to you, and I'm not looking for this to be anything serious, but I don't want to compete with a ghost. I don't want to be with you, and know that you're thinking about her."

The left side of Grey's mouth quirked up in a small smile, and she shook her head almost sadly as she reached up to tuck an errant curl behind Lauren's ear. She lingered in the touch for a moment before she let her hand fall away. "It wouldn't be like that."

Lauren sighed. There was an openness in Grey's expression that told her it was the truth, but she was still not convinced that this was the smart thing to do. For as much as she enjoyed kissing Grey, and for as much as she was sure she would enjoy doing more than just kiss, she did not want to do anything that would hurt her in the end. "So what do you want to do?" she asked, leaving the ball in Grey's court, trusting that she would make the decision that was best for her.

Grey's smile widened as she leaned in and captured Lauren's lips in a slow kiss that simmered with relief and possibilities. "Whatever we want," she murmured as she pulled away. The sound of excited voices had her looking up toward the back deck, and she sighed as she spotted three little tow-heads bounding into the salon.

"We're baaaaaaaack!" Peyton and Max sing-songed, swinging t-shirts over their heads excitedly and slashing at the air with plastic pirate swords. "We got shirts and swords!"

"Me too!" Reid echoed, jumping up and down and waving his prizes in the air.

Grey took a discreet step away from Lauren, who was running her hands through her hair to try and put herself back together, and smiled at the boys. "Lemme see 'em!"

They both listened intently as the boys rehashed their entire trip ashore, including an animated discussion of whether or not the bearded man they saw in one of the stores was a "real life pirate!", and Lauren smiled when Will and Kim ushered the boys toward their rooms to get ready for bed. "Are you guys going to want a nightcap and dessert or anything?"

"If it's not too much trouble, that would be great." Will tipped his head in thanks. "The boys ended up hogging the sundae we got to share at the restaurant."

"That explains their energy," Lauren chuckled. She waved at him to go after the boys, and turned toward the fridge. The small of her back felt heavy with the weight of Grey's eyes on her, and she sighed as she pulled the fridge door open. "You know, I can feel you watching me."

"Really?" Grey smirked and glanced over her shoulder to make sure they were alone as she sidled up behind Lauren. She ran a light finger down Lauren's spine and chuckled softly at the way Lauren twitched under the playful touch. "Can you feel that too?"

"Yes." Lauren let out a shaky breath as she leaned back into Grey. The chill pouring from the fridge stood in stark contrast to the heat coming off the woman behind her, and she shook her head. "And I really need you to stop that now."

Grey's eyes fluttered at the roughness in Lauren's tone, and she could not resist leaning in to brush a soft kiss across her cheek. "Are you sure about that?"

"Go give your mom a kiss goodnight," Will's voice carried through the salon.

"Unfortunately," Lauren whispered. "We are not alone, and if you keep teasing me…"

A wolfish grin pulled at Grey's lips. "What?"

Lauren shuddered as the many possibilities of what she could do flashed through her mind. "Grey," she said, the brunette's name a warning. "Please? I need to make this dessert for Will and Kim."

"Fine." Grey nodded as she backed away. "Later?"

"I'm shakin' my hiney!" Peyton sang at the top of his lungs. "I'm shakin' my hiney!"

Grey and Lauren turned to find him standing in the middle of the salon in his Spiderman pajamas, wiggling his little ass and grinning like a maniac.

Lauren laughed and reached out to give Grey's hand a gentle squeeze as Will swept the hiney-shaking boy into his arms and "flew" him into his bedroom. "Later sounds wonderful. Maybe when we're alone?"

"Yeah," Grey sighed and shook her head, not even bothering to try and hide the longing she could feel burning in her gaze. "Later."

Chapter 19

The sound of the sliding doors to the salon closing drew Lauren's eyes away from the plate she was busy drying. It was impossible to keep from smiling when Grey turned toward her with a playful grin, and she took a deep breath as she forced her attention back onto her work. Although her eyes were on the plate she was drying, she was acutely aware of Grey's presence, and her pulse picked up speed with every quiet footstep that approached her. The hairs on the back of her neck stood on end when Grey stopped behind her, close enough to feel the warmth of her body, but just far enough away to not be physically touching. An expectant shiver rolled down her spine when Grey's hand landed lightly on her hip, and she licked her lips as she set the plate in her hand down and turned to look at Grey.

Grey wrapped her other hand around Lauren's waist and stepped into her so that their hips were pressed lightly together. She dipped her head to let her lips hover tantalizingly over Lauren's, and smiled at the sound of Lauren's breath catching. The last two hours had been torture, forcing herself to play the attentive hostess when all she wanted to do was pin Lauren to the nearest surface and kiss her until they were both completely out of breath. "So…is it 'later' yet?"

The feeling of Grey's breath against her lips kick-started Lauren's idling libido, but she did her best to not let that show as she gave a small, noncommittal tip of her head. "It is later, yes. And I'm quite tired." She feigned a dramatic yawn, stretching her arms over her head and pushing her chest out toward Grey. "Was there something you needed?" She bit the inside of her cheek to keep from laughing at the absolutely flabbergasted look that flashed across Grey's face when the brunette pulled back to look at her.

The small twitch at the corners of Lauren's lips told Grey that she was messing with her, and she smiled as she dropped a quick, friendly kiss to Lauren's forehead. "Nah, I'm good. See you in the morning," she said as she stepped away from her.

Should have known she'd call me on it, Lauren thought as she reached out and wrapped her hand around Grey's bicep, pulling her to a gentle stop.

Grey smirked and stepped back into Lauren, closer this time, so that she was pressed flush against her. "Was there something you needed?"

Lauren shrugged playfully. "I don't know. I feel like there's *somebody* I should be doing, but…" She let her voice trail off as Grey let out a bark of laughter, and grinned. "Do you have any idea who that is?"

"Hmm…" Grey smiled and wrapped her arms around Lauren's waist. She leaned in like she was going to kiss her, but pulled away at the last minute, laughing softly at the disappointment that flashed across Lauren's eyes as she did. "I don't know…"

"Goddamn it, Wells," Lauren muttered as she locked her arms around Grey's neck and held her in place. "Just kiss me already."

Despite the tension and awareness that had simmered between them all night, the kiss started slowly. Just the briefest clasping of lips that repeated over and over again, each tender connection lasting longer than the last until their mouths opened and their tongues danced lightly together in the space between their parted lips. The passion that had flared between them earlier sparked back to life with every slow, teasing swipe of their tongues, and Lauren sighed as the hands on her hips pressed her back against the edge of the countertop.

One of Grey's hands once again found its way into Lauren's hair, her long fingers threading through wild curls, and Lauren adjusted her stance so that one of Grey's legs could slip between her own. Their kisses grew deeper as their hips rocked together in a slow grind, their hands wandering over unexplored curves and valleys, fingers gripping, stroking, teasing, and pinching as the need for more flared between them.

"My god," Lauren murmured, her head falling back as Grey's fingers closed with a delicious roughness around her nipple.

Grey smiled at the breathy exhalation, and dipped her head down to pepper Lauren's throat with kisses as she continued to tweak and pull at the rapidly hardening nub. She moaned softly at the feeling of Lauren's pulse pounding beneath her lips, and sucked hungrily against the sensitive spot before soothing it with the flat of her tongue. She blew lightly over the pinked flesh, and her nipples tightened at the way Lauren gasped and shivered against her. Grey brushed her lips over the curve of Lauren's jaw and back to her mouth. She sighed at the way Lauren's head turned just enough for their lips to meet, and an intoxicating warmth spread through her as Lauren's tongue stroked boldly against her own. A shiver tumbled down her spine at the feeling of Lauren's fingers playing with the short hairs at the back of her neck when they finally broke apart, and she nuzzled Lauren's cheek as she whispered, "Come to bed with me."

Lauren nodded and kissed Grey softly. "Yes."

"Good." Grey flicked the tip of her tongue over Lauren's lips, and she chuckled at the way Lauren groaned in response. "Come on, Murphy," she murmured playfully as she took Lauren's hand into her own and led her toward the stairs.

Lauren was painfully aroused just from kissing Grey, and her pulse throbbed between her legs as she followed Grey down the steps. It had been far too long since she gone to bed with another woman, and she managed to make it to the small landing between their cabins before the urge to touch, taste, and consume overwhelmed her. She used the hold she had on Grey's hand to pull her to a stop, and she smiled when Grey turned toward her.

"Yes?" Grey asked softly, her voice ringing with amusement.

Words were unnecessary as Lauren swept forward, claiming Grey's lips in a kiss that was instantly deep and wet and probing. She did not miss the low growl that rumbled in Grey's throat when she used her body to pin her to the cabinets against the outer wall, nor did she miss the way Grey yielded to her, sinking back against the cabinets as she let Lauren control the kiss. Lauren smiled as she rubbed herself against Grey, letting their hips slide sensuously together as she ran her hands over Grey's torso until she was cradling two perfect breasts in her hands. Her thumbs had no problems seeking out the straining nipples beneath Grey's shirt, and she swallowed thickly at the way Grey arched into her hands.

"Fuck," Lauren rasped as Grey's hands latched onto her ass and pulled her forward roughly, the brunette's hips rotating in a slow, circular grind against her own as their kisses grew sloppier and more desperate.

Grey's eyes rolled back in her head as she felt Lauren's hand drop to her waist, tickling the flat of her stomach, and her grip on Lauren's ass tightened as she felt the button on her slacks pop open.

"Tell me to stop and I will," Lauren murmured against Grey's lips as she began to slowly unzip her slacks.

"Don't stop," Grey whispered as Lauren's fingers dipped inside the open V of her fly and began rubbing her lightly over her underwear. She rolled her hips into the touch and groaned when it disappeared. "Wha—" Her question broke off as Lauren's hands began working at the buttons of her shirt.

"Want to see you." Lauren sucked on Grey's lower lip as she worked at the buttons on her shirt, her fingers flying from one button to the next until the shirt was hanging limply from Grey's shoulders. Her eyes swept over tanned, defined abs and settled on Grey's breasts, and she smiled as she noticed the front clasp on Grey's bra, which she wasted no time popping it open. "Gorgeous," she breathed as she dipped her head to take Grey's left nipple into her mouth.

"Shit," Grey hissed, biting her lip to keep from making any other noise as Lauren sucked hard on her nipple. The electric pull tugged at her clit, sending another wave of desire crashing wetly between her thighs, and she groaned as she threaded her fingers into Lauren's hair, holding her in place. She clapped her free hand over her mouth to muffle the sounds she was making as Lauren pulled back to blow gently over her nipple, the cool air coaxing the already rock-hard point even tighter, and even the hand over her mouth did little to dampen the sound of her moan when Lauren's right hand slipped back down her stomach.

Pleased by the effect she was having on Grey, Lauren eased her hand into the brunette's underwear, and hummed approvingly at the moisture she found waiting for her. She lifted her head to brush a quick kiss over Grey's lips as she began rubbing her fingers in quick, light circles. She covered Grey's right breast with her free hand, her fingers wasting no time pulling, twisting, and tweaking the previously neglected nipple. "You are so goddamn sexy," she murmured, using her chin to nudge Grey's hand away from her mouth so that she could kiss her.

Grey melted into the kiss, her hips rocking in time with the hand between her legs, grateful for the cabinetry at her back because that was pretty much the only thing keeping her upright at this point. She whimpered when the kiss eventually broke, and her eyes rolled back in her head at the feeling of Lauren's fingers sliding over her. "Oh my god."

"Hmm?" Lauren murmured, smiling against Grey's lips as she angled her hand lower to push inside her.

Before Grey could answer, however, a tiny, sobbing voice called out, "Mooooooom!"

Lauren froze at the sound, momentarily confused as to where it came from. A few seconds later, another little voice called out as the sound of retching filtered down to them, and Lauren closed her eyes in disbelief as she leaned her forehead against Grey's shoulder. "Would it be bad if we went into your cabin and locked the door behind us?"

"No." Grey shook her head and rocked her hips desperately against Lauren's hand. "Fuck, Lauren, please…"

Heavy footfalls pounded through the salon as one of the boys' parents rushed to their aid. The "Oh geez!" that followed answered Lauren's question for them. It would be one thing to hide from what was happening, but the haze of blind passion that had surrounded them disappeared completely at the continued, agonized retching sounds that seemed to multiply.

"Max is using the potty, try and hit the tub, Pey!"

"Christ," Grey muttered, squeezing her eyes shut as she tried to ignore what was happening upstairs. It did not work.

Lauren pulled her hand gingerly away from Grey as she took a small step back, the look on her face a cross between concern, disbelief, and wry amusement at their situation.

"I'm thinking 'later' needs to be when we're alone, alone." Grey sighed as she began putting her clothes back in order, resigned to the fact that no matter how much she wanted it, she was not getting off any time soon. "Like, nobody on the boat but us, alone."

Lauren sighed and ran a hand through her hair. "Yeah." She chuckled at the absolute absurdity of being cockblocked by a puking kid who was not even hers, and shook her head as she leaned in and kiss Grey softly. "I'm sorry."

"Me too," Grey grumbled, rolling her eyes.

"Yeah." Lauren kissed Grey again as the sound of more retching and Will's half-frantic instructions to the boys filtered down to them. "Should we go see if they need some help?"

"Probably should. Unless you want to be mopping floors later," Grey replied dryly. She sighed and stole one last quick kiss. "We *will* continue this later."

"Bet your ass we will," Lauren breathed. She instantly missed the warmth of Grey's body and she sighed as she turned and started up the stairs to see what she could do to help.

Chapter 20

"So, what's the plan?" Lauren asked as she sat down in the barstool beside Grey and handed her a steaming cup of coffee. The dark circles under Grey's eyes matched her own, and she shuddered at the memory of the last twelve hours. She would have never imagined that little kids could throw up that much. But they were sleeping now, and the sun was already well above the eastern horizon, which meant that it was time to begin another day—whether they were ready to face it or not.

Grey shrugged and sipped gratefully at the coffee. "The plan was to jump up to The Baths on Virgin Gorda for a day of exploring and stuff, but I think it's safe to say that the boys won't be up for that."

"Can we just stay here?"

"I only reserved this spot for the one night. We need to be out of here by ten." Grey ran a hand through her hair and sighed. "I guess we can always just head up to the North Sound. We are supposed to tie up there tonight anyways, and there are usually more than enough mooring balls at Bitter End. It's a longer sail than I would normally try and fit into one go, just because clients like to stop and do things, but if going ashore isn't really an option anyway..."

"May as well try and stick to the original itinerary as much as possible?"

"Exactly." Grey glanced around the empty salon and smiled as she leaned in to press a quick kiss to Lauren's lips. The easy comfort she felt when she was with Lauren was exhilarating, and she smiled as she pulled back to look at her. "Good morning."

Lauren reached up to lightly drag the fingers of her left hand down Grey's jaw. "Good morning to you." She chuckled at the feeling of Grey's hand sliding slowly up her leg, long fingers dipping beneath the edge of her shorts to tickle her inner thigh. "Whoa there, tiger." She covered Grey's wandering hand with her own. "For as much as it seems like it at the moment, we are not alone."

"But I want to touch you," Grey murmured, squeezing Lauren's leg. Her smile grew wider at the shiver she felt roll through Lauren's body, and she wiggled her fingers playfully under Lauren's hand. "Do you want me to touch you?"

"God yes," Lauren whispered, her hold on Grey's hand unconsciously relaxing, giving her enough slack to slide her fingers high enough that they brushed against her panties. "But…" Her argument died in her throat at the feeling of Grey's fingers lightly stroking the length of her.

Grey smiled as she focused her attention on Lauren's clit, rubbing slow, soft circles on the hidden bud. "Hmm?" she teased as she watched Lauren's eyes flutter and her mouth fall open.

Really, Grey knew that she was pushing it. If anything, last night had proven exactly how careful they needed to be, but the soft pants falling from Lauren's lips made it all but impossible for her to exercise caution. She pressed harder, her stomach clenching at the low moan that rumbled in Lauren's throat, and she swore softly as the sound of a cabin door opening and closing interrupted them.

Her own disappointment was nothing compared to Lauren's, though, judging by the annoyed ire flashing in the redhead's eyes when they snapped open, and she chuckled at the death glare Lauren shot her as she quickly pulled her hand from her shorts. "Sorry?"

"You're a tease," Lauren grumbled, doing her best to not shift in her seat.

Grey smirked and gave Lauren's leg a gentle squeeze. "You like it."

Lauren laughed in spite of herself and nodded. "I do. But beware what you ask for, Captain Wells…"

"Mmm, is that a challenge?" Grey whispered huskily in Lauren's ear as she slid out of her chair, purposefully rubbing her chest against Lauren's arm.

"If you would like it to be," Lauren retorted with far more confidence than she actually possessed. Her pulse jumped under Grey's knowing gaze, and she held her breath as she refused to look away. The stare was a challenge, plain and simple, and she was determined that she would not lose. Seconds seemed to last for hours, and Lauren finally let the breath she had been holding go when the sound of a third person entering the salon reached their ears, drawing Grey's attention away from her.

Lauren followed Grey's gaze, and a sympathetic smile pulled at her lips when she spied Kim shuffling across the salon in a pair of black running shorts and a t-shirt emblazoned with the 2012 Miami Marathon logo. The woman looked like she was dead on her feet, and Lauren could not help but wonder why in the world she was even awake since the boys were all asleep.

"Good morning," Grey greeted their guest.

"Morning," Kim mumbled. "I was just going to grab a cup of coffee before I showered."

"You want me to get it for you?" Lauren offered.

"It's okay, I got it," Kim said, waving the offer off with a sleepy hand.

Once Kim was distracted with the coffee machine, Grey leaned down and flicked her tongue over the shell of Lauren's ear. Her eyes fluttered closed for the briefest of moments at the quiet sound of Lauren's breath hitching, and she hummed softly as she nipped at her earlobe. She chuckled at the low growl that rumbled in Lauren's throat, and gave her side a discreet squeeze.

Kim looked up from the coffee machine, too sleep-deprived to notice what was happening in front of her. "I know the plan was to head over to those caves to go exploring today, but the boys aren't going to be up for much more than watching movies."

"We figured as much," Grey said, nodding. "Instead of stopping at The Baths, we'll just make the jump up to Bitter End, since the plan was to moor there tonight anyways. Hopefully they'll be back to themselves tomorrow, and you guys will be able to do all the water-sports you had planned. The itinerary has us spending tomorrow night there too, so we'll just jockey down and hit The Baths on Thursday," she said, doing some quick mental calculations as she adjusted their agreed-upon itinerary. "I figure we can tie up at Jost Thursday night and clear customs there. Friday we can head on over to Saint John, and then we'll head back to Charlotte Amalie on Saturday." She shrugged. "Not a big deal at all."

Kim smiled. "Okay. Good. I am sorry about all this."

"Please," Grey scoffed, shaking her head. "Like you really planned for the boys to spend the night channeling the Exorcist."

"They really did, didn't they?" Kim chuckled. She poured some milk into her coffee and sighed as she lifted the mug to her lips. "God, that sucked."

"Yeah it did," Lauren muttered under her breath, her cheeks flushing a little as her mind flashed back to what she had been doing when puke-a-palooza had begun. She looked up to find

Grey watching her, and she cleared her throat softly as she reached out to stroke the side of her left index finger up and down Grey's leg.

"Tell me about it," Grey whispered in agreement.

"Well," Kim said, flashing a curious look at Grey and Lauren, "since all of my boys are sleeping, I am going to go shower in peace."

Once they were alone, Grey hooked a finger under Lauren's chin and gently guided her face upwards. "I really do want to touch you," she whispered, smiling as she leaned down to claim Lauren's mouth in a slow, sweet, kiss that thrummed with the promise of more. She smiled as she pulled away just far enough to nuzzle Lauren's cheek, her next words falling in seductive waves over Lauren's lips. "I want to see all of you, touch all of you..."

Lauren groaned.

"And I really, really want you to finish what you started last night," Grey continued in a husky whisper. "But, unfortunately, if we're really going to wait until we are 'alone alone', we have another four and a half days to wait until that can happen."

"Oh god."

Grey chuckled and pressed one last lingering kiss to Lauren's lips. "Tell me about it."

Chapter 21

After receiving mooring instructions from the Bitter End harbormaster, Grey clipped the radio back into place and turned around in her seat to look for Lauren, who had spent the majority of the morning camped out on the starboard dive platform with Reid while Kim and Will attended to the older boys, whose stomachs did not appreciate the gentle pitch and roll of the boat as they sailed. Grey had watched off and on during the trip as Lauren taught Reid how to cast a fishing line that was rigged with only a light casting weight, nothing heavy enough to get caught in their wake and pull the rod out of his hands, and he was now casting and reeling-in his line like a pro.

Though she hated to break up his fun, Grey needed Lauren's help to get them hooked up to their assigned mooring ball in the harbor, and she sighed as she slid out of her chair. "Lauren!"

Lauren looked up to where Grey was standing on the bridge, and shielded her eyes from the sun with her hand left hand even as she fisted her right around one of the straps that ran along the back of the lifejacket Reid was wearing so that she had a good hold on him. "Yeah?"

"Harbormaster just gave me our mooring assignment. I'm going to need your help."

"Got it," Lauren hollered back as she turned to Reid, who was still casting and reeling-in his line with a wide smile on his face. "Hey, buddy. I gotta go help Grey, so we're going to have to stop fishing for a little bit. Do you want to go up to the bridge with Grey, or do you want to go inside and try to find your mom?"

Reid frowned thoughtfully as he spun the handle on his reel, his eyes glued to the water as he looked for his bright yellow casting weight. "Can I go up with Grey?" he finally asked once the weight was snug against the tip top of the pole.

"Of course you can." Lauren smiled and took the pole out of his hand. She looked up at Grey, who was still watching them from the bridge, and pointed first at Reid and then at her, the unspoken message clearly received when Grey nodded and waved him up. "I'll put this away someplace safe," she told Reid, "and you head on up to Grey."

Lauren followed Reid up onto the deck and waited until he was working his way up the stairs before she started toward the forward storage compartments for the boat pole she would need to capture the buoy attached to the mooring ball. She set the pole down on the trampoline and hurried to ready the port and starboard bow lines that she would use to tie off with. She worked quickly and efficiently, her every movement so fluid and natural that, to anyone who did not know better, she looked like she had done this particular task every day for years. She glanced up at the bridge when she finished readying the lines, and her stomach fluttered at the appreciative tilt of Grey's lips. It was patently unfair that she should be so affected by just a look, and she sighed as she turned away.

Head in the game, Murph, she lectured herself as she crouched on the end walkway that cut between the trampolines at the bow of the boat. She sat back on her heels and let her gaze slide over the bustling harbor as Grey motored toward their assigned buoy.

A resort ran along the eastern half of the beach, the red tile roofs of its buildings standing out against the lush green foliage of the island, and she counted twenty pyramid-shaped roofs poking through the treetops higher up in the hills. There was a short dock that jutted out from the western edge of the resort that had space for a handful of boats, but mooring balls seemed to be the preferred anchoring choice.

The feeling of the boat's engines reversing, slowing the *Veritas* to a crawl before Grey eased the throttle forward again, drew Lauren's attention back to her task, and she licked her lips as she surveyed the water in front of her. She picked up the boat pole as she edged closer to the edge of the trampoline, searching for the pick-up buoy. She spotted it a few feet away, and waved her left hand over her shoulder in a small 'go-go' motion as she adjusted her grip on the boat pole. When the buoy was just below the bow, she held up a fist to tell Grey to stop as she snagged the buoy and hauled it onto the trampoline. She quickly slipped the port-side bow line through the pivot and tied it off to its cleat before doing the same with the starboard line, and she turned around to give Grey a thumbs up when she was done.

The sight of Reid jumping up and down and cheering her efforts made her laugh, but her laughter died in her throat when her eyes landed on Grey. Butterflies once again took flight in her stomach at the small smile Grey was giving her, and she sucked in a deep breath as she held her gaze.

Grey was vaguely aware of the bouncing bundle of energy beside her as she stared at Lauren, but the majority of her focus was directed toward the woman below. The air between them sparked with electricity, warm and alluring, and Grey knew that she was being sucked into a rip current of emotions that were bound to overwhelm her in the end. And, as she watched the wind tug at the loose curls that had fallen from Lauren's ponytail, she was surprised to realize that she was perfectly okay with that.

"Nicely done, Ms. Murphy," Grey called out, her smile widening at the way Lauren ducked her head in either thanks or embarrassment at the praise.

"Yay!" Reid yelled, his little arms thrown victoriously in the air. He grinned as he looked up at Grey and added, "Can I go fish more now?"

Grey ruffled his hair and nodded. "'Course you can, buddy."

Reid bounded down the stairs to the back deck, and Grey hurried after him, a soft smile tugging at her lips when her eyes again locked onto Lauren's as she wound her way down the stairs. They were drawn to one another like magnets, and Grey felt a thrill shoot through her at the feeling of Lauren's hand reaching back to tickle her thigh as she joined her on the deck.

Though her eyes were trained on Reid, who was already down on the dive platform with the fishing pole she had stashed near the stairs earlier, Lauren was still achingly aware of Grey's presence as the brunette sidled in behind her. She had caught Grey watching her several times while they sailed up the coast of Virgin Gorda, and while she had enjoyed spending time with Reid, she had wished that she could be up at the helm with Grey instead. But, now that they were finally close enough to touch, she was glad that circumstances had kept them apart. The urge to touch Grey was so strong that it took all of her willpower to try resist it, and she knew that, if she were given the opportunity to actually put her hands on Grey's body that she would not want to stop.

Grey was fighting a similar impulse, but she rolled her eyes as she gave in to it, reaching out to wrap a light hand around Lauren's hip. Reid was distracted with his casting and, even if somebody were to come out onto deck from the salon, her body was shielding the touch. She gave Lauren's side a quick squeeze and smiled at the way Lauren leaned back into her. "Hi."

"Hello." Lauren glanced over her left shoulder at Grey, and smiled at the way Grey's thumb dipped beneath the hem of her t-shirt to rub soft strokes against her side. "Can I help you with something?"

"I wish," Grey muttered as she let her pinky trail along the waistband of Lauren's shorts.

"Grey…" Lauren warned, but whatever she was about to say next was interrupted by Will calling to Reid as he ambled out onto the deck.

"I know," Grey grumbled, letting her hand drop as she discreetly moved away from Lauren. She forced herself to smile as she looked at Will. "How're Max and Peyton doing?"

"Better," Will said, smiling gratefully at both Lauren and Grey. "Thank you for keeping an eye on Reid for us so we could deal with them."

"It wasn't a problem at all," Lauren assured him. "He was great."

"Daddy! Watch this!" Reid yelled as he scrambled to his feet and lifted his little fishing pole above his left shoulder. He reared back and then flicked the pole forward, and whooped in excitement when his casting weight went flying out into the harbor. "Did you see that?!"

"Good job, Reid!" Will cheered. He looked over at Lauren and Grey and added, "Kim and the older boys are napping inside, so I'll take over with this guy for a bit."

"Sounds good." Grey watched him head down the steps to the dive platform to stand by his son, and pushed her sunglasses up onto her head as she turned toward Lauren. "Looks like we are relieved of Reid-duty."

"I heard. I'm just going to head into the galley—" Lauren hooked a thumb over her shoulder, "—and make something for all of us to snack on before I get working on dinner prep."

"You want some help?"

The throaty timbre of Grey's voice made Lauren's mouth go dry, and she nodded jerkily as she turned on her heel to make her way inside. The salon was silent, so much so that Lauren could hear the soft pad of Grey's shoes on the hardwood behind her. The quiet fall of each footstep, rubber landing in near silence against the polished wood floor, drove Lauren's anticipation higher with each step she took until she was aware of nothing but Grey. She braced a hand on the edge of the counter at the feeling of Grey's fingers sliding around her waist, and closed her eyes when Grey pressed up against her back.

"What do you want me to help with?" Grey asked in a low whisper as she brushed her lips over Lauren's ear.

"Jesus," Lauren breathed, her eyes fluttering shut at the feeling of Grey's hips rolling against her ass.

Grey smiled and flicked her tongue over the shell of Lauren's ear. "You want me to talk to you about our Lord and Savior Jesus Christ?"

Lauren laughed and shook her head. "No."

"Good, because I don't really know that speech." Grey dropped her mouth to Lauren's pulse point and began teasing the sensitive spot with gentle licks and sucks. "I know that you like this, though."

"I do," Lauren admitted, leaning her head back against Grey's shoulder as the brunette's mouth continued to work its magic. "We should probably go downstairs."

Grey hummed and blew softly against the slightly pinked skin she had been teasing. "I thought we were waiting until we're alone?" she asked, even as she allowed Lauren to pull her toward the stairs.

"We are." The hold on her waist loosened as Lauren descended the stairs, and she used the opportunity to turn and face Grey once she had reached the short hall between their cabins. "I just *really* want to kiss you," she whispered huskily as she wrapped her arms around Grey's neck.

"I like kissing." Grey grabbed onto Lauren's hips and pushed her back against the closed door to her cabin. She leaned in and let her mouth hover above Lauren's, letting the anticipation build. The feeling of warm breath dancing across her lips made her pulse race, and she groaned as she finally surrendered to her desire to capture Lauren's lips with her own.

The kiss was slow, deep, and hungry, a desperate combination of lips and teeth and tongue that left no question as to where things between them were headed. Lauren sank back into the door, a ragged sigh escaping her at the feeling of a toned thigh slipping purposefully between her legs. Strong hands sliding heavily up her sides sent a shiver cascading down her spine, and her eyes rolled back in her head when Grey's fingers wrapped around her wrists and lifted her hands up over her head, pinning them to the door. Her heart jumped into her throat when Grey's fingers threaded through her own, and she moaned when Grey's hips began thrusting lightly against her. It would be so easy to let things go further, to reach down and open the door, spilling them into the cabin where she could lose herself in everything that was Grey Wells. The idea was tempting, impossibly so, considering the way her hips were now rolling to meet each of Grey's thrusts, and Lauren groaned when it all suddenly disappeared. She blinked in confusion as she opened her eyes to find Grey smiling at her. "What…?"

Grey shook her head and brushed a chaste kiss over Lauren's lips. "We should probably stop."

Lauren knew in the back of her list-filled mind that Grey was right, but she still asked, "Why?"

"Because—" Grey slipped her hands from Lauren's and let them drop to the redhead's hips, "—if we don't stop this now, I won't want to. And," she added, tilting her head toward the salon, "we are not alone."

Understanding dawned on Lauren's face, hard and more than just a little frustrated. "Fuck."

Grey chuckled and canted her hips into Lauren one more time. "Can we make cookies?"

Lauren frowned. "I…you…what?"

"Cookies," Grey repeated, her eyes wide and entirely too innocent for the things they had just been doing. "For snack?"

"You know what, Wells…" Lauren shook her head as her voice trailed off. "You suck."

"I do," Grey agreed, stroking her hands over Lauren's hips as she leaned in to press a quick kiss across her lips. "And many other things, as well. And I can't wait to do it all to you, but we really do not have the time right now."

"You are enjoying this way too much," Lauren grumbled, her tone annoyed, but it was softened by the amused smile that was starting to tug the corners of her lips.

"Maybe a little," Grey admitted with a laugh. "So…cookies?"

Lauren threw her arms in the air in defeat and shrugged. "Sure. Why not? Let's go make cookies."

Chapter 22

Later that night, after the dinner dishes had been cleared and the Muellers had all disappeared to their cabins to try and make up for the sleep they did not get the night before, Grey found Lauren lying on her back on the starboard trampoline at the front of the boat. Lauren's hands were folded behind her head, her long legs stretched out in front of her and crossed at the ankle, and her eyes were trained on the stars overhead. She looked relaxed and at ease with the world, like the breeze blowing out of the east that tickled her toes and snaked over her body did so at her behest.

"Are you going to stand there and stare at me all night, or are you going to come out here?" Lauren asked, her voice soft and amused as she finally turned her head enough to look at Grey.

Grey smiled and shrugged. "Both options have their merits."

"Yeah, well," Lauren drawled, looking back up at the sky, "just lemme know what you decide."

There was an aloofness to Lauren's tone that made Grey's stomach drop, and she frowned as she stepped onto the trampoline. The fabric dipped slightly beneath her feet, each step rippling outward and making Lauren bounce with her progress. Despite this, Lauren gave no indication that she felt Grey's approach, and Grey sighed as she lowered herself onto the mat beside her. "Are you mad about earlier?" she asked as she lay down beside Lauren, mirroring her posture as she folded her hands behind her head and looked up at the sky.

"No, I'm not mad." Lauren offered her a small smile as she pulled her right hand out from beneath her head and slipped it into Grey's left. Their fingers threaded together as if it were the most natural thing in the world and not the first time they had actually held hands, and Lauren's smile softened as she gave Grey's hand a gentle squeeze. "Really. I'm not mad. I was the one who said I wanted to kiss you in the first place. Just…you do realize that I was not actually challenging you to a duel to see who could tease the other into complete insanity first, right? It was just sass."

"I like your sass," Grey murmured. "And I know you weren't throwing down a challenge this morning. I just…I meant what I said. If we were going to keep kissing like that, I would not have wanted to stop; and I don't want to be worried about somebody walking in on us, or needing something from us, or whatever. But, at the same time—" she blew out a loud breath, "—I really just want to kiss you and touch you and…" Her voice trailed off and she shrugged, letting the silence finish the thought for her.

"Me too." Lauren looked down at their joined hands and slowly stroked her thumb over the side of Grey's index finger.

"So, what do you want to do?" Grey asked as she watched Lauren study their hands. "Because, I gotta tell you, that feels really good."

Lauren looked up at Grey, and her breath caught in her throat at the look of blatant desire that was staring back at her. Whatever it was between them, it was too strong for her to resist, and she wordlessly released Grey's hand and rolled onto her side so that she was lying half on top of her. The thought of possibly being discovered fled her mind completely as she stared down at

Grey, and she smiled as she dipped her head to capture her lips in a searing kiss. "I want to do this."

"Me too," Grey whispered, stroking her hands over Lauren's back. She rolled her right leg out to the side as she drew Lauren down into her, and she sighed at the feeling of Lauren's leg slipping between her own. "Kiss me."

Lauren's nipples hardened at the plea, and she groaned as she claimed Grey's lips in a series of slow, deep, heavy kisses that stole the air from both of their lungs. "Goddamn," Lauren whispered when she finally pulled back far enough to draw a proper breath.

"Tell me about it," Grey muttered, smiling against Lauren's lips.

"Maybe later." Lauren relaxed and settled fully atop Grey, letting the brunette take her full weight. She smiled as she threaded her fingers through Grey's hair, giving the short strands a gentle tug as she lowered her mouth to kiss her again.

The longer they kissed, the more their hands began to wander, fingertips digging lightly into heated flesh. Grey moaned softly at the first gentle thrust of Lauren's hips against her, and wasted no time matching her rhythm. She dropped her left hand to Lauren's ass, encouraging her to thrust harder, while she slid her right up over Lauren's ribs to her breast. She gave her captured prize a gentle squeeze, and smiled at the way Lauren gasped softly in response.

Lauren shuddered at the feeling of Grey's thumb stroking almost lazily back and forth across her nipple and swallowed thickly as she pulled back far enough to look into her eyes. She could feel the heat of Grey's arousal against her leg, and she wanted to feel that warmth against her skin. Around her fingers. On her tongue. "Grey?"

"Hmm?" Grey smiled up at Lauren as she gave her nipple a quick tweak.

"Shit," Lauren grunted, her hips bucking into Grey at the rougher touch. "Do you want to take this inside?"

"God yes," Grey breathed, lifting her head to suck at the spot on Lauren's neck that had driven her crazy that afternoon.

"Fuck," Lauren hissed, biting her lip to try and muffle the sound as her head dropped to Grey's shoulder. A none-too-gentle nip made her squirm, though whether it was to escape Grey's mouth, she was not sure. "I'm not kidding, Grey," she warned. "You keep doing that and we won't make it inside."

Grey chuckled. "If we were alone, I'd love nothing more than to have you right here. Your skin glowing in the moonlight, the breeze off the water tickling every beautiful inch of you as I made you come over and over and over again."

Oh, yes please, Lauren thought, her hips jerking forward into Grey as a fresh wave of arousal crashed between her legs. "Grey…"

"Hmm?" Grey teased, flicking the tip of her tongue over the edge of Lauren's jaw.

Lauren's hips bucked again, and she groaned as she pushed herself up to her feet. Grey looked absolutely luscious laid out against the white trampoline, dark hair mussed from where her fingers had been twisted in it and her sun-bronzed skin standing in stark relief to the pale fabric. Yeah, when they were alone, they would definitely act out the little scenario Grey had just painted in her mind, but for now…"Bed."

"Aye, aye," Grey said, smiling as she took Lauren's outstretched hand and pulled herself to her feet.

Chapter 23

Lauren felt like a teenager sneaking around under the nose of an unsuspecting parent as she and Grey tiptoed through the salon and down the stairs to the brunette's cabin. The light from Grey's en suite spilled into the room, providing more than enough light to see while still leaving shadows to soften any perceived imperfections. She watched Grey close the door behind them, effectively shuttering them from the world, and felt her heart swoop up into her throat as Grey turned toward her.

The sound of the lock engaging was like a starter's pistol, and Lauren wasted no time reacting to it. Want like she had never experienced before burned in her veins as she closed the distance between them, her eyes darting over Grey's face as she slipped her right hand around the back of her neck and pulled her in for a deep, probing kiss that was surprisingly gentle in its ferocity.

Grey sank into the kiss, her hands reaching for the hem of Lauren's shirt and ripping it off up over her head. She made quick work of Lauren's bra as well, and smiled as she tossed it over her shoulder. "Much better," she murmured as her covered Lauren's breasts with her hands. She ran the pads of her thumbs over swollen nipples, and hummed softly at the way Lauren arched into the touch.

"You too," Lauren muttered, sucking Grey's lower lip between her teeth and biting down gently on it as she reached for her shirt. She soothed the bite with the flat of her tongue as her fingers dragged it up over lusciously defined abs. She pulled back just far enough to yank Grey's shirt off, and her mouth went dry as her eyes swept over Grey's body. "Fuck," she breathed, licking her lips as her eyes locked onto Grey's. The brunette's eyes were dark as pitch in the dim light, and Lauren felt herself clench at the promise that was burning in their obsidian depths.

A low groan rumbled in the back of Lauren's throat as Grey's lips descended on her own with an urgency that made her eyes roll back in her head. The kiss grew deeper as they stumbled toward the bed, hands roaming with heavy purpose over smooth skin and gentle curves. Shorts and underwear were removed and kicked unthinkingly aside as they shuffled across the small space, and they were completely naked by the time they reached into bed.

Grey smiled against Lauren's lips as she crawled onto the bed after her. She kissed Lauren firmly, using that connection to guide the redhead down onto her back, and settled her hips between Lauren's open thighs. She shivered at the feeling of blunt nails scraping down her back, and groaned when Lauren's hands latched onto her ass and tugged at her. Warm, slick arousal painted a stripe down her lower stomach as she thrust her hips forward, and she groaned as she tore her mouth away from Lauren's to blaze a fiery trail of kisses over her jaw to the sweet spot on her neck. She sucked a deep breath in through her nose, inhaling the unique blend of vanilla-scented shampoo and Coppertone that she would forever associate with Lauren, and brushed the lightest of kisses over the sensitive hollow.

Lauren turned her head to the side as Grey began licking, sucking, and nipping at her throat in earnest. Every rough scrape of teeth over her skin was like an electric shock to her system, making her pulse speed and her clit jump. She tightened her hold on Grey's ass as the brunette began rocking into her, hips rotating in a slow grind as nimble fingers skated down her side and over her hip. She bit her lip to try and muffle the moan that escaped her when Grey's fingers brushed over her clit, lightly at first before settling into a series of slow, heavy circles that made her hips buck. "Grey, please," she whimpered, rolling her hips in a desperate attempt to force Grey's hand lower.

Soft heat surrounded Grey as she thrust into Lauren, and she sighed as she lifted her head from the sweet curve of Lauren's neck to look into her eyes as she finished that first thrust with a light tap of the heel of her hand against the redhead's clit. "Better?" she asked, arching a brow playfully as she pulled out slowly, letting her fingertips drag over hidden ridges that made Lauren twitch.

Lauren shook her head. Later, they would have time to play, but she was already wound so tight that she did not have the patience for it. "God, Wells, just fuck me already," Lauren groaned, rocking herself against Grey's fingers.

"Christ," Grey breathed, her eyes fluttering closed for the briefest of moments before she used her hips to drive herself forward. Her palm slapped wetly between Lauren's legs as she finished the thrust, and she was honestly not sure which of them moaned louder at the contact.

It did not take them long at all to find a rhythm, their bodies rocking together with a fluidity and ease that belied the fact that this was their first time together. Lauren fisted her hands around the pillow beneath her head as she lifted her hips to receive each of Grey's thrusts, drawing her in as deep as she possibly could. The feeling of Grey's nipples dragging over her skin drove Lauren higher, stoking the white-hot heat that was beginning to build low in her hips, and she was only vaguely aware of the sounds she was making as she was swept away by her pleasure.

The litany of words that spilled from Lauren's lips, pleading and profane, all wrapped erotically around her name, spurred Grey onward. Ignoring the burning in her forearm, she drove herself forward again and again, harder, faster, deeper. She wanted nothing more than to watch Lauren come undone, to hear the sweet sound of her release, to feel her tremble and shake with the force of her climax. And then, with one last long, hard grind of her hand, Lauren came with a scream that was so intense that Grey gasped as a smaller orgasm swept through her in response.

Lauren moaned as the hand between her legs gentled, Grey's thrusts becoming coaxing rather than demanding, as she rode out her release. Her throttling grip on the pillow relaxed as the last wracking spasm left her feeling boneless and blissfully sated, and she smiled as she reached up to run a soft hand over Grey's jaw. She used that hold to guide Grey's lips to her own, and her stomach fluttered at the tenderness in Grey's kiss.

"You are beautiful," Grey whispered, a small smile quirking her lips as she nuzzled Lauren's cheek.

"Thank you," Lauren breathed, her heart thudding heavily at the earnestness in Grey's tone. She sighed and recaptured Grey's lips in a kiss that was slow and sweet, letting that touch convey how much she appreciated the compliment, and smiled when the need for a proper breath drove them apart. Lauren held Grey's gaze captive as she trailed her hand down the slope of the brunette's neck to her chest, and her smile widened at the way Grey's eyes fluttered shut when she gave her nipple a light pinch. "Let me have you."

Grey nodded and rolled with Lauren's twisting hips, stroking her hands over Lauren's sides as she settled back against the pillows. Lauren's lips were on hers almost immediately, and she moaned softly when the kiss finally broke and Lauren began moving lower, peppering her throat with kisses and nips that made her eyes roll back in her head. She continued to run her hands over Lauren's sides as the redhead moved lower, dull teeth dragging over her collarbone, and she could not contain the whimper that escaped her when Lauren's hungry mouth dropped to her chest.

Lauren covered Grey's left breast with her hand as she sucked and tongued the right, bringing both of Grey's nipples to hard, tight points before switching sides and beginning the whole process over again. She looked up into Grey's eyes as she dragged the flat of her tongue over her nipple, letting it strain against the touch before bouncing back into place, and her breath caught at the desire burning in Grey's eyes. She pressed a quick kiss to the nipple she had been teasing before she slid lower, her gaze locked onto Grey's as she laid a wet, heavy kiss to her stomach. "Is this okay?" she asked, her meaning clear as she moved lower, running the tip of her tongue over the ridges of Grey's abdomen.

"Yes." Grey dropped her head back to the mattress and rolled her body beseechingly up toward Lauren.

"Good." Lauren smiled and flicking the tip of her tongue over Grey's belly button. She moved lower, lips dragging lightly over smooth skin, teeth scraping over a protruding hip bone. She laid a string of slow, wet, open-mouthed kisses to the line where Grey's leg and torso met, and she hummed softly as the musky scent of Grey's arousal flooded her senses. She kissed her way lower, wrapping her arms around Grey's legs as she settled between her thighs.

Grey groaned at the feeling of Lauren's tongue swiping lightly through her, spreading her open before sliding in a slow circuit around her clit.

Emboldened by Grey's reaction, Lauren tightened her hold around Grey's legs and pulled herself in closer. She sucked Grey's clit between her lips and teased the swollen bundle with the tip of her tongue, flicking and tapping against it, loving the way Grey's hips rocked against her mouth.

Grey fisted her hands in the sheets as Lauren's tongue was suddenly *everywhere*, tasting, touching, teasing every inch of her. A strangled moan escaped her at the feeling of Lauren's tongue thrusting inside her, once, twice, three times, just enough to make her need more before sweeping higher to lap heavily at her clit. She gasped as the firmer touch made lights flash behind her eyes and rolled her hips away from Lauren's mouth. The loss of sensation was just as shocking as having too much, however, and she rocked her hips back up in a blind search for more.

In what seemed like no time at all, Grey felt the familiar warmth of release spreading down her thighs and up into her chest, and she covered her mouth with her hand as she came undone with a scream that would have otherwise certainly carried beyond her cabin. Her head spun with the force of her orgasm, and she reached down blindly with her other hand to grab onto Lauren's, needing to feel anchored as pleasure coursed through her. Her heart raced even as her orgasm eased, her breath coming in quick, shallow gasps as she welcomed the weight of Lauren's body atop her own. She moaned at the taste of herself on Lauren's tongue as they kissed, and sighed when she opened her eyes to find Lauren smiling at her. "Hmm?"

"Nothing," Lauren murmured as she nuzzled Grey's cheek with her nose. She stroked her right hand over Grey's stomach, idly tracing the ridges of her abdominals, enjoying the way they bunched and twitched under her touch. Grey was lax beneath her, and she hummed softly as she dipped her hand between Grey's legs to play in the wetness that was still pooled there.

"Oh god," Grey moaned, her eyes fluttering shut again as her leg rolled automatically to the side.

"Close. Lauren," Lauren teased, smirking as she flicked her tongue over the shell of Grey's ear. She sighed as swollen lips wrapped invitingly around her fingers, and she eased her hand lower, wanting nothing more than to see how many times she could make Grey come before the brunette begged her to stop.

Chapter 24

Grey woke up well before dawn the next morning, her internal clock jolting her from sleep in spite of the fact that she had dropped off only a few hours earlier. She stretched carefully, pointing her toes and extending her legs beneath the sheet that was bunched at her waist, mindful of the sleeping woman beside her. The light in her bathroom was still on, casting enough light into the cabin to see everything clearly without being disruptive, and Grey took advantage of it as she turned onto her side to look at Lauren.

Lauren was lying on her stomach with her arms folded up over her head, and there was the softest of smiles playing at her lips. Her hair was splayed in wild tangles over her shoulders, and the sheet that covered them both was bunched low enough that the little dimples at the small of her back were visible. She looked relaxed, sated, and oh-so-beautiful, and Grey's fingers twitched with the need to reach out and touch, to draw familiar shapes amongst the smattering of pale freckles that dusted Lauren's pale skin.

She needs to sleep, Grey told herself, fisting her hand under her chin to keep from reaching out for Lauren.

Her eyes swept slowly over Lauren's body, running in slow circuits from her closed eyes, past her smiling lips and down over her shoulder, along the long, gentle curve of her back to the sheet that blocked the rest of what she wanted to see from her view, and then back again. Up and down, tracing and re-tracing those same curves, committing every detail to memory. Her body throbbed with the need to feel Lauren again, to touch that soft skin with her fingers, and to taste it against lips. After a few minutes of such longing perusal, her fingers reached for Lauren without her conscious approval, daring to lightly trace the gentle curve of her shoulder.

Her heart skipped a beat when Lauren hummed quietly at the touch, and she leaned in to press a gentle kiss to the soft swell of muscle she had just been caressing. She lingered in the kiss, her tongue peeking out to graze over skin that tasted like sweat and sex, and her eyes fluttered closed as she moved her lips a few centimeters to the right and kissed her again. And again.

And again.

She shifted, balancing her weight on her left elbow as she reached over Lauren to brace her right hand on the redhead's other side, and ghosted her lips around the edge of a shoulder blade. She held herself above Lauren as she feathered kisses across the span of her upper back. Lauren shifted beneath her, spreading her legs wider, her sleeping body unconsciously reacting to Grey's soft, barely-there kisses. Grey smiled and carefully maneuvered herself between Lauren's legs, shoving the sheet that had been covering them down to their feet as she began laying an unhurried line of kisses down Lauren's spine. Her goal was not to awaken, or even to arouse, she just selfishly wanted this moment to enjoy the feeling of happiness that filled her.

Lauren stirred as she reached the curve of her lower back, the most adorable little mewl escaping her as she gave a small stretch, and Grey smiled as she dragged her lips lower so that she was able to lick the dimples above Lauren's ass. "Good morning."

Lauren smiled at the feeling of Grey's breath against her skin and relaxed into the mattress. "Morning," she replied sleepily.

"Is this okay?" Grey whispered, laying another lingering kiss to the soft skin in front of her.

"Mmm. Yeah," Lauren hummed, her eyes drifting shut when Grey moved lower, warm lips and a hot tongue grazing over her ass. She drifted along the line between sleep and true wakefulness as Grey's mouth moved slowly over her backside, enjoying the tender press of Grey's lips against her skin. Every kiss was both relaxing and arousing, and Lauren sighed when Grey's tongue painted a languid stripe over the line where ass and thigh met to flutter for the briefest of moments between her legs. She rolled her right leg out wider, her hips canting up off the bed in a quiet plea for more, and moaned when Grey's tongue swept deliberately over her clit and up through the length of her.

Grey looked up toward Lauren's face as she dragged her tongue through damp folds one more time before she finished the lick with a wet kiss to Lauren's left cheek. She smiled at the way the muscle flexed beneath her lips, and captured it playfully between her teeth. "You're not falling asleep on me up there, are you?" she teased, her voice light as she took the pinked skin she had just bitten into her mouth and sucked hard enough to leave a mark.

"Totally," Lauren drawled, smirking as she picked her head up and looked over her shoulder at Grey. There was a softness in Grey's eyes that made her heart swoop up into her throat, a hint of something far more serious than the casual nature of their relationship warranted, but she forced those thoughts aside as she watched Grey crawl back up over her, the brunette's tongue drawing a thin line up her side. The feeling of Grey's breasts dragging over her skin sent pleasant shivers rolling through her, and she groaned when Grey's lips finally reached her own. The kiss was as achingly gentle and unhurried, and Lauren sighed when it eventually broke. "Hi."

"Hi," Grey murmured, dropping her mouth to Lauren's shoulder as she ran her right hand down the redhead's side and slipped it between her and the bed. She nipped at the skin beneath her lips as she eased her hand lower to rub a lazy circle over Lauren's clit. "Okay?"

"Fucking perfect," Lauren sighed, lifting her ass up into Grey and giving the hand between her legs a little more room. Her eyes fluttered closed at the feeling of Grey's fingers dipping lower and then sliding wetly over her, and a low moan rumbled in her throat when Grey's body curved around her own, hips pushing into her ass as full breasts pressed against her back.

The flexing of Lauren's fingers against the sheet drew Grey's attention, and she covered Lauren's left hand with her own. She kissed Lauren as she threaded their fingers together, the simple hold and the feeling of their bodies fitted together ratcheting up the unexpected intimacy of the moment as Grey's continued to rub lazy circles over swollen nerves.

They rocked together at an easy pace, their joined hands pressing into the sheets, fingers curling together and then relaxing as they traded wet, languid kisses, both of them more than content to let things build slowly. To bask in the softness of each touch, and to revel in the feeling of warm, smooth skin.

Lauren turned her head into the pillow and groaned when she felt her orgasm begin to crest, and she cried out softly as she crashed gently over her. It was as close to perfection as it was possible for the moment to be, and she let out a shuddering breath when she collapsed to the bed.

The smile tugging at Lauren's lips told Grey everything she needed to know as she draped herself over Lauren's back, and she grinned as she pressed a lingering kiss to Lauren's cheek. "Good morning," she murmured playfully.

"I'll say." Lauren tried to roll over, and laughed when Grey refused to budge, somehow managing to become even more of a dead weight against her back. "Are you not going to let me return the favor?"

Grey shrugged and buried her face in Lauren's hair. "Dunno." She thrust her hips into Lauren's ass and added, "I'm comfy."

"You're adorable," Lauren countered, squeezing the fingers that were still interlaced with her own. She laughed at the playful raspberry Grey blew at her, and sighed when her eyes landed on the alarm clock nestled into one of the alcoves just above her head. She was going to have to get up soon to start breakfast.

"What was that sigh for?" Grey asked, sweeping Lauren's hair aside to suck on her earlobe.

"It's getting late," Lauren said, her voice tinged with annoyed acceptance. No matter how much she would rather spend the day in bed, there were three loud little boys who would be expecting food soon.

Grey cracked an eye open to look at the glowing orange numbers on her alarm clock, and groaned as she snuggled into Lauren. "Can't they just have cereal or something today?"

"I wish." Lauren rocked her butt up into Grey. "Let me roll over."

"Fine," Grey grumbled dramatically, like doing so was an incredible inconvenience, and pushed herself up enough to allow Lauren to turn onto her back. The maneuver ended with her straddling Lauren's hips, and she waggled her eyebrows suggestively as she leaned in and kissed her.

Lauren wrapped her left hand around the back of Grey's neck, holding her close as she opened her mouth to deepen the kiss. She slipped her right hand down between Grey's legs, and rested the back of her wrist against her stomach as she stroked through the length of her. Lauren smiled at the way Grey moaned and curled into her, hips pressing down as her back arched up in pleasure. "What would you like?"

Grey leaned her forehead against Lauren's as she ground herself against the redhead's hand. "I just want you to touch me."

"I can do that," Lauren murmured. She cupped Grey more fully, pressing her middle finger between swollen lips, and began rubbing her in a languorous massage. "Good?"

"Amazing," Grey breathed, dropping to her forearms.

Lauren smiled and lifted her chin to capture Grey's lips in a deep, lazy kiss as the brunette began rocking against her. Time seemed to stand still as they moved, breaths cascading in synchronized waves over parted lips as they moved to a rhythm that was all their own.

It was, Lauren thought as Grey's hips bucked harder against her hand, almost frightening how well they fit together, how in tune she was to what Grey needed. She rubbed harder, pressing the heel of her palm against Grey's clit as she eased two fingers inside her, moving in quick, shallow thrusts that she knew would bring her crashing over the edge.

Lauren slipped her hand from between them when Grey's trembling eased, and wrapped her arms around Grey's waist as the brunette collapsed on top of her. Her stomach fluttered at the feeling of soft lips against her throat, and she sighed as she ran a light hand down Grey's back, turning her head to the side as a nimble tongue flicked over her pulse point. "I don't think we have time for that," she pointed out softly, though she made no move to pull away.

"I know." Grey sighed and dropped her head to Lauren's shoulder. "I just…"

"Yeah," Lauren agreed. "Trust me, I know. But, for now…"

"Work," Grey grunted, making the word sound like a curse. She picked her head up and glared at her alarm clock as it snapped to life.

Lauren smiled at Grey's antics and gave her ass a playful slap. She knew that, if left to their own devices, they would never get out of bed and that was, unfortunately not an option for them at the moment. "Come on, Wells. Get that gorgeous ass of yours into the shower, and I'll make waffles for breakfast."

Chapter 25

"I'm surprised you wanted to do this." Lauren waved a hand at the orchid-festooned woods that surrounded them. A morning hike had not been on her to-do list, though she did have to admit that it felt good to stretch her legs a bit. She usually started her day back in New York with a jog through Central Park, but an early morning run had obviously not been an option since she boarded the *Veritas*.

Grey looked over at Lauren and shrugged. Because the twins were feeling better, the Muellers were spending the morning at the yacht club, taking advantage of the rentals offered to do some parasailing and kayaking. She had one kayak on board the *Veritas*, but Max and Peyton had been fighting over it for pretty much the whole trip, so this way they would both be able to paddle to their hearts' content. "Why not? It beats sitting on the boat waiting for the Muellers to radio and say they're ready to come back for lunch. We *are* kind of at their disposal for the week, ya know."

"I know." Lauren's lips curved in a lecherous smirk and she added, "It's just that, well, I'm sure we could have found *something* to do to keep ourselves occupied while we were waiting around on them."

"Oh, I don't doubt that." Grey grinned and hopped over a particularly tricky section of tumbled boulders. "I just don't trust the Cockblock Crew down there to leave us alone when everybody's awake. And I, for one, do not want to get blue-balled again."

Lauren laughed and nodded as she followed Grey's path over the boulders to the uneven trail on the other side. The Muellers did have quite a knack for interrupting them. "Fair point," she admitted as she eyed the steep slope in front of them. The majority of the climb had been manageable, but this last three-quarter mile section was pretty much a straight, unforgiving, boulder-strewn shot to the peak. "Isn't there an easier path up there?"

"You tired?" Grey teased, brow arched in mock disbelief even as she pretended that her legs weren't burning from the climb. "Want to go back down?"

"Well, I really do like going down," Lauren drawled.

Grey laughed and shook her head. "I have yet to meet a lesbian who doesn't like going down, Murphy."

They traversed the next section side-by-side, witty banter forgotten as they concentrated on where they were stepping. The trail eventually opened up into a steep, relatively smooth path to the peak, and Grey nudged Lauren with her elbow. "Last one to the top goes down first?"

Lauren looked at Grey and smirked. "Okay." She bolted up the hill, laughing at the sound of Grey's surprised gasp as she left her in her wake.

Grey gritted her teeth as she started up the path after Lauren, ignoring the way her quads protested the more vigorous pace. To be honest, she was more than a little surprised at how lithely Lauren was scampering up the hill. Lauren had admitted to being a klutz, but she sure did not look like one now. Grey bore down when she was but ten yards from the edge of the peak, digging deep into her reserves to try and overtake Lauren, but her extra burst of speed was not enough to hurtle her into victory.

"Shit." Grey set her hands on her hips and shook her head at the way Lauren was trotting around the small clearing, arms held victoriously aloft à la Rocky Balboa. "Way to be a gracious winner, Murphy."

"Yup," Lauren agreed, finishing her mini-celebration by doing a small lunge and fist-pump. She looked up at Grey and grinned as she sauntered over to her. "I win."

"You do." Grey smiled and wrapped her arms around Lauren's waist. She leaned in like she was going to kiss her, but pulled back at the last instant and chuckled at the small pout she got for her antics. "What?"

"Nothing," Lauren said, shaking her head as she tried to pull away. The arms around her waist held her tight, however, and she sighed dramatically as she sank back into Grey. "What do you want?"

Instead of answering, Grey sucked Lauren's lower lip between her own and gave it a playful nip. "You." She smiled as she kissed Lauren again, deep and unhurried, and hummed when she eventually pulled away. "While I have every intention of paying up on our wager, I'm guessing that you don't want me to do it here," she murmured as she kissed Lauren again softly.

"Probably wouldn't be the wisest idea," Lauren said, remembering the three families they had passed on their way up. She cupped Grey's face in her hands and smoothed her thumbs over her cheeks as she kissed her again. "We should really stop doing this, then."

"I know," Grey whispered, even as she leaned in to recapture Lauren's lips with her own. This kiss was slower, sweeter, one that hinted at softer desires, and she sighed when she pulled away for good. Grey's stomach fluttered at the delicate flush on Lauren's cheeks and the way eyes had darkened with need, and she cleared her throat softly as she slipped out of her embrace. Silence, warm and thick with longing surrounded them, and Grey had to force herself to look away to break its spell. "So…not a bad view, huh?" she asked as she folded her hands behind her head and walked up to the edge of the cliff, hoping that a little fresh air and distance would help clear her head.

"Not at all," Lauren agreed, her voice noticeably rougher than usual as her eyes swept over Grey's body. Grey was not wearing anything special, just a pair of royal blue Nike shorts and a red tank, but she really was spectacular. Tan skin and toned muscles, with her hair blowing lightly in the breeze, Grey was a vision to behold.

Grey turned to Lauren, and smiled at the almost dazed look on her face. "Come on." She beckoned her closer. "I won't let you fall."

Lauren shook her head and walked over to where Grey was standing. She avoided Grey's questioning gaze as she crept closer to the edge, and she gasped when she truly took in the view. Bitter End stretched out beneath them, the water in the harbor a clear, crystalline blue and the beach a golden strip of heaven dotted with lounge chairs and umbrellas. There was a handful of boats dotting the harbor, and Lauren nodded as her eyes landed on the *Veritas*, easily picking it out from the rest. "It's stunning."

"It is," Grey agreed softly, her gaze locked onto Lauren's face. She smiled when Lauren turned and looked at her, completely unashamed at having been caught staring. "So is this worth the climb?"

"Yeah." Lauren nodded and looked back over the scene below as she pulled her phone from the pocket of her shorts. She thumbed the camera app open and smiled shyly at Grey. "Can you take my picture?"

Grey nodded and held her hand out. "Of course." Grey took the phone from Lauren and held it up in front of her face. She pushed it closer to Lauren and then pulled it back, forcing the camera to focus, and smiled as she called out, "Say…blowjob!"

Lauren let out a bark of laughter and shook her head at Grey as she took her phone back to check the shot. "Blowjob? Really?"

"Best way to get people to smile for pictures," Grey replied seriously. "Of course, for kids I say 'underpants'. Kids think underwear is frickin' hilarious for some reason."

Pleased with the way the picture had turned out, Lauren flipped the camera to the front-facing lens and asked Grey, "Take a picture with me?"

"Can we say blowjob?" Grey asked, grinning as she moved in closer to Lauren. She wrapped her arms around Lauren's waist and pressed a wet kiss to the sensitive spot below her ear. Her grin widened at the way Lauren's breath hitched, and she hummed softly as she covered the spot with her mouth and sucked against it. "Or, how about orgasm?"

Lauren groaned. "God."

"That's not very smile-inducing," Grey murmured as she pulled back and blew lightly over the damp skin, a thrill shooting through her at the way Lauren moaned softly and shuddered in her arms.

"Hey! We'll do you if you do us!" a new, unfamiliar voice called out.

Lauren looked up in surprise at the two men who were walking across the small clearing toward them. She had been so wrapped up in Grey that she had not even noticed them approaching. "Um…sure," she said, ignoring their knowing smirks as she re-orientated the camera and handed the phone to the guy who had called out to them. "Thanks."

"Not a problem, mate," he replied, winking as he backed up and held the camera in front of his face. "Say cheese!"

Grey whispered, "Pussy," in Lauren's ear, and grinned when Lauren burst out laughing.

"Excellent," the guy drawled, nodding at the picture on the screen before he handed it back to Lauren. "Now us?"

"Damn it, Grey," Lauren muttered, blushing as she took her phone back.

"What?" She waved her hand at the screen. "That's a good picture."

And, Lauren hated to admit it, but it was. They were both smiling widely, their eyes were twinkling with laughter, and looking at the image of herself in Grey's arms sent a wholly unexpected feeling of warmth rushing through her. They looked really good together, and she ignored the little voice of reason in the back of her head that was telling her the whole thing was only temporary as she shoved the phone back into her pocket. "Still…"

"Whatever, Murphy," Grey chuckled, giving Lauren's side a squeeze as she pulled away. "You guys have a camera?"

"Phone," the guy who had taken their picture for them said as he pulled his cell from his pocket.

Grey took the phone from him and smiled as the two men assumed a pose that clearly suggested that they were much more than just friends on vacation. "Ready?" she asked, once they were both looking at her.

"Yeah," they chorused.

"Say cheese," Grey called out, smirking at the way Lauren huffed beside her. "Please. I'm not going to tell a couple guys I don't know to say 'blowjob'," she muttered under her breath.

"Probably a smart idea," Lauren said, tipping her head in agreement.

"Cheers," the man said as he took his phone back from Grey.

"Not a problem," Grey assured him with a smile. The guys walked over to another vantage point, leaving them alone, and she waggled her brows suggestively as she looked at Lauren. "You ready to go down?"

Lauren laughed. "You first, Wells. I won, remember?"

"I remember." Grey stole a quick kiss. "Trust me, I'm looking forward to it."

Lauren's stomach flip-flopped in anticipation, and she nodded. "Me too."

Chapter 26

Lauren looked over at Grey as they made their way down the final, gently sloping section of the trail that would deposit them on the beach. Grey had slipped on a rock and ripped a nice little gash in her knee, deep enough that there was a steady trickle of blood coursing down her lower leg to her ankle, where the top of her sock was already stained a deep crimson. "Are you sure you're…?" she started to ask for the third time, and rolled her eyes when Grey waved her off again.

"It's just a little cut, Lauren. I'm fine. Really."

They cleared the tree line, and Lauren turned toward the dock where they had left the dinghy. "Fine. But you do know that you falling on your ass was not the 'going down' I was looking forward to, right?"

"It wasn't?" Grey shot Lauren a look of playful surprise. "Because that was *so* totally what I meant…"

"Yeah, I'm sure."

Grey smiled as she looped an arm around Lauren's shoulders and brushed a wet kiss over her cheek. "Don't worry. I'll still be able to go down later."

"You better," Lauren sassed. "Injured or not, I expect you to pay up. I won that race fair and square."

Grey laughed and gave Lauren's shoulders a squeeze. "You sure did. I was surprised, to be honest."

"That I won?"

"Well, yeah. I mean, before you almost cut your thumb off the other day, you were telling me how you fell down all the time playing basketball…"

"It was because I was still growing into my legs," Lauren grumbled. "Once I stopped growing, I stopped falling down so much."

Grey pulled away and gave Lauren's legs a thorough ogling. "You definitely grew into them, all right."

"Horndog."

"Says the woman telling me that I *have* to go down on her later this evening," Grey retorted. "Pot, meet kettle."

"Oh my god!" Lauren laughed. "Grey!"

Grey smirked. "What?"

Lauren wanted to pretend to be annoyed, but she could not help but smile at the mischievous twinkle in Grey's eyes. Really, she had walked right into that one, and she knew it. "Nothing. You win."

"If it makes you feel any better, you'll be winning later."

"Damn right I will be," Lauren muttered, chuckling under her breath as she side-eyed Grey. She tipped her head at the Muellers, who were just up ahead. "Now, behave. Time to put your captain's hat back on and pick your mind up out of the gutter."

Grey looked at their guests and grinned. "Hate to break it to you, but my mind is pretty much always in the gutter."

"For some reason, that doesn't really surprise me," Lauren said as she waved at the boys, who were now sprinting toward them.

The boys slowed when they saw the blood on Grey's leg. "You okay?" Max asked.

"Nothing a band-aid won't fix," Grey assured him. "So, how was kayaking?"

"Awesome!" the boys chorused as they began leading the way back to their parents, each of them trying to talk over the other as they relived everything that had happened, including Will capsizing his kayak, spilling both him and Reid into the water, and then swimming over to dump Kim into the water for laughing at him.

"I bet that didn't go over well," Lauren chuckled as they stopped beside Will and Kim's loungers.

"It didn't," Kim confirmed with a smile and a pointed look at her husband.

"Totally worth it, though," Will added with a smirk as he high fived Peyton.

"Lauren?" Reid piped up.

Lauren looked down at the youngest boy and smiled. "What's up, buddy?"

"Can we have a picnic on the beach?"

Lauren glanced at Kim to make sure that she was okay with the idea, and then nodded. "Absolutely. What do you want to eat?"

"Sandwiches are fine," Kim answered for him. "The boys just want to play on the beach a little longer, and then Pey and Max are going to try parasailing this afternoon with Will."

"I'm not old enough," Reid pouted.

"What if," Lauren said, squatting down in front of the boy to catch his eye, "you help me make cookies when they're doing that?"

Reid's eyes lit up with excitement. "Can I lick the mixer thing?"

"If you can get to it before Grey does," Lauren said as she threw a teasing look over her shoulder at Grey.

"Can I help make dinner, too?" Reid asked hopefully. Out of all the boys, he enjoyed helping to cook the most and, more often than not, he wandered into the galley while Lauren was cooking just to watch.

"I'm sure we can find something for you to do."

"What are we going to make?"

Lauren sighed, knowing that her answer was going to push Grey's mind right back into the gutter. "Tacos." Sure enough, Grey sniggered, and Lauren rolled her eyes as she slapped at her leg and continued, "And those roasted veggies you guys like, and some rice, and maybe we'll take those cookies you're gonna help me with and make sundaes with them. Whattaya think?"

Reid grinned and threw his arms around Lauren's neck. "Awesome!"

"Good." Lauren hugged him loosely and gave his back a light pat. "So, you guys go play, and I'll make you a picnic. And then later this afternoon you can be my sous chef. Sound good?"

Reid nodded and took off toward his brothers who were digging a giant hole near the water's edge.

"Thank you for that," Kim spoke up, giving Lauren an appreciative smile.

"Not a problem at all. So, I'm assuming PB and J for the boys since that's their favorite," Lauren said as she pushed herself back to her feet. "How about you guys? I can make a chicken salad, or…"

"Some kind of a sandwich is fine, really," Kim said, shaking her head. "Just throw in some snack-type things to go with them and some bottled waters and we'll be good."

Lauren nodded slowly. "Okay, if you're sure…"

"I'll bring it all back over to you guys in a few," Grey told the Muellers with a smile as she and Lauren started toward the dock where their dinghy was tied up. "So…tacos for dinner, huh?"

she asked once they were in the dinghy and on their way back to the *Veritas.*

"Shut up."

"At least you didn't say we were 'eating out' tonight," Grey mused loudly.

"Damn it, Wells…"

"Going downtown?" Grey laughed at the annoyed look Lauren shot her, and killed the outboard engine as they coasted toward the starboard dive platform on the yacht. "Just get on the boat, Murphy."

Lauren rolled her eyes and climbed out of the dinghy. "You think you're funny."

"I'm hilarious," Grey said as she tied the little inflatable off to a cleat near the platform.

Lauren looked back at Grey as the brunette leapt gracefully onto the dive platform, and was about to respond when she was interrupted by her cell phone ringing. "That's weird," she murmured as she pulled it from her pocket.

"There is cell service here, ya know," Grey pointed out as she followed Lauren up the stairs to the back deck. "Big tourist resort and all. But, it's a British tower…"

"I added international roaming for the month. And that's not what I meant," Lauren said, frowning as she looked at her best friend's name on her screen. Jen Collins worked with her at Clarke's, and was taking care of her cat for her while she was gone. "What's up, Jen?" she answered the call, shooting Grey an apologetic look. She knew that Jen would only call her if it was something important.

"Oh, thank god," Jen said without preamble. *"What vet do you take Jenks to?"*

Lauren's frown deepened. "West Side Vets. It's just down the block from the restaurant. Why?"

"Because the little bastard snuck out the front door and into the hallway when I opened it to get the paper, and then decided to try and throw down with old Mrs. Schwartz's terrier."

"Is he okay?"

"He's fine. He just got bit on the paw when he was trying to use George's nose like a punching bag. I don't think it's a big deal, but I want to get him checked out anyways, just in case."

Grey gave Lauren's waist a light squeeze as she eased past her into the salon. "I'm gonna go get cleaned up."

Lauren nodded and sat down at one of the outside banquettes. "Okay."

"Is this a bad time?" Jen asked.

"No. You're fine. I'm just about to make some lunch," Lauren told her. "Is Jenks using the paw?"

"Yeah, and the bleeding stopped, but…"

"Just watch him. If he doesn't act bothered by it, you don't need to take him to the vet," Lauren told her. Her cat had a habit of sneaking out and picking fights, and George the terrier was far from his first sparring partner.

"You're sure?"

"Positive," Lauren assured her. "Is everything else okay?"

"It's all business as usual," Jen said. *"Nothing exciting to report. How about you? How's it going there?"*

"It's going well," Lauren said. She smiled as she looked at Grey, who had the first aid kit on the peninsula counter. Grey's injured leg was propped on a barstool, and she was cleaning it with what looked like a damp paper towel. "Really well."

"You got laid," Jen said, her tone both amused and congratulatory. *"Who'd you bone?"*

"I did not…" Lauren started to argue.

"Not buying it, I know that voice," Jen interrupted her. *"So, spill. Who? When? Was it good?"*

"You should not be this invested in my personal life," Lauren pointed out.

"Shush. I'm married. I gotta live vicariously through you. So…tell me!"

"I can't," Lauren said in a low tone that she hoped would not carry. "She might hear me."

"You boned one of the guests on the boat? Wow, talk about full-service!"

"I did not bone a guest. It's a married couple and their three small boys…don't be gross." She sighed and, knowing that Jen was not going to let the matter drop, added quietly, "It was Grey."

"The captain? I thought the captain was a guy?"

Lauren hummed under her breath as she looked at Grey. "Mmm, no. Grey is definitely a woman."

"Well, then…was it good?"

"Incredible."

"Is she hot?"

"Gorgeous."

"Am I going to get more than a one-word answer out of you?"

Lauren smiled and shook her head. "No."

"Will I at least get to see a picture of her when you get home?"

"Sure."

"Sweet!"

"You're ridiculous."

"You love me," Jen retorted. *"And that was two words, so feel free to speak in complete sentences now. So, besides banging the super-hot captain, anything else happening?"*

Lauren shook her head as she watched Grey finish bandaging her leg. "Not really. Am just enjoying a lot of fresh air."

"And orgasms, apparently."

"Jennifer Jean…"

"What?!" Jen laughed. *"It's good. You deserve to be happy, Lo. Really."*

"Thank you," Lauren muttered, rubbing a hand over her forehead. "I, uh, should probably go, though. I need to make a picnic lunch for the guests."

"Sounds good," Jen said. *"Have fun. Have lots of orgasms, and I will see you at La Guardia when you get back."*

"Right," Lauren said, a small smile quirking her lips. "Thanks. Take care of my boy for me, okay?"

"Will do. I'll talk to you later."

"Yeah…bye," Lauren murmured, her eyes glued to Grey as she disconnected the call. Grey looked up and smiled at her, and she sighed as she pushed herself to her feet, purposefully trying and failing to ignore the feeling of unease that swept through her when she thought about returning to New York.

Chapter 27

Lauren was in the middle of preparing their lunch when Grey returned to the *Veritas* from delivering the Muellers' picnic to the beach, and she hovered in the doorway to the salon to watch her work. Ever since Lauren wandered into the galley after talking on the phone, there had been a distance in her eyes that gave Grey pause. Lauren had joked and smiled while prepping the Muellers' lunch, but it was clear that something was weighing on her mind.

Grey smiled when Lauren looked up to see her loitering on the threshold, and gave a small wave as she ambled into the salon to sit at one of the barstools facing the galley. "Lunch is delivered," she reported. "Kim wanted me to tell you that a plain ol' turkey sandwich would have been fine, but that the turkey melts looked great. And the boys were especially excited about the cookies you stashed in the bottom of the basket."

"Well, you know, I promised Reid that we would make more later, so I kinda had to empty out the cookie jar to make room," Lauren said with a smile that did not quite reach her eyes as she transferred their sandwiches from the grill pan onto plates she had already laid out on the counter.

Grey nodded as she watched Lauren cut the sandwiches into triangles. "Yeah. I figured as much. Thanks." She took the plate Lauren nudged toward her. "Looks delicious."

"It's nothing special." Lauren brushed off the compliment with a wave of her hand as she pulled a couple bottles of water from the fridge.

"Doesn't mean it won't be good." Grey took the water Lauren held out to her. She twisted the top off as Lauren rounded the peninsula to sit in the empty chair on her right, and she arched a brow questioningly as she turned to look at her. "Is everything okay? You've seemed a little off ever since you got off the phone."

Surprised that Grey had picked up on her mood, Lauren shook her head. "Yeah. No. Everything's fine. My cat is just a punk and decided to brawl with my friend's neighbor's dog."

"Is he okay?"

"He's fine." Lauren rolled her eyes and picked up her sandwich. "The dog bit him on the paw and I guess it was bleeding pretty bad, so my friend Jen who is watching him for me freaked out and was going to rush him to the vet. I told her to just watch him and see how he acts, because he probably doesn't need to go in. He's a jerk, but he's tough."

"Sounds like it. What's his name?"

"Jenks." Lauren smiled at the way Grey shook her head and chuckled under her breath. "What?"

"With that name, I would be disappointed if he wasn't a total punk."

"I'm impressed you know where I got it from. Not a lot of people do."

Grey shrugged, her smile dimming as a memory of Emily, eyes twinkling with playful amusement as she threatened to withhold sex until Grey read those seven battered paperbacks flashed across her mind. Emily had sworn off the series at that point, but she still made Grey read and suffer through it all with her. "Emily made me read them."

Lauren's smile faltered at the mention of Emily. They had avoided talking about her ever since the night they had first kissed, and she was unsure how to respond. "Oh. Did..." She cleared her throat softly. "Did you like them?"

"I did, until it became obvious that the author was never going to give Ivy a happy ending," Grey said. She rolled her eyes, because this was a conversation she had had many times over with Emily, and it never failed to leave her feeling frustrated and annoyed. "I mean, it would be one thing if they weren't so perfect for each other. They made the damn bells ring, ya know? I just, sometimes I really want to find the lady who writes the books and smack her upside the head."

"Yeah, well, if you ever do decide to do that, lemme know. I'll go with you. I wanna get a shot in too," Lauren said as she took a bite of her sandwich. She chewed thoughtfully as she watched Grey out of the corner of her eye, wary of doing or saying something that might upset her.

"Deal." Grey sighed and studied her sandwich with far more intensity than a simple turkey and bacon melt required. She had been doing well just focusing on Lauren, but now that she was thinking about Emily, it was hard to stop. The memories were not as painful as they had once been, but they were there. Warm. Bittersweet. Making her breath feel light and her heart ache. "I miss her."

Lauren smiled sadly as she set her sandwich down and pulled Grey into her arms. "I know, sweetie," she whispered as Grey leaned into her. She closed her eyes at the feeling of Grey's face burrowing into her neck, and sighed as she held her tight. "It's okay."

"I'm sorry."

Lauren pressed her lips to Grey's cheek and smoothed a hand over her back. "Don't be. It's okay, Grey," she repeated gently. "Do you want to talk about it?"

Grey shook her head.

"Okay." Lauren brushed another kiss across Grey's cheek.

"It was cancer," Grey said, the words spilling from her mouth without her consent. She had not really talked to anyone about those last few months—even Kip had not been able to coax it out of her—but there was something about Lauren that made her want to share. "We caught it late. Like, crazy late. She was already in stage four when she was diagnosed. It had spread everywhere. Her brain, her lungs, her bones…" Her voice trailed off, and she sucked in a ragged breath as her eyes stung with tears.

"Oh, Grey," Lauren breathed as her heart broke for the woman in her arms.

"They gave her six months, but she didn't even make it four," Grey whispered. "She was on so many drugs at the end that she slept pretty much all the time, and when she was awake, you could just see how much it hurt in her eyes. I still don't know how we didn't realize something was wrong sooner. She had had some headaches and stuff before she was diagnosed, but nothing unmanageable—but as soon as the tests came back saying cancer, it was like her symptoms exploded out of control. It was fucking awful, waking up every day, seeing her in so much pain. Wishing there was something I could do to make it stop, but selfishly wanting her to fight because I didn't want to lose her."

Lauren swallowed thickly and had to fight back her own tears at the absolute agony in Grey's voice.

"I was so afraid of losing her that I barely slept those last few weeks. I was terrified that she would die while I was sleeping and that I wouldn't know about it until I woke up. I just…my every breath was hers. If I could have taken the pain from her I would have, but I couldn't, and three months and eleven days after she was diagnosed, she was gone." She cleared her throat and pulled back to wipe at the tears that were now coursing freely down her cheeks. "It was just so fast," she added softly as she stared unseeingly at Lauren's collarbone, her vision blurred by the tears she could not keep from falling. "One day she was fine, we had just gotten engaged, and then she was gone. Just like that. It was so fucking fast…" Her voice trailed off into a sob.

Lauren felt utterly useless as she watched Grey fall apart in front of her. Fat tears poured from Grey's eyes as she stared into a past that Lauren knew would haunt her forever. Lauren reached for her, needing to ease some of her pain. "Oh, sweetie," she murmured as she wrapped her right hand around the back of Grey's neck and drew her forward. "I'm so, so sorry, Grey," she whispered as she pressed her lips to Grey's forehead. "I'm so sorry."

"Me too," Grey rasped. She sniffled and shook her head. "God, I am so sorry," she muttered as she pulled away and pressed the heels of her palms into her eyes, as if she could stop crying by sheer force alone. "You don't need to deal with my shit."

"Hey." Lauren tugged gently at Grey's wrists, and smiled sadly when watery brown eyes reluctantly met her own. "I want to deal with your shit."

"Why?" Grey blew out a loud breath and looked at Lauren in pure disbelief. "Why would you want to deal with any of this?"

Lauren shrugged. "I just do." She knew that answer was completely inadequate, but she did not know how to even begin to explain it.

"You're insane," Grey muttered in a rough, slightly awed voice.

"That is entirely possible," Lauren agreed, her heart lifting at the small smile that quirked Grey's lips. "Come here," she said as she pushed herself to her feet. She was pleased when Grey followed without question, and she hummed under her breath as she pulled Grey into her arms.

Grey wrapped her arms around Lauren's neck and melted into the embrace. She closed her eyes and buried her face in the crook of Lauren's neck, greedily taking the comfort Lauren offered. Her heart broke all over again as she thought of those final moments she had with Emily and the days that had followed, and she was only vaguely aware of the gentle hand that was sweeping up and down her back as she cried. Eventually her tears dried up, and Grey let out a shuddering breath as she pulled away. "Thank you."

"No thanks necessary." Lauren brushed a tender kiss across Grey's forehead. "You okay?"

"I will be," Grey answered softly. It was what she had assured everybody who had asked after the funeral, but this was the first time that she actually believed it. She nodded, almost as if to assure herself that her words were true, and let out a soft sigh as she leaned her forehead against Lauren's. "I will be."

Chapter 28

Lauren hovered in the doorway to Grey's cabin with a bottle of the brunette's favorite scotch and two glasses in her hands. Grey was lying face-down on the bed, her arms folded up under the pillow her face was buried in, and if it were not for the rhythmic movement of her right foot sliding back and forth across the edge of the mattress, Lauren would have thought she was sleeping. She had not been surprised when Grey had claimed a headache and disappeared to her cabin as soon as the dessert dishes had been cleared. To be honest, Lauren was surprised that Grey had not done so earlier. Grey had put on a brave face and pretended that everything was fine, but Lauren had not missed the way her eyes would cloud over whenever she stopped moving and her mind was allowed to drift to thoughts of Emily.

Staying on deck and pretending to be unaffected by the knowledge that Grey was upset and alone was torture. She had been beyond grateful when Kim looked pointedly at the salon and told her that they were just going to play a quick game of Go Fish with the boys before calling it a night, and that she was more than welcome to retire for the evening. Lauren had smiled at her gratefully and had to resist the urge to run as she turned and went in search of Grey.

"Hey."

"Hey." Grey's voice was muffled by the pillow, but she knew that Lauren would be able to hear.

"Can I come in?" Lauren waited until she saw Grey nod once before she stepped into the cabin and used her heel to close the door after herself. She padded quickly across the room and sat on the edge of the bed beside Grey. "How's the head?"

Grey turned her head to look at Lauren, and she smiled when she saw the bottle of scotch in her hand. "Full."

"I'll bet." Lauren watched quietly as Grey sat up and stacked the pillows against the cubbies that made up her headboard. Grey's eyes were tired yet grateful when she leaned back against the pillows, and Lauren smiled as she handed her one of the empty glasses. "Thought you could maybe use a drink."

"You thought right." Grey sighed and patted the bed beside her. "Make yourself comfortable."

Lauren slid into the empty spot beside Grey and placed the glass in her hand between her legs so that she could unscrew the cap on the bottle of scotch. She poured a generous amount of the rich, ocher-colored liquor into each of their glasses before she quickly re-capped the bottle and leaned over to set it onto the floor beside the bed. Lauren glanced over at Grey as she settled back against the pillows beside her, her body automatically mirroring Grey's relaxed posture as she stretched her legs out in front of her and crossed them at the ankle.

Grey could feel Lauren's eyes on her, and her lips curled in a small smile as she reached out for her, taking Lauren's left hand into her right and twining their fingers together. She gave Lauren's hand a light squeeze but said nothing as she sipped at her scotch, and her mind, which had been spinning with memories of Emily, finally going still at the feeling of comfort that flooded through her from Lauren's touch. The soft brush of Lauren's thumb over the back of her hand soothed her and, after a few minutes of sitting together in silence, Grey turned toward Lauren and gave her a small, grateful nod. "Thank you."

"You're welcome." Lauren gave Grey's hand a gentle squeeze. "You okay?"

"Yeah. I mean, I will be." Grey looked down at their hands that were resting on the warm skin of Lauren's thigh and sighed. Though Lauren had said that she did not mind, Grey still felt bad that she was spending her vacation dealing with all of her drama. "I am sorry about all this."

"Oh, Grey." Lauren set her glass onto a shelf behind her head and ran her fingers down the curve of Grey's jaw. "You don't have anything to be sorry about."

Grey closed her eyes and leaned into Lauren's hand, unable to resist the warmth of her touch. "I miss her."

"I know." Lauren's lips ticked up in a small smile as she cradled Grey's jaw in her hand and smoothed her thumb over Grey's cheek. "I know you do. It's okay."

"How are you so cool with all this?" Grey asked, blinking her eyes open to look at Lauren, whose eyes were overflowing with understanding.

"What else can I be?" Lauren shook her head as she saw Grey preparing to argue, and slid her hand down to press her index finger against Grey's lips to silence her. "I mean, seriously. You have every right to mourn, and there is no time limit on something like that. Emily is a part of you. She is a big, wonderful part of your life that helped you become the woman you are now, and it's *okay* for you miss her. You *should* miss her."

Grey pressed a kiss to the finger against her lips and sighed when Lauren pulled it away. "You are too understanding."

"I'm not," Lauren assured her. She smiled sadly and brushed her lips across Grey's forehead, steeling herself to say the words she knew she needed to say. "You are an amazing woman, Grey, and I have really enjoyed everything that we've done together, but if you're not okay with this anymore, if it's something that is going to cause you too much stress or heartache, we can stop."

"It's not that." Grey shook her head. "It's not you…"

"It's me," Lauren finished with a wry grin. "Yeah. I've heard that one before."

"No." Grey shook her head again and chugged what was left of the scotch in her glass, the alcohol warming her belly and strengthening her resolve. She set the empty tumbler down on the shelf beside Lauren's and turned into her, bracing her left hand on the bed beside Lauren's hip so that she was hovering in front of her. "That's not what I meant," she whispered, holding Lauren's gaze. Her eyes dropped to Lauren's lips and then back up to her eyes, and she smiled. "I miss her. But I also don't want to stop doing what we're doing, either."

Lauren's eyes danced over Grey's face as she tried to gauge the truthfulness in her words. "You're sure?"

"Yeah." Grey nodded and leaned in closer until their lips were only a hair's breadth apart. "I'm sure."

Lauren knew that she should call an end to whatever this was, but there was something about Grey that called to her, and her pulse began to race as she realized that, right or wrong, she just could not resist Grey Wells. "This is probably a really bad idea."

Grey grinned and pressed the softest of kisses to Lauren's lips, the caress a defiant confirmation of the fact that she knew Lauren was right, and that she did not care. "Do you want to stop?"

"No." Lauren reached up and wrapped her right hand around the back of Grey's neck, holding her in place. She knew that it was the absolute wrong thing to say, but she did not care. For the first time in her life, she was going to do the reckless thing. The stupid thing. She wanted Grey. And, judging by the swirling desire burning in Grey's eyes, Grey wanted her too. And, for now, that was enough. "I don't want to stop."

"Good." Grey kissed Lauren again. It started out as just a simple clasping of lips, a chaste confirmation that this was what they both wanted, but it did not take long at all for it to become something more as that indefinable spark that drew them together flared.

A shiver rolled down Lauren's spine at the feeling of Grey's hands slipping beneath her shirt, long, strong fingers digging possessively into her sides, and she took advantage of their positioning to help Grey out of her shirt and bra. The rest of Grey's clothes hit the floor not even a minute later, and Lauren smiled as she twisted her hips and forced Grey to roll onto her back.

Grey smiled as she relaxed back onto the bed, enjoying the sight of Lauren hovering above her. "Yes?"

Lauren's eyes dragged over Grey's lean, tan body, tracing the subtle lines of toned muscle and soft, feminine curves. Her heart thudded heavily in her throat as an unexpected feeling of tenderness swept through her the moment their eyes met, and she shook her head as she dipped down to capture Grey's lips in a kiss that was so much softer than the ones they had been trading only moments before.

The quiet affection in Lauren's kiss made Grey's heart flutter up into her throat, and she melted into it, meeting each languid swipe of Lauren's tongue with one of her own. She undressed Lauren with little thought as to what she was doing as her fingers slid over warm, soft skin, drawing little gasps and soft groans from Lauren's lips, and she sighed when she was eventually rewarded with the soft press of Lauren's body against her own. "Lauren…"

"Let me," Lauren whispered, dragging the tip of her nose over Grey's cheek as she stared into Grey's eyes.

The gentle warmth burning in Lauren's gaze took Grey's breath away. "Okay."

"Thank you." Lauren pressed a soft kiss to the left corner of Grey's lips, and then the right, before claiming them again completely.

Grey wrapped her hands around Lauren's hips as they kissed slowly, each lingering connection bleeding into the next until it became impossible to identify where one kiss ended and the next began. She held Lauren to her, delighting in the soft, electric pulse that would shoot through her body every time their nipples grazed together. Her breath caught in her throat at the feeling of Lauren's fingers dragging lightly down her arms, and she moaned softly when Lauren's hands wrapped lightly around her wrists and guided her arms up over her head.

"Okay?" Lauren asked softly as she threaded their fingers together, pinning Grey's hands to the sheets beside her head.

"God, yes." Grey squeezed Lauren's hands and nodded, surprising herself at how badly she wanted to give up the control she usually held in an iron fist. She sank into the bed as their kisses grew impossibly slower, their bodies settling into a gentle rocking motion that began and ended with a gentle squeeze of their joined hands.

Fiery kisses blazed a lazy trail down her throat, and Grey let out a shuddering breath when Lauren's fingers slipped from her own to drag lightly down her arms as Lauren languorously mapped the plane of her chest with her mouth. The feeling of Lauren's lips covering her breasts with the same reverent attention made Grey's eyes roll back in her head, and her heart stopped beating for an infinite second when a lingering kiss was pressed to the valley between her breasts, shattering what was left of her heart and somehow managing to fit those broken pieces back together at the same time. "Lauren…"

The desperation in Grey's voice made Lauren freeze, and she picked up her head to really look at her. Grey's lips were pressed tight together and turned down at the corners, and Lauren's stomach twisted as she thought that she had done something wrong. Grey had such a good heart, even broken as it was, that she just… God, what had she been thinking? Of course it was too much. She rocked back up so that she could look Grey in the eye. "I'm sorry."

"Don't be," Grey whispered, shaking her head. "I just…I need you closer."

Lauren nodded and settled onto the bed so that she was draped over Grey's right side. "Better?"

"Much." Grey laid her right hand into her left above her head, leaving herself open for Lauren's touch. Her heart beat a disjointed rhythm as Lauren hesitated for a moment, but it settled once again when Lauren relaxed against her. "Please don't stop."

The openness in Grey's gaze assured Lauren that she truly did want to continue, and she licked her lips as she leaned in to kiss her again.

Grey sighed as Lauren's right hand began to slide over her body, touching, teasing, caressing. Her eyes rolled back in her head at the feeling of Lauren's fingers spiraling slowly around her breasts in swooping circles and lazy figure-eights, every touch so achingly tender and unhurried, like the bounds of time and the universe had no bearing on them in this moment. It was both liberating and terrifying how free Grey felt under Lauren's hand, and she sighed against Lauren's lips as that blissful touch eventually dipped lower, ghosting over her stomach and down over her hips to dance along her inner thigh. "Lauren…"

"I'm here." Lauren brushed a gentle kiss over Grey's lips. She watched Grey's face intently as she slid her hand higher, dipping her fingers into the slick warmth that waited for her, and her throat grew tight at the way Grey smiled and whimpered at the touch. Lauren kept her touch light as her fingers skated through swollen folds, stroking and rubbing, up and down and back again, over and over, every pass as unhurried and gentle as the one before.

"God, Lauren," Grey sighed, her eyes rolling back in her head as Lauren's fingers skated higher to rub broad, light circles over her clit. Each circuit sent sparks of desire through her, and she reached up with her left hand, blindly seeking *something* to hold onto. She sighed when her fingertips ghosted across Lauren's, and she tangled their fingers together, using that hold as an anchor as she began to feel like she was floating away. A gentle, reassuring squeeze of her hand made Grey's heart skip a beat, and she sighed as she threaded the fingers of her right hand through Lauren's hair, pulling her down and claiming her lips in a kiss that was soft and deep and pure surrender.

Lauren smiled when the kiss broke and rested her forehead against Grey's. The warmth staring back at her took her breath away, and she bit her lip as she eased her middle finger lower. "You are beautiful." She pressed firmly against the sensitive ring of muscle, teasing it with a couple feinting thrusts before finally slipping inside. "So beautiful," she breathed, her pulse jumping at the flash of ecstasy that bolted through Grey's eyes at her first careful thrust.

"More," Grey rasped, tugging imploringly at Lauren's hair.

"Trust me," Lauren replied softly as she continued to thrust into Grey with just the one finger.

"I do," Grey whimpered, arching her back off the mattress as she rolled her hips against Lauren's hand. "Please."

Unable to resist the blatant need in Grey's voice, Lauren sighed and nodded, adding a second finger on her next thrust. She watched Grey's face with unabashed affection as she resumed her languid pace, wanting nothing more than to extend this moment for as long as possible. When the walls around her fingers began to flutter, she curled her fingers and dragged them over hidden ridges, making Grey's hips twitch. "Just let go, baby," she murmured encouragingly, the endearment slipping out so naturally that she did not even notice.

Grey moaned and squeezed her eyes shut, focusing the entirety of her attention on the heat building low in her hips. She clutched Lauren to her as her climax began to crest, and she let out a quiet gasp when it crashed through her in gentle waves.

"I've got you," Lauren promised, the words falling lightly against Grey's lips as the brunette trembled and shook in her arms. She sighed when Grey's body went lax beneath her, Grey's grip on her slackening as her entire body sank back into the bed, and carefully pulled her fingers free.

Grey could feel Lauren's eyes on her as she drifted, her mind and her body content to savor the blissful afterglow of her release. She stroked her fingers through Lauren's hair as she kissed her lazily, their tongues dancing together in the space between their parted lips. Grey held Lauren tighter and kissed her harder whenever she thought that Lauren was going to pull away, afraid that, when the moment ended, the lightness she felt suffusing her body would disappear as well.

Eventually, they did break apart, and Grey held her breath as she looked up at Lauren. She looked like an angel, pale skin glowing in the light of the moon that spilled through the windows along the outer hull, and Grey's breath caught in her throat at the tenderness that she could see lighting Lauren's eyes.

"You okay?" Lauren asked softly.

Grey nodded. "Yeah."

"Good."

Grey yawned widely, the day catching up to her in a rush, and rolled her eyes as she muttered, "Sorry."

"Don't be," Lauren said as she snuggled into Grey's side. "Sleep. Rest."

Grey frowned and ran a single finger up Lauren's spine. "What about you?"

Lauren shook her head. "Later." She brushed the lightest of kisses over the point of Grey's cheek, and smiled at the way the furrows in Grey's forehead deepened. "I promise."

"You're sure?"

"I am." Lauren smiled and nodded reassuringly as she traced the line of Grey's jaw with her fingertips. She could not resist leaning in to steal one last kiss, and she sighed against Grey's lips when it eventually broke. "Sweet dreams."

Grey lifted her chin to kiss Lauren again quickly, and smiled as she pulled away. "You too," she whispered as she rolled onto her side, her right hand grabbing hold of Lauren's and pulling it over her stomach. It was not often that she allowed herself to be held like this, but as Lauren's body pressed up against her back and molded to her own, Grey felt safer than she had in years.

Lauren knew the moment sleep claimed Grey completely, and she sighed softly as she pressed a gentle kiss to her shoulder.

"What are we doing?" she wondered quietly. Grey shifted in front of her, drawing their joined hands up to rest between her breasts, and Lauren closed her eyes as she held Grey tighter. Whatever it was they were doing, it was too late for her to even consider stopping now.

Chapter 29

Lauren squeezed her eyes shut against the sunlight streaming into the cabin and buried her face in a pillow. Her limbs felt heavy with sleep and her muscles sore as she stretched, pointing her toes and arching her back as she tried to wake up. She groaned as she smoothed a hand over the bed beside her, and was surprised to find it empty. It was then that the sunlight filling the room actually registered with her tired brain, and she frowned as she pushed herself up onto her forearms to look at the clock above the bed.

It was already after eight o'clock.

"Fuck," she hissed as she slammed her forehead back onto the bed. She had slept through breakfast.

She turned her head to the side and looked at the spot where Grey had laid the night before, idly wondering why in the hell Grey had not woken her up. Her gaze landed on a folded note sitting proudly on Grey's pillow, and she smiled as she reached for it. There was a grinning narwhal drawn on the front flap, its pale blue body a perfect complement to its rainbow-colored horn, and Lauren's smile widened as she opened the note to see what Grey had written on the inside.

Good morning, beautiful. You
looked so peaceful sleeping that I just didn't

have the heart to wake you. Don't worry about breakfast—I took care of it. Cheerios for everybody!

Just kidding... I'm going to make pancakes. There will be a plate keeping warm in the oven for you whenever you're ready.

~G

Lauren sighed and reread the note, both loving and hating the way her heart fluttered at the words written in Grey's tidy scrawl. The unease that had settled in her stomach the night before returned as she ran the pad of her index finger over the G at the bottom of the page, and her pulse sped as she remembered the way Grey had looked when she came undone beneath her. Even now, hours later and alone in Grey's bed, the memory filled her with such affection for the brunette that she knew her decision to give in to her desire for Grey was the only one she could have possibly made.

Though, she was sure, it would end up to be precisely the wrong one when it was time for her to return to her life in New York.

She rolled out of bed and slipped into her clothes from the night before, making sure to take Grey's note with her as she ducked across the hall to her cabin to shower and dress for the day. Once she was presentable, Lauren made her way up to the salon. She smiled and waved at the twins, who were sprawled across the couch with their tablets playing Minecraft, and nodded hello to Kim, who was sitting at one of the barstools. Grey was standing beside the sink, leaning against the counter and chatting with Kim, and Lauren's breath caught in her throat at the smile

Grey shot her. "Good morning," she murmured, a light blush creeping up her neck at the feeling of Kim's eyes on her.

"Hey sleepyhead," Grey teased.

Lauren rolled her eyes as she brushed past Grey to get to the coffee machine. "Yeah. I know. Sorry about that."

"Don't worry about it," Kim said, brushing off the apology with a wave of her hand. "We managed just fine on our own."

"Grey makes *awesome* chocolate chip pancakes!" Max and Peyton chimed in.

Lauren arched a brow and looked at Grey, who was grinning proudly and giving the boys two thumbs up for their support. "Good to know. Maybe I'll let her wake up early every morning to cook and I'll just sleep in."

"Yeah, nice try," Grey retorted, her eyes twinkling with amusement as she turned back to Lauren. The urge to take Lauren into her arms and kiss her good morning was nearly overwhelming, and she cleared her throat softly as she jammed her hands into her pockets. "Pancakes are the extent of my culinary prowess when it comes to breakfast food."

"Damn," Lauren muttered, just loud enough for Grey and Kim to hear. She laughed along with them as she prepped her coffee, busying her hands with the simple task so that she did not reach for Grey. Beyond the fact that she did not know how the Muellers would react to the idea of her and Grey being together, she found the idea of flaunting it to be entirely unprofessional. But that did not stop her fingers from itching to take Grey's hands into her own.

She wanted something deeper and more meaningful than playful banter. Be it a simple hug that started too tight and melted into something softer, or a kiss that held some small fraction of the tenderness they had shared, she craved some sign that the connection she had felt with Grey the night before had been real.

The subtle darkening of Lauren's eyes did not escape Grey's attention, and she nodded minutely, assuring Lauren with a look that she was feeling the same thing. But, no matter how much Grey wished otherwise, now was not the time for the things she really wanted to do, and she instead focused her attention on trying to keep things between them light and playful. "So—" she drawled, tipping her head at the oven where, as promised, a stack of pancakes was being kept warm for Lauren, "—you want to try my awesome pancakes?"

Kim, who had been watching Grey and Lauren with a small, knowing smile curling her lips, laughed. "Yeah, she would," she muttered before Lauren could answer for herself. Her eyes went wide as Grey and Lauren turned to her, shock clearly written on their faces, and she groaned. "I said that out loud, didn't I?"

"I…" Lauren frowned and shook her head. "How?"

Kim shrugged and offered the couple a small smile. "Well, I mean, come on. It *is* pretty obvious. The looks, the touches, the way you both seem to gravitate toward each other…" She chuckled at their matching surprised expressions. "You two just have really great chemistry."

Lauren bit her lip and became intensely interested in the floor as Grey gaped at their guest. Out of everything she had expected to happen that morning, waking up alone and being called-out on what she and Grey were doing together had not even made the list.

Grey cleared her throat uncomfortably. "Okay…?" she replied, her brows scrunching together and setting deep creases in her forehead.

Kim nodded and leaned back in her chair. "Of course. I mean, I get that some people are assholes—"

The twins, who had been ignoring the adult conversation up until that point, looked up and pointed at their mother with triumphant grins. "Dollar!"

"Shit," Kim muttered.

"That's another one!" Peyton pointed out gleefully as he high-fived his brother.

Kim smiled sheepishly at Grey and Lauren. "The boys got in trouble at school for repeating some of my more colorful language, so we made a deal that they have to give me a dollar if I hear them swear, and vice-versa. Little monsters are making out like bandits," she added under her breath. "I'll pay you guys later," she told the boys in a louder voice.

"Yeah!" Max cheered.

"We're going to the pirate beach today, right?" Peyton added, looking expectantly at Grey.

Grey nodded, grateful for the change in conversation. "Absolutely, buddy."

"And you'll show us skull rock?" Peyton pressed.

"I will," Grey assured him. She looked at Lauren and sighed as she allowed herself to reach out and give her hand a gentle squeeze. She wanted more, but the touch was enough to tide her over for the time being. "You okay if I start getting ready to head out?"

Lauren nodded, her eyes dropping to the way Grey's fingers curled around her own. "Of course. You want me to throw the lines?"

"I can do it." Grey shook her head and brushed her thumb over the back of Lauren's hand one last time before letting go. "Sit. Eat. It's fine."

"You're sure…?"

Grey nodded. "Yeah. Totally."

Kim chuckled softly and shook her head.

"What's so funny?" Will asked as he walked into the salon with Reid.

"You owe me a hundred bucks," Kim answered her husband.

Lauren's jaw dropped as she looked at Kim. "Seriously?"

Will's gaze slipped from his wife, who was looking far too pleased with herself, to Lauren and Grey, who looked mortally embarrassed, and he sighed. "Fuck."

"Dollar!" all three boys yelled happily.

Grey looked at Lauren, and shook her head as she chuckled softly under her breath. She loved the unpredictability of her job, but this morning definitely took the cake. Granted, all things considered, it went better than it could have, but still. "I think I'm gonna throw those lines and head up to the bridge."

"Can I help?" Reid asked.

"Us too!" Max and Peyton called out, turning off their tablets and tossing them onto the couch cushions as they bolted to their feet.

"I'll help supervise," Will said as he followed his sons out onto the deck.

"Have fun," Kim told her husband as she picked up her coffee cup and took a languorous sip. She laughed at the way Will shook his head and flipped her off over his shoulder, and sighed as she leaned back in her chair. "Peace at last."

Lauren slid her coffee cup and plate to an empty seat at the bar and nodded. "Yeah…"

After a few minutes of companionable silence, Kim said, "I'm sorry if I embarrassed you guys. Sometimes the filter on my 'thinking bubble'—" she surrounded the phrase with little air finger quotes, "—as the kids call it, doesn't work too well."

"No. It's fine. Really," Lauren said. After a beat, she added, "It's just…complicated."

"Everything worth having is," Kim said softly. She smiled at Lauren and sighed as she slipped out of her chair. "I should probably go help with the boys before they decide to use Reid as shark bait or something."

"I'll take care of the dishes," Lauren said, tipping her head at Kim's mug. "Don't worry about that."

"You're sure?" Kim asked. "It's not hard to put it in the dishwasher."

"I'm sure. And, thanks."

Kim nodded. "No problem," she replied lightly as she spun on her heel and walked out the open doors to the deck beyond.

Chapter 30

Grey slipped the backpack she was wearing from her shoulders and pulled a small wooden treasure chest from the largest compartment. She smiled at Lauren as she handed her the bag, and tipped her head at the skull-shaped rock in front of them that looked like it was right out of the movie *Peter Pan.* "I'm just going to hide this where I told Will and Kim it would be, and then we can go back to The Baths, if you'd like. Or, we can keep going down the trail to Devil's Bay and have a look around there. Whichever you'd prefer."

"No. That's fine. We can head back to The Baths," Lauren said. They had hustled through caves so quickly to hurry and hide the "pirate treasure" for the boys that she had only gotten a quick glimpse at the stunning natural grottoes that overlooked the sea, and she was looking forward to spending some time really exploring them.

"All right." Grey winked at Lauren as she left the backpack in the dirt and scampered off to the side of Skull Rock to hide the treasure chest full of replica doubloons in the lush foliage that surrounded the rock. She brushed her hands off on the back of her shorts as she made her way back onto the trail, and smiled. "Done."

"Will anyone else pick it up?" Lauren wondered aloud as she watched Grey zip the backpack shut and hoist it back onto her shoulders. While the national park was not overrun with tourists, they were certainly not the only ones there, and she was worried about how the boys would take coming back empty-handed after Grey had gotten them so hyped to find 'real pirate treasure'.

Grey shook her head. "Nah. You'd have to know it's there to find it. And—" she checked her watch, "—they should be on their way up here soon. They were just going to hang back for twenty minutes or so to explore the caves and give us time to do this, and then they were going to make their way down to the bay so the boys can snorkel and stuff."

"If you say so." Lauren fell into step beside Grey and smiled at the way the brunette's hand slipped into her own. "Can I help you with something?" she teased as she gave Grey's hand a squeeze.

"Oh, I'm sure I'll be able to think of something."

"Says the woman who left me alone in bed this morning."

"I let you sleep," Grey pointed out. "I didn't just abandon you to go fishing or something. I was nice and let you sleep-in while I slaved away in the kitchen making breakfast for everybody."

Lauren chuckled and bumped Grey's shoulder with her own. "Pancakes is hardly a 'slaving away' type of food."

"Yeah, well, we can't all be professionally-trained gourmet chefs. Some of us had to learn one burnt grilled cheese sandwich at a time." Grey stopped at the head of a set of stairs that led from the outside trail to The Baths and waved for Lauren to go first. "Even you have to admit that those pancakes were good, though."

"They were decent," Lauren allowed as she started down the ladder.

"Not cool, Lauren Whatever-you-middle-name-is Murphy."

"It's Rose," Lauren supplied with a smile. She hopped down to the sandy floor below, skipping the final few steps, and ran her hand through her hair as she looked up at Grey. Like herself, Grey was barefoot, wearing only a pair of shorts and a bikini to make navigating the water-filled grottos more comfortable, and Lauren licked her lips as she appreciated the subtle sway of Grey's breasts as she descended the stairs.

Grey smirked at Lauren as she stopped in front of her. "See something you like?"

"Wouldn't you like to know, Ms. I-left-Lauren-alone-in-bed-this-morning."

"Oh my god!" Grey laughed, reached out to grab onto Lauren's hips, and shook her head as she pulled Lauren into her. "It's not like I abandoned you," she pointed out as she brushed her lips over Lauren's. "I made breakfast. And, I left you a note. Doesn't the note count for something?"

Lauren sighed and nodded as she looped her arms around Grey's neck. She would have kept up the ruse, but the warm press of Grey's skin against her own made it hard to breathe, let alone think. The note was cute, and she would never admit that she had carefully placed it between the pages of her copy of *Fodor's U.S. and British Virgin Islands* that was sitting in one of the cubbies above her bed, but what she had really wanted was this. The feeling of Grey's body pressed against her own, so firm yet soft at the same time, strong fingers curling into her sides as deliciously tempting lips ghosted over her own.

A pleased smile quirked Grey's lips and she hummed as she rolled her hips into Lauren's. "What was your favorite part? The drawing, or what I wrote?"

"Fishing for compliments is not at all sexy," Lauren muttered, rolling her eyes, but she was unable to keep from smiling as Grey nuzzled her cheek. "But both. Okay? I liked both."

"I like you," Grey murmured softly, honestly.

Lauren smiled. "I like you too."

"Good." Grey tightened her hold on Lauren's hips and kissed her again, deeper, slower, every swipe of her tongue around Lauren's an apology for not being there when she woke up.

Lauren groaned when her back came into contact with one of the cool boulders that made up the grotto, and she threaded the fingers of her right hand through Grey's hair to hold her close. She knew that this was not the place for them to lose control, but it was impossible for her to pull away. There was so a tenderness to the kiss that made Lauren weak in the knees, and the feeling of Grey's breath cascading over her lips in trembling waves was nearly enough to make them buckle.

"Grey..." The brunette's name was the only word Lauren could manage, but it was enough. She whimpered softly as Grey's mouth descended back on her own with a gentle urgency that made her toes curl.

"Eww, kissing!" little voices cried out.

Grey groaned. She recognized those voices.

"Told you," Kim's voice added smugly.

"Damn," Will muttered.

"Dollar!"

Lauren's cheeks flamed with embarrassment as Grey reluctantly pulled away from her, and she rolled her eyes as she offered the Muellers a small wave. "Hello."

Will smiled sheepishly and waved. "Hey."

Kim chuckled. "We're on our way over to Devil's Bay."

"Sounds good." Grey ran her hands through her hair and looked at the boys. "You guys have that map I gave you?" It was crude, just black Sharpie on a piece of parchment textured printer paper, but she had tried her best to make it look like an actual treasure map.

Thankfully, the boys were young enough that they did not question the authenticity of the map. "Yup!" Peyton answered, waving the page in the air.

The 'map' was now wrinkled, no doubt from the boys fighting over it, and a little wet, and Grey had to admit that it made it look more authentic. "Awesome. Good luck then. Hopefully you guys will come back with some treasure, huh?"

"Yeah!" the boys chorused as they took off up the stairs at a sprint.

"We'll probably spend the day at the beach," Kim told Lauren and Grey with a pointed look as Will scampered up the stairs after the boys. "So, you know, don't feel like you need to hang out here on our behalf if you'd rather go back to the boat. I have the walkie-talkie. I'll just buzz when we're done."

"Oh my god," Lauren muttered as she rubbed her hand over her forehead.

Grey cleared her throat loudly and nodded. "I…uh…got it. Thanks."

Kim grinned. "See you two later!"

Lauren and Grey watched Kim jog up the stairs with matching dumbstruck expressions on their faces and, once Kim had disappeared from sight, Lauren turned to look at Grey. "Did she really just do that?"

"She did."

"Wow."

Grey nodded. "Yeah." She laughed and shook her head. The whole thing was utterly insane, but she had to admit that she greatly appreciated Kim's not-so-subtle-suggestion. "So, since we have been effectively relieved of duty for most of the day, what do you say we finish exploring these caves and then head on back to the boat for a bit?"

Lauren looked around the grotto and smiled. "We can explore on the way back to the boat. Once you've seen one rock grotto, you've seen them all…right?"

"Pretty much," Grey agreed with a chuckle. She tipped her head at the triangular opening that led them back toward the beach where their dinghy was moored, and waved for Lauren to go first. "After you, milady."

Chapter 31

"Oh my god."

Lauren chuckled and pinched the sensitive skin of Grey's throat between her teeth. The tender emotion that had flowed between them ebbed as they made their way out of The Baths, morphing with every stolen kiss and knowing smirk into something that was much easier to understand. Desire. Pure, wanton, naked desire. "Yes?"

Grey bit the inside of her cheek and tried to focus on maintaining a straight course toward the *Veritas*, which was increasingly difficult with the way Lauren's fingers were tweaking and rolling her nipple. Lauren pinched harder, and Grey groaned as she reflexively jerked the rudder to the left before quickly correcting it.

"Are you having issues?" Lauren smiled as she brushed her lips higher, fluttering her tongue over the sweet spot below Grey's ear before raking her teeth over the line of Grey's jaw. "We seem to be swerving all over the place…"

"Tell me about it," Grey laughed. She used her free hand to pull Lauren's from her breast, and smiled as she pressed a wet kiss to the center of her palm. "You do realize that once we get back on the *Veritas,* you are mine, right?"

"Is that so?"

"It is." Grey flicked her tongue along the seam between Lauren's index and middle fingers. "I have a bet to pay up on, and the egregious sin of leaving you alone in bed this morning to make up for."

"Oh." Lauren licked her lips as an expectant shiver rolled down her spine and curled low in her hips. "Really?"

"Really." Grey gave Lauren a thorough once over as she killed the engine to let the dinghy drift the final few yards to the *Veritas'* stern, and smirked at the sight of Lauren's nipples straining against the flimsy fabric of her bikini. "We do have the boat to ourselves for the next few hours, after all."

Lauren laughed and shook her head in amusement even as her stomach fluttered with anticipation. "Few hours, huh? Somebody's feeling ambitious."

"You have no idea." Grey winked at Lauren as she dropped her hand and edged toward the bow of the dinghy to soften their landing. She tied the bow line to a cleat by the dive platform, and tipped her head toward the *Veritas*. "Well…shall we?"

"I guess," Lauren replied with a dramatic sigh as she made the small hop onto the yacht. She smiled over her shoulder at Grey as she started up the stairs. "I mean, there's really nothing *else* to do…"

Grey laughed and hurried after Lauren, easily catching up to her by the time she had reached the back deck. She wrapped her arms around Lauren's waist from behind, and pressed her lips to the curve where Lauren's neck and shoulder met. "You don't want this?"

"I never said *that*." Lauren relaxed back into Grey, and sighed when Grey's fingers began slowly massaging her stomach. "That feels good," she breathed.

"You know what would feel even better?" Grey brushed her lips over the shell of Lauren's ear and chuckled at the way Lauren groaned.

"Hmm?"

"You…coming against my tongue," Grey answered in a low, seductive purr.

Just the idea of it made Lauren clench, and she groaned as she spun in Grey's arms. The playfulness in Grey's eyes had turned darker, hungrier, and Lauren surged forward with a whimper to crush their lips together. Her hips jerked forward at the feeling of Grey's hands sliding up her spine, and she moaned against Grey's lips when the brunette's nimble fingers made quick work of the ties holding her top on. "Bed?"

Grey shook her head and pulled back just far enough to look Lauren in the eye. "Trust me?"

"Of course." The answer was given without thought, and Lauren's eyes widened as Grey tugged her toward the stairs to the bridge.

Grey's heart thudded heavily in her chest at the way Lauren followed her without question, one arm demurely covering her naked chest as she climbed the stairs after her. She stopped beside the sunbathing mat that took up the front half of the bridge, and smiled reassuringly at Lauren as she took her back into her arms. "Okay?"

Instead of answering, Lauren simply smiled and used her right hand to guide Grey's left to her breast. She gave Grey's hand a light squeeze, and sighed when Grey picked up the motion.

"Good?"

"So good." Lauren smiled and flicked her tongue over Grey's lips as she pulled Grey's top off. "Much better."

Grey laughed and pressed a hard kiss to Lauren's lips as she dropped her hands to the clasp on Lauren's shorts. Topless was definitely a step in the right direction, but she wanted more.

Desire, hot and slick crashed between Lauren's legs at the feeling of the wind sweeping over her skin when she kicked her shorts and bikini bottoms aside. She had not expected to be so aroused by the feeling of the sun and the air on her body, warming and caressing areas that were usually hidden behind layers of clothing. It was freeing and invigorating, and she felt herself grow even wetter when Grey guided her down onto the sunbathing mat. Lauren settled back onto the mat, her legs falling half open as she looked up at Grey. The brunette was an absolute vision, all sun-kissed skin and taut, sinewy muscle, and she licked her lips as she watched Grey's fingers curl around the snap on her boardshorts.

Knowing that she had Lauren's full attention, Grey undressed slowly, pushing her shorts and bikini bottoms down over her hips inch by teasing inch until gravity took over and carried them to the ground. Her eyes roamed over Lauren's body as she crawled onto the mat, sliding her knees between Lauren's legs as she held herself up on half-extended arms so that their nipples raked lightly together. She dipped her head like she was going to kiss Lauren but pulled away at the last second, and chuckled at the disgruntled huff that tumbled from Lauren's lips. "Yes?"

"Just kiss me." Lauren wrapped her right hand around the back of Grey's neck and drew her down into her. The kiss was deep and hungry, a toe-curling mix of tongues and teeth and unrestrained desire, and she groaned when it eventually broke. "Fuck, Grey."

"Maybe later," Grey murmured. She used her chin to turn Lauren's head to the side, and brushed her lips over the shell of Lauren's ear. "You are so fucking sexy."

Lauren bit her lip and moaned.

Grey hummed and nuzzled Lauren's ear as she nipped at her earlobe. "I am going to make you scream," she promised in a husky whisper before she moved lower, wrapping her mouth around Lauren's pulse point and sucking against it hard enough to leave a mark.

Lauren threaded the fingers of her right hand through Grey's hair when the brunette's mouth descended upon her breast. Every lick, nip, and suck made her clit jump, and she sighed as she closed her eyes and surrendered herself to Grey's touch.

Pleasant sparks shot down Grey's spine at the feeling of Lauren's fingers scratching her scalp. She hummed as she sucked hard on Lauren's left nipple, and pulled her head back to stretch the bud to its limit before letting it fall from her lips. "Gorgeous," she muttered under her breath as she blew lightly over the swollen nub. She looked up at Lauren through her lashes as she began moving lower, and froze for a moment at the look of absolute ecstasy that was painted across the redhead's features.

It was so different from the look of tender understanding Lauren had worn the night before, and a gentle affection bloomed in Grey's chest as she pressed a soft kiss to Lauren's belly before she dragged her teeth over a protruding hipbone. She watched Lauren's face as she kissed her way lower, and she was not sure which of them moaned louder at the first slow swipe of her tongue through her. Grey cradled Lauren's hips in her hands, holding loosely when she lapped lightly at Lauren's clit and tightening her grip when she ran her tongue in bold, heavy strokes through swollen folds. She purposefully kept her touch varied and her tempo unpredictable, so that it was impossible for Lauren to find any kind of rhythm that might hasten her release.

She wanted this to last.

The irregularity of Grey's touch had Lauren bucking against her mouth as she sought that perfect combination of speed and force and friction that would send her flying. Her every attempt failed miserably, however, and she groaned as she lifted herself up enough to look down her body at Grey. Grey's lips were curled in a smile as she teased her with quick, light flicks, and Lauren bit her lip as she reached down to thread her fingers through Grey's hair. Her eyes fluttered closed when Grey's tongue dragged heavily over her clit, and she let out a shaky breath as she forced them back open. "God."

"Yes?" Grey's smile widened at the way Lauren's eyelids fluttered when she circled her opening with her tongue. She dug her fingers into Lauren's hips as she pushed inside, wiggling the tip of her tongue against clinging velvet, and hummed when she pulled out.

Lauren whimpered at the loss, and dropped her head back to the mat. "Don't stop," she begged as she lifted herself toward Grey's mouth. "God, please don't stop."

More than happy to oblige, Grey slid her hands lower, cupping Lauren's ass in her palms and lifting the redhead's throbbing center to her mouth. The keening moan that was all but shouted at the heavens when she resumed fucking Lauren with her tongue made Grey clench, and she tightened her hold on Lauren's ass as pushed as deep inside her as she possibly could. She fucked her slowly, firmly, drawing out each short thrust until Lauren writhed against her.

White heat, soft and powerful, spread through Lauren's body, thrumming with the promise of ecstasy. She rocked her hips desperately against Grey's mouth as her climax began to crest, the muscles of her lower abdomen tightening until there was nothing left to do but snap. She cried out as she came, her body freezing for an extended heartbeat before relaxing and succumbing to the waves of pleasure that were coursing through her.

And then, just when her orgasm began to ease, Grey's tongue curled and twisted inside her, and a second orgasm, more powerful than her first, slammed into her. Lauren screamed, unable to hold back as every synapse in her body exploded in a burst of overwhelming pleasure.

Grey eased Lauren through the length of her release and, when the last spasm left Lauren gasping and completely relaxed in her hands, she gently lowered her to the mat and kissed her way back up Lauren's body. She smiled at the look of pure contentment that lit Lauren's face as she captured her lips in a slow, deep kiss, letting Lauren taste herself on her tongue.

Lauren moaned softly and stroked her hands up and down Grey's sides as they kissed, basking in the pleasant buzz that was still thrumming in her veins. "Oh wow," she breathed when the kiss finally broke.

"Told you I was going to make you scream," Grey murmured as she nuzzled Lauren's cheek.

"You did." Lauren dragged her nails up Grey's stomach, and smiled at the way Grey's hips jerked forward. "I want to taste you."

Grey groaned. "Please."

"Good," Lauren muttered, her nipples tightening at the unfettered need in Grey's voice. She reached down to grab onto Grey's hips, and stroked her thumbs over the smooth skin before she gave them a tug. "Up."

What Lauren meant was clear, and Grey's pulse pounded forcefully between her legs as she crawled slowly up Lauren's body until she was kneeling above her mouth. She reached down with her right hand and tangled her fingers in Lauren's hair as the redhead's hands rubbed broad, soft circles over her ass, and she could not contain the moan that escaped her when Lauren's tongue finally slid through her.

Lauren smiled at the sight of Grey above her, back straight, chin dropped to her chest as she held her gaze. Grey's skin seemed to glow in the sunlight, and Lauren ran her hands over every inch that she could reach as Grey's hips began rolling against her mouth. The feeling of Grey's thighs against her cheeks was electric, the taste of her intoxicating, and Lauren strained to get as close to her as possible.

"Yes," Grey hissed as Lauren's fingers clamped onto her nipples at the same time her clit was sucked between soft, hungry lips. "Lauren..." Her eyes fluttered shut when she was answered with a low moan that reverberated through her.

"Let go," Lauren encouraged, sliding her hands down to Grey's hips and pulling her into a faster rhythm. She hummed softly when Grey began moving with her, and lapped eagerly at every inch of skin that came within reach.

Grey's head fell back as she gave in and began really riding the ravenous mouth between her legs, her hips canting back, drawing attention to her clit before rocking forward when the sensation became too much. It did not take long at all for release to sweep through her, and she cried out Lauren's name as she came.

Lauren moaned softly at the sound of her name being torn from Grey's throat, and she watched with unabashed awe as Grey came undone above her. She felt powerful, even though she was not in the position of power at the moment, and she sighed when Grey's hips rolled away from her.

"Jesus." Grey flopped onto her back on the mat beside Lauren. She laughed at the feeling of Lauren's fingers tickling her inner thigh, and shook her head as she covered Lauren's hand with her own. "Lauren."

"Tell me about it." Lauren chuckled softly under her breath as she rolled onto her side and pressed a wet kiss to Grey's thigh. "We definitely need to do that again," she added with a smirk as she laid her head on Grey's hip.

Grey smiled as she combed her fingers through Lauren's hair. "Which part?"

"All of it," Lauren answered without hesitation. She winked at Grey as she moved just enough to flick the tip of her tongue over Grey's clit.

Grey groaned as her body reacted immediately to Lauren's touch. "Don't go starting anything you can't finish, Murphy."

"Who says I can't finish this?" Lauren slid the tip of her tongue around the swollen bundle of nerves, and smiled at the way Grey's legs spread wider for her. "I think you like this."

"I have no idea what you're talking about," Grey deadpanned. Her breath hitched at the feeling of Lauren's lips brushing the lightest of kisses over her, and she sighed as she ran her free hand over the back of Lauren's thigh. She wrapped her fingers around Lauren's knee and gave it a light tug. "Me too."

"So ambitious," Lauren teased, letting Grey's hand guide her as she rolled onto her knees and wrapped her arms around Grey's thighs.

"Absolutely," Grey agreed, her breath falling in warm waves over Lauren's center. She smiled as she slid her hands over Lauren's thighs to her hips, pulling Lauren down to her mouth. And, as she began to match Lauren lick for lick, she could not help thinking that it was going to be a long, glorious afternoon.

Chapter 32

The sound of happy voices made Lauren look up from the plate of apple nachos she was making, and she smiled at the boys as they skipped merrily into the salon. "Hey, guys. How was the beach?"

Reid's eyes grew wide when he spotted the snack Lauren was making, and he grinned as he scampered for the middle barstool. "Apple nachos!" Apple nachos—apple slices drizzled with caramel and chocolate sauce and topped with chocolate chips—were his favorite snack that Lauren made for them.

"We found the treasure!" Peyton and Max added as they climbed up into the chairs on either side of their little brother, greedily grabbing at the apple slices and trying to hoard the ones with the most chocolate chips.

"Dad has it," Reid shared.

"Well done, you guys." Lauren leaned forward to give each of the boys a high five. "You'll have to show me later." Movement in her periphery caught her attention, and she looked up to see Grey walking into the salon with Kim and Will. She blushed at the knowing smirk Kim shot her, and turned to wet some paper towels for the boys to use as napkins.

"Lauren made nachos!" Reid announced to his parents.

"I see that," Kim said. Reid's face was already smeared with caramel and chocolate, and the twins looked like chipmunks with their cheeks stuffed to bursting. She chuckled under her breath as she shook her head and ruffled the boys' hair. "So, good afternoon?" she asked Lauren with a sly grin.

Lauren's blush deepened, and she nodded. "Very good," she conceded with a smile. Though, to be fair, even calling the afternoon 'very good' was an understatement. She was honestly impressed that she was able to walk.

"What'd you do?" Reid asked. "Did you swim at the beach too? I saw a shark!"

"It wasn't a shark, Reid." Peyton rolled his eyes and slapped his forehead dramatically. "It was just a fish."

"It was a shark!"

"Was not!" Max argued.

"Quiet game on three!" Kim yelled. "One…two…three!"

All three boys shut up and glared at each other.

"God, I love that game," Kim muttered as she reached past the boys to snag a piece of apple.

Lauren laughed. "My parents used to do that one to us, too. And then it changed into the 'who can hold their breath the longest' game."

"I'm gonna remember that one," Kim said, nodding as she looked at her sons. "Of course, with these three, they'll probably hold their breath so long that they pass out."

"But, they won't be fighting." Will grinned and flashed Lauren a thumbs up. "Thanks for the idea."

"My pleasure." Lauren looked past the Muellers to Grey, who was running a hand through her hair as she looked at one of the screens at the navigation center. "Everything okay?"

"Yeah." Grey nodded as she turned to face the group. "Was just checking some things to make sure that we'll be okay to jump over to Road Town before it gets dark."

"We get to go more sailing?" Reid asked.

Peyton and Max grinned victoriously as they slapped the table and pointed at him, clearly celebrating the fact that he was out of the game because he talked.

"We do," Grey told him. She turned her attention to Will and Kim and smiled. "If you guys want, Lauren and I can watch the boys tonight and you two can go have a night out on your own. It will be our last night in a port with any kind of nightlife, and we—" she waved a hand between herself and Lauren, "—thought that you guys might like a little grown-up time."

"That would be great, thank you," Kim said, smiling at Grey and Lauren before looking at her husband. "Whattaya say?"

"I never turn down offers for free babysitting," Will answered with a grin.

It was hardly free babysitting, considering how much they had paid to charter the yacht for the week, but Grey just smiled and nodded. "We kinda figured we owed you one."

"So do we clear out of British customs tonight?" Will asked.

Grey shook her head. "First thing tomorrow morning. I want to get there right when the office opens. Then we gotta head over to Cruz Bay on Saint John to clear-in with U.S. customs. We can do lunch aboard the boat, or else you guys can grab something in town—there are quite a few family-friendly restaurants that are pretty good right by the customs office—and then we'll skip over to Christmas Cove."

"Are there reindeer there?" Peyton asked excitedly.

Max threw his hands up in the air and did a little victory dance in his seat. "I win!"

"Well, the silence was nice while it lasted," Kim sighed.

"No reindeer, sorry buddy," Grey told him with a regretful smile. "But, there are some really cool fish, and if we're lucky there might be a few sea turtles."

"Turtles are cool," Max said, grinning at his brothers, who nodded their agreement.

Grey smiled. "Good. So—" she clapped her hands and looked pointedly at Lauren, "—I'm gonna throw the lines and get us moving. We have a spot reserved in the harbor, but I want to try and get there before it gets too packed to maneuver."

"I can throw the lines for you, if you want," Will offered.

"That would be great," Grey said. "Thanks."

"Us too!" The boys yelled as they hurried to shove what was left of the apple slices into their mouths.

"Finish chewing before you get out of those chairs," Kim warned. She shook her head at the way her sons groaned and began chewing with a vengeance to try and finish first. "It is not a race."

"Yeah right," Will chuckled. "Have you met our kids?"

Kim just rolled her eyes. Everything with the boys was a race. Whether it was seeing who could get dressed the fastest, or who got to the bathroom first to brush their teeth, nothing was done without it being some kind of competition. "Yeah."

"Here, guys," Lauren told the boys as she set open bottles of water in front of them. She smiled at the mumbled *'fanks'* she got from the trio, whose mouths were still full despite their best efforts. "How many apples did you fit in there?"

"You don't want to know," Kim answered drolly. "They watched the Nathan's Hot Dog contest on the fourth with their cousins, and it's been all downhill from there."

"Better than when they watched Ninja Warrior with your brother," Will pointed out. "At least we haven't taken any trips to the ER for this one…"

"Yet," Kim added with a resigned shake of her head. She looked at Lauren and explained, "The boys thought it would be fun to climb their doorframes like the 'ninjas on TV'—" she framed the words with her fingers, "—and Max fell and broke his wrist."

"Ouch," Lauren muttered. "Me and my brother used to do that, though. Would drive my mom nuts."

"Done!" Peyton announced. He looked at his brothers, who were still chewing like maniacs, and grinned. "I win."

"Not a race, Pey," Will droned.

Peyton just grinned. "Hey, Dad. Can I have the treasure chest?" He held his hands out as his dad pulled the box out of their beach bag. "Grey, come look!"

Because the salon-side of the counter was crowded with the Muellers, Grey walked around the peninsula to stand by Lauren in the galley so they could be appropriately wowed by the boys' find. She smiled at the way Lauren leaned into her when she put a hand on the small of her back, and leaned forward interestedly. "Whatcha got?"

Reid finished chewing in a hurry so he could answer Grey's question. "Dubballoons."

"Duh-bloons," Peyton corrected.

"That's what I said!" Reid argued.

"No it's not," Max said.

"No backing out of that babysitting offer," Kim told Lauren and Grey.

"Wouldn't dream of it," Grey assured her. "Like I said, we owe you some alone-time." She smiled at the boys and added, "So, who's gonna help me get this boat moving?"

"Me!" the boys all shouted as they leapt from their chairs and took off running out the door.

Grey chuckled and gave Lauren's side a quick squeeze before she started after them. "I'm gonna keep them so busy this afternoon that they'll pass out as soon as they've finished dinner," she told Kim.

Kim just laughed. "Good luck with that," she told Grey as the brunette disappeared onto the back deck.

Chapter 33

The Muellers' last day aboard the *Veritas* was a hectic whirlwind of island-hopping and clearing customs, and by the time they were anchored in Christmas Cove, everybody was ready to just relax. That meant more swimming for the boys and their father, while Kim stretched out on the trampolines to watch them as she soaked up the last few rays of the day.

Because Lauren was busy in the kitchen preparing a special dinner for the family's last night aboard the boat, Grey gathered bottles of root beer for the boys and a couple bottles of Saint John's Ale for Will and Kim and carried them out to the front of the boat. Seeing the family enjoying themselves made her smile, and she laughed out loud as she watched Peyton go flying off the starboard pontoon with an excited, "Watch this!" before landing a textbook belly flop.

"That had to hurt," Grey commented as she set the tray of drinks down onto the small walkway that cut between the forward trampolines. She grabbed one of the beers and held it out for Kim. "Here you go."

"My son, the rocket surgeon," Kim chuckled as she sat up and took the bottle from Grey. "Thank you. And, thanks again for watching them last night so we could go out."

"It was—"

"Wonderful," Kim interrupted. She sighed and peered over the edge of the boat to where Peyton was cry-laughing in his father's arms. When she was convinced that he was okay, she rolled her eyes and turned back to Grey. "The boys cannot stop talking about how much fun they had making pizzas with you two and playing games, and I just want you to know that Will and I really appreciated the opportunity to spend a little time alone."

Grey smiled. "It really wasn't a problem at all. They're good kids. We had fun, too."

"Still… Thank you."

"It was our pleasure," Grey assured her with a small tip of her head as she looked out over the cove. Despite the fact that nearly every one of the twenty-two mooring balls that dotted the cove were taken, there was still an air of tranquility about the place that she loved. And she needed that tranquility, especially after dealing with customs and busy ports all day. Her personality was best suited for small groups and open space, so having to maneuver through crowded harbors and hordes of people always left her feeling exhausted. She needed to recharge her batteries, to sit with a bottle of beer or a glass of scotch and enjoy the feeling of the sun on her skin and the wind in her hair, but that would have to wait until later. For now, a few quiet moments with Lauren would have to suffice until the workday was officially at an end. "Well," she murmured after a beat, "I should probably go see if Lauren needs any help with dinner. If you guys need anything, just holler."

"Will do."

"Moooooommy!" Max yelled, and Grey chuckled when Will echoed the call.

Kim sighed and set her beer back on the tray. "Looks like I'm up," she drawled wryly as she laid her sunglasses beside the bottles and walked over to the edge of the boat. "What's up, Max?"

"Come swimming!" all three boys chorused.

Grey laughed. "Have fun."

"Yeah. You too," Kim said, winking at Grey before she leapt off the side of the boat, knees tucked to her chest as she cannonballed her entire family.

Grey shook her head as she made her way back down the length of the boat to the back deck. She enjoyed the majority of the clients she ferried about the islands, but Kim really was one of a kind. Grey's step faltered when she spotted Lauren dancing in the kitchen, hips swaying almost in time with the beat of the music playing from the salon's speakers, and she smiled to herself as she leaned against the doorframe to watch.

Even though she had lived every second, it was hard for her to believe that only a week had passed since she first laid eyes on Lauren. She had gone from both hating and craving the sight of Lauren because the redhead reminded her of Emily, to seeing the differences between the two women, and then seeing and appreciating Lauren for who she was. She still missed Emily, but the hurt she used to feel whenever she thought about her had become a dull, pleasant ache. She was moving on, learning to live again in Lauren's understanding arms.

The song playing changed to an old Killers tune, and Grey covered her mouth with her hand to stifle her laughter at the way Lauren started bopping her head with the intro. A wooden spoon became a microphone as Lauren began singing and dancing in earnest. Grey had thought that what she needed was quietude—it was, after all, her usual method of dealing with days like the one she had just had—but as her feet carried her toward the galley, she realized that she did not need a few peaceful moments alone to recharge after the long day.

She simply needed Lauren.

Her smile grew as she sidled into the galley, close enough to touch Lauren if she were to just reach out her hand. The song began building toward the chorus and she waited, purposefully hovering beyond Lauren's line of sight, until she began singing along. "Somebody told me, you had a boyfriend, that looks like a girlfriend…"

Lauren whipped around, wooden spoon held threateningly in the air, and froze when she saw Grey standing behind her. Grey's hands were held up in front of her, ready to block any blows that might be directed her way, and Lauren shook her head as she tried to glare at her. "Don't scare me like that!"

"Come on, Murphy." Grey tugged the wooden spoon from Lauren's hand and tossed it into the sink as she started dancing up against her. "Dance with me."

"I don't…" Lauren began to argue, but her voice trailed off when she realized that, contrary to every other person who had ever seen her dance, Grey was not laughing at her. The look in Grey's eyes cajoled her to join-in, and she was helpless to resist. She was impossibly self-conscious as she started dancing again, her every movement much more muted than it was before, but as the song played on, she found herself letting go until she was dancing like she had been when she realized she was not alone.

"Oh, I love this one," Grey said when the music changed. She laughed and captured Lauren's lips in a playful kiss as she reached for the redhead's hips and pulled her flush against her. "Come on, Murphy. Show me whatcha got."

The feeling of Grey's leg slipping between her own made Lauren gasp, and she froze as Grey began grinding against her. She could do silly dancing-in-the-kitchen dancing, but not this. She shook her head and stammered, "I…I don't…"

"Yes you do," Grey said, easily reading the apprehension in Lauren's eyes. "Trust me."

Lauren bit her lip and allowed the hands on her hips to guide her into motion. Her heart hammered with nerves when Grey's hold relaxed and she was left controlling her own movement. She felt awkward and uncoordinated as she tried to keep pace with Grey, and just when she was about to pull back and give up, Grey's lips covered her own, effectively holding her in place.

"You're doing great," Grey murmured reassuringly.

"I don't know how to dance," Lauren argued weakly.

"You do." Grey wrapped her right hand around Lauren's neck and pulled her in for another kiss.

The longer Grey kissed her, the less concerned Lauren became with the quality of her dancing. She looped her arms around Grey's neck and deepened the kiss, and her body began moving of its own volition to the beat of the music and the rhythmic press of Grey's hips against her own. The music became nothing but background noise, something loud and brash to contrast the soft moans and ragged breaths that filled their air between them. Their hips slowed to a gentle grind that was more akin to foreplay than dancing, and Lauren whimpered at the loss of Grey's lips when they broke apart.

Grey smoothed a hand over Lauren's cheek. "That was fun."

"It was," Lauren agreed softly. Her eyes flitted over Grey's face and she smiled. "Thank you."

"For what?"

Lauren shrugged and looked away. "Not laughing at me."

"Oh, Lauren," Grey sighed, hooking a finger under Lauren's chin to lift her eyes up to her own. "You move beautifully." She could see that Lauren was ready to protest her assessment, and she cut her off with another quick kiss. "You do."

Lauren wanted to argue, but the earnestness in Grey's gaze brokered no dissent, and she relented with a small nod. She knew that it was a lie, but she appreciated it all the same. "Thank you."

Grey smiled and pulled Lauren into her arms. Her heart swelled at the way Lauren sank into her, clearly needing the physical reassurance, and she sighed as she brushed a light kiss over her ear. "You're welcome."

Chapter 34

Lauren was surprised by how hard it was to say goodbye to the Muellers once they were back in Charlotte Amalie. She should have been ecstatic because their leaving meant that she and Grey would finally be alone for a few days, and she was, but there was also a part of her that hated seeing them go. She was going to miss the boys and their enthusiasm about everything, Will's easy-going nature, and even Kim's knowing little smirks and playful comments. They had been the perfect buffer during those first few days of awkwardness, and their acceptance these last few days had been a blessing.

"Goodbye, Lauren," Reid pouted as he fell into her arms. "Thank you for making us yummy food."

"You're welcome, buddy," Lauren murmured, giving the boy a good squeeze before letting go. She watched him turn to his brothers, who were hovering near the bottom of the port-side dive platform, looking reluctant to leave, and shook her head as she looked at Will and Kim. "Thank you guys, for everything."

"Thank you," Will stressed, shaking her hand. "Everything was amazing," he added as he turned his attention to Grey.

Kim just pulled Lauren into her arms and hugged her tight. "Thank you. And good luck," she added softly.

"Thanks." Lauren's gaze flicked over to Grey, and she cleared her throat softly as she backed out of Kim's embrace. "Have a safe trip home."

"We will," Will assured her as he watched his wife hug Grey goodbye as well. "Really, the trip was amazing. We may just have to come back next year and do it again."

"I'll be here," Grey told him with a smile.

It did not escape anyone's attention that Lauren remained silent, and that was enough of a push to finally send the Muellers on their way. Lauren wrapped her arms around herself as she watched Will hop onto the dock to help the boys make the jump over, and she sighed at the feeling of Grey's hand ghosting over her hip as Kim followed them. She did not want to think about the fact that her time aboard the *Veritas* was already halfway over, or that she would soon have to go back to New York.

Grey's lips were warm and welcoming when Lauren turned to capture them with her own, and she purposefully ignored the idea that it was because Grey was feeling the same things she was. A small shiver rolled down Lauren's spine as Grey's mouth opened over hers, the brunette's tongue both ardent and demanding as it stroked along her own, and she gave as good as she got as she spun and fisted her hands in the collar of Grey's shirt. Thoughts of New York tried to push their way back to the forefront of her mind, but they were quashed by the overwhelming need she had for Grey. Lauren kissed Grey until her head spun, and she let out a shuddering sigh when she finally pulled back far enough to draw a proper breath.

"Goddamn," Grey muttered as she nuzzled Lauren's cheek.

Lauren pulled back just far enough to run the pad of her thumb over Grey's lips as she nodded. "Yeah."

"Is there anything you'd like to do or see these next couple days?"

"You."

Grey laughed and pressed a quick, playful kiss to Lauren's lips. "Well, duh. But, seriously. We need to be back here around noon on Thursday to get everything ready for the next cruise, but tonight, tomorrow, and Wednesday are all ours. Anything you want, and it's yours."

"I just want you," Lauren answered honestly. She smirked and added, "Preferably naked."

"That can definitely be arranged," Grey assured her. "But…"

Lauren silenced Grey with a kiss. She had come down to the islands with a list of things she wanted to see and try, but everything on that list paled in comparison to the woman in front of her. "I just want you."

The earnestness in Lauren's voice was unmistakable, and Grey nodded. "Okay. I know of a nice little bay over on Saint John that's about as secluded as you can get during the high season. What do you say we pick up some provisions and then head over there tomorrow? We can grab a mooring ball and just hang out."

Lauren smiled and kissed Grey softly. "That sounds absolutely perfect."

"And…even though it's like, the least sexy thing in the world, I really need to do some laundry."

"Me too," Lauren admitted with a small laugh.

"Okay." Grey kissed the tip of Lauren's nose playfully. "So, laundry, then some grocery shopping, and then, tonight, will you let me take you out to dinner?"

Lauren nodded. "I would like that."

Grey could not contain her smile as she lifted her chin to press a sweet kiss to Lauren's lips. "Me too," she whispered, the words barely audible over the pounding of her heart.

Chapter 35

Grey glanced at Lauren as she pulled to a stop in front of the valet station and put the car into park. Though neither of them had dared refer to the evening as a date, it did not escape her attention that they had both dressed as if it were one. Lauren was stunning in a knee-length black dress that had a soft, flowing skirt and was fitted through the bodice, and Grey licked her lips as her eyes traced the curve of the neckline that revealed just the barest hint of cleavage. The dress was simple, classy, and ridiculously sexy, and Grey smiled as she imagined unzipping it slowly and watching it fall to the floor later. "I know I already told you this," she said as she reached out and ran a gentle finger down Lauren's thigh, "but you really do look beautiful tonight."

A light blush crept up Lauren's cheeks at the sincerity in Grey's tone. She had thrown the dress into her bag at the last minute—more of a 'why not?' than anything else—and she was glad now that she had. "Thank you." Lauren ignored the sound of her car door opening and let her eyes sweep slowly over Grey's body. Grey had opted for a pair of tailored black slacks with pale gray pinstripes and a white oxford that was rolled to just below her elbows and had one button too many left open at the neck. She looked good enough to eat, and Lauren felt her pulse jump as she imagined all the ways their night might end. "You too," she added quietly, but a slight huskiness to her voice gave away some of what she was thinking.

A second valet had appeared to handle Grey's door, and Grey sighed as she gave Lauren's thigh a quick squeeze before climbing out of the car. She met Lauren under the portico that ran from the drive to the doors of the restaurant, and she tipped her head invitingly as she offered Lauren her hand. "Shall we?"

"Of course," Lauren murmured, a small smile quirking her lips as she slipped her hand into Grey's.

Bluewater was the signature restaurant at Kipling Resort in Frenchman's Cove, the Kipling family's most exclusive hotel on the island. It was always packed, getting a reservation usually meant calling weeks in advance if you were not a hotel guest, and Grey was grateful for her connections when the maître d' led them through the crowded dining room to an intimate corner of the patio that overlooked the ocean.

They took their seats at a table surrounded by manicured plants that sparkled with strings of white lights, and Grey nodded her thanks to the maître d' as she took the menu he held out for her, not even pretending to listen as he prattled on about that night's specials. Nothing the kitchen prepared could ever be more delectable than the woman beside her, who was wearing the most alluring smile lifting as she listened intently to the description of each dish.

After he had left them with the promise of their server arriving shortly, Grey set her menu on the table and reached out to cover Lauren's hand with her own. She had been a little worried that her choice in restaurants might be too much given their situation, but she knew that Lauren would appreciate the five-star cuisine, and she wanted to give her a nice night out. "Thank you for coming out with me tonight."

Lauren looked up at Grey through her lashes, and leaned forward and kissed Grey softly, lingering in the connection for a few moments before pulling back with a small sigh. She smiled and ran a light hand over Grey's jaw. "Thank you for asking."

Movement in her periphery made Grey pull away from Lauren's touch, and she rolled her eyes when she saw a familiar blonde approaching their table with a bottle of wine in her hands. "Surprise, surprise," Grey drawled as she pushed her chair back and stood to hug her friend hello.

"Like you could really call Jonathan for a reservation and not have me hear about it," Kelly Kipling replied as she returned the hug. She looked at Lauren over Grey's shoulder, and sighed. She had spent the last week worrying about how Grey, and seeing Lauren in person did little to assuage her. Lauren was not as identical to Emily as she had feared, but the resemblance was close enough to give her pause. Kelly gave Grey a searching look as she slipped out of her embrace, and pursed her lips thoughtfully as she turned her full attention to Lauren. "Chef Murphy, it is nice to actually meet you."

"Ms. Kipling?" Lauren guessed, correctly assuming that the blonde was the woman who had interviewed her over the phone.

"Kelly, please," Kelly insisted with a small, saccharine smile. "I'm glad to see that you're enjoying your stay in the islands."

Grey groaned. The jab at her…whatever it was she had with Lauren was clear, and she shook her head. "Kip, come on."

The comment could have been considered playful, but the caustic edge to Kelly's voice told Lauren that the blonde did not approve of what she had walked-in on. And, knowing hard it had been for Grey to even be around her those first few days, she understood. Were their situation reversed, she knew that she would be just as protective of Grey. Lauren sighed and nodded. "I am."

Kelly looked poised to respond, and Grey sighed. She flashed an apologetic smile at Lauren before she turned and gave Kelly a withering glare. "Let me walk you to the bar to get that bottle opened," she said, looking pointedly at the bottle of wine in Kelly's hands. "We'll be right back," she told Lauren, wishing she could do something about the concern that was clearly visible in Lauren's eyes as she ushered Kelly toward the bar.

"I do employ a sommelier," Kelly drawled as she led the way across the patio.

"Yeah, and a wicked tongue," Grey muttered as she sidled up to the outdoor bar beside her friend.

"Sweet talker," Kelly jibed as she handed the bottle to the bartender to open.

Grey watched the bartender as he uncorked the bottle, and waited until he had made a discreet exit to respond. "Kelly."

The use of her first name told Kelly that Grey had had enough, and she relented. "Okay, fine. But, seriously, are you sure about whatever it is you're doing with her?"

Grey shrugged and ran her hands through her hair. Just the mention of Lauren had her turning to look at the redhead. "Yeah. No. I dunno. It's just…"

"What?" Kelly prompted when it seemed like Grey was not going to finish her thought.

"Inevitable," Grey murmured as she turned back to Kelly. "Look, I know you're being all mama bear and everything and, while I appreciate it, I just…I care about her. She's a sweet girl and she just…" Grey smiled sadly and shook her head. "She doesn't need this shit. I was the one who kissed her first. She already knew about Emily and she gave me an out, but I didn't want it. I still don't want it. I know this is probably not going to end well," she added softly, finally giving voice to the truth that lurked in the background of every moment she and Lauren had shared over the last few days, "but I can't stay away from her. I don't want to."

Kelly gaped, floored by the fact that Grey had not only said Emily's name—something she had not done since the funeral—

she had also apparently talked to Lauren about her as well. "Well…fuck."

"Yes, there's been quite a bit of that, too," Grey muttered dryly, hoping to lighten the mood.

Kelly chuckled. "You getting laid is not the most revelatory information, Wells."

"Shut up," Grey muttered.

"You love me." Kelly looked over at Lauren and sighed. "So, you're boning the chef, huh?"

Grey rolled her eyes. "I wouldn't put it so crudely, but yes."

"Please," Kelly scoffed. "You just said you guys have been fucking. How is boning any worse? But, most importantly, is the sex good?"

"Amazing. But that's all I'm telling you." Grey blew out a quiet breath and smiled. "I'm a big girl, Kip. I know what I'm doing, even if it isn't the smartest thing I've ever done."

"Yeah, well—" Kelly reached out and gave Grey's hand a gentle squeeze, "—I'm still gonna worry about you."

"I know," Grey said. "And I love you for that."

Kelly sighed and looked over at Lauren. Grey's assurances that she knew what she was doing did little to alleviate her apprehension about what Grey was doing with Lauren, but she also knew that Lauren had to be something special if she was able to get Grey to actually talk about Emily. "I guess I need to go apologize for being such a bitch, huh?"

"That would be nice."

"Dinner on the house?"

"That would be even nicer." Grey laughed softly and pulled Kelly into a fierce hug. "Thank you for looking out for me. I know I haven't been the easiest to deal with these last few years."

"Yeah, well, that's my job." Kelly smiled as she pulled back to look Grey in the eye. "I mean, I've been looking out for your sorry ass since I got stuck with you as a roommate, freshman year. Who the hell else is gonna do it?"

Grey laughed and shook her head as her gaze drifted to Lauren. "I don't know," she whispered.

Kelly glanced from Grey to Lauren and back again, noting the way Grey's eyes had grown soft when she looked at Lauren. "You wanna talk about that?"

"Not really, no."

"Okay." Kelly picked up the bottle of wine she had brought with her left hand and motioned toward Lauren with her right. "Let's go get that apology out of the way so you two can enjoy the rest of your night." She smiled at Grey and rolled her eyes. "God, I hate apologizing."

"I know," Grey chuckled as she fell into step beside her friend.

They made their way back through the maze of tables filling the patio, and Kelly cleared her throat softly as she approached the table where Lauren sat fiddling with her napkin on her lap as she looked out over the water. "I'm sorry."

Lauren looked up, her gaze flitting between Kelly and Grey, who were standing beside the table. Kelly looked perfectly contrite, though there was something about the way she held herself that said it was begrudgingly done, and while Grey did not look as relaxed as she had been before her friend had surprised them, she did have a small, genuine smile tugging at her lips. Lauren sighed when Grey's hand landed lightly on her shoulder, and could not help but lean into it. "Yeah. Me too," she murmured.

It was obvious from the way Lauren had reflexively relaxed under Grey's hand that Lauren could no more avoid Grey than Grey could avoid her, and Kelly shook her head as she silently cursed the Fates for dealing Grey yet another spectacularly fucked-up hand. "Right, well—" she made a show of checking the time on her watch, "—I should probably get going." She tipped her head at Lauren in a small bow. "Chef Murphy, it was nice to meet you."

"Lauren, please," Lauren replied with a small smile. "And it was nice to meet you, too."

"Grey." Kelly looked at her old friend. "Take care of yourself, and call me later."

"I will," Grey assured her.

Kelly smiled and leaned in to brush a quick kiss across Grey's cheek. "Be good," she murmured affectionately.

"When am I ever good?" Grey quipped, her tone holding the same warmth. She nodded in response to the questioning look in Kelly's eyes, assuring her that she would be okay. "I'll talk to you later."

"Yeah. Enjoy your meal."

Grey retook her seat as Kelly made her way across the patio and into the main dining room with long, purposeful strides, and sighed as she reached for Lauren's hand. "I'm sorry about that."

"Don't be." Lauren shook her head as she stroked her fingertips over Grey's palm. "She's a good friend."

"Yeah, but still. You didn't need that."

"Honestly, if I were here, I would've done the same thing," Lauren said. "She's just looking out for you."

Grey gave Lauren a small smile as she leaned in and dropped a quick kiss to her lips. "I know." She ran the backs of her fingers over Lauren's jaw and kissed her again softly. "But I don't need to be protected. I know what I'm doing."

"Grey…"

"Lauren." Grey brushed her thumb over the corner of Lauren's lips.

Lauren's eyes danced over Grey's face. Her eyes were warm and soft, her expression sure, and Lauren sighed as she nodded. "Okay."

"Good." Grey stole another soft kiss, and then forced herself to pull away and sit back in her chair. She shook her head as she picked up her menu, already missing the feeling of gentle contentment that filled her whenever she touched Lauren. She looked up at the sound of Lauren's chair scraping across the patio beside her, and smiled when Lauren's hand slid lightly over her thigh. She held Lauren's gaze as she reached down and covered the hand on her leg and gave it a gentle squeeze. "Kip is buying us dinner to make up for being a bitch earlier," she shared, keeping her tone purposefully light as she tried to steer their evening back to where it was before Kip had shown up. "So I am going to order the most expensive thing on the menu. What looks good to you?"

Lauren stared at Grey for a moment longer, and then shrugged. They both knew that their situation was far from ideal, but as neither of them were willing to put an end to things, there was really no point dwelling on the fact. All that they could do was enjoy the moments they had, and hope that the memories they made would be enough to make it all worthwhile. "I don't know." She picked up her menu. "What do you suggest?"

Grey smiled and tickled her fingers over Lauren's. "Me."

Lauren laughed. "Really?"

"Absolutely."

"While that is an incredibly tempting idea," Lauren drawled as she let her eyes drag over Grey's body, deliberately lingering on the ample swell of her breasts, "I think I'll save you for dessert."

Chapter 36

As it turned out, it was remarkably easy for Lauren to pretend that the end of her tenure aboard the *Veritas* was not growing steadily closer with every passing second. When it was just the two of them, it was easy to imagine that the soft hiss of the swinging pendulum of Time that would ultimately tear them apart was simply the wind that was skipping over the waves and filling their sails.

The trip from Charlotte Amalie to Hawksnest Bay had been smooth, and they rounded the rocky cape at the southern end of the bay before midday. Lauren sat up on the sunbathing mat where she had stretched out at the sound of the sails furling overhead, and let her eyes sweep over their surroundings. The water was the clear, gradient hues of turquoise and blue that Lauren had become accustomed to during her time in the islands, and the mooring field near the center of the bay was empty. Lush, rich, green vegetation cascaded down the mountains to a pristine stretch of pale golden sand that wrapped along the curve of the bay, and Lauren could already picture herself spending a lazy afternoon on the warm sand, listening to the hypnotic crash of waves lapping at the shore.

"It's beautiful," Lauren said, smiling as she turned to look at Grey.

"It is," Grey agreed, ignoring the scenery around them as she watched the sails overhead retract with a careful eye in case any of the mechanicals that allowed her to solo-sail the *Veritas* malfunctioned. In reality, the bay was not that much different from any of the others they had visited over the last week, but it felt much more secluded, which was something she always appreciated whenever she visited.

"Is it always like this?" Lauren asked, waving a hand at the empty mooring field.

Grey bounced her head from side to side and shrugged as she powered up the *Veritas'* twin engines. "It depends, really," she said as she made for the buoy at the southernmost edge of the mooring field. "Most of the time, though, yeah. Hawkshead is too far south for charters to use as a mooring spot on cruises out of Charlotte Amalie, because it's easier to jump from Saint John to the other islands if you go a little further north, like we did with the Muellers. It's also too far north to use as an anchorage to dink down to Cruz for customs, so there's none of that mess to deal with, and it doesn't get a lot of foot traffic because there aren't any hotels on the bay."

"It's perfect," Lauren declared, turning back toward the shoreline.

"Yeah," Grey murmured as she looked at Lauren, her gaze soft behind the reflective lenses of her sunglasses. She stared at Lauren for a few seconds longer before she sighed and turned her attention back to the water in front of the bow. "Absolutely perfect."

Lauren slipped on her deck shoes when Grey backed the engines down to a crawl as they approached the edge of the mooring field, and then smiled at Grey as she made for the stairs. "I'll go tie us off."

Grey watched her go with a smile, thinking that a string bikini and a pair of Sperry's had never looked so good together.

She slid out of her chair and stood behind the wheel when Lauren knelt at the end of the starboard trampoline with the boat pole in her hand. Grey followed Lauren's hand signals as they neared the buoy, tapping the throttle with each 'go-go' wave of Lauren's hand and finally throwing the engines into reverse when Lauren held up a fist, bringing the seventy-five foot catamaran to a complete halt.

Once the bow lines were secured to the mooring buoy, Grey turned off the engines and caught Lauren's eye. "Well done, Ms. Murphy."

"Thank ya, ma'am," Lauren drawled, bowing with a flourish. She laughed at the way Grey shook her head at her, and waved a hand beckoningly. "Come on."

"Down there?" Grey teased, her gaze drifting over Lauren's shoulder to the water beyond. Her skin itched from the sun and the wind that had battered her on the sail over, and she smiled as an idea for how to remedy that came to mind.

"Yes. Down here."

"Well, gee, I dunno," Grey joked as she toed off her shoes and shucked the shorts she had been wearing over her bathing suit. She carefully removed and folded her sunglasses, and stored them in a small cubby at the helm. "What's in it for me?"

Lauren laughed and shook her head. "What do you want?"

"You."

"Then come down here," Lauren repeated, holding her arms out to either side of her in a 'what are you waiting for' type of gesture.

Grey climbed onto the side of the bridge and balanced on the small ledge that ran along the outside of the railing. She could see all the way to the sand and coral dotting the bottom of the bay below, and she smiled as she looked back at Lauren. "Okay," she said as she lifted her arms over her head and dove off the side.

"Damn," Lauren murmured as she watched Grey's body arc smoothly through the air, her natural athleticism on display as she sliced into the water, her body in perfect alignment from her fingertips to the tips of her toes. She hurried to the edge and waited for Grey to reappear, and laughed when Grey's head finally broke the water. "You're nuts!"

Grey shrugged, reached behind herself, and tugged at the strings of her bikini top. "Probably." She tossed the wet top at Lauren and grinned as it landed wetly at her feet. "Come on, Murphy! The water's great!"

Lauren smiled and cocked her head to the side as she looked down at Grey, who was treading water a few feet away from her. "How great is it?" she asked, toeing off her shoes and flicking them into the center of the trampoline.

"Amazing."

"Really?" Lauren teased, holding Grey's gaze as she removed her top. She winked at her as she tossed it over her shoulder, and arched a brow challengingly as she dropped her hands to her hips.

"Is that all you got?" Grey worked her bikini bottoms down her legs and flung them up onto the boat as well.

Lauren laughed as she shucked the rest of her suit and kicked it aside. "I guess not."

"Get down here."

"What's in it for me?" Lauren teased, putting an extra sway in her hips as she ambled toward the bow of the boat and prepared to jump.

Grey smiled. "Me."

"I dunno…" Lauren tapped a contemplative finger on her chin.

"Really?" Grey laughed, sending a splash of water in Lauren's direction.

"Okay, fine." Lauren winked at Grey as she leapt feet-first off the side. The feeling of the warm water sliding over her skin was refreshing after the morning's sail, and she laughed when Grey's hands landed on her waist the moment her head broke the surface. Before she could say anything, Grey's lips were on hers, both gentle and demanding, and she sighed as she wrapped her arms around Grey's neck and yielded to the kiss.

"Glad you decided to join me," Grey murmured.

Lauren toyed with the short hairs at the back of Grey's neck. "Me too."

A small shiver rolled down Grey's spine at the softness in Lauren's gaze, and she sighed as she kissed her again. The hand on the back of her neck tightened, holding her in place as Lauren's mouth slanted over her own, deepening the kiss, and Grey groaned when Lauren edged close enough that their breasts brushed lightly together. "Lauren…"

"Yes?" Lauren hummed, her lips quirking up in a small smile at the feeling of Grey's hands sliding over her ass.

"If you're going to keep kissing me like that, we're going to have to get out of the water."

"What? You can't do this and keep your head above water?" Lauren teased, kicking idly to keep afloat as she dropped her right hand between Grey's legs and gave her a playful squeeze.

Grey laughed and reached down to pull Lauren's hand away from her. "No. I can't."

"Me neither," Lauren admitted, shaking her head as she pulled her hand from Grey's grip. "So I guess we should probably stop."

"Or we can get out of the water."

Lauren's eyes flicked toward the dive platform at the stern of the boat. "That works too."

"Good." Grey pressed a quick kiss to Lauren's lips and grinned when she pulled away. "Race you there!"

"Like that's really fair!" Lauren laughed and started after Grey, not even bothering to try and win despite the fact that she could tell Grey was holding back. She watched Grey flip the swim ladder down once she reached the stern of the boat, and she stopped moving altogether when Grey climbed out of the water, her smooth skin and toned muscles glinting in the sun. The sight of Grey standing on the platform, wet and naked, with a lazy smile quirking her lips waiting for her, spurred Lauren forward, and she closed the final yards separating her from the *Veritas* in what seemed like a blink of an eye.

Grey's mouth went dry as she watched Lauren emerge from the water. Her eyes were glued to the way rivulets of water coursed slowly over Lauren's body, around her breasts and down the plane of her stomach, and she cleared her throat softly when Lauren finally stood in front of her. "God, you're beautiful."

"You are too." Lauren smiled as she stepped into Grey and ran a light hand over her hip. She leaned in and brushed a soft kiss over Grey's lips, and her nipples tightened at the way Grey whimpered quietly when she pulled away. "Come on," she murmured, pressing on Grey's hip, knowing that they were not going to be able to remain standing on their own much longer.

Grey's eyes remained locked on Lauren's as she backed up the stairs to the deck, and she wasted no time pulling Lauren into her once she had cleared the final step. "Kiss me," she growled, even as she wrapped a hand around Lauren's neck and claimed her lips in a deep, bruising kiss.

Lauren let Grey direct the kiss as she guided her backwards. She smiled when they bumped into a table, and used her body to pin Grey in place. Lauren nipped at Grey's lower lip as she ran her right hand up the brunette's thigh. Grey shifted in front of her, widening her stance, and Lauren hummed as she tickled her fingers up between her legs. She wrapped her left arm around Grey's waist and held her close as she stroked through the arousal that waited for her. "You feel so good."

Grey chuckled and leaned her forehead against Lauren's as she slipped a hand between her legs. "You too," she murmured, her voice low and rough and dripping of sex as she rubbed firm circles over Lauren's clit. "So wet."

"God, Grey," Lauren groaned, her hips bucking wantonly against Grey's hand. She dipped her head enough to reclaim Grey's lips in a kiss that stole the air from her lungs. They worked each other higher and higher, mirroring the other's touch until it became impossible to tell who was leading and who was following.

"Fuck. So close," Grey grunted, tearing her mouth away from Lauren's. She squeezed her eyes shut as she bit down on Lauren's shoulder, trying to hold herself back, and redoubled her effort to make Lauren come first.

"Come with me," Lauren pleaded, pressing her lips to Grey's ear. "Come with me, Grey. Come with…" Her voice trailed off in a silent scream as orgasm ripped through her, the quiet filled by the sound of Grey moaning her name like it alone held the brunette's salvation. She clung to Grey as their lips crashed together again, tongues sliding sloppily around each other as they rode out their release, and she let out a shaky breath when her orgasm finally eased. "Holy fuck."

Grey chuckled and buried her face in the crook of Lauren's neck. She sighed as she cradled Lauren to her, enjoying the soft press of Lauren's body against her own. She brushed her lips over the hollow of Lauren's throat, and smiled as she felt Lauren's breath catch in response. "Tell me about it."

Chapter 37

The afternoon passed in a blur of tangled limbs and feverish kisses, and the sun was inching toward the western horizon, casting shades of red and gold across the sky when Grey entered the salon later that evening to find Lauren working in the galley. Her lips curled in a soft smile as her eyes swept slowly over Lauren's body, tracing the long legs that only hours before had been spread invitingly to her, up over the swell of Lauren's ass and along her spine that was hidden by the thin tank top she was wearing. Lauren's hair was pulled up in the messy bun Grey adored, and she winced at the sight of several faint purple marks dotting Lauren's throat.

"Are you going to stand there all night, or are you going to come help?" Lauren asked, smiling over her shoulder at Grey.

Grey laughed and padded into the galley to stand behind Lauren. She wrapped her arms around her waist, and hummed softly as she brushed a tender kiss over the darkest of the marks marring her throat. "Sorry about these."

"Don't be," Lauren murmured. "They're so light that they probably won't even be noticeable by the time we head back to Saint Thomas and, for now, I…" She set the knife she had been holding down onto the cutting board beside the Ahi steaks she had been trimming and covered Grey's hands at her waist with her own. "I like seeing them there."

"Seriously?"

The obvious surprise in Grey's tone made Lauren smile. "Yeah. Why not?"

"I dunno." Grey nuzzled Lauren's neck. "I guess I just didn't think that you'd like being marked."

"I don't, usually," Lauren admitted softly. "But I liked seeing them when I looked in the mirror earlier. And I really like the way it feels when you're kissing them like that…" Her voice trailed off into a low moan at the feeling of Grey's tongue sweeping lightly over one of the marks.

"I like seeing them on you too," Grey whispered.

"Yeah." Lauren sighed and leaned back into Grey, her eyes fluttering closed as she relaxed in the warmth of her gentle embrace. "This is nice."

"Yeah, it is." Grey dropped her lips to the curve where Lauren's neck and shoulder met and held her tighter. "Very nice," she muttered, closing her eyes as she inhaled the sweet scent of Lauren's shampoo.

A warm shiver rolled down Lauren's spine at the feeling of Grey's lips against her skin, and she turned carefully in her arms until she was able to wrap her arms around Grey's neck. Being held felt nice, but she wanted to hold, too.

"Can we just stay like this all night?" Grey nuzzled Lauren's cheek with her nose.

Lauren pressed a soft kiss to Grey's ear, and her heart swelled with affection for the woman in her arms. "We can certainly try."

"Good," Grey muttered.

Lauren hummed and leaned back against the counter, accepting Grey's weight as she stroked a gentle hand up and down her back, more than content to lose herself in the quiet intimacy that wrapped itself comfortingly around them.

The moment eventually came to an end when Grey's stomach growled loudly, and she smiled sheepishly as she pulled back just far enough to look Lauren in the eye. "Sorry."

"You have nothing to be sorry about." Lauren smiled and dusted a soft kiss across Grey's lips. "We had quite the workout this afternoon."

"Mmm, we did," Grey purred, rolling her eyes as her stomach once again made its presence known.

Lauren laughed and reluctantly released her hold on Grey. "It's okay. I'm getting hungry too, to be honest."

"Well, at least it's not just my stomach ruining the mood, then." Grey chuckled sardonically as she glanced over Lauren's shoulder to the cutting board on the counter. "Ahi, huh?"

"Yeah, it sounded good," Lauren replied with a shrug. "I was thinking of just doing some rice with it. Keep things simple for tonight?"

"Works for me." Grey smiled and darted in to steal one last kiss. "Is there anything I can do to help?"

"You can get the water going for the rice, if you want," Lauren offered as she picked up her knife and turned her attention back to the fish on the cutting board. "I mean, there's really not a lot to do here. I'm just going to make a quick ginger-wasabi rub for the tuna, and then sear the steaks right before the rice is done."

"I think I can manage to boil some water," Grey said as she reached for the measuring cup Lauren had already set out beside the sink. She poured two cups of water into a saucepan and set it on the range to boil. "How about some music?"

"Sure."

"Are you in the mood for anything in particular?"

Lauren shook her head and smiled at Grey. "Not really." She laughed at the look of playful annoyance Grey shot her. "Really, Grey. Whatever you want is fine with me."

"So…metal?" Grey smirked over her shoulder at Lauren as she made her way over to the stereo tucked into the shelving behind the sofa.

"If that's what you want," Lauren replied serenely, knowing full-well from having looked through Grey's iPod that there was not any metal on it.

"Wait." Grey snapped her fingers. "I know…elevator music."

Lauren laughed and nodded. "Go for it."

"God, you're really not going to make this easy for me, are you?" Grey grumbled as she scrolled through her playlists. She glanced up at Lauren, who was watching her with the most beguiling smile, and sighed. "Come on. Give me a little help?"

"Okay, fine. Not elevator music."

"Big fucking help that is," Grey muttered, looking back down at her iPod. She was not in the mood for classical, but did not particularly feel like listening to anything super up-tempo either. "How's piano pop sound?"

"That'll work," Lauren agreed as she turned to pull a knob of ginger out of the fridge. Music began playing as she bumped the door closed with her shoulder, and she smiled as she immediately recognized the song. She bobbed her head with the opening vocals as she pulled a grater out of the cupboard below the peninsula where she had been working, and caught Grey's eye across the salon when the chorus kicked in. "I've got my little black dress on…"

"That was a great dress."

"I'm glad you liked it." Lauren winked at Grey and then she turned her attention back to their food.

Grey sat down at the barstool opposite where Lauren was standing and folded her arms on the counter as she contented herself with watching Lauren work. They chatted amiably as dinner cooked, conversation flowing from comments about whatever song was playing to whatever happened to cross their minds at that particular moment, and Grey marveled at the comfortable domesticity of it all. They had only known each other for a short time, but it felt like they had been doing this particular dance for years.

Once they had finished eating and everything was cleaned and put away, Grey grabbed two tumblers from the cupboard by the sink and the bottle of Auchentoshan from the liquor cabinet. She smiled at Lauren and waved the bottle of scotch at the back deck. "After you."

Lauren tipped her head and wandered out onto the deck, calling over her shoulder, "Bridge, or tramps?"

"Whatever you want is fine with me," Grey drawled with a smirk, throwing Lauren's words from earlier back at her.

"Ooh, you sure got me there." Lauren chuckled as she bypassed the stairs to the bridge and started down the side of the starboard hull. She smiled at the sound of Grey laughing behind her as she stepped onto the trampolines at the bow. "It really isn't that funny, Wells," she said as she dropped to the mat.

"Says you," Grey retorted as she sat down beside Lauren. She arched a brow challengingly and handed Lauren the glasses she was carrying. "I thought it was pretty funny."

"Yeah, well, whatever makes you giggle." Lauren held the tumblers out for Grey to fill and gave them a wiggle.

Grey poured a generous serving of scotch into each glass, and gave Lauren her most smoldering look as she capped the bottle and set it onto the hull beside her. "You like it."

There was really no point trying to deny it, and Lauren sighed as she nodded and leaned over to press a chaste kiss to Grey's lips. "Yeah. I like it."

Grey smiled and kissed Lauren again, tilting her head to the side and deepening the kiss as Lauren's mouth opened invitingly under her own. She sighed under her breath when she eventually pulled away, and dropped a playful kiss to the tip of Lauren's nose. "I like that."

"Me too," Lauren agreed softly, licking her lips as she looked out over the silhouette of the island in front of them. She took a sip of her drink and glanced back at Grey, and was not at all surprised to find that Grey was watching her. Her heart fluttered as she leaned back into Grey, unable to do anything but give in to the overwhelming desire that consumed her.

They kissed slowly, deeply, every clasping of lips and every sweep of their tongues speaking a truth neither of them felt comfortable admitting. Grey was the first to pull away, and she smiled as she leaned her forehead against Lauren's. She reached up with her free hand to run her fingers over Lauren's jaw, and her heart skipped a beat at the way Lauren's eyes fluttered closed under the gentle touch. "So beautiful," she murmured adoringly.

Lauren was glad for the shadows that hid her blush as she opened her eyes to look at Grey. "Thank you," she whispered.

"Thank you." Grey cupped Lauren's face in her hand and pressed a chaste kiss to her lips. "I didn't think I'd ever feel like this again."

"Like what?"

"Whole." Grey sucked in a deep breath and held it for a moment before letting it go. "Like I can actually breathe again. I don't know what it is about you that got behind my walls like you did, but I am so glad that it happened."

"Oh, sweetie," Lauren murmured, her gaze softening as she mirrored Grey's pose and cupped the brunette's face with her free hand. She smoothed her thumb over Grey's cheek and shook her head. "You are an amazing woman. You know that, right?"

"I'm a mess."

"No, you're not," Lauren argued in a gentle tone. "You are an amazing, smart, beautiful, funny, sexy as hell woman who deserves to be happy."

The sincerity in Lauren's tone took Grey's breath away, and she looked away as she admitted softly, "I am." She took another deep breath and forced herself to meet Lauren's gaze. "Happy, I mean. You make me happy."

"You make me happy too." Lauren lifted her chin and brushed a tender kiss over Grey's lips, and sighed as she pulled away, her eyes drifting to the stars overhead. The moment was becoming far too serious, and she wracked her brain for something to lighten the mood. "Do you see that star up there?"

Grey understood what Lauren was doing, and she was thankful for it as she leaned into her to look along her arm that was stretched toward the heavens. "That's Sirius." She laughed at the surprised look Lauren shot her and pecked her lips affectionately. "I do sail for a living, you know. I spend a lot of time out here looking at the sky."

"Should have known," Lauren grumbled.

"Sorry." Grey grinned and leaned her forehead on Lauren's shoulder. "You can still teach me about the constellations if you want."

"Now you're just patronizing me."

"Maybe." Grey rolled away from the elbow Lauren aimed at her side and chuckled as she darted a hand out to tickle Lauren's leg. "Is that all you got, Murphy?"

"Oh, don't you wish you knew." Lauren arched a brow challengingly and lifted her glass to her lips.

"You betcha," Grey said in her best Minnesotan accent.

"Oh, yeah, doncha know." Lauren laughed and shook her head. "Would you believe that I actually don't know a lot of people under sixty who talk like that at home?"

"That is very disappointing."

"I'm sure it's not," Lauren retorted dryly, smiling as she took another sip of her drink.

"It is!"

Lauren rolled her eyes. "Just drink your scotch, Wells."

"Are you trying to get me drunk because your 'impress the girl with your knowledge of astronomy' move failed so epically?" Grey asked, smirking as she held Lauren's gaze and took a healthy swallow of her drink.

"It was not a move. It was a change of topic."

Grey sighed and nodded. "I know." She finished off the alcohol in her glass and lay back on the trampoline, watching Lauren out of the corner of her eye as the redhead did the same. Once Lauren was lying beside her, she reached out and threaded their fingers together.

"Smooth," Lauren murmured, turning her head to look at Grey as she gave her hand a light squeeze.

"I try." Grey sighed and looked back up at the stars, her lips quirking up in a small smile. "You see that bright light there?"

"I see lots of stars, Copernicus."

"Well, that one there—" Grey lifted their joined hands and pointed at the glowing orb high in the eastern sky, "—is Jupiter."

"Really?" Lauren asked, cocking her head to the side as if that slight change in angle would help her tell if Grey was pulling her leg or not.

"Yup. And if you look really carefully, you can see Aries and Pisces on either side of it."

Lauren sighed dramatically and looked over at Grey. "Fine. I'll admit it, your star game is better than mine."

Grey smiled and lifted their joined hands to her lips so she could press a lingering kiss to the back of Lauren's knuckles. "You can always do the ol' yawn and stretch maneuver next time, if you want."

"I'll keep that in mind."

"You do that." Grey pointed their hands at a bright star near the horizon. "That's Venus."

"Now you're just making shit up," Lauren grumbled.

"I'm not!" Grey laughed. "But I can always stop, if you want."

"No, that's okay," Lauren said, smiling as she scooted closer to Grey so that she could rest her head on Grey's shoulder. "You may proceed to amaze me with your impressive knowledge of astronomy."

"If I do, will I be getting lucky later?" Grey smirked.

"Maybe."

Grey kissed Lauren softly. "What if I just want to hold you as you fall asleep?"

Lauren's heart fluttered at the tenderness shining in Grey's eyes, and she smiled as she whispered, "You better have a killer star-game for that one."

"Well then…" Grey cleared her throat softly and pointed their hands at a collection of stars high overhead. "You see that constellation there…"

Chapter 38

The sun was reaching its apex the next day when Grey led Lauren out of the thinning trees and onto a crop of black, volcanic rock at the end of the path they had been following. She waved a hand at the vista in front of them and grinned as she looked back at Lauren. "See?"

Lauren nodded as she took it all in. A calm sea stretched between them and the handful of small islands that dotted the horizon, and Lauren smiled as she crept closer to the edge. Grey had promised her a killer view, and she had to admit that Grey had certainly delivered. "It is pretty perfect."

"Yeah," Grey murmured as she sat down on the rocks. She stretched her legs out in front of her and crossed them at the ankles as she leaned back on her hands, making herself comfortable as she drank in the view. The rocky point at the southern edge of Hawksnest Bay was one of her secret spots, a haven of tranquility that let her feel both connected to the earth and apart from it at the same time.

"So, how did you find this place?" Lauren asked as she sat down beside Grey.

"You mean, besides the fact that I routinely sail by here?" Grey teased as she bumped Lauren's shoulder with her own.

Lauren chuckled and rolled her eyes. "Yeah. I mean besides that."

Grey shrugged. "Lucky accident, I guess."

It was obvious that there was more to the story, but Lauren knew better than to press, and she sighed as she looked out over the water. It was as if the entire world were spread out before her, full of opportunity and adventure, daring her to do something worthy of being remembered. It was humbling, to sit there and realize that she had never done one thing worthy of being remembered by anybody. "I feel so small, sitting here."

"Yeah," Grey agreed, her tone much lighter than Lauren's. She had found this spot during a weekend bender with Kip not long after Emily had died. She had wanted to come alone, but Kip had invited herself along—no doubt to make sure that she did not drink herself into a stupor, fall overboard, and drown.

Which was, she had to admit, something that could have very well happened.

Grey had sailed by the point more times than she could count, but she had never bothered to actually seek it out until that weekend. The hike that day had been Kip's idea—something to get her out and moving instead of just sitting on the boat drinking herself to death—and though Grey had cursed her friend the entire time, she had been thankful for it ever since. It probably did not make sense to a lot of people, but Grey *liked* feeling insignificant. In the months after Emily's death, it had been a relief to be faced with the fact that her pain did not matter in the grand scheme of things. That no matter how she felt, the tide kept turning. The wind continued to blow.

That life, in all its forms, soldiered on.

Lauren watched Grey out of the corner of her eye as they sat in an easy silence, each lost to their own thoughts. A part of her expected to see the shadow of melancholy that always hovered at the edges of Grey's personality to appear, to darken her features and weigh heavily on her shoulders, but it never happened. The small smile tugging at Grey's lips made Lauren smile as well, and she could not resist reaching out and wrapping an arm around Grey's shoulders. "Thank you for showing me this," she whispered as she drew Grey into her and pressed a light kiss to her temple.

A feeling of utter peace swept through Grey as she leaned into Lauren, like this was exactly where she was supposed to be, and she closed her eyes as she tried to commit every detail of the moment to memory. "Thank you for coming with me."

"There is nowhere else I'd rather be." Lauren rested her temple against the top of Grey's head and held her close as the truth in her own words rocked her to her core. Her dreams were within her grasp back in New York, just waiting for her to return and take them, and yet she found herself wishing that this moment could last forever.

The fact that it could not settled heavily on her heart, and she squeezed her eyes shut to try and block out the painful truth. *One more week*, she told herself. *You have this for one more week. Don't think about New York. Just enjoy the moment.*

Grey felt Lauren stiffen beside her, and she sighed as she opened her eyes. "You okay?"

"Yeah," Lauren whispered. "Just…"

The silence at the end of Lauren's thought told Grey all she needed to know, and she nodded understandingly. "I know." A large body surging out of the ocean in front of them drew her attention, and she smiled as she pointed at it, grateful for the distraction. "Look."

"What?" Lauren lifted her head and looked at the spot in the ocean where Grey was pointing.

"Just…there." Grey smiled as a humpback whale breached right in front of them. "See it?"

"Kinda hard to miss," Lauren chuckled, her brows lifting in surprise. "I didn't realize there were any whales in the Caribbean."

"Usually just sperm whales," Grey said, her smile growing wider as another whale leapt out of the water, not far away from the first. "But humpbacks come to the Caribbean during the winter to mate. It's pretty early for them to be out here though, they don't usually show up until at least January."

"Still…" Lauren sat up straighter and leaned forward to stare at the now placid waters in front of them, as if by sheer force of will alone she could make the whales reappear. "That's pretty amazing."

Grey looked over at Lauren, whose face was lit with wonder, and nodded. "Yeah. Amazing."

"I have never seen anything like that before." Lauren glanced at Grey, and blushed when she found the brunette staring at her. "What?"

"Nothing." Grey shook her head. She leaned in and kissed Lauren softly. "Is it wrong that I like looking at you?"

Lauren smiled shyly and shook her head. "No."

"Good," Grey whispered, smiling as she cradled Lauren's face in her hand and guided the redhead's lips back to her own. They kissed slowly, lazily, their tongues stroking idly together, and Grey sighed when she finally pulled away. She ran the backs of her fingers over Lauren's jaw and kissed her again. "We should probably stop this."

"Says the woman who keeps kissing me," Lauren pointed out in a husky whisper.

"I can't help it," Grey retorted, kissing Lauren again for emphasis.

Lauren laughed. "You're ridiculous."

"Ridiculously sexy?"

Grey's expression was adorably hopeful, and Lauren shook her head as she pressed a hard, chaste kiss to her lips.

"Ridiculously silly." She kissed her again, more tenderly this time. "And pretty damn perfect."

"Smooth talker," Grey murmured.

Lauren smiled and kissed Grey again, the caress even gentler than the last, and she held it until her head began to swim. "You know it. Now, be good. These rocks are not comfortable enough for the things that'll happen if you keep kissing me like that."

"Yeah, because I'm the one doing all the kissing here," Grey grumbled playfully as she pulled away. She winked at Lauren and added, "If I'm not allowed to kiss you, what do you want to do?"

"I dunno." Lauren shrugged and shot Grey a sly look. "You could always tell me a joke or something."

Grey smiled. "You want a clean one, or a dirty one?"

Lauren laughed and shook her head. "Why am I not surprised you have a catalogue of both? I dunno, Wells, surprise me."

"Okay…" Grey's voice trailed off for a moment as she mentally rifled through her options, and she clapped her hands when she decided what joke she was going to tell. "There were these two whales swimming around off the coast of Japan. We'll call them Hubby Whale and Wifey Whale."

Lauren sniggered. "Okay."

"Hush. So, one day, they're swimming around, bored out of their minds, and Hubby Whale spies a whaling ship. 'Hey,' he says to his wife, 'you wanna have some fun?' Wifey Whale, used to his idiotic ideas, rolls her eyes and asks, 'What do you have in mind?' 'Well,' Hubby Whale drawls, 'those fishermen are always messing with us—let's go have some fun with them.' Still not convinced, Wifey Whale says, 'Like what?' Hubby Whale starts giggling like an idiot and says, 'Let's go capsize their boat!' Wifey rolls her eyes again. 'Capsize their boat?' 'Yeah,' he insists. 'It'll be easy. We just take a big breath, swim under the boat, and blow real hard. The bubbles will capsize the boat and it'll be AWESOME!'"

"Whales say 'awesome', huh?" Lauren chuckled.

"These do. Now stop interrupting," Grey admonished with a smile. "So…after going back and forth over it, Wifey Whale finally agrees to help capsize the boat. They each take a big breath, swim under the boat, and blow as hard as they can. And, sure enough, the damn thing pitches right over and all the sailors fall into the water. 'See!' Hubby Whale shouts victoriously, 'It worked!' Wifey Whale smiles and says, 'Okay, that was kind of fun.' 'Told you," Hubby says, his eyes drifting toward the sailors splashing around in the water. 'You know…I am kind of hungry.' 'No,' Wifey says immediately. 'Just, no'. 'But why?' Hubby asks in the most pathetic whiney-little-kid-type voice ever. And Wifey just shakes her head and says, 'While I have no problem blowing, I refuse to swallow seamen.'"

Lauren chuckled and shook her head. "Oh my god. I did not see that coming."

Grey grinned. "Ba-dum-dum."

Lauren laughed harder. "Okay, that was good."

"Right? Kip told me that one," Grey shared. "Your turn."

"I don't remember this being a quid pro quo type arrangement," Lauren pointed out.

"Come on, Murphy," Grey cajoled. "You gotta have one dirty joke in your repertoire."

Lauren sighed. "Okay, I have one…but it's not exactly dirty."

Grey nodded. "All right. Wait—it's not the lesbian dinosaur one, is it?"

"Um no." Lauren shook her head. "I don't know a dinosaur joke. It's about a nun."

"Well, that's a classic start," Grey said, nodding. "Okay, go."

"Right." Lauren cleared her throat. "So one day, Sister Marie Clarence, a nun from a convent in a small town in France, walks into a liquor store. The guy working the counter looks surprised to see her in his store, and when she asks for a fifth of bourbon, he looks positively scandalized. 'But sister,' he says, aghast, 'why in the world would you want the devil's drink?' Sister Marie Clarence looks at him and says, 'It's for the Mother Superior.' 'I don't believe you,' the shopkeeper says, shaking his head. 'The good Mother would never want for poison such as this. I am going to report you to the Monsignor!'

"Sister Marie Clarence smiles her most sincere smile at the man and shakes her head. 'I speak the truth. The Mother Superior is quite constipated, and this bourbon will help cure her of her ills.' The shopkeeper looks properly abashed and reaches beneath the counter for a fifth of his finest bourbon. He slips it into a paper bag and hands it to the nun. 'Of course, Sister. I apologize for doubting the strength of your faith. Here, take this to the Mother Superior.' Sister Marie Clarence nods her thanks at the man, tucks the bag into her habit, and discreetly leaves the store.

"Later that night, when the shopkeeper is walking home after closing up for the night, he passes by the convent. There's a large crowd gathered at the gates, so he wanders over to see what's going on. He pushes his way through the crowd, and his eyes just about pop out of his head when he sees Sister Marie Clarence wearing nothing but her veil, dancing naked in the courtyard and singing the most bawdy bar song he had ever heard. 'SISTER!' the shopkeeper yells at the clearly inebriated nun. 'What in the world are you doing? I thought that bourbon was for the Mother Superior's constipation?' Sister Marie Clarence turns to him and gives a little shimmy. 'Oh, it is,' she assures him with a grin. 'When she sees me, she's going to shit!'"

Grey let out a bark of laughter and clapped her hands. "Okay, seriously, that is my new favorite joke."

"I'm glad you liked it." Lauren smiled, obviously pleased, and cleared her throat as she looked back out over the water. It was still early in the day, and she was not ready to let this moment end. "So, what's the lesbian dinosaur one?"

Grey held up a finger as she tried to get her laughter under control. Once she succeeded, she heaved a large sigh and smiled. She had not expected to spend the afternoon sitting out here telling jokes, but like everything else that happened when she was with Lauren, it just felt too right to even question. "It's stupid, really."

"So? It's a joke, Grey…"

"Okay, fine." Grey tucked her knees up to her chest and looked over at Lauren. "How about this—if you can guess the punch line, I'll make you dinner tonight."

Lauren grinned. "You're on."

Chapter 39

"I can't believe it." Of all the dishes Grey could have messed up for the dinner she had made for Lauren, it was the rice that did her in. Not the Mahi-mahi, or the lemon, garlic, and wine reduction she had finished the fish in, but the rice. "This is so embarrassing."

Lauren smiled and took another bite of the ruined rice. It was chewy, yet somehow undercooked at the same time, and she reached out to place a reassuring hand on Grey's arm as she swallowed. "It's not that bad."

"You don't have to eat it," Grey muttered. "Really. You're going to make yourself sick trying to choke any more of that down."

"Nobody's getting sick." Lauren chuckled and rolled her eyes. "It's just rice, Grey."

Grey groaned and ran a frustrated hand through her hair as she glowered at the offending side dish, as if it was the rice's fault that it had not turned out right. "I'm sorry."

"It's fine." Lauren used the side of her fork to cut into her fish, and she looked at Grey as she speared the bite on the tines. "The Mahi turned out really well. And this sauce is incredible," she added as she swirled the fish in the excess sauce pooled on her plate.

Grey blew out a loud breath and forced a small smile, embarrassment still written clearly on her face. "Thank you."

"Thank you for a lovely dinner," Lauren replied, her eyes soft and her tone warm.

"I…" Grey started to argue that the dinner she had made was anything but lovely, but she held back. Lauren was clearly not bothered by her lack of culinary skills, and her wallowing in self-pity was only going to ruin their last night alone together. She sighed and reached for her wine glass. Rice was apparently too difficult for her to manage, but she knew how to pick a good wine, and the pinot noir she had paired with the meal was outstanding. Grey met Lauren's gaze as she lifted her glass, letting it hover in the candlelit air between them, and said, "To lovely dinners with even lovelier company."

"Hear, hear!" Lauren murmured, lifting her glass to lightly tap it to Grey's. She smiled at her as she took a sip, and sighed softly when she set her glass back onto the table. "Did I ever tell you about the time I made Yorkshire pudding soup?"

"I didn't realize that was a thing." Grey's brow furrowed, and she shook her head. "I've heard of Yorkshire Pudding, but…"

"It's not a thing," Lauren interjected, shaking her head. "My first week in culinary school, we had to make Yorkshire pudding, which is just a million shades of awesome when done right." She forked a another small bite of fish into her mouth and, when she had swallowed, continued, "So, Chef gives us the recipe, and sends us off to our stations. I still swear that I did everything right, but when it came out of the oven, even though the outsides were cooked, the middles weren't. It was disgusting."

"What happened?" Grey asked.

"To make the dish go wrong?"

"Yeah."

Lauren shrugged. "Haven't a clue. Probably pulled them a couple minutes early, but whatever the case, they were still soup. Chef cut into one and it poured onto the plate. I was mortified."

"And yet you still went on to finish first in your class," Grey pointed out.

"One mistake doesn't have to ruin everything," Lauren said. She sighed and shook her head. "Anyways, this sauce. Tell me how you made it. Since, you know, you banned me from the galley so I didn't get to watch."

After Grey explained her technique to Lauren, about which the redhead had a million questions, half of which Grey did not see the point of even though she answered them as best she could, they moved onto easier topics. First cars. Worst date they had ever been on. Favorite holiday and, because Lauren loved food, favorite holiday dish. For as well as they knew each other physically, and for as comfortable as they were together, they were still learning about each other as people, and the easy back-and-forth helped fill in some of those gaps.

Grey was finishing reliving, in all its gory detail, the train wreck of her first serious relationship as they put the last of the dinner dishes away, and she arched a brow at Lauren as she used her heel to close the dishwasher door. "And she threw my MacBook at me—thank god I caught it—and that was it. So…your turn."

"I'm still friends with my first serious girlfriend." Lauren smiled at the look of surprise on Grey's face and reached for her glass of wine. "We dated for pretty much my entire freshman year. We met at a party at NYU—my roommate at CIA was from New York, and her best friend from high school was at NYU and invited us to a thing her dorm was doing. Rachel was a theatre student there, and we just…hit it off. Things were good. Simple, as they are when you're nineteen, but good. Even though she was only a freshman as well, Rachel auditioned for and got a lead in a musical on Off-Off. That started taking up all of her time and things with us just…fizzled. No harm, no foul. It just didn't work."

"Well, that's disappointing," Grey teased. She topped off their glasses and tipped her head at the salon doors. "Go out to the tramps?"

Lauren nodded. "Sure."

"So…is she still on Broadway?" Grey asked as she stared toward the front of the boat.

"She won a Tony last year," Lauren said with a smile.

"Damn."

Lauren chuckled. "Yeah. So...anyways, that's it. No real drama. Sorry."

"You can make it up to me," Grey said, winking at Lauren as she took the glass of wine from her hand and set it down on the side of the boat. "Dance with me."

"There's no music," Lauren pointed out as Grey stepped into her, the brunette's left hand slipping possessively around her waist.

"Don't need it," Grey whispered. She took Lauren's left hand in her right and stepped into her, tucking their joined hands between them. Grey shifted her weight to her right foot, then her left, and smiled when Lauren naturally followed. "See?"

"I do." Lauren pressed in closer, leaning her forehead against Grey's as they swayed to the music of the breeze tumbling around them. Her heartbeat slowed to match the even cadence of their movement, and she closed her eyes as she soaked it all in. The strength of Grey's hand wrapped around her own, the firm press of Grey's body, the feeling of Grey's breath landing so lightly upon her lips. They moved in small, uneven circles across the trampoline, and Lauren let out a shuddering sigh when Grey's lips landed on her own.

They stopped moving altogether as their kisses became slower, deeper. Grey released her hold on Lauren's hand to reach up and lightly drag the backs of her nails up the curve of the redhead's jaw before cradling it gently in her hand. She brought her left hand up to mirror her right, her thumbs stroking softly over Lauren's cheeks as she poured herself into the kiss.

Lauren whimpered when Grey pulled back by a fraction, warm breath cascading in quiet pants against her lips. She lifted her chin and recaptured Grey's lips, eager to taste them again. She slid her hands over Grey's back, her right dropping low enough to grab a firm cheek as she pressed her left between winged scapulae and tried to draw her in closer.

Grey used her tender hold on Lauren's face to keep the raging fire that seemed to perpetually burn between them at bay. It would be so easy to just give in to it, to strip them both bare and fuck until exhaustion made it impossible to move, but she wanted more than that. She teased Lauren's lower lip with her tongue as she trailed her hands slowly down Lauren's throat, lingering to feel the heavy beat of Lauren's pulse against her fingertips. Her fingers bumped over the ridges of Lauren's collarbones and swept around the swell of her breasts before skating across the expanse of her abdomen to dip beneath the hem of her shirt. "May I?" she asked as she lifted the shirt by a fraction, already certain of the answer, but wanting to hear it just the same.

"Yes."

Lauren's voice was soft, breathy, and Grey smiled as she inched the shirt higher, her fingers following their previous path back up Lauren's body until she was able to push the shirt off over her head. She pulled back to look at Lauren as her arms dropped, the shirt fluttering from her fingertips to land forgotten at their feet. Lauren's skin was radiant in the soft light of moon, her naked chest lifting and falling with each breath, her nipples growing hard as the cooler night air swept over them. "You're perfect."

"Hardly," Lauren muttered, shaking her head as she reached for Grey. She removed the brunette's tee quickly, and sighed when Grey stepped back into her. "Much better." She ran her hands over Grey's sides and pulled her in closer.

Their kisses remained deep and unhurried as they undressed each other, each of them taking the time to stroke and caress newly revealed skin before they pushed more clothing off and away. Grey used her body to guide Lauren down onto the mat, their lips never breaking contact as she stretched out on top of her. A shiver rolled down her spine when Lauren's nails scratched a light line down the length of her back, and she sighed as she dipped her head to kiss her again softly.

The blatant emotion in Grey's kiss made Lauren's head spin, and she drew a ragged breath when Grey's lips left her own to blaze a languid trail down her throat. She drew random circles on Grey's back as the brunette moved lower, sure hands cupping her breasts, nimble fingers rolling and tweaking one nipple while Grey tongued and sucked at the other.

After lavishing attention on each breast in turn, Grey moved lower, watching the way goosebumps erupted in the wake of every slow, wet kiss she pressed to Lauren's skin. She paused only for a moment to flick her tongue in Lauren's belly button before continuing on, her fingertips sliding slowly down Lauren's sides the lower she went. Grey looked up at Lauren's face as she nuzzled her thigh, and her heart skipped a beat as she leaned in further, letting her breath play over damp, swollen folds as she moved slowly closer to where they both wanted her to be. The gasp that escaped Lauren at the fist light swipe of her tongue made Grey's stomach clench, and she groaned as she wrapped her hands around Lauren's legs and pulled herself in closer.

"Oh, yes," Lauren moaned, her voice low and rumbling with desire as she rolled her hips up against Grey's mouth. The feeling of Grey's fingers digging firmly into her thighs, pulling her open wider, and the soft flick of her tongue was electric, and Lauren's eyes fluttered closed as she reached down to comb her fingers through Grey's hair.

Grey worked slowly, methodically, lapping lightly at Lauren's clit and then sucking it into her mouth before pulling back and running her tongue through the length of her. The soft sighs and whimpers raining down on her from above were like a symphony, and she greedily wished that it would never end as she let her hands wander, stroking every inch of skin within her reach as she guided Lauren closer and closer to the edge.

The gentle affection in every electric swipe of Grey's tongue or fingertips made Lauren's head spin, a fog of feelings and sensation swirling inside her mind that made cogent thought all but impossible. All she could focus on was Grey's touch. The warm, firm press of her tongue, the slightly calloused hands wrapped lightly around her hips, holding her gently in place as release swept through her in surprisingly gentle waves.

A quiet moan tumbled from Grey's lips at the feeling of Lauren coming against her tongue, and she eased her middle finger inside her, moving in long, slow strokes as Lauren trembled with her release. When the final spasm eased, Grey looked up into Lauren's eyes that burned bright in the moonlight, and smiled as she added a second finger to her thrusts. "Good?"

"So good," Lauren purred, her hips lifting to meet each slow, deep thrust of Grey's fingers.

"Good," Grey whispered as she curled her fingers and dragged them heavily over hidden ridges, making Lauren gasp and twitch. She smirked as she dipped her chin and sucked Lauren's swollen clit between her lips, teasing the bud with the tip of her tongue as she held Lauren's hips down with her free hand.

Even though her body was still pulsing with the aftereffects of her first orgasm, the heavenly combination of Grey's mouth and fingers soon had Lauren rushing headlong into a second. Her hips rocked wildly against Grey's mouth as she sought that perfect rhythm that would send her flying, and she was only vaguely aware of the desperate words falling from her lips as her body strained to reach that euphoric edge. Her mouth fell open in a silent scream as she curled in on herself, her body wrapping around Grey as it exploded in pleasure, and she could hear nothing but the pounding of her heartbeat in her ears as the first violent spasm eased and she sank limply back onto the mat.

Grey looked up at the feeling of Lauren's hand tugging at her hair, and she obediently moved higher, dragging her lips and chin over the plane of Lauren's stomach, leaving a trail of sticky wetness in her wake. She smiled as she hovered above Lauren, and sighed as she dipped down to claim her lips in a deep, lingering kiss.

The feeling of Lauren sucking on her tongue made Grey's nipples tighten and her clit jump, and she groaned as her body remembered that it had not yet found its peak. Unable to ignore the throbbing between her legs any longer, Grey shifted above Lauren, using her right knee to push the redhead's left leg out wider as she lifted her hips higher and then canted them down into Lauren.

"Oh god, again?" Lauren whimpered, even as she curled her hips to meet Grey's. Slick warmth covered her, and she bit her lip as Grey ground down into her.

Grey rolled her hips slowly, her desire spiking at the feeling of Lauren's arousal mixing with her own, and she let out a sharp gasp when she finally found her mark. Her back bowed as she dropped her head, and she smiled at Lauren as she began rolling her hips against her in a hard, steady rhythm. "Okay?"

Lauren nodded. "Yes." She reached up and wrapped her right hand around the back of Grey's neck. "You feel so good."

"Lauren," Grey moaned, her eyes fluttering shut. A part of her wanted to draw things out like she had for Lauren, but her body, already well past the limits of restraint, had other ideas.

"I know," Lauren murmured. Though it was too dark for her to see the flash of ecstasy that she knew would flare in Grey's eyes when the brunette came, Lauren still gave the back of her neck a squeeze and whispered, "Look at me, Grey."

Grey forced her eyes open and her breath caught in her throat when her gaze locked onto Lauren's. Already so perilously close to release, the visual connection seemed to tug at her very soul, anchoring her in that moment to the woman spread beneath her. Her hips continued to rock without any conscious effort as she stared into Lauren's eyes that reflected the moon and the stars back up at her. "Lauren," Grey breathed, the name falling from her lips like a prayer as she raced toward her climax. "Oh, Lauren."

The emotion in Grey's voice made Lauren clench, and she whimpered as her left hand shot out to latch onto Grey's hip. The promise of a third orgasm thrummed in her veins, just waiting to explode, and she moaned as Grey's breath fell in hot, ragged pants against her lips. "Please don't stop. God, Grey, please don't stop."

Grey chuckled and nodded. "I won't," she promised, rolling her hips down harder for emphasis. Tension coiled low in her hips, threatening to snap, and she licked her lips as she stared down at Lauren. "Are you close?"

"So close," Lauren rasped as she clung to Grey.

"What do you need?"

"You. Just you," Lauren sighed, fighting to keep her eyes open as her rising pleasure began to crest.

"You have me." Grey pressed a hard, desperate kiss to Lauren's lips. "You have me." She took a deep breath and groaned. "Shit. Lauren, I'm…" Her voice trailed off into a deep, keening moan as her climax overwhelmed her. She tried to keep looking at Lauren, but her eyes snapped shut as her body shook and trembled, though the feeling of being tied to Lauren remained.

Lauren used her hold on the back of Grey's neck to pull the brunette down into her, their heated kiss muffling the sound of the moan that escaped her as she followed Grey over that blissful edge.

Chapter 40

Grey awoke slowly the next morning, and rolled onto her side to look at Lauren, who was stretched out on her stomach beside her, one fist tucked beneath her chin as she dreamed. Her eyes roamed slowly over Lauren's face as memories from the night before washed over her, filling her with a feeling of warm contentment. Her heart fluttered as she remembered the passion that had filled Lauren's kisses once they had finally made their way back inside, every press of lips searing its way to her soul with the unspoken emotion that had burned like wildfire between them on the trampolines. Her skin broke out into small goosebumps at the memory of Lauren's hands, so strong and sure against her hips, guiding her back onto the bed. The entire night had been so much more than just sex, and a small, sad smile lifted Grey's lips as she reached out to tenderly brush a stray curl away from the corner of Lauren's mouth.

"I wish we could just stay here forever," Grey whispered as her eyes lingered on the soft curve of Lauren's lips.

The hushed confession lingered in the air, an unrealistic longing that Grey knew would never be realized, and she sighed as she lightly traced the ridge of Lauren's knuckles with her index finger. The physical connection eased the ache that had built in her chest, and so she did it again. And again. Bumping down over each knuckle and then skating lightly along the smooth skin behind them. Her breathing slowed to match the progress of her touch, measured and even, in and out, until she was able to convince herself that this was enough. That these last few days, this moment, and the next too-short cruise were more than she had ever expected to experience again, and that she would be fine.

She knew that it was a lie, but it gave her comfort anyway.

Eventually Lauren began to stir, and Grey dropped her hand to the mattress as hazel eyes soft with sleep slowly opened. "Good morning."

Lauren reached out and covered Grey's hand with her own. "Good morning to you, too," she whispered. She rubbed her thumb over the back of Grey's hand and smiled. "Last night…"

Grey smiled and leaned in to nuzzle Lauren's cheek with her nose. "I know," she murmured as she finally closed the distance between them and captured Lauren's lips in a sweet kiss.

"Yeah." Lauren rolled onto her back and hummed approvingly at the way Grey moved with her, the brunette's right leg slipping between her own as she settled on top her. Grey's lips were so soft and gentle against her own that Lauren felt her heart skip a beat, and she sighed as she melted into it.

Grey knew that they were on a tight schedule, that the cleaning crew she employed would be at the dock in Charlotte Amalie ready to prepare the *Veritas* for its next charter at noon, but that knowledge meant very little when Lauren was so warm and naked beneath her. She wanted nothing more than to steal a few more moments of happiness, and she had no trouble ignoring her responsibilities as she began thrusting her hips gently into Lauren, painting her thigh with the sweet essence of the redhead's desire. Their kisses grew deeper as they moved together, and Grey smiled at Lauren when she pulled back to look at her. "Okay?"

"Mmm, yes." Lauren held Grey's gaze as she ran her hands down the length of Grey's arms to tangle their fingers together beside her head.

"Good," Grey murmured, giving Lauren's hands a gentle squeeze. She rested her forehead against Lauren's as they resumed their slow dance, their hips rolling and grinding together as they stared unblinkingly into each other's eyes. The raw emotion burning in Lauren's gaze stole the breath from Grey's lungs, and she whimpered as she pressed a hard kiss to her lips. "Lauren…"

Lauren moaned, her hold on Grey's hands tightening as the speed and force of their thrusts increased. She would have gladly stayed in this moment forever—pinned beneath Grey and staring up into eyes so dark that only the merest ring of brown was visible—but her body had other ideas. "No," she groaned as she felt her orgasm begin to crest.

"Yes," Grey rasped, pressing her forehead harder against Lauren's as she ground their hips together. "God yes. Please, baby."

"Oh, Grey…" Lauren's voice trailed off into a moan as she rocked against Grey's thigh. "You?"

Grey gritted her teeth and nodded. She stared imploringly into Lauren's eyes as their hips rotated together, and she finally let the breath she had been holding go when she felt Lauren begin to pulse against her thigh. A low moan rumbled deep in her throat as her own release swept through her, and she smiled against Lauren's lips as they clung to each other, their gazes locked as ecstasy flared like fireworks in their eyes.

"My god," Lauren sighed when Grey collapsed on top of her.

Grey chuckled and flicked her tongue across the hollow of Lauren's throat. "Yeah."

"I think I'm ready to go back to sleep," Lauren teased as she pressed her lips to the top of Grey's head.

"Can't." Grey shook her head and pushed herself back up to look at Lauren. "We need to head back to Saint Thomas."

"I know." Lauren smoothed a hand over Grey's jaw and sighed. She was not ready for her final cruise aboard the *Veritas* to begin. She was not ready for this to end. "What do we need to do today?"

"More of this," Grey said, kissing Lauren softly. She smiled and nuzzled Lauren's cheek affectionately.

"I like this," Lauren whispered.

"Me too." Grey sighed and kissed Lauren again. No matter how much she liked it, however, the reality of their situation could not be pushed aside any longer. In an ideal world, they would stay holed up in one secluded bay after another, hiding from the world and losing themselves in each other, but she had long ago been forced to come to terms with the fact that hers was not an ideal world. "But, we also need to do some grocery shopping to restock the pantry and the liquor cabinet for the next cruise. I figure we can hit the farmer's market tomorrow morning like we did before the Muellers' cruise, that way everything is as fresh as possible, and then we'll be ready to shove off as soon as the guests arrive tomorrow morning. Do you have a general idea of what you'll need?"

Lauren nodded. She had received menu questionnaires—allergies, preferences, likes and dislikes—when she accepted the position aboard the *Veritas*, and had already planned out the menus for each of the cruises. The Muellers were the more difficult to plan for, with having small children and the family planning on eating almost every meal aboard the boat, but their next charter was a trio of married couples who wanted to spend their days on the water and their evenings in various ports exploring the local nightlife. That meant she only had to really plan for breakfast and lunch, with enough supplies for a few dinners just in case the guests decided to dine on the *Veritas* before they headed into town for the night. "Yeah."

"Good." Grey smiled and brushed one last kiss across Lauren's lips before forcing herself to roll off of her. "So, you ready?"

No, Lauren thought, even as she said, "When you are, Captain Wells."

Chapter 41

Lauren jolted awake the next morning to the sound of Grey's alarm clock going off, and groaned as she pulled her pillow over her head to try and block out the noise. Her head was pounding, and her mouth tasted like something had crawled into it and died while she slept. "Fucking vodka."

After running errands the day before, they had gone to a hole-in-the-wall restaurant not far from the marina that was popular with the locals for its roti—curried vegetables and meat wrapped in a thin dough. The food had been good, but the band playing was better, and somehow 'a quick dinner out' turned into dancing and shots.

Lots and lots of shots.

Grey cracked an eye open and grunted as she slapped at her alarm. She ran her tongue over the top of her mouth and grimaced. "What did we drink?"

"Too much," Lauren grunted.

"Yeah, got that," Grey muttered, scrubbing a hand over her face.

Lauren peeked out at Grey from beneath her pillow, and saw that Grey looked as rough as she felt. They probably should have skipped that last round of Lemon Drops. "God, I hate vodka."

Grey chuckled as she flopped back onto the bed and curled up against Lauren's side. She wrapped an arm around Lauren's waist, and closed her eyes as she pressed a lingering kiss to her shoulder. "I think this is the tequila's fault."

"I think we'll just have to agree to disagree." Lauren pushed the heel of her hand against her forehead and squeezed her eyes shut. She relaxed into Grey, relishing the warmth of the brunette's skin against her own as Grey's fingers began scratching lightly across her stomach. She was so comfortable that she was close to drifting off to sleep again when the alarm blared back to life.

"Sorry," Grey whispered as she released her hold on Lauren to slap at the alarm again. "I hate to say it, but we need to get up."

"I know," Lauren grumbled as she rolled onto her back. Her head throbbed at the movement, and she groaned as she forced herself to climb out of bed. "Oh, this is gonna suck."

"Tell me about it," Grey said as she rolled to her feet. She ran a hand through her hair as she looked at Lauren, and smiled in spite of her hangover. "I had fun last night."

"Me too." Lauren stepped over their clothes that had been strewn across the floor in their haste to get each other naked the night before, and slipped into Grey's waiting arms at the foot of the bed. "No vodka next time, though."

"Deal," Grey murmured, even though they both knew that there would not be a 'next time'. She pressed a chaste kiss to Lauren's cheek and sighed. "If you get the Tylenol out of the medicine cabinet, I'll go grab us a couple bottles of water from the fridge."

"Sounds good."

"You wanna just pick up some breakfast on our way to the farmer's market?" Grey asked as she started for the door.

Lauren's eyes swept over Grey's naked body and she smiled in spite of her pounding headache. "If I wasn't so hung-over right now, I'd have you for breakfast."

"Promises, promises," Grey chuckled, her gaze trailing lazily over Lauren's body.

Lauren laughed and shrugged. "Sorry?"

"No you're not." Grey waved a hand at the bathroom. "You can have first shower."

"We can always shower together," Lauren offered as she started for the en suite. "I'm too hung over to do more than just shower, but…"

Grey nodded. She did not have the energy to do more than simply shower either, but she would never pass up the opportunity to spend more time with Lauren. "I'll meet you in there."

Lauren was just climbing into the shower when Grey returned with the bottles of water, and Grey smiled when she spotted three Tylenol laid out on the counter for her. She swallowed the pills dry and chased them down with half of one of the bottles of water before opening the shower door and climbing into the stall with Lauren. "Hey, sexy."

"Hey, yourself," Lauren said as she watched Grey climb into the shower. She smiled at the way Grey's hands slid over her sides, and groaned when Grey's mouth dropped to her clavicle. "We're just showering," she reminded Grey when dull teeth nipped at her skin.

"I know." Grey soothed the spot with her tongue and stood up to look Lauren in the eye as she reached for a bottle of shampoo. She poured a generous amount into her left hand and brushed a soft kiss across Lauren's lips as she started rubbing the soap into her hair.

The feeling of Grey's fingers massaging her scalp was heavenly, and Lauren moaned softly as she reached out and held onto Grey's hips for balance. "God, that feels good."

"Good." Grey smiled as she watched Lauren's eyes flutter shut, her face a mask of absolute pleasure as she began to lightly sway with her touch. She took her time massaging the vanilla-scented shampoo into Lauren's hair, scratching her nails over her scalp and rubbing her thumbs lightly over Lauren's temples. She kissed Lauren once she was done, using that pressure to guide her back beneath the spray. Grey smiled against Lauren's lips as she smoothed the bubbles from her hair, and sighed when she pulled away.

Lauren blinked her eyes open, her gaze immediately locking onto Grey's. The brunette's eyes were warm and soft, swirling with a gentle affection that took her breath away. "Wow."

"I'm glad you liked it," Grey murmured as she reached for Lauren's body wash, which had migrated into her shower over the last few days as well. She squeezed some of the pink gel into her hand and set the bottle back onto its shelf. "Trade places with me, please," she instructed as she poured some of the soap from her left hand to her right. "I'm going to need the spray at my back for this part." She chuckled at the look Lauren shot her and shook her head. "We're just showering, remember?"

"If I was just showering, I would have been done by now," Lauren pointed out playfully as she squeezed past Grey to the back half of the small shower stall.

"I know." Grey smoothed her hands over Lauren's shoulders, digging her thumbs into tight muscles as she went. "But isn't this better?"

"So much better," Lauren agreed in a breathy whisper.

"Can you get your hair up somehow?"

Lauren nodded and twisted her hair up on itself so that it was off her neck.

"Perfect." Grey dropped a quick kiss to the newly exposed skin before she began squeezing that same spot with her right hand in a gentle massage.

Lauren braced her hands on the wall in front of her as Grey's thumbs dug into the muscles at the back of her neck. She groaned when Grey began working at a knot in her upped back, and let her head fall forward as she gave herself over to Grey's touch. Grey's hands sliding over her skin was both relaxing and arousing, and Lauren could not have contained the little moans that kept escaping her even had she wanted to.

"Mmm, hi," Lauren hummed when Grey's hands skated over her hips to tickle her stomach. She rocked back into the brunette, pressing her ass into Grey's hips as strong arms enveloped her middle.

Grey rubbed her hands over Lauren's stomach and nipped playfully at her earlobe. "Just showering."

"I know." Lauren looked over her shoulder at Grey and grinned when she saw how close she was. "Kiss me," she whispered, even as she lifted her lips to Grey's.

Grey did not need to be told twice, and she moaned softly as she covered Lauren's lips with her own. They kissed languidly, tongues flicking idly together as Grey's hands continued to stroke with a quiet passion over Lauren's body, sweeping down over her hips to tickle her upper thighs before sliding higher again. Lauren whimpered and bucked back into her when she spiraled her fingers around her breasts, and she smiled as she covered them with her hands and gave them a gentle squeeze. "Just showering," she murmured as she dropped her hands back to Lauren's waist.

"Just showering, my ass," Lauren muttered as she turned to face Grey.

"I washed that too."

Lauren rolled her eyes, and instantly regretted it as the move made her headache pulse viciously. She sighed and reached for Grey's shampoo. "I know," she said as she poured the shampoo into her hand. "Hair wet, please."

Grey smiled and did as Lauren asked, closing her eyes as she tilted her head back into the stream.

"God, I wish I wasn't so hung-over," Lauren muttered as she watched the way the water course in thin lines around Grey's breasts. She licked her lips as she stepped into Grey, letting their nipples brush lightly together as she began massaging the shampoo into her hair, just like Grey had done to her. Lauren took her time washing Grey, lingering on the spots that made her whimper or moan until she finished with her hands on Grey's breasts. She gave them a light squeeze and leaned her cheek against the back of Grey's shoulder as she closed her eyes and just basked in the feeling of warm skin against her own and the joy that filled her because of it.

"This is nice," Grey whispered as she lifted her left hand to cover Lauren's right.

"Yeah." Lauren pressed a lazy kiss to Grey's back and smiled. The Tylenol she had taken before climbing into the shower was finally beginning to kick-in, but she had no desire to do anything more than this. Just holding Grey under the warm spray of the shower was enough. "Can we just stay here all day?"

Grey blew out a soft breath and spun in Lauren's hold so that she could look her in the eye. She smiled as she cradled Lauren's face in her hands and smoothed her thumbs over her cheeks. She captured Lauren's lips in a kiss that was achingly tender, full of everything she was feeling that she was too afraid to put into words, and she sighed when she eventually pulled back to drag her nose along the side of Lauren's. "I would like nothing more than to stay right here with you."

"But we can't," Lauren finished for her. "I know."

"I'm sorry."

"Me too." Lauren stole one last kiss as she reached behind herself to turn off the water. She shivered when she opened the shower door, letting cool air into the warm stall, and quickly wrapped a towel around herself. "Here you go," she said as she passed Grey's towel back to her.

Grey took it with a smile, and quickly began drying herself off. "Thanks."

"You're welcome." Lauren she reached out to run her hand through Grey's wet hair, toying with the short strands, unwilling to let this moment end just yet. Grey's eyes were fathomless, and Lauren's heart swooped up into her throat as she looked at her. She shook her head and sighed as she pulled her hand away, and cleared her throat softly as she began toweling herself dry. "What time are they all getting here?"

"Eleven-ish."

Lauren groaned. She knew that the alarm went off at six, which meant they would be hard-pressed to get everything they needed done before it was time for their guests to arrive.

"Exactly." Grey smiled and darted forward to peck Lauren's lips with a quick kiss. "So, it's time to get that marvelous ass of yours into gear, Ms. Murphy. We have work to do."

They finished getting done in companionable silence, stealing glances and kisses and sneaking soft touches whenever the opportunity allowed. They moved easily around each other, and in what seemed like no time at all they were making their way out of the salon to the back deck.

Grey squinted out at the busy harbor through the dark lenses of her sunglasses as she locked up after them, and was glad to see that the large cruise ship that had been docked across the water the night before was beginning to slowly make its way toward open water. That would make her life much easier later on when it was time for them to set sail.

Because they had walked to dinner the night before, Grey's car was still parked in its spot in the marina lot, and she smiled at Lauren as she held the passenger door for her. "Is there anything that's sounding good for breakfast?"

"Honestly?" Lauren laughed. "Is there a McDonald's anywhere around here?"

Grey chuckled knowingly. "Ah, the ol' McMuffin and hash brown hangover cure."

"I think it's the Diet Coke I get with it, honestly, but yeah," Lauren agreed with a smile. "I mean, the Tylenol is helping but…"

"We have to be functioning adults for the rest of the day." Grey grinned and started the car. "There's a McD's on the way to the farmer's market. We can stop there first, and then try and hurry through the rest of the things we need to do."

Lauren adjusted her sunglasses and nodded, resigned to officially starting their day. "Sounds good to me," she murmured as she looked out the windshield.

Chapter 42

Lauren looked out the galley window at Grey, who was leaning against the deck railing at the stern and chatting amiably with their guests. The sun was setting behind Grey, painting a golden stripe across the indigo waters of Saint Frances Bay, and Lauren idly wondered where in the world the day had gone. It seemed like only a couple of hours had passed since she and Grey had showered together, and yet the sun sinking toward the horizon was proof enough that the day had indeed passed them by.

She frowned and turned her attention back to the appetizer she was plating, wishing that she could turn back time to when it was just the two of them cocooned in the serenity of Hawksnest Bay. At the time, she had been too engrossed in living every moment to really recognize how special that time was, but now, looking back on it all, she knew that those few days were ones she would never forget. She blew out a frustrated breath as she arranged the last few pieces of coconut shrimp around a small ceramic bowl filled with a tangy orange dipping sauce.

Despite the fact that Lauren wished she and Grey could magically go back in time to when it was just the two of them aboard the boat, she had to admit that she was enjoying the company of their latest guests. David Yi, Harrison Coppes, and Rob Schwartz had been fraternity brothers at Yale, and they and their wives Julie, Mia, and Lily got together once a year to catch up and cut loose, free from the responsibilities of their careers and their children. They were an outgoing group that talked loudly and laughed raucously, and Lauren smiled in spite of herself as she remembered the way they had gathered around the peninsula in the galley to knock back two rounds of tequila shots before the *Veritas* had even left its slip in Charlotte Amalie.

Once she was pleased with the presentation of the appetizer, Lauren gathered herself with a deep breath, picked up the plate of shrimp, and carried it out to the deck. David and Julie were seated at the port-side table, while Harrison and Mia were seated at the other with Rob and Lily, and Lauren looked between the two tables before deciding to set the platter down on the table with more people. "Coconut crusted shrimp. Enjoy."

Mia smiled at Lauren as she picked up a shrimp and dipped it in the sauce, and she moaned appreciatively at her first bite. "This is amazing."

"I'm glad you like it." Lauren smiled and tipped her head in thanks even as her gaze locked onto Grey's. After days of being able to touch and kiss Grey whenever the urge struck, it felt strange to have to hold herself back, and she sighed when she saw a similar emotion flickering in Grey's eyes.

"Don't eat it all," Mia's husband, Harrison, teased as he and the rest of the group all reached for the shrimp. "Save some for the rest of us."

"Move faster next time." Mia waved him off with a smirk and reached for a second shrimp, playfully batting her husband's hand away and stealing the one he had been going for.

Lauren laughed and turned to head back to the galley. No matter how amusing the mini-slap-fight the group was now engaged in was, she still had to finish preparing the evening's main course. "Dinner will be ready in about half an hour."

With the group happily converged on the appetizer Lauren had brought out, Grey pushed herself off the railing she had been perched on and started toward the salon. The minutiae of running a floating bed and breakfast had kept her occupied for most of the day, and she had not had one minute alone with Lauren from the moment their newest guests had set foot aboard the *Veritas*. "Anybody need another drink?"

Julie chuckled and shook her head. "Not until I get a little more food in me."

"Yeah. Me too," David chimed in, glancing at the others, who all nodded their agreement. "You mix a strong margarita, Grey."

Grey nodded and started toward the salon. "Just let us know if you guys need anything else." Her eyes flicked briefly over the group one last time and, once she was convinced that they would be fine for a while, she disappeared inside. Her gaze immediately landed on Lauren, who was leaning against the edge of the counter waiting for her, and she smiled as she closed the distance between them in four long strides.

"Took you long enough," Lauren murmured as she looped her arms around Grey's neck.

"Sorry." Grey wrapped her arms around Lauren's waist and pulled her in close. She held Lauren's gaze as she leaned in until their lips were almost touching, and sighed as she nuzzled Lauren's cheek with her nose. "I had to make sure they were good for a while so that I could do this."

"Is this really all you want to do?" Lauren smirked and pulled back to arch a playful brow at Grey.

"God, no." Grey surged forward and captured Lauren's lips with her own. She smiled at the way Lauren whimpered into the kiss, and she tightened her hold on Lauren's waist as she ran the tip of her tongue along the seam of Lauren's lips.

Lauren opened her mouth to Grey, tilting her head to the side to take Grey deeper as the firm press of the brunette's body urged her backwards. She gasped softly when her back came into contact with the cool steel door of the refrigerator, but the small sound of surprise quickly became a rumbling moan when Grey's body molded to her own, pinning her to the door as strong hands wrapped possessively around her hips.

The sound of laughter filtering through the open galley window reminded Grey that they were not alone, and she lifted her hands to cup Lauren's face as she gentled her kisses until they were nothing more than a lazy string of tender pecks. "I missed that," she whispered as she leaned her forehead against Lauren's.

"Me too." Lauren lifted her chin and kissed Grey softly. After a day spent apart, filled with hours that seemed to fly by in mere seconds, this connection that made her breath light and her heart beat heavily in her throat was all that she wanted. She threaded the fingers of her right hand through the short hairs at the back of Grey's neck, scratching lightly as she brushed their lips together, drawing the moment out for a few seconds longer.

Grey smoothed her thumbs over Lauren's cheeks and smiled at the soft sigh the gentle touch coaxed from her lips. "Did today seem to go way too fast?"

"Yes." Lauren nodded. "Way too fast." She blinked her eyes open and sighed. "I need to make dinner."

"Yeah." Grey leaned in and kissed Lauren softly. "Do you need any help?"

"Nah, that's all right. I got it. You can stay and keep me company, though."

"You don't trust me with the rice, do you?"

"Not at all." Lauren laughed and stole one last kiss before patting Grey on the shoulders. She smiled at the way Grey huffed dramatically as she took a step back, and shook her head as she turned to open the fridge.

"So, what are you going to make?" Grey made her way to the barstools on the other side of the counter so that Lauren had the room she needed to work.

Lauren pulled a Ziploc bag full of scallops that she had picked up that morning from the fridge, along with an onion and another baggie filled with an assortment of mushrooms, and set it all on the counter in front of Grey. "Scallops and mushroom risotto."

"So…fancy rice."

"It's really not," Lauren said, shaking her head as she pulled out a cutting board. "Actually, could you grab me two large boxes of beef broth and the Arborio rice from the pantry?"

Grey nodded and slipped off her stool to retrieve the requested items. "Why beef?" she asked as she set it all onto the counter beside Lauren.

Lauren nodded her thanks and began dicing the onion. "I could use vegetable broth, but the beef broth pairs well with the mushrooms and adds a better flavor to the dish. If anyone was vegetarian, I would go with the other, but since I'm not working around that restriction, I just like this way better."

"Okay." Grey retook her seat opposite Lauren and watched with open interest at how quickly she was able to cut up the onion. "That's impressive."

Lauren looked up at Grey through her lashes and smiled as she pushed the pile of onion she had just diced into a pile at the corner of the cutting board. "Thank you." She dumped the bag of mushrooms onto the cutting board and gave them a rough chop into large, bite-sized pieces. "You want to help with the risotto?"

"You don't trust me with regular rice, but you're going to trust me with risotto?"

"I am offering to teach you how to make risotto."

"Will you be pressed up against my back helping me stir?" Grey asked with a sultry smile.

"I could be," Lauren chuckled. "Would you like that?"

Grey laughed and nodded. "Probably way too much," she admitted. "But I'm game if you are."

"Okay." Lauren set a large saucepan and a medium-sized stockpot onto the stove. "You can pour the broth into the saucepan," she instructed as she pulled a knob of butter from the fridge and dumped it into the stockpot. She drizzled a two-count of oil on top of the butter and turned on the flame.

"Now what?" Grey asked once she had finished with the stock.

Lauren handed Grey a wooden spoon and reached in front of her to turn the flame on under the stock. She moved behind Grey and whispered in her ear, "Start by sautéing the onions."

"Oh, I'm gonna like this," Grey murmured as a shiver rolled down her spine.

"Me too."

"Ooh, what are you making?" a new voice called out.

Lauren's stomach dropped as she turned and found Lily standing on the other side of the peninsula with the now-empty appetizer platter in her hands. "Mushroom risotto."

"Is it hard?" Lily asked, clearly intrigued.

"Not at all." Lauren looked at Grey and sighed. "You want to watch? I was just going to teach Grey how to make it."

Lily grinned and nodded. "Yes, please. That would be great."

"And here we go again with the cockblocks," Grey muttered under her breath, just loud enough for Lauren to hear.

"We weren't going there right now anyways." Lauren laughed and gave Grey's hip a light squeeze. "Besides, you have to admit that this is better than puke-a-palooza."

Grey shuddered and nodded in agreement. "Anything is better than that."

"So what do you do first?" Lily asked as she sidled up beside Lauren and Grey at the range and peered into the two pots.

"Well—" Lauren took a discreet step away from Grey so that she was no longer pressed against her back, "—you start by sautéing an onion, which is what Grey's doing now."

Forty minutes later, Lauren looked over the eight perfectly-plated dishes of risotto and scallops and smiled as she gave Lily a high five. "It looks awesome."

"Thank you for teaching me how to make it," Lily said with a small tip of her head. She looked at Grey, who was on the other side of the counter, preparing to take the dishes outside, and added, "I'm sorry I took over your lesson."

"Don't worry about it." Grey waved her off with a smile. "I was glad to hand over the whole stirring thing…it was kind of warm standing over the stove like that."

Lauren laughed. "There's a reason risotto always falls to one of the line chefs."

"And the truth comes out at last," Grey chuckled.

Lily laughed and picked up two bowls to take outside. "It was worth it. Thanks again for letting me help."

Lauren smiled and tipped her head in a small bow. "It was my pleasure." She watched Lily triumphantly carry the bowls she was carrying outside to her friends, and sidled up beside Grey to drop a chaste kiss to her cheek. "I'm sorry your cooking lesson got hijacked."

"It's okay." Grey sighed and reached out to give Lauren's hand a gentle squeeze. "I honestly didn't care too much about the lesson. I just wanted to spend the time with you"

"Me too." Lauren stole a quick kiss and glanced out the doors to the deck as she pulled back. "Later? You, me, no interruptions?"

Grey nodded and picked up a couple of bowls to take outside. She smiled at Lauren as she passed by her, and murmured, "I'm looking forward to it."

Chapter 43

Grey smiled to herself as she looked over the group piled into the dinghy with her, pleased to see that they were enjoying themselves. They had left Saint Frances right after breakfast and headed over to Jost Van Dyke to clear-in with British customs. The group spent the middle part of the day enjoying a lazy lunch and drinks at Foxy's, and had ended up sleeping off their midday cocktails on the quick jump from Jost to Cane Garden Bay on Tortola. As a general rule, there was not a lot of 'nightlife' to be found in the islands, where a fun night out usually meant drinking the night away at one of the many beachside bars that dotted the shores. But Quito's Gazebo on Tortola was one of the few exceptions to that particular rule, especially on Friday and Saturday nights when he played with his reggae band, Quito and The Edge.

She angled the dinghy toward the strip of beach in front of the restaurant and tapped Harrison, who was sitting closest to her, on the shoulder. "That's Quito's."

Harrison looked at the bright yellow two-story building on the beach that Grey was pointing at, and then back at her with a wide grin. "Cool."

"Yeah." Grey bumped the engine into neutral and let the dinghy coast toward the sand. Once she felt the bottom of the bow scrape against the bottom, she killed the engine and let the boat's momentum carry it forward until it stopped. "All ashore that's going ashore."

Julie, who had been seated in the bow, gathered her sandals in her hand and leapt from the boat to the sand with a dancer's grace. Grey waited until the rest of the group had made the jump before she followed, and she looked at Julie as she ran a hand through her hair. "You have that cell I gave you?"

"Right here," Julie said, patting her purse.

"Excellent." Grey nodded. The walkie worked well enough in areas where cell service was sometimes sketchy, but Tortola had towers everywhere and the small cell phone was much easier for guests to manage on trips ashore like this one. "So, if I don't hear from you, I'll be back here at midnight to pick you up." She ran a hand through her hair and shrugged. "Otherwise, just give me a call and I'll come when you need me. Sound good?"

"Perfect." David said. "Do you need help pushing off?"

Grey smiled her thanks and shook her head. "I got it. There's no reason for any of you guys to get wet before dinner."

"You're sure?" Harrison asked. "It's not a big deal."

"Positive." Grey waved him off. "I got this."

She waited by the bow until they had started toward the restaurant, and then turned and gave the dinghy a good shove to work it free. Once it finally began sliding from its temporary berth, she hopped back in and quickly turned the engine over, revving it in reverse until she was sure it was safe to whip the dinghy around without the outboard's prop digging into the bottom.

As she skipped across the bay toward the *Veritas*, Grey's thoughts turned to Lauren and the fact that, once again, their time together seemed to be passing far too quickly. Despite the fact that they never talked about Lauren leaving at the end of the cruise, she was keenly aware that the few precious moments they had left together were slipping through their fingers. She knew that Lauren was feeling it too, because every hug they shared lasted a little too long, and every kiss simmered with an unmistakable desperation to not think too hard about the future.

It blew her mind to think that, just fourteen days ago, she had longed for the end of Lauren's term aboard the *Veritas*. She remembered how she had struggled those first few days to come to terms with Lauren's uncanny resemblance to Emily. How she had run from her time and again, terrified of her attraction to the beautiful redhead and what it meant. She remembered how she had fought to hang on to the pain of Emily's loss that she had grown to cherish, only to find that, once she did let go, she was left with even sweeter memories, free of the shadow of death that had haunted her for so long.

Lauren was like a beautiful ray of sunlight breaking through the dark clouds that hung low over storm-tossed seas. She was everything that had been missing in Grey's life over the last three years. Hope. Happiness. A warm smile and a gentle hug that Grey felt safe enough to break down in. Every moment Grey spent with Lauren made her feel alive.

She just wished there were more moments left available to them.

The sight of Lauren standing at the stern of the *Veritas* waiting for her as she approached drew Grey's thoughts back to the present, and her heart leapt into her throat at the view. Lauren's hair was blowing lightly in the breeze, tickling her face and shoulders and glowing like fire in the evening sun. Her smile was soft and warm and just a little bit sad, and Grey found herself mirroring the expression as she killed the engine and hurried to the bow to grab onto the railing beside the dive platform. She tied the dinghy off quickly and hopped onto the platform with a practiced ease honed by years of repetition, and hurried up the stairs to where Lauren was waiting for her.

Grey was aware of nothing but Lauren's golden-hued eyes watching her as she closed those final steps separating them, and her heart, which had begun racing for some reason as she climbed the stairs, beat once, heavily, as she pulled Lauren into her arms, and then skipped what felt like the next six beats. She buried her face in the crook of Lauren's neck as she held her tight, and she let out a shuddering breath when Lauren's arms wrapped around her just as fiercely. They lingered in the embrace, drawing strength from the other's presence, until Grey pulled back just far enough to press a soft kiss to Lauren's lips. "Hi."

Lauren smiled and kissed Grey again. "Hi."

"That was quite the welcome," Grey murmured as she nuzzled Lauren's cheek with her nose.

"I'll say." Lauren huffed a quiet laugh and leaned her foreheads against Grey's. Her stomach twisted uncomfortably at the sadness in Grey's gaze, and she sighed as she closed her eyes to block out the sight. "Grey…"

"I know," Grey whispered. She reached up to tuck Lauren's hair behind her ears as she kissed her again. Her eyes fluttered shut as she lost herself in the sweet taste of Lauren's lips and the feeling of Lauren's hands fisting her shirt at her waist, tugging her closer as the futility of their situation threatened to overwhelm them both. She kissed Lauren harder, pouring herself into the caress as her eyes stung with tears she refused to shed. "What do you need, sweetie?"

"You." Lauren used her hold on Grey's shirt to tug her toward the salon.

"You have me," Grey whispered. She fused their mouths together again as they stumbled backward step-by-step, the promise of physical contact a balm to their slowly breaking hearts. The irony of the situation did not escape Grey as they stripped each other down in her cabin, fingers skimming over soft skin in a desperate bid to forget. To pretend that everything was okay. She had lost herself in this particular dance too many times to not recognize it.

"God, Grey, please," Lauren breathed as Grey settled on top of her.

"I know," Grey whispered. She nipped at Lauren's throat as their hands moved in concert down each other's bodies in a blind search for the softness and heat that would chase away their demons, if only for a little while.

Chapter 44

Grey dropped onto one of the banquettes on the back deck, and groaned when the movement made the beer in her hand bubble over. She set the bottle onto the table as she flicked her hand twice to shake most of the spilled beer off before wiping it dry on her shorts. "Perfect."

At this point, she was not even surprised that something else had gone wrong. The day had been a mess from the moment she and Lauren had slept through their alarm. Once they scrambled out of bed, the morning passed in a blur of blueberry pancakes and choppy seas on the sail from Cane Garden Bay to Sandy Spit. What should have been an easy sail was anything but, and instead of enjoying a few hours alone while their guests frolicked on the islet, Grey and Lauren ended up playing hostess to Mia and Harrison, who had stayed back on the boat, looking more than a little green-in-the-gills from the rough ride. Things had thankfully gotten better after the group returned to the boat for a late lunch. The sail back over to Soper's Hole had been much calmer, and by the time she and Lauren finished securing the last mooring line at their reserved slip in the marina, Mia and Harrison had recovered enough to join their friends for their already planned night out. Grey had never been so relieved to see her guests off as she had been when she pointed the group in the direction of Pusser's Landing and bid them goodnight.

"Everything okay?" Lauren asked as she wandered out of the salon with a bottle of Blackbeard Ale hanging limply from her fingers.

Just the sight of Lauren made Grey smile, and she slid further into the banquette and patted the seat beside her. "It is now."

Lauren made a small sound of understanding as she sat beside Grey. She glanced at Grey out of the corner of her eye as their legs brushed together, and smiled when Grey's right hand dropped to her thigh. Lauren sipped at her beer as Grey's fingers began stroking lightly over her leg, and looked out over the boardwalk that was already teeming with tourists, despite the fact that twilight had not yet fallen. Reggae music from the band at Pusser's drifted over the water, faint and indistinct, though Lauren imagined she could hear the rattle of the snare drum and the heavy beats laid down by the bass guitar.

Grey stroked her fingers over Lauren's thigh as she sipped her beer, down around the curve of her knee, up to the hem of her shorts, and back again, grateful that Lauren seemed content to just sit with her for a while. She tried to focus on the feeling of Lauren's skin beneath her fingertips as she drew lazy spirals and swirls on her leg, but her thoughts nevertheless drifted to the fact that this was Lauren's next-to-last night on the boat.

A lump lodged itself in Grey's throat, and she took long swallow of her beer to try and force it down. She was determined to take what time they had left together and cherish every moment. Grey blinked hard and let out a quiet, shuddering breath as she valiantly tried to control herself. She and Lauren had talked earlier about going into town and grabbing dinner at Pusser's, but she did not want to share Lauren with anyone else. She wanted to be selfish. To keep Lauren to herself. To lose herself in the taste of her kiss, and hopefully forget, if only for a little while, how much it was going to hurt to watch her walk away. "You wanna just stay-in tonight?"

Lauren looked over at Grey, who looked as haunted, unable to even force a fake smile, and nodded. "Sure."

"Good." Grey finished her beer and set the empty bottle onto the table. Her fingers pressed into the soft skin of Lauren's inner thigh as she brushed a kiss over the corner of Lauren's mouth, and she sighed when Lauren's lips turned to meet her own. They kissed slowly, heads inclining together as mouths opened and tongues stroked against each other in a familiar, graceful dance that was about so much more than simple desire.

It did not take long for their kisses to become deeper as they turned toward each other, fingers digging into flesh and fabric in a desperate attempt to find a level of closeness that just did not physically exist. The sweet promise of blissful escape laced every clash of lips, and Lauren whimpered when Grey's hand on her thigh moved higher, long fingers dipping beneath her shorts to tease her through her panties. She gasped when Grey's touch slid high enough to make her hips twitch, and pulled back just far enough to whisper, "Take me to bed," before reclaiming Grey's lips with her own.

The sound of the cabin door clicking shut went unheard by either of them as they shuffled together toward the bed. Clothes fell to the floor in random bursts, a shirt here, a pair of shorts there, until there was nothing left between them. The sheets were cool to the touch as Grey guided Lauren back onto the bed, their lips clasped in a kiss that was a potent mix of desperation and pure emotion.

Lauren wrapped her hands around Grey's hips and pulled the brunette down on top of her as she lay back on the bed, and her breath caught at the feeling of Grey's settling so naturally in the cradle of her thighs. Their kisses gentled to a degree that made

Lauren's heart ache, and she swallowed thickly around a lump that had lodged itself in her throat as Grey's lips began trailing over her jaw.

Grey's hands wrapped lightly around Lauren's ribs as she kissed her way down her throat, lingering on the spots that made Lauren gasp before moving on, every brush of lips a tender declaration she did not have the courage to speak aloud. She flicked the tip of her tongue over the hollow at the base of Lauren's throat, and dragged her nose over the line of her sternum. A lingering kiss was pressed to the spot above Lauren's heart before Grey moved on, mapping the supple curves of Lauren's body in a languid exploration. Wet kisses and gentle nips that left Lauren's skin pink and glistening marked her path, one that she silently prayed no one else would ever follow.

Her pulse slowed to a steady, heavy beat as she worshipped Lauren with lips and teeth and tongue. She lost herself in the sweet taste of Lauren's desire, was lulled by the feeling of strong hips rolling against her mouth. The silky brush of Lauren's thighs against her cheeks was hypnotic; the soft whimpers and mewls tumbling from her lips more enchanting than any siren's song. Her stomach fluttered at the feeling of Lauren's fingers combing lightly through her hair, and her stomach clenched at the sight of Lauren arched above her with her head thrown back in pleasure.

She was entranced. Ensnared. And she never wanted to break free.

Grey knew by the quickening of Lauren's hips that she was close, and she brought her over the edge with a few final tender flicks of her tongue. She watched, spellbound as Lauren trembled above her, the sounds of Lauren's pleasure stoking her own until her body seized with a gentler, sympathetic orgasm.

She eased Lauren through the length of her release and then, when her trembling eased, leaned her cheek against Lauren's inner thigh, content to watch her bask in the afterglow.

This is all I need, she thought to herself as her eyes swept over Lauren's spent form, tracking the gentle rise and fall of her chest. *Just this. Just her.*

Her heart began to beat faster with the realization that Lauren was leaving soon, heading back to New York and a life that did not include her, and she sucked a sharp breath in through her nose as reality slammed back into her with all the force and forgiveness of a runaway train.

She turned her head into Lauren's leg and squeezed her eyes shut against the sting of tears that threatened, but it did no good as a few leaked out anyway. She bit the inside of her cheek to keep the whimper she could feel bubbling in her throat from escaping. Ever since Emily had gotten sick, she had not expected much of the world beside hurt and pain. She had been content to drift from one moment to the next, occasionally finding a rare burst of happiness, but mostly just existing in a world painted gray. But here, now, with tiny fissures spreading across the surface of her heart—her heart that Lauren had somehow made whole again—she allowed herself to hope for something more than the half-life she had been living.

Her gaze landed on Lauren's, and her heart skipped a beat. She knew that she should not do it, but hope had sprung recklessly in her veins and she could not resist its seductive pull. "Stay." The plea was a shaky whisper that barely tumbled past her lips, but she knew Lauren had heard by the way her mouth fell open and her eyes widened in surprise.

"Grey, I…" Lauren shook her head, wishing that things were that simple.

Grey's heart pounded wildly in her throat as she swept up Lauren's body to press their foreheads together. "Please," she begged softly, laying her heart on the line as she stared beseechingly into Lauren's eyes. "Stay with me."

Lauren sighed, hating how, just at the sound, Grey seemed to deflate in front of her. "I can't."

It had been a foolish hope, Grey knew, but that did little to stem the icy tide of rejection that washed through her. Grey shook her head and pulled away from Lauren, her heart seizing painfully with the final dying beat of the hope she had allowed to bloom inside her. Grey bit her lip, growing more frustrated with herself by the second for daring to ask Lauren to stay. Of course Lauren was not going to. She had known all along that this was temporary, and she had been stupid to ever think that it might be something more. "Yeah. I know."

"Do you?" Lauren challenged, sitting up and ducking her head to catch Grey's eye.

"Yeah, of course," Grey brushed her off and tried to slip out of the bed, the urge to flee and protect herself too strong to resist, but a gentle hand on her arm stopped her.

"No." Lauren hooked a finger under Grey's chin, lifting the brunette's eyes to her own. She knew exactly how hard it must have been for Grey to open herself up like she just had, and she would be damned if she let Grey think that she had rejected her because she did not want her. "I don't think you do. The idea of staying here with you is tempting—so very, very tempting—but I just can't. Not right now, anyways."

Grey blew out a loud breath and ran a hand through her hair. She understood where Lauren was coming from, but understanding did not make it any easier to hear. "I get it," she said, her voice carrying none of its usual strength. She had hoped and lost, and now she was just looking to survive. "I get it, I do. I just…" She shook her head, defeat clearly written in her expression as she looked into Lauren's muddy hazel eyes. "I don't want to lose this."

"Me neither," Lauren whispered, her heart breaking as she adjusted her hold so that she was gently cradling Grey's jaw in her hand. She smoothed her thumb over Grey's cheek, hoping that the tender touch would provide some kind of comfort. "But, sweetie…it's only been two weeks. I can't possibly just walk away from everything I've worked so hard for because I spent the two happiest weeks of my life in the Virgin Islands with you."

Grey turned her face into Lauren's palm and pressed a soft kiss to the middle of it. "I know." She sighed and looked back into Lauren's eyes, wishing that things were different. "It just…"

"Sucks," Lauren supplied.

"Yeah," Grey agreed softly. She huffed a mirthless laugh and shook her head. "So what do we do now?"

"I don't know. I guess it depends on whether or not we want to put the time in and see if this thing between us is real."

"Do you?"

Lauren nodded. "Yeah. I do." She finally gave in to the urge to try and kiss the frown from Grey's lips, and her stomach fluttered hopefully at the way Grey responded to her.

They kissed slowly, sweetly, every brush of lips a silent confirmation that what they shared was something worth fighting for, and Grey let out a shaky breath when they finally broke apart. "Me too."

"Good." Lauren smiled sadly and nodded. "Do you think you'd be able to get up to New York any time soon to visit?"

Grey blew out a loud breath and ran a hand through her hair as she tried to picture her schedule for the next few months. "I think I have a four-day block off in early February. Nothing before that though, because it's the high season. Those three days off we just had are rare. My charters are usually booked back-to-back."

The idea of not seeing Grey for a couple months made Lauren's stomach drop, but it was better than nothing. "Okay." Lauren brushed a soft kiss across Grey's lips. "Would you come up then?"

"In February?"

"Yeah."

Grey nodded. "Yeah."

Chapter 45

Lauren looked toward the western horizon that had already swallowed half of the setting sun and sighed. Her last full day aboard the *Veritas* had passed in exactly the same manner as the three previous days: much too quickly.

The throaty rumble of an outboard engine drew her attention toward the stern, and her breath caught at the sight of Grey expertly steering the small craft toward her. Grey was an absolute vision with her windblown hair and toned physique, and Lauren felt her heart stutter as she looked at her.

Knowing that leaving was the right decision did little to ease the ache that settled squarely in her chest, and Lauren shook her head as the urge to stay swept through her. She had been the strong one the night before, thinking rationally, doing the smart and mature thing, but it had not been easy. She had lain awake all night in the safe haven of Grey's arms, letting her tears fall silently to her pillow as she wondered where she would find the strength to actually go back to New York.

She lifted her hand in greeting as Grey killed the dinghy's engine and drifted toward the *Veritas*, and felt her stomach drop at the pained smile she got in return. The day had not been easy for either of them, and she knew that Grey was thinking the same thing she was.

Their time was almost up.

Lauren folded her arms over her chest as she watched Grey tie the dinghy's bow line off to the cleat by the dive platform, and tried to force a small smile when Grey started up the stairs toward her. "Hey."

"Lauren," Grey sighed as she stepped onto the back deck. Her stomach twisted violently at the pained expression on Lauren's face, and she shook her head as she pulled Lauren into her arms. "Come here, baby."

The day had been long, and Grey tried to console herself with the idea that watching Lauren walk away the next morning would not be goodbye—but that did little more than take the worst of the sting away. Because no matter their promises to call, email, text, and Skype as much as possible, the fact remained that, after tomorrow, Lauren would not be aboard the *Veritas* with her.

Lauren melted into Grey's embrace, which was far gentler than any they had shared all day, and her heart broke a little bit more as she buried her face in the curve of Grey's neck. *God, I am going to miss this.*

"Shh, I know." Grey rubbed Lauren's back gently. "It's okay." She blinked back her tears and leaned her cheek against the top of Lauren's head. "It's okay."

"What time do you have to go back and pick them up?" Lauren mumbled into Grey's neck.

"They'll call. I have a feeling it will be late since this is their last night in the islands."

Lauren sniffled and lifted her head to offer Grey a watery smile, and her stomach dropped when she got an identical smile back. "Good."

The sight of Lauren's tears made Grey's spill free, and she swallowed around a lump in her throat as she pressed a tender kiss to Lauren's forehead. "Please don't cry."

"I can't help it," Lauren half-laughed, half-sobbed, feeling like an idiot because she had been the one to insist that she return to New York. "I just…"

"I know." Grey's voice was just as rough as pulled back and took Lauren's hands in her own. She tugged her toward the salon, and was relieved when Lauren followed her. A feeling of peace swept over her when she closed the cabin door behind them, and she sighed as she pulled Lauren into her arms once more. It felt so right to hold her, and she wanted to do nothing else for the rest of the night. She brushed her lips over Lauren's ear and whispered, "Cuddle with me?"

Lauren traced Grey's jaw with her fingertips and nodded. "Of course."

Grey toed off her shoes and climbed onto the bed, and smiled sadly when Lauren did the same. "Come here," she whispered as she drew Lauren into her, wrapping her arms around her waist and holding her close.

The feeling of Grey's arms around her was instantly relaxing, and Lauren curled herself around Grey's side. She rested her head on Grey's chest, and let the slow, steady beat of Grey's heart calm her. She sighed softly at the feeling of Grey's fingers stroking lazily up and down her spine, the touch so gentle and reassuring, and she let her eyes drift shut as she selfishly took the comfort Grey was offering her. "That feels good."

"Good." Grey brushed her lips over Lauren's forehead and, on her next pass, slipped her fingers beneath the hem of her shirt. "Is this okay?" she asked as she stroked the soft skin of Lauren's lower back.

"Yes," Lauren breathed. She licked her lips and let her left hand, which had been splayed across Grey's stomach, drift beneath the brunette's shirt as well. "This?"

Grey closed her eyes at the feeling of Lauren's fingers tracing the line of her right oblique and sighed. "Absolutely perfect."

"Good." Lauren turned her head to press her lips to the underside of Grey's chin. One kiss became two, and she whimpered when Grey shifted and the brunette's lips landed lightly on her own. The kiss was achingly tender, and she pulled back with a gasp when Grey's tongue flicked across her lips. Grey's eyes were swirling with so much emotion that it stole the breath from her lungs, and she could not hold back the quiet groan that rumbled in her throat as she gave herself over to it.

Grey melted into the bed as Lauren rolled more fully on top of her, the redhead's hand inching up her stomach until her fingertips tickled the underside of her breast. "Please," she whispered, arching up into the touch.

"You're sure?"

"Yes." Grey covered Lauren's hand with her own and pulled it higher. A shaky breath escaped her at the feeling of Lauren's palm dragging over her nipple, and she nodded, answering the question she could see shining in Lauren's gaze. She wanted this. Wanted her. It might be the thing that broke her completely, but she needed to fall apart under Lauren's hands one more time before she watched her walk away. The next few months before she could make it up to New York to see Lauren again were going to be hell, and she wanted this memory to help her through them. "God, Lauren. Please touch me."

Lauren's heart thudded heavily in her throat at the desperate edge in Grey's voice, and she moaned softly as she squeezed the breast under her hand. "Okay."

They undressed each other slowly between languid kisses, fingers trailing lightly over warm skin as they gave up all pretense of control and lost themselves in the moment. Every touch burned with a depth of affection neither was willing to voice, but it was conveyed all the same in the soft sighs that tumbled from their lips.

Lauren's head fell forward, her forehead bumping against Grey's as long fingers pushed slowly inside her, and she immediately mirrored the touch, thrusting swiftly into the wet warmth that waited for her. Her heart fluttered at the feeling of Grey's body drawing her in deeper, and she moaned as Grey's free hand curled around the back of her neck and pulled her down into a kiss that was so deep and passionate that it made her head spin.

It did not take long for their bodies to fall into the easy rhythm that was theirs and theirs alone, and Grey gasped as her heart skipped a beat at the feeling of Lauren's fingers filling her so completely. She opened herself to the woman above her, taking all that Lauren had to give and giving all of herself in return. She matched Lauren's slow, deep thrusts stroke for stroke as they eased each other higher and higher, and she groaned when the white heat of impending release began to spread through her. "No. Not yet."

"Yes," Lauren encouraged softly, dusting the lightest of kisses over Grey's lips.

"I'm not ready." Grey squeezed her eyes shut and threw her head back against the mattress, straining against the traitorous euphoria building inside her. She wanted more, wanted more time to commit the feeling of Lauren's fingers inside her to memory, to burn the feeling of Lauren's body rocking against her own into her brain so that she would be able to remember every last detail without any effort at all. "Not yet."

Lauren's smile was sad as she brushed her lips over Grey's chin. "Sweetie…"

"Please, Lauren," Grey whispered, rolling her hips away from the hand between her legs, trying to lessen the sensation building inside her. She cried out softly as it instead sent bolts of electricity arcing through her. She clung to Lauren as release swept through her without her permission, suffusing her body with pleasure even as her heart broke all over again.

"I know," Lauren whispered, nuzzling Grey's cheek with her own as she cradled the brunette to her, her eyes squeezed shut against the truth they could no longer ignore. "I know."

Chapter 46

If Lauren had thought things between her and Grey had been uncomfortable her first few days aboard the *Veritas*, those days had nothing on her final morning. Waking up in each other's arms only served to highlight the fact that it was the last time they would be doing so for the foreseeable future. They showered together, letting the water washing over them clear away their tears as they took advantage of their final time alone, fingers reverently tracing every curve and valley in an attempt to stave off the inevitable.

Breakfast had been an utter failure. Lauren had made waffles because they were Grey's favorite, but neither of them felt much like eating. The desperate kiss they had shared in the doorway of Lauren's cabin after the breakfast dishes were cleared was wet with their tears, and it took Grey more than a minute after they broke apart to get enough control of herself to make her way up to the helm.

Lauren spent the sail back to Charlotte Amalie packing. She wanted to spend the time with Grey, but she had put the task off for far too long already, and if she did not do it then, she would most likely miss her flight. Retrieving all of her things that had migrated across the small hall to Grey's cabin had been pure torture, and she was so blinded by tears when she returned to her own cabin that she just blindly shoved the toiletries and random articles of clothing into her bag to get them out of her sight.

She had managed to put on a brave face that fooled nobody as they said goodbye to their guests, and had turned back to the salon the moment they were gone to try and hide her tears. The feeling of strong arms wrapping around her waist from behind shattered what was left of her control, and she let out an anguished sob as she turned in Grey's arms to bury her face in the sweet curve of the brunette's neck. She knew that she needed to do this, that if what they had was truly meant to be that they would find a way back to each other, but at the moment it just felt like her heart was being ripped from her body. "I gotta…"

"I know." Grey squeezed Lauren tightly and then relaxed her hold, letting the redhead slip from her grasp. *This is not goodbye. It's just a see you later*, she reminded herself as she watched Lauren trudge slowly down the stairs to her cabin to retrieve her bag.

Lauren looked around the cabin she had only stayed in for a few short days before she began spending her nights in Grey's arms, and shook her head as she picked up her duffel. It was disproportionally heavy in her hand, as if the bag was protesting what was about to happen, and Lauren felt her heart lurch painfully in her chest when she returned to the salon where Grey was waiting for her. The sight of Grey standing there, back straight, her beautiful face twisted in a mask of resigned agony, made Lauren's grip on her bag slip for the briefest of moments as the weight of what she was about to do made her knees buckle.

The voice of reason inside her head was resolute in reminding her that it was absolutely ridiculous to throw away her career for what essentially amounted to a summer fling. That no matter how much affection she felt for Grey, she would regret not returning to her life in New York. That two weeks of happiness did not constitute enough of a reason to throw away everything she had worked so hard for.

She did not want to leave, but she was going to. They would talk, get to know each other more, and in a few months they would see each other again. Somehow she knew that these next few months would do little to change how she felt about Grey, but she was determined to do the rational thing—no matter how badly she wished to be utterly irrational.

Grey tensed as she heard Lauren's duffel hit the floor with a quiet *thud*, and she drew a deep breath as she turned to look at her. Lauren was as beautiful ever, even with her lower lip trembling and tears pooling in her eyes, and Grey opened her arms, beckoning her closer with a look because her throat was too tight to allow her to speak.

Words were unnecessary as they held each other, their faces buried in the sweet curves where neck and shoulder met. Grey's heart clenched at the feeling of Lauren's tears soaking the collar of her shirt, and she swallowed thickly as she tried, and failed, to stem the tide of her own tears as she held her close. It was patently unfair that, after years of simply existing, she should learn to live again in the arms of a woman destined to leave her, but she had long ago learned that life was anything but fair.

The only bright spot in their situation was that it did not have to be permanent. It was not that final line demarking life and death that could not be crossed; it was just a few latitudinal lines on a map that would separate them. And those lines, while imposing, could be crossed.

But to cross that line, it had to be drawn, and Grey pressed her lips to the sensitive hollow beneath Lauren's ear, lingering in the touch for a moment before she pulled away to look her in the eye. "Call me when you get to New York?"

Lauren did not bother to wipe at the tears running down her face as she nodded. "Of course." She knew that she needed to go if she was to catch her plane. Knew that she had already stayed much longer than was prudent simply because she could not stomach the idea of actually leaving, but she could not move.

Grey smiled sadly and kissed away Lauren's tears. "It's okay, baby. You need to go if you're going to get to the airport on time."

"I know," Lauren whispered. Her feet remained rooted to the spot as she kissed Grey softly, the gentle caress a promise that it would not be the last. "I'll talk to you soon, okay?" she asked as she took that first small step away from Grey.

"Okay." Grey wrapped her arms around her waist to keep from reaching for Lauren again.

"I…" Lauren's voice trailed off as she bent down to pick up her bag. "Grey…"

The anguish in Lauren's voice made Grey's heart break, and she blinked hard as she tipped her head at the door. "It's okay."

Lauren knew that everything was as far from okay as it was possible to be, but she still gathered her bag in her hand and, with one last deep breath to steel her resolve, walked out the door.

It was, she deluded herself into believing, the right thing to do.

Two weeks was not nearly enough time to make any kind of life-altering decision. It was impossible to fall in love with somebody in such a short amount of time. It was all lies, but Lauren held onto them like they were the most impeccable of truths, needing the strength they gave her as she made her way down the stairs and hopped onto the dock. Her strength faltered at the sound of Grey's agonized sob coming from inside the salon, the sound more akin to one a wounded animal might make than a woman, but she did not dare look back.

She knew that if she did, she would never leave.

She stumbled into motion, her footsteps slow and heavy, her body leaning forward in resistance to the force that tried to pull her back into Grey's arms. She made her way down the dock, resolutely moving one foot in front of the other, determined to do the mature, rational thing—no matter how much it hurt.

Chapter 47

When Lauren had arrived in Manhattan at eighteen, she was young and the crowds and the noise were invigorating. It was a far cry from her quiet, suburban, Midwestern life, and she loved it. And after her first year in the city, she had grown so used to the hustle and bustle, to the screech of brakes and the revving of engines, that all of it had disappeared into the background. It was just life. Busy, chaotic, wonderful life that left her feeling like she could conquer the world.

Now it was just loud. Glaringly, gratingly loud. Even at one in the morning, as she made her way back to her apartment after her first shift back in the kitchen at Clarke's since returning from the islands not even twenty-four hours earlier. She had stumbled through the day in a fog, her mind constantly replaying the voicemail Grey had left her when she slept through her phone ringing. Two weeks of minimal sleep, combined with a long plane ride and the emotional toll of leaving had left her exhausted, and she had not awoken until well after noon. Grey had not sounded upset at her not answering, more concerned than anything else, but when Lauren called her back it went straight to voicemail. She figured it was because Grey was busy sailing from one location to another, and she had left her a message promising to call again once she finished her shift.

The door to her building closing behind her muted the noises of the city, and Lauren sighed as she crossed the lobby to the elevator that rattled and clacked all the way up to the fifth floor. Her apartment was dimly lit by the city lights that burned outside the floor-to-ceiling windows that ran the length of her apartment, leaving a crisscross grid of murky yellow light across the hardwood floors that were close enough in color to those on the *Veritas* to make her heart ache. She did not bother to turn on any lights as she toed off her shoes and left them on the mat beneath her hanging coats, content to let the cool gray dim of her apartment wrap around her like a blanket as she padded down the hall to her bedroom.

The shadows creeping from the corners, bleeding up over the ceiling and seeping in uneven pools across the floor reminded her of the way the salon of the *Veritas* would look bathed in moonlight, and if she tried hard enough, she was almost able to pretend that she was not in New York.

She stripped off her work clothes as she stood in front of her closet, the bedroom lit by the same muddy yellow light as the rest of the apartment. The chill in the air had her reaching for her most comfortable pair of sleep pants, and her fingers automatically sought and found her favorite gray Henley. The one that still smelled like the detergent Grey favored. The familiar scent was both a balm to her battered soul and a knife to her heart, and she blinked back the tears that threatened as she climbed into bed, so that she could lie down as she talked to Grey and pretend that Grey was beside her, and not thousands of miles away.

Her call was answered on the first ring, and she smiled at the sound of Grey's sleepy voice. "Hey, you."

"Hey," Grey murmured. *"You home now?"*

"Safe and sound," Lauren assured her. "How was your day?"

"Long. Had to jump from Charlotte Amalie to Tortola to pick up the charter, and then over to Peter Island for the night."

"That's different," Lauren said, closing her eyes as she leaned back against her pillows.

"Yeah." Grey was quiet for a moment. *"How about you? How was your day?"*

"Long," Lauren said, smiling at the way Grey chuckled softly. "I forgot how tiring New York is."

"It's definitely not the islands," Grey agreed softly. *"Work good?"*

"Yeah. It was just work. Nothing exciting."

"All fingers and thumbs still attached?"

Lauren blew a raspberry into the phone. "Yes. All digits are uninjured and accounted for."

"Good." Grey sighed, and Lauren pictured her running a hand through her hair. *"I have plans for those fingers when I get up there in February."*

"Do you, now?" Lauren chuckled. She looked up at the feeling of Jenks landing lightly on her legs, and she patted the bed beside her, calling him closer. She smiled at the way he purred softly and nuzzled her face, his bright blue eyes filled with the kitty equivalent of concern. "Hey, buddy," she whispered as she scratched behind his ear.

"Jenks?"

"Mmm, he's giving me snuggles."

"Lucky bastard," Grey muttered.

Lauren smiled. "If it makes you feel any better, yours are better."

"Damn right they are." Grey blew out a soft breath. *"I miss you."*

Sheets rustled as Grey tried to make herself comfortable, and Lauren smiled sadly as she imagined how beautiful Grey must look in that moment. She rolled onto her side, facing the half of the bed that Grey had always taken, and closed her eyes. "I miss you too."

It was too late for idle small-talk but neither seemed particularly eager to lose the tenuous connection they shared, so they fell into an easy silence, listening to the other breathe as they each pretended that they were together. Lauren was not sure when she fell asleep, but she woke up some time later to find her phone on the mattress beneath her chin. The screen was dark, and she blinked sleepily as she swiped it open. Instead of the open call screen she saw a text notification, and she smiled as she read Grey's message.

Sleep well, beautiful. Skype date later?
Will be moored in Jost by 1500…

Three o'clock gave Lauren a few hours before she was to report back to Clarke's, and she grinned at the idea of actually seeing Grey—not just talking to her.

It's a date. I'll be waiting, call when you can.
Be safe.
XO

She fell back asleep with her smile still firmly in place, her right hand curled loosely in the middle of the bed as if she were waiting for Grey to reach out and take it.

Chapter 48

Lauren fell back into her usual routine of visiting vendors with Paul Laine—the executive chef at Clarke's—first thing in the morning for fresh ingredients they would need for that night's menu, and then going for a run through the park afterwards. She ate lunch at home with Jenks sitting on the table in front of her, and then tried her best to not stare at the clock as she waited for Grey to call. After a week of falling asleep with the phone at her ear, she and Grey agreed to check in with each other during the late-afternoon, after Grey had moored the Veritas for the night and before Lauren had to leave for work. There were days where the ability to call just did not happen, of course, that was the unfortunate truth of their situation, but for the most part it worked out nicely for each of them. Lauren missed falling asleep in the early hours of the morning knowing that Grey was just on the other end of the line, but she comforted herself with the knowledge that at least Grey was getting a good night's rest.

The holidays had come and gone in a blur, and it was strange for her to think that she and Grey had spent three times the number of days apart than they had together, but every day she found herself missing Grey more. It would have been easier for both of them if their separation had dulled the connection they felt, but it only grew stronger with every passing day. Christmas gifts had been exchanged via Skype, and New Year's had been rung in over the phone as Lauren snuck off into the alley behind the restaurant at midnight to call Grey and wish her a happy New Year.

They had broached the subject of what they should do the week after New Year's—but they had yet to come to any kind of an agreement. The *Veritas* was booked for the rest of the season, which meant that Grey was stuck in the islands until at least July, and Lauren had heard her name being mentioned several times as a potential replacement for an executive chef who was on their way out.

The only thing they both could agree on, was that they were anxiously looking forward to the day when Lauren would pick Grey up at La Guardia. Their time together would be short, but after so long apart even four days together sounded like heaven.

Lauren was sitting on the couch in her living room on a Wednesday afternoon the week before Grey was scheduled to visit, listening to a nature track she had purchased off iTunes on repeat—pretending that the sound of the waves crashing from her speakers were real and remembering the way Grey looked standing at the helm of the *Veritas* as they raced over the waves under a full sail. She smiled as her phone on the coffee table in front of her buzzed and came to life, rich violin slurs filling the room and announcing that it was Grey on the other end. "You're early today."

"I am," Grey replied, her voice light with the sound of her smile. *"Do you need me to call back later?"*

"I want you to call whenever you can. Even when you're drunk," Lauren said, chuckling softly at the memory of the night of Grey's seemingly endless drunk dials that had started with Grey confessing how much she missed Lauren and ended with phone sex. "How was your day?"

"The usual. Just kicked the last group off the boat in Charlotte Amalie, which is why I was able to call earlier than usual. You want to Skype?"

"Of course," Lauren said. She sat up and reached for her laptop that was sitting on the coffee table in front of her. She closed out her iTunes and smiled when a familiar rectangular box popped up on her screen. "There you are," she murmured when Grey's face came up on the screen. Grey was sitting at one of the tables on the back deck, and Lauren's stomach lurched at the sight. God, she missed that.

"Here I am," Grey said with a soft smile.

Lauren licked her lips and nodded, taking a moment to just look at Grey. Even though Grey was smiling, her eyes were sad, and Lauren understood without having to ask why that was. Technology was great and it made being apart at least somewhat bearable, but looking at Grey's image on her computer screen also drove home the fact that they were thousands of miles apart. Her fingers itched to touch, to comb through Grey's hair, to wrap around the curve of her jaw and hold her close as she kissed her slowly, thoroughly, making her whimper, and Lauren cleared her throat softly as she forced herself back to the present. "Hi."

"Hi," Grey whispered. "How was your morning? Anything exciting happen at work last night?"

"Work was work. Jen and I went out for drinks afterwards, so that was nice, I guess."

"Did you not have fun?" Grey asked, her expression clearly concerned.

"I did. It's just…" Lauren rolled her eyes. "It's just weird."

"Why?"

Lauren shrugged. "I don't know. I mean, we went to our usual bar after work, sat at our usual table, and had our usual drinks just like we usually do. She talked about her husband and I talked about you—she liked that whale joke of yours, by the way—and it just…it just made me miss you more. You would think that I would've gotten used to this by now, but I would rather be spending the time talking with you."

"Oh, Lauren." Grey lifted her hand like she was going to reach for Lauren, only to end up running it through her hair instead. "I miss you too. But, hey, there are only nine days until I'll be up there to see you."

Lauren smiled at the thought. "I know. I can't wait."

"Me neither," Grey whispered, her eyes dancing over Lauren's face They talked for another half an hour about everything and nothing at all, comfortable silence filling the void between topics as they just looked at each other, their expressions conveying everything they were thinking.

Lauren let out a soft, regret-filled sighed when her phone on the table began to beep. "I'm sorry. That's my work alarm. I'm going to have to get going."

"It's fine. Usual time tomorrow?"

"Of course." Lauren smiled. "It's the best part of my day."

"Mine too," Grey whispered. "Have a good night at work."

"I'll try. What do you have going on tonight? Anything?"

"Nothing special." Grey shook her head. "Am just going to go over to Kip's for dinner and hang out for a bit. Head out again tomorrow morning, but will be in Leinster in plenty of time to call.
"

Lauren nodded. "Have fun. Tell Kelly I say hello."

"Will do." Grey pressed two fingers to her lips and then touched them to the screen, and smiled when Lauren did the same. "Tomorrow?"

"Tomorrow," Lauren promised, hating the way her stomach sank at the knowledge that she would not see Grey again until the following afternoon.

"Goodbye, beautiful," Grey whispered.

Lauren smiled sadly and nodded. "Bye." She blew out a loud breath as she closed up her laptop to keep Jenks from making a bed of the keyboard, and set it down on the table. She propped her elbows on her knees and let her head drop into her hands as she tried to refocus herself on the things she needed to do. Work was a nice distraction from how much she missed Grey, and she had grown to crave the chaos of the kitchen. She sucked in a deep breath as she let her hands fall, and looked at Jenks, who was watching her carefully. "Right, buddy. Time to get ready for work."

She pocketed her phone as she made her way down the hall to her bedroom, and she smiled at the sound of Jenks trailing behind her. She dressed quickly, knowing that things were going to be hectic that night because Laine was planning on trying a new recipe. The special the week before had been one of hers, and it had been so well-received that she knew he was going to be hovering over everybody's shoulders, barking orders and making sure that everything was perfect, trying to solidify his position as her better.

She finished dressing quickly, and threw a few treats into Jenks' bowl as she passed through the kitchen to the front door. She had just pulled on her coat when her phone began ringing with the default tone assigned to the majority of her contacts, and she answered it distractedly as she stepped into her shoes. "Hello?"

"Chef Murphy?"

Lauren frowned. She did not recognize the voice on the other end. She pulled the phone away from her ear to glance at the number, and her frown deepened as she failed to recognize it as well. "Yes."

"My name is Jason Whitmore. I'm the owner and general manager of Café Belle."

Café Belle was a French/American fusion restaurant on the Upper West Side that was on the verge of breaking into the elite upper echelon of restaurants in the city. The rumor mill had been churning for the last year with speculation of Marcus Adrian leaving his position as executive chef at the café to strike out on his own, and Lauren's pulse jumped as she realized those rumors might actually be true.

"I'm sure you've heard the rumors about Chef Adrian leaving Café Belle to open his own restaurant..."

Lauren nodded slowly. "I have..."

"Would you be interested in interviewing for the position?"

"Of executive chef?"

"Yes," Whitmore replied, his tone amused.

"Of course," Lauren answered automatically, her pulse racing with excitement.

"Excellent. Would you be available to interview tomorrow morning?"

"I...yes. Of course. What time?"

"How does eleven o'clock sound?"

"That sounds great."

"Perfect. Then I shall see you tomorrow morning, Chef Murphy."

Lauren stared at the wall in front of her for a moment as she processed what had just happened. She had an interview to become the Executive chef at Café Belle. She danced giddily in place, and then froze as her eyes landed on the wallpaper on her phone. It was a selfie-shot she and Grey had taken while in Hawksnest, just the two of them cuddled up together on the trampolines at the front of the boat. Grey's smile was radiant, and Lauren's heart sank as she looked at it.

"Shit." Her legs threatened to give out beneath her, and she leaned against the wall for support. "What am I going to do?"

Her phone beeped again with her 'you better move your ass or you're going to be late' alarm, and she shook her head as she dropped the phone into her purse and finished getting ready to leave. That same question played on an infinite loop as she made her way to work on auto-pilot, weaving her way through the crowd that filled the sidewalk between her apartment and the restaurant.

What am I going to do?

Cross the street. Dodge a creepy looking guy who was not going to alter his course.

What am I going to do?

Wait at a red light. Slow down, duck around the tourists taking a picture of a building.

What am I going to do?

She had yet to find any kind of an answer by the time she walked into Clarke's, and she made a beeline through the empty dining room before shouldering her way through the swinging door to the kitchen. The small locker room area at the back of the kitchen was empty when she walked inside, and she continued to mull over her dilemma as she stored her things. She had just closed her locker when a gentle hand on her shoulder made her jump, and she swore softly under her breath as she turned to find her best friend standing behind her.

"Sorry," Jen murmured, smiling apologetically. She leaned back against her locker and gave Lauren an appraising look. "Everything okay? I said hello three times and you never heard me."

"Yeah. No." Lauren shook her head. "Everything's fine. I'm just thinking."

"About Grey?"

"Yes…and no." Lauren blew out quiet breath and shook her head as she pulled her hair up into a bun. "Jason Whitmore called me right when I was leaving to come here tonight. I have an interview tomorrow morning for the executive chef position at Café Belle."

Jen's eyes went wide and she stood up straighter. "Lo, that's awesome!"

"Yeah, I know," Lauren murmured, her brow furrowing as she nodded. "I know it is."

Jen sighed, understanding without having to be told why Lauren looked so conflicted about it all. It was clear to her from listening to Lauren talk that things between her and Grey were growing more and more serious. They existed in a state of flux, neither doing anything that would force the other's hand, but it could not go on forever. "What are you going to do?"

"I don't…what do you think I should do?"

"Only you can answer that one, kiddo," Jen said gently. "I know the whole Grey thing is a mess right now, but you said that she was at least open to the idea of maybe moving up here this summer. I know the idea of another six months of being thousands of miles away from each other isn't the most fun, but it's also do-able."

Lauren nodded. "Yeah. I know."

"I do think that you need to go to the interview and at least hear Whitmore out, though. See the kitchen and the dining room. Understand what it is you would be losing if you didn't do it. And," Jen added seriously, "you really need to talk to Grey about this."

"I know," Lauren whispered, her stomach twisting at the thought. The noise in the kitchen beyond the locker room door became louder, and she shook her head as she hurriedly rolled her sleeves to her elbows. It was time to go to work. "I'll talk to her about it tomorrow."

"You can call her now, if you want. I'll cover for you."

Lauren shook her head. "No. Thank you, though. This is…this is not a five-minute conversation, and she's having dinner with a friend tonight. I'll just talk to her tomorrow afternoon when she calls. And, besides…"

"You don't know what you're going to do yet," Jen finished for her.

Lauren smiled sadly and nodded. "Yeah."

Chapter 49

Lauren had no better idea of what she was going to do by the time she arrived at Café Belle the next morning, and her first real look at the restaurant did little to add any clarity to her thinking. The facilities were impressive—the dining room was of decent size, cozy, yet intimate, and the kitchen was a chef's dream with its surprisingly large footprint and gleaming, top-of-the-line equipment—and Lauren found herself liking Jason Whitmore as he gave her a quick tour before beginning they sat down to talk. He was an older gentleman, with salt-and-pepper hair, an infectious smile, and an obvious love for the industry, and she could tell after spending only ten minutes with him that he would be a joy to work for.

After the brief tour the settled down at a table near the kitchen to begin the actual interview process. Lauren tried not to look too pleased when he rattled off the finer points of her résumé from memory, including the mention she had received in *New York Magazine* earlier that year, and she fielded his initial questions easily. She had strong ties to local vendors, so she knew who had the best product at the best price, and had no problem offering up sample seasonal menu ideas. His smile grew wider with every answer she gave, everything about his demeanor telling her that 'yes, you are the one', which made her feel more and more queasy.

She still had no idea if this was even what she wanted anymore.

"I must say, I have been quite impressed with your answers so far, and I think you will make a most excellent addition to our staff." Whitmore leaned back in his chair and played with the stem of his water glass. "I just have one more question for you, if you don't mind."

Lauren nodded and folded her hands on the table. "Of course."

He smiled. "Tell me about your favorite meal you cooked. Who was it for, and what was the menu?"

Lauren's drifted to a quiet night in Hawksnest Bay and the feeling of Grey's arms around her waist, as soft lips brushed lightly over her neck, teasing the marks that had been left there. She remembered the way Grey smiled at her and the way the brunette's eyes burned with a quiet affection as they ate at the counter, legs brushing together as, even after an afternoon of making love, they had been unable to resist touching each other some more. She remembered the way she felt when Grey confessed to being genuinely happy, how their being together helped her feel whole. She remembered their astronomy lesson, making out under the stars, and the aching softness of Grey's hands on her later that night, every touch a silent declaration of deeper emotions neither of them had felt comfortable confessing at the time.

"I…" Lauren cleared her throat softly. She finally had her answer and, to be honest, it was one that she had known in her heart all along. "I'm afraid, sir, that my favorite meal had nothing to do with the food and everything to do with the woman I made it for. The meal itself was simple—lightly seared Ahi steaks that I had rubbed with a ginger-wasabi blend and some jasmine rice on the side—but the company…" Her voice trailed off again, and she flashed him an apologetic smile. "If you had called me about this position two months ago, I would have jumped at the opportunity. Your restaurant really is incredible. This dining room—" she waved a hand around them, "—gorgeous. The kitchen is a chef's dream." She shook her head and sighed. "But it's not my dream anymore, I'm afraid."

"I see," Whitmore murmured. His smile turned softer, and he nodded. "I met my wife the summer before I was to study abroad at Oxford for a year, and I know that look in your eyes well. Young love certainly does leave a special glow on us all. I must admit that I am disappointed you will not be joining Café Belle, but I do understand. If you ever change your mind and decide that this is something you are interested in pursuing, please do not hesitate to give me a call."

Lauren smiled, touched by his offer. He really was a rare gem of a man in an industry as cut-throat as theirs. "Of course. Thank you, sir."

"Jason, please." He stood and held out his hand. "I wish you the best of luck in your future endeavors, Chef Murphy."

Lauren took a deep breath and she shook his hand. "Thank you."

Somehow, Lauren was not surprised to find Jen waiting on a bench outside the restaurant when she stepped onto the sidewalk, and she smiled as she caught her eye. "Are you stalking me?"

"I am." Jen grinned and nodded. "So…how'd it go?"

"Really, really well," Lauren said, glancing over her shoulder at the glass door behind her. She tucked her hair behind her ears and sighed as she turned back toward Jen. "But I turned him down."

Jen arched a brow in surprise, though she really was not all that surprised. She had known this day was coming ever since Lauren came back into the kitchen after wishing Grey a happy New Year, looking like she had been kicked in the gut because she did not get to ring it in with a kiss. "You turned him down?"

"I know, Jen." Lauren interrupted her with a smile. "I do." She took a deep breath and smiled as, for the first time since she landed back in New York, she finally had a clear idea of what she wanted. "Believe me, I know what I just did. I just…" She shrugged. "I don't want this anymore."

"Well, fuck," Jen muttered, smiling as she shook her head. "So what are you going to do?"

"I dunno."

Jen chuckled. "Bullshit. You've made up your mind. I can see it in your eyes. Say it, Lo."

"I want Grey." Just saying it out loud made Lauren feel lighter than she had since she returned to New York, and she threw her head back and laughed. "I want Grey. I want to spend my days sailing around the Caribbean with her. I want to wake up in her arms every morning, listening to the sound of the ocean slapping against the hull of the boat."

Jen nodded and pulled Lauren into a quick hug. "I'm glad you've finally figured it out."

"I have," Lauren whispered.

"So…what now?" Jen asked as she backed out of the hug and started walking toward the subway entrance at the end of the street.

Lauren sighed and shook her head as she fell into step beside her. "I don't know. I'll need to find somebody to take Jenks because he can't go with me…"

"You know I'll take him. I love that little bastard like he's my own. Besides, he wrapped Ben around his finger when we watched him for you while you were gone. So, don't worry about him. Jenks will be fine. Assuming, of course, that he stays away from old Mrs. Schwartz's terrier. Your apartment?"

"I'll have to sell it or find a renter. What do you think?"

"If you can rent it out for the price of your mortgage, I'd do that. You know real estate around here is only going to get more expensive. And, besides… I'm not saying things between you and Grey won't work out, but if they don't, you would have something to come back to."

"Yeah, I know. I don't think that's going to be a problem, though."

"Me neither, to be honest. But it's good to have a backup plan, just in case. And, you know, investments and grown-up shit like that. So, are you going to tell her when she comes up next week?" Jen asked as she swiped her MetroCard through the scanner and pushed through the turnstile.

Lauren chewed her lip thoughtfully as she followed her onto the other side. They had made it this long already so another nine days would not mean much in the grand scheme of things, but she also did not want to wait. "I don't know. I kinda want to just go down there now and find her and tell her."

"Well, in that case," Jen said with a smile. "Let's see what we can do about making that happen. You'll have to quit Clarke's."

"And pack."

"A get your place on the market. You going to try rent it furnished?"

"I think I'll just put everything in storage. Can always sell it later on, or have my brother come pick it up to take to the cabin or something. Do you still have your realtor's number from when you and Ben bought last summer?"

Jen nodded. "Yep. You want her number?"

"Is it in your phone?" Lauren asked, and when Jen nodded, she just smiled and held out her hand. "Gimme."

"Impatient little thing, aren't you," Jen teased as she handed it over.

Lauren winked and lifted Jen's phone to her ear. "Maybe just a little."

Chapter 50

Once Lauren had made up her mind about what to do, it was almost too easy to set it all into motion. By Thursday evening she had arranged to get her apartment up on the market and given notice at Clarke's. She offered them one week, and had been pleasantly surprised when Sam Clarke, the restaurant's owner, told her that he would be happy if she just worked through the weekend. She had, of course, jumped at the offer. Sunday afternoon she took Jenks and all of his things over to Jen and Ben's apartment, and she was proud of herself for managing to not sob her eyes out until she was in the elevator afterwards. A moving company was scheduled to come the following week to box up her things and move them into storage, and all that was left was for her to pack her clothes and the few things she could not leave behind.

The hardest part out of all of it had been not letting on to Grey what was happening during their daily calls. Jen had thrown the idea of her surprising Grey out as a joke—a 'hey, wouldn't it be cool if you…' kind of thing—but Lauren immediately fell in love with the idea and had run with it.

It was just after noon when Lauren's plane touched down in Charlotte Amalie the following Monday, and she jogged through the terminal to baggage claim to pick up the one large suitcase she had brought with her. She slowed to a walk as she entered the baggage area, and waved when she spotted a familiar face in the crowd. While she had not told Grey that she was coming back, she had called Kelly Kipling because she knew that would need her help. The blonde had access to resources Lauren could only dream of having, and she smiled as she walked up to her. "Hey."

"Hey yourself," Kelly drawled, her lips curled in a warm, welcoming smile. "How was your flight?"

"Long," Lauren admitted with a small laugh. She had barely slept the night before due to her excitement about seeing Grey again, and that anticipation had intensified with every mile her plane had covered.

Kelly chuckled and nodded. Lauren's eyes were twinkling, her smile wide, and it was clear that she could not wait to surprise Grey. "You're adorable. Let's get your bag and get going. Peter Island, right?"

"Yeah." Lauren nodded. "She said her guests were going to be spending the day at the resort, and that they would leave there for Tortola tomorrow."

Kelly looked at the luggage carousel, which had just jolted into motion. "She is going to flip her shit when she sees you."

"I sure hope so," Lauren murmured.

"She will." Kelly wrapped an arm around Lauren's waist and pulled her into a light hug. "Trust me."

Lauren nodded and pointed at a silver hard shell suitcase that had just spilled down the conveyor to the carousel. "That's me."

"Well, grab it, and let's go," Kelly said. "Lots of things to do still."

Once Lauren had her bag, Kelly led the way out of the airport to where she had parked her car, and they then headed to a smaller private airfield where the Kipling helicopter was waiting for them. The green and white Bell 206 was sitting empty on a pad outside a large hangar, and Lauren whistled as Kelly rolled to a stop in front of it. "Wow."

"Just you wait." Kelly patted Lauren on the leg. "You're going to be my copilot for this jump."

Lauren's eyebrows lifted over the frame of her sunglasses as she turned to look at Kelly. "You fly that thing?"

"Damn right I do." Kelly shouldered her door open and flashed an expectant look over her shoulder at Lauren. "Well, do you want to go get your woman, or what? Let's go!"

"Damn right I do," Lauren muttered as she slipped out of the passenger seat and walked around the back of the Range Rover to retrieve her suitcase.

A middle-aged man with jet black hair in a pair of khaki shorts, blue polo shirt with the airfield's logo stitched onto the right breast, and a pair of mirrored aviators drove up in an open Jeep just as her bag hit the pavement, and Lauren smiled gratefully to him when he took her suitcase and lifted it into the cabin. She stood back and watched as Kelly and the man went through the preflight checklist, double-checking everything to make sure the helicopter was ready to fly, and her heart leapt into her throat when Kelly turned and held a gleaming white helmet out to her.

"You're sure about this?" Lauren asked as she inspected the helmet.

"Helmets are kind of required equipment."

"I didn't mean that. I meant having me copilot."

"I'm not going to make you fly it or anything, I just figured you'd rather sit up front with me. And the helmet has a com, so we'll be able to talk on the way over."

Lauren nodded and jammed the helmet onto her head. She looked up at Kelly, who was fastening her own chin strap, and grinned, her excitement getting the better of her as she got one step closer to finally seeing Grey. "Thank you for doing this."

"You keep Grey happy, and we'll call it even," Kelly said with a soft smile.

"I'll do my best," Lauren promised with a small nod. She took a deep breath and turned toward the helicopter. "Right. Well, shall we?"

"We most definitely shall." Kelly walked around the nose of the helicopter to her preferred half of the cockpit and climbed inside. Once Lauren was buckled-in beside her, she turned on the engines and began easing the throttle forward to lift them off the ground.

Kelly spent the flight from Saint Thomas to Tortola explaining what she was doing and answering Lauren's questions. She did not miss the way Lauren's attention never wavered from the water beneath them, actively looking for the *Veritas* even as she held up her half of the conversation, and Kelly chuckled at the way Lauren sat up straighter when she announced that they were coming up on Peter Island.

Lauren's pulse jumped as a populated bay came into view, and she could not contain the smile that lit her face when she spotted a familiar red and white catamaran tied up at the end of a T-shaped dock. "There it is."

Kelly leaned forward to look, and nodded when she spotted the *Veritas*. "That it is. You ready?"

"Oh yeah," Lauren muttered, nodding as she looked over at Kelly. "More than ready."

"Let's go get you your girl, then."

Chapter 51

Grey had the *Veritas* to herself for the afternoon because her guests and the chef she had hired for the trip were all off exploring Peter Island's impressive amenities. It was a nice change of pace after two months of constant charters, and she took advantage of the calm to begin packing for her upcoming trip to New York. She was kneeling at the bow of the port-side hull with her head shoved in one of the storage areas looking for the bag of cold-weather clothes she kept for random trips back home to Newport but which rarely saw any use because her family preferred to visit her in the Caribbean during those months.

"There you are," she muttered as she spotted the vacuum-sealed bag she was looking for, and she grunted as she leaned further into the hatch to grab it. She startled when the phone in her pocket began ringing, jolting upright and banging the back of her head on the edge of the hatch. She swore softly under her breath as she sat up and rubbed at the spot with her left hand while she used her other hand to pull her phone from her pocket. "What's up, Kip?"

"Not much. Just checking in. How's everything going?"

Kip's tone was playful, and Grey sighed as she pushed herself up to her feet. She picked up the bag of clothes she had injured herself retrieving, and flipped the hatch shut with her foot.

"Everything's fine. Guests are off doing the spa thing on Peter Island, and I'm just rummaging through the storage holds for the clothes I'll need when I go visit Lauren in a few days. What's going on?"

"Am I not allowed to just call and shoot the shit?"

"You are, but you never do," Grey pointed out with a laugh as she worked her way down the hull toward the stern. The marina was calm, the water off to her right perfectly smooth as everybody moored in the lagoon for the day was off exploring the resort. She fisted the edge of the bag in her hand tighter so that it would not drop in the water, and shook her head. "Seriously, is everything okay?"

"Yep. Great, actually. Best day ever type of shit. Hey, do me a favor and go out onto the back deck…"

"I'm on my way there now. Kip, what's going on?" Grey asked, but her question was answered the moment she jumped onto the back deck and saw a familiar face with a riot of wild red curls standing on the dock just off the stern. The bag she had been so careful to not drop in the water slipped from her grasp, and she barely had the wherewithal to set her phone onto the table before it, too, tumbled to the deck. She opened and closed her mouth a couple times as she tried to find her voice, but her surprise had rendered her completely speechless.

Lauren laughed at Grey's gobsmacked expression and waved. "Permission to come aboard, Captain?"

"You…" Grey hurried down to the starboard dive platform and jumped onto the dock. Her eyes danced over Lauren's face as she stopped in front of her, and she shook her head as she pulled Lauren into her arms. "You're really here."

"I am." Lauren smiled and pressed a soft kiss to Grey's lips, and her eyes fluttered shut when Grey's hands tightened around her waist to pull her in closer. Their kiss became deeper almost instantly, mouths slanting and lips parting as they lost themselves in the heady feeling of finally being back together. Lauren's head spun from the passion in Grey's kisses, and she swayed slightly on her feet when they slowed to a string of lingering pecks. "My god…"

Grey's eyes were soft as she ran a tender hand over Lauren's jaw. "What are you doing here?"

"I wanted to see you."

Grey nodded and kissed Lauren again, more softly this time, letting the caress convey exactly how much she had missed having her close like this. "How did you even get here? Don't you have to work tonight?"

Lauren shook her head and smiled at the way Grey's forehead wrinkled in confusion. "I quit my job at Clarke's."

"You quit?"

"Well, technically," Lauren murmured as she nuzzled Grey's cheek with her nose, loving the feeling of being able to actually touch her again, "I turned down an offer for an executive chef position." She brushed a soft kiss over the corner of Grey's lips. "And *then* I quit my job."

Grey gaped. "You…what?"

"Mmm." Lauren smiled and kissed Grey again.

"You're not making any sense," Grey muttered, keeping her arms around Lauren's waist as she pulled back to look her in the eye. "You turned down an executive chef position?"

"I did."

"Why?"

Lauren's smile softened, and she sighed as she tickled her fingers through the fine hairs at the nape of Grey's neck. "The general manager was wonderful, the restaurant itself was perfect, the kitchen was an absolute dream, and I was tempted to do it. But then he asked me what my favorite meal I'd ever made was, and who I made it for…" Her voice trailed off and she shrugged. "If I had been asked that question two months ago, I would've rattled off a dish without even having to stop and think about it. But now…my *first* thought was of you. Of how good it felt for you to hold me in your arms, and how wonderful it felt when you kissed me. I eventually got around to the food, but it was not what was important. And that was when I knew…"

The look in Lauren's eyes was unmistakable, and Grey's heart flew up into her throat. "Knew what?"

"That I don't need a fancy title or a professional kitchen to be happy." Lauren took a deep breath to steady her nerves. "I love you, Grey Wells. More than cooking or—"

Grey silenced Lauren with a kiss that was filled with every ounce of love she could pour into the caress. "I love you too," she whispered against Lauren's lips, sealing the oath with another kiss that made the world around them disappear and left them both completely breathless. She laughed softly and brushed her lips over Lauren's forehead. "God, do I love you."

Lauren smiled and melted into Grey's embrace, basking in the warm, familiar press of the brunette's body against her own. Oh, how she had missed this.

The sound of footsteps echoing down the dock toward them made Grey look up, and she shook her head when she saw Kip walking toward them. "I should have known you were involved in this."

"Yeah, well," Kelly drawled, smiling at the couple, "somebody had to get her out here."

"Thanks again, for that," Lauren said, snuggling into Grey's side as she turned to half-face Kelly.

"My pleasure." Kelly cleared her throat loudly and gave Grey a serious look. "So…you gonna give the girl a job, or can I have her?"

Grey laughed, feeling lighter than she ever thought she would again, and shook her head. "No dice, Kip. She's mine." She pressed a light kiss to Lauren's lips. "Whattaya say? You want to be the executive chef aboard the *Veritas*?"

Lauren smiled and nodded. "I do."

"Good." Grey lifted a hand to Lauren's face, and smoothed a thumb over her cheek. Her eyes danced over Lauren's face as she leaned in closer, and she sighed as she kissed her again softly, pouring everything she was into the kiss, leaving no doubt in either of their minds that this arrangement was permanent. She had loved and lost and somehow been blessed to love again—and she knew that she would love Lauren Murphy for the rest of her life.

Acknowledgements

Many, many thanks to my wonderful betas, without whom this story would have never seen the light of day. To Amy, thank you for…everything. I look forward to tackling many more projects with you in the future. To Rae D. Magdon, thank you for sharing your impressive knowledge of grammar, and enlightening me to the ways of the Editor. To Jade, thank you for the much-needed pats on the head as I fumbled through getting this story from my head and onto paper. And last, but most certainly not least, thanks go to Wye for taking the time to read through this multiple times, and for your honesty in the face of potentially thrown objects.

CPSIA information can be obtained
at www.ICGtesting.com
Printed in the USA
LVHW092219010721
691731LV00013B/285

9 780692 023969